"He wanted her dead, just like Gwen did . . . he'd take Becky away from us if he could. How could he live with her knowing I'm her father, and that his dead wife's her mother?"

Cruel, heartless laughter echoed in my ears. But what Jason had said was the truth, and there was something in Father's eyes that made me realize how uncertain Becky's future would be if we stayed here.

"He doesn't know what he's doing, Quinn. Please, I beg of you. Your brother's not well, and he won't get better on his own."

"How can you even say such a thing?" I shouted through my tears. "He's my brother, my only friend, and I'll make him well because I love him."

"I love him, too," Father insisted.

But by then I knew it was a lie.

by J.S. FORRESTER

A JAMES A. BRYANS BOOK
FROM DELL/EMERALD

This is a work of fiction. All the characters and events portrayed in this book are fictional, and any resemblance to real people or incidents is purely coincidental.

Published by
Dell Publishing Co., Inc.
1 Dag Hammarskjold Plaza
New York, New York 10017

Dell ® TM 681510, Dell Publishing Co., Inc.

ISBN: 0-440-08056-8

Printed in the United States of America
1991 EDITION
LEISURE ENTERTAINMENT SERVICE CO., INC.

For Steve & Henry
and
Jack & Marc

PROLOGUE

The road leading back to the Valley is full of pitfalls. The rubble-strewn path is proof of decay, with great yawning cracks in the asphalt, and deep, jagged-edged holes into which rocks and gravel have tumbled. When I returned many years after my brother Jason and I fled late one summer's afternoon, time was at a standstill, and everywhere I looked the Valley seemed the same. The oatmeal-colored chaparral, parched and dry, caught the sound of the wind in its thorny branches. The dense, tangled canopy of brush whispered of secrets that I had spent the better part of my life trying desperately to forget. But secrets inevitably possess a life of their own. They demand to be retold, to be passed on from one ear to the next until they become secrets no longer.

I could hear them the day I returned, and I remember pulling over to the side of the road and listening intently. I turned off the engine, and for several minutes the motor pinged and a fan continued to spin beneath the hood. But gradually the silence engulfed me. Then the wind came up, very faint at first, and hardly noticeable. I heard it off in the distance, at the far end of the Valley where I had once scampered among the lichen-encrusted rocks and boulders. Here there were caves and secret niches, hiding places scooped out of the granite hillside where Jason and I had played out our innocent games of childhood, never suspecting we would soon become unwitting participants in a terrifying nightmare.

Everywhere I looked the Valley shimmered magically in the golden light of afternoon. The ring of hills which encircled it, keeping it safe from prying eyes, were tinged with a soft and delicate shade of purple. Sage and manzanita grew thick and wild, the land untouched for generations. Here my great-grandfather, a stern and forbidding figure, had come to build his fortress, a gabled Victorian mansion of sharp angles and secret rooms, hidden passageways along which rats now crawled, but where Jason and I had once made our frightened way.

I gripped the steering wheel tightly, afraid that if I didn't I might go spinning off into the past, never to return. Perhaps it was the quality of the light, for nowhere else did it seem quite the same as here, in the Valley where I was born and where I learned what it was to be victimized by deceit. Or perhaps it was the faint winy scent of vegetation, the subtle green fragrance which drifted down the granite hillsides, floating across the floor of the Valley. I hadn't been here in so long, and yet as I looked out on the silent splendor of what I had run away from, I knew that one part of me had remained behind, waiting for my return.

Do you remember what happened? Shall I refresh your memory and recount it to you again, that spider's web of falsehoods and vicious accusations? We were running away not from danger so much as deceit. We were lied to, Jason and I, told our beautiful mother was dead when she was not. And when she was finally returned to us, it was only to be taken away again—so suddenly, so cruelly and unexpectedly, that thinking about it now makes my head throb with bitter anguish.

How could any of it have happened to us when we had done nothing to deserve such punishment? We were father's golden children, his pride and joy, the very strength and comfort of his life. But he had deceived us, and in so doing had brought grief and tragedy upon us all.

For years I had stayed away, trying to make a new life for myself and my dear little Becky, who was both my sister and my niece. She was the living proof of Jason and Mother's love, a love whose twisted, unhappy roots had brought her into being. Father had not wanted her to live, and Aunt Gwen, Mother's spoiled and willful sister, had called the precious infant a monster, someone to be smothered until there was not a trace of breath left in her body.

That was why we had to run away that day, when all the nightmares came crashing down on us. I wasn't even thirteen then, and yet I felt much older than my years, having lived through a summer of terror I was only all too eager to escape. As a child I thought I could forget, and in time the horrifying memories would fade away. My life would stretch before me without anything to cloud the promise of happiness I was certain could be mine. How naive I was then, how sad and foolish to think the past would never catch up to me.

It did catch up.

It caught up to all of us—Father and Aunt Gwen and my darling Jason, even Becky too, though at first she was much too young to understand.

And now I had to see it for myself, this place that once held so much happiness for me, the pleasure of waking up on a spring morning when the air carried the fragrance of rebirth, each day more joyous than the next.

I got out of the car and walked the rest of the way, tracing the footsteps of my youth, certain I could see their faint outline in the dusty path along which I seemed to be traveling back into the past.

Up ahead the black wrought-iron fence was as much a part of the landscape as the scrub oak and thorny chaparral. Like some strange hell-born plant, the sharp-crowned pickets thrust themselves out of the ground to stand rigid and inflexible, daring me to pass beyond their inhospitable palisade.

But as I drew near I saw it as it really was, merely an old and rusty picket fence, sagging in places, the spear points broken off in others. The gate stood ajar, as if inviting me to enter. The dark, upright shapes of tombstones, slabs of pitted black marble whose weathered inscriptions reverberated like the echo of voices in my mind, leaned in all directions. It was as if someone had come here long before me, trying to topple the stones and thus obliterate the past.

But these monuments to the dead were much stronger than the efforts of the living. Here, one moonlit night when I was just a child, Jason and I had made our way, determined to discover the truth of our mother's death. Here we had dug deep into the hard-packed earth while poor-wills called in the distance, and a chorus of cicadas and crickets added their sad raspy music to our dreadful task. The yapping of a coyote tumbled down from the hills as we dug deeper, until at last we uncovered the coffin where Father had told us Mother had been laid to rest.

Do you recall what happened? Shall I tell it to you again, the nightmare of deception that all but destroyed my brother's sanity, my own as well? When I saw it as I did late that one afternoon, with the silent hillsides my only witness, I had to wonder if indeed any of it had actually taken place. Perhaps my tortured childhood was something I'd imagined, a complex, multilayered dream that had gradually assumed the guise of reality.

REBECCA HOWE LEFLAND, the stone read.

The once precisely chiseled letters had lost their sharp edge. Although less than ten years had passed, to look at the tombstone one would have thought Mother had been dead as long as Josiah and Hepzibah, founders of our accursed Lefland clan.

I'd brought along a bouquet of flowers, and as I knelt before Mother's grave I laid the roses and babies'-breath at the base of the marble stone. I felt the warmth of the earth against my knees, and the land was like a living, breathing creature, conscious of my presence.

How we miss you still, I thought as my eyes clouded over, and tears began to well up under my lids. They said you were sick, hopelessly ill, and that your madness turned you into someone we wouldn't recognize. But we knew you as you really were, Mother, and that was something neither Jason nor I could ever forget. And oh, if you could see your Becky now, how proud you'd be of her. She looks so much like you it's startling, with that same profusion of golden hair, those same crystal blue eyes, as sharp and clear as a mountain stream. Even her voice reminds me of you, so that when I hear her speak I know you never meant to leave us.

With a trembling finger I traced the letters of her name, and thought of all that had happened to us in the years since Father had taken her away. He had told us she was dead, when in truth he'd committed her to an asylum.

Incurable, that's what they called her. Hopelessly insane. But the real insanity was what he had done to us, saying it was for our best interests, when what he really meant to say was that it was best for him, not anyone else.

For a long time I knelt there, trying to make some sense of my life, to come away with an understanding of all that I had gone through, and all that Father had made me suffer. Yet even though I'd made this pilgrimage in search of answers, by the time my shadow crept across the face of Mother's gravestone I still lacked that basic understanding I'd come here to find.

The lies perpetrated in the past continued to haunt me. There was no escaping them, just as there was no escaping the fact that I was a Lefland, and always would be. Jason had said it was in our blood, and that no matter what we did we could never escape that accursed heritage that was our birthright. I had refused to believe that, but in the ten years since leaving the Valley I'd finally come to accept the wisdom of his words. Yet we both had tried, and no one could ever take that away from us. We had struggled against terrible odds, never able to forget what we had run away from.

Maybe I was still running, even after all these years. I was a woman now, but as I knelt before Mother's grave I could just as easily have been a child. My arms slipped around the stone. I pressed my face to the sun-warmed marble and tried to recall the softness of Mother's cheek, and how comforting it was when she held me in her arms. If only tears could have brought her back I would have wept for days on end. But though tears can moisten the earth and sometimes even bring up life, they can't recall the dead.

When I got to my feet the sun was beginning to set. Its

reddish glow suffused the hillsides, a faint, bloody wash of color that crept mournfully across the chaparral. I turned away, knowing there were no answers here, just as I must have known even before I made the decision to return.

But one day I would be back to claim what was mine. One day I would stand again before Mother's grave and calmly recount the story of my life, the life that Father had not allowed her to share with me. Perhaps then the demons of the past would finally be laid to rest, and Mother's troubled spirit would at last be at peace.

I could wish for nothing better, for whatever was worse had already taken place.

PART I

ESCAPE

CHAPTER ONE

Later, he would plead that it was all Warren's doing, not Dr. Warren the psychiatrist whom Mother had trusted, and who had thought nothing of betraying her, but Warren the evil and self-destructive little boy who lurked within my brother's mind, eager to gain control of him. It was this demon Jason had named Warren who made my brother plunge the knife into Father's side. It was this dreadful imp, this creature of utter cruelty and perversity, who took charge of things the day Father returned to the Valley to confront all the horror he had brought into being.

It was dusk when we heard the tires screeching along the gravel, and then Father's big cheery hello as he bounded up the front steps. Jason and I were waiting for him in the entrance hall, the pendants of the crystal chandelier scattering broken rainbows across the walls. They made me think of half-hearted promises, the glowing colors as uncertain as my frame of mind.

But you remember all this, don't you? Father followed us upstairs, staring with both horror and disbelief at the newborn infant I held in my arms, protecting Becky from the rage I saw behind his grim, shocked expression. He was trying to control his feelings, but Jason wasn't about to be deceived and neither was I. And when we led him upstairs to Mother's room—You remember that too, don't you?—Father could no longer pretend that his life would ever be the same, and that our family would once again be happy and whole.

Mother was dead. The lipstick and rouge and eye shadow we had applied to her face could not conceal the truth from his eyes. Father looked at the corpse we had propped up in bed and began to whimper like a child. Then he buried his face in his hands and wept for all that he had done to us, and all that he had done to her, his beloved Rebecca.

But it was much too late for forgiveness. Jason had told me that, and I recognized the simple truth of his words. You know what we had gone through those past few months. You know all of it. The mock funeral Father had staged. My discovery of Mother's diary and its subsequent disappearance. The threatening notes we had each received. And of course the night we exhumed her coffin and found that all it contained was a pile of stones. Mother had escaped from Dr. Warren's hospital, and had barely managed to survive until finally Jason coaxed her out of hiding and brought her home. You know of Aunt Gwen too, and what my brother had done to her just a few hours before Father returned to the Valley. All these things I've told you, trusting you as perhaps I've trusted no one else.

I see it now as I saw it then. The knife that Warren had forced into my brother's hand, the knife that plunged deep into Father's side. The blood that drenched his shirt, collecting in a thick, treacly puddle on the floor. The look of anguish on his face as he lay there, trying to stanch the wound.

"We'll send a doctor over as soon as we get to Juniper

City," Jason was saying, so calm and collected I could hardly believe my ears.

He started to the door, urging me to follow. It was already getting dark, and the sooner we got going, the better.

"Don't listen to him, Quinn," Father called out to me. "He doesn't know what he's saying. The only way to help him is to help me."

I didn't know what to do.

There was Jason, standing by the door and ever so carefully wiping the blood off the bone-handled dirk he'd given me for my birthday. And there was Father, Bennett Lefland, stretched out on the floor with his blood-stained hand pressed tight against the wound in his side.

Then, without any warning, Jason suddenly lost control. The mask of reserve slipped off his face, revealing the raw emotions he could no longer hide from view.

'He's a liar, Quinn!" my brother screamed. His voice was as raspy as a file, pitched on the edge of hysteria. "He's a filthy liar and he knows it, too! Don't you see? He'll send me away, lock me up like he tried to do with Mom. She's dead, and it's all his fault, Quinn, every bit of it. All he wanted to do was get rid of her, anyway, so he could marry Aunt Gwen, that evil bitch."

"What have you done to her?" Father demanded, unable to raise his voice above a pathetic and pain-racked whisper.

"Just what you'd like to do to me," Jason hissed. "She's up in the attic, behind the wall where she deserves to be."

He bent down and began to rifle Father's pockets, removing the car keys as well as his billfold. Then he looked over at Mother, watching us with dead, unseeing eyes.

"It's what you told me to do," my brother said to her, almost as if he actually believed she were still alive. "Now you can rest, knowing he's been punished."

Father begged me not to listen. I looked at him and then at Jason, torn between the two. Then Becky opened her mouth and began to cry, her tiny fists flailing at the air.

"He wanted her dead, just like Gwen did," my brother reminded me. "He'd take Becky away from us if he could, because how could he live with her knowing I'm her father, and that his dead wife's her mother?"

Cruel, heartless laughter echoed in my ears. But what Jason had said was the truth, and there was something in Father's eyes that made me realize how uncertain Becky's future would be if we stayed here by his side.

"He doesn't know what he's doing, Quinn. Please, I beg of you. Your brother's not well, and he won't get better on his own. Your mother didn't, despite all I tried to do for her. And Jason won't, either."

"How can you even say such a thing?" I shouted through my tears. "He's my brother, my only friend, and I'll make him well because I love him."

"I love him, too," Father insisted.

But by then I knew it was a lie. I knew it from the look of revulsion he had shown the baby, and from the hate that seeped out of his voice the way blood continued to seep from his wound. We had spoiled everything for him, don't you see? We had ruined all his carefully laid plans, this new life he was going to make for himself and his sister-in-law, the future and second Mrs. Lefland. We had interfered, and Bennett was not the kind of man who took interference lightly. For several days, several weeks even, he would no doubt pretend that everything was all right. He would try to make it up to us, lavishing gifts on us as if material things could make us forget what he had put us through. But then one day Jason would be dragged away, just as Mother had, and I would never see my brother again.

"You'd send him away and keep us apart for the rest of our lives," I told him. "But now we'll be together because we love each other, and our love is much stronger than your hatred, Father."

I picked up the baby, cradling her in my arms. Becky Hope Lefland, I thought, we're going to protect you. We'll never let him hurt you. You're not a monster, even if that's what he thinks. You're our precious Becky, and we'll never let him take you away from us.

"Quinn, you can talk to him," Father pleaded. "You can make him understand—"

"Understand what? That his father lied to him, that his father wants him locked up like a mad dog?" I said, my voice as shrill and vindictive as Jason's.

Was that sadness I saw in Father's eyes, or merely the fear that we were going to leave him here to die? Jason kept insisting it was a superficial wound, that it looked much worse than it really was, and that we'd phone the doctor as soon as we reached town.

I started to the door, still conscious of Father's imploring eyes, trying to pin me to my place.

"Don't try to find us," I warned him. "We don't want you to. We don't want anything to do with you. You're not our father, Bennett Lefland. You're no one's father, not ever again."

Jason knew how to drive, and as the sky darkened in the west, and reddish clouds swept across the rim of the Valley, we set off for Juniper City. I glanced behind me, staring at the house where I had spent my life, never dreaming that one day I would be forced to flee from all that was dear to me. There was my room on the second floor, the curtains with the little blue flowers neatly framing the windows. There was Jason's room, where of late I'd heard him sobbing in his sleep, unable to accept what had happened to us, and what was happening still.

He sat very stiff and tense behind the wheel, clutching it so tightly I wondered if he'd ever be able to uncurl his fingers. His knuckles were white and bloodless, and he kept clenching his jaw, gritting his teeth until the sound he made was like chalk on a blackboard, and I had to beg him to stop.

The road to Juniper City was deserted. I wondered what would happen once we got to town, if someone would try to stop us before we had a chance to phone the doctor. Jason had cut the telephone wires back at the house, so there was no danger of Father calling the sheriff and alerting him to our arrival.

Again I glanced behind me, but by then the house was no longer visible. The Valley too was gone, while ahead the road unraveled like a spool of thread, a broken yellow line dividing one lane from the other.

"Try not to think about it, Quinn. You know as well as I do we didn't have any other choice."

He sounded so rational that for a moment I forgot all about Warren, certain my brother had banished ..im to the farthest reaches of his mind. But perhaps Warren was much cleverer than I gave him credit for being. What if he was masquerading as my brother, pretending to be the Jason I loved and understood, when in fact he was the very opposite?

Warren was the dark side of my brother's personality

that lurked within him like the beast in the jungle, just waiting for the chance to spring. Jason had told me he'd found some pills in Mother's medicine cabinet, and that after he took one Warren had gone to sleep. But had the pill worn off? Had Warren awakened, flexing his muscles and eager to regain control?

Although I was reluctant to bring it up, I knew I had to.

"Is Warren still asleep, or am I talking to him now?"

My brother took his eyes off the road for just an instant.

"He's gone away, Quinn, I swear he has."

There was utter conviction in his voice, and I began to breathe a little easier. But then reality reared its ugly head. I wasn't even thirteen years old. Jason had only just turned fourteen, and though he might be able to pass for fifteen, he still didn't look old enough to drive. What if we were stopped? He had no driver's license, no birth certificate, no proof of any kind. Thank God it was already dark, for perhaps if we drove at night we wouldn't draw attention to ourselves.

But what would happen in the morning? How long could we hide? How far away could we run? It was suddenly becoming clear that what we were doing was doomed to failure. We were children. We had close to five hundred dollars, and when that ran out what would we do then? Jason might be able to get a part-time job, but even if he did where would we live? Who would rent an apartment to two children? Why, people would laugh in our faces if we tried to find a place of our own.

I held Becky in my arms, knowing that soon I'd have to feed her again and change her diaper. If Jason and I were the only ones running away it might have been easier for us. But with Becky it only made our situation all the more difficult. She was our responsibility now, and everything we did had to take her welfare into account.

Jason must have sensed what was on my mind, unless of course he was thinking about the same things I was. He reached over and patted my cheek, then urged me to snuggle up to him. I leaned my head against his shoulder, trying not to let my fears get the better of me.

"You'll see, it'll all work out for the best," he promised. "We'll just take things one step at a time. We'll get through today and then we'll get through tomorrow."

"And what about the day after that?"

Jason laughed, but it was strained and hollow sounding, something he was forcing himself to do.

"First Juniper City . . . then the world," he said with a grin.

But what if the world didn't want any part of us? Even Jason didn't know the answer to that.

If you blinked you'd miss Juniper City entirely.

Main Street consisted of a general store, a supermarket that was more the size of a grocery, a hamburger stand, and a gas station. Several other establishments lined the only paved street in town, including the sheriff's office, the one place we made sure to stay as far away from as we possibly could.

Jason parked the car on the outskirts of town, then told me to leave Becky behind, bundled up on the front seat.

"Nothing's going to happen to her," he insisted when I started to object. "We'll only be gone ten or fifteen minutes at most."

I had to buy formula and diapers, and I guess he had a point. Everyone in town knew who we were, and if I showed up at the market with a newborn infant in my arms, I would surely attract more than just idle curiosity. So I made certain she was comfortable, and leaving the window open a crack for air, followed my brother into town.

While Jason went off to phone the doctor—he really didn't want to, but I made him promise that he would—I slipped into the market, hoping I wouldn't draw attention to myself. But when my cart was loaded up with Pampers and formula, a voice suddenly called out from the opposite end of the aisle. For a second I pretended not to hear, and continued toward the checkout stand.

"Quinton? That is you, isn't it, dear?"

I turned around and forced myself to smile. Evelyn Chatsworth, the town postmistress, steered her overflowing shopping cart in my direction. She was a tiny bird of a woman, deceptively frail-looking, and though it looked like she hardly ate, the groceries in her cart proved otherwise.

"Why, I haven't seen you in months," she exclaimed, making it sound as if we were the best of friends, when in fact we were merely acquaintances. "How is everything out your way?"

"Oh fine, thank you," I murmured.

It was then that she glanced at the cartons of diapers and cans of formula. I knew what she was thinking, and so before she had a chance to ask I hurriedly explained that our aunt was visiting with her baby. I guess she believed me, because she made no further mention of it, asking instead how Jason and I were, and saying how terribly sorry she was to hear of our loss.

"Do remember me to your father," she went on.

Her long, bony fingers clutched my arm, just like a bird perching on the branch of a tree. For a moment I had the strangest feeling she didn't intend to let go, but was going to hold onto me until the sheriff came to take me away.

"I certainly will, Miss Chatsworth. I'll tell him as soon as I get home. Well . . . it was nice seeing you again."

By the time I paid the girl who worked the cash register I was shaking so hard that I was sure Miss Chatsworth would notice. But when I looked over my shoulder she was busy peering into the ice cream bin, trying to decide between chocolate and vanilla.

I was starting out the front door when suddenly I noticed a pickup truck parked on the other side of Main Street. Panic overwhelmed me, and I couldn't even breathe.

What were they doing back so early? They were supposed to be down in L.A., not here in town. There was no one behind the wheel, and I stepped cautiously to the edge of the narrow sidewalk, holding the grocery bags in front of my face just in case one of them was nearby.

Anna and Will Darby, our housekeeper and handyman, had gone off to Los Angeles on a wild goose chase, for Jason had sent them a telegram that pretended to be from their son. But Harry was dead, something they would soon enough discover for themselves. I didn't want to think about him, or the terrible accident that had claimed his life. I didn't want to think about anything but getting away from here, and as fast as I could.

There was no one else on Main Street, but any second I had a feeling my luck would change. Why, they must have driven straight through, because it was a good four hours to Los Angeles and then another four to come back. If

Mrs. Darby saw me here she'd know something was up, and I couldn't take the chance.

And where was Jason? Had he already bumped into them, was that what had happened?

The way my heart was pounding it felt as if it would tear right through my sweater. But finally I gathered up my courage—what little was left of it, that is—and dashed down the street. Moments later I heard footsteps, but I didn't dare look back. Even though I wanted to break into a run I was afraid of being too conspicuous.

Yet as fast as I walked, the footsteps were just as rapid. There was an eagerness to them too, and I knew that whoever was behind me was trying to catch up. What would I tell Mrs. Darby? How would I explain? I wouldn't even know where to begin, and realizing that made me feel so helpless I hardly knew what I was doing.

The Pampers and formula and baby supplies were getting heavier by the minute. My arms felt like they were about to snap in two like a pair of rotten twigs. If I could only get off Main Street I'd be all right. But instead of receding, the footsteps continued to grow louder, until suddenly I felt a hand on my shoulder and I all but cried out in fear.

"I—"

But I didn't know what else to say. If I started to run she'd only chase after me, and then I'd end up leading her straight to the car.

"Christ almighty, it's only me."

I heard myself groan, but at least it was a groan of relief. Jason took one of the bags from me and pulled me along.

"You scared the daylights out of me," I told him, annoyed that he hadn't called out my name, and angry at myself for not having had the courage to look back. "Didn't you see whose truck is parked back there?"

Jason emptied half a bag of M & M's into my hand and shook his head.

"The Darbys," I whispered, glancing nervously behind me.

At the far end of Main Street, where the commercial district ended and an unpaved road led out of town, I thought I saw a door opening. Without thinking twice about it I dragged Jason back into the shadows.

"How the hell did they get back so fast?" he asked.

He sounded less concerned about their presence than I was, and munched contentedly on the candy as if he didn't have a care in the world.

"I don't know, but they did. And if they see us here—"

I didn't have to say anything else, because by then Jason was walking so quickly I could barely keep up with him. By the time we reached the car I was out of breath, and when I heard Becky crying I started to fear the worst.

As soon as my brother unlocked the door I slid into the car and cradled her in my arms. Her frightened little cries slowly tapered off, and as I rocked her back and forth I whispered that everything was all right. Jason was here and so was I.

My brother reached over and switched on the radio, spinning the dial back and forth. But all he could get was a gospel station. I sat back and listened to a threatening voice warn me how the devil was a tempter, and that if I didn't follow the straight and narrow I would never find salvation. When I looked at Jason he was smiling, and there was something about his expression that gave me goosebumps. Was he the Tempter in disguise? It was a thought that made my blood run cold, and rather than dwell on it I turned off the radio.

"What are we going to do, Jason?"

For a long time my brother stared straight ahead, following the curves of the road as if he were steering us up and down a roller coaster.

"Are we just going to drive all night?" I went on.

"I don't know."

I couldn't help getting angry.

"Well, if you don't know, how in the world do you expect me to?" I demanded.

In the darkness of the car his green eyes looked much lighter than they actually were. When he glanced at me they seemed colorless, as if I were gazing into a bottomless pool, the water so cold it would take my breath away, freezing the blood in my veins.

"I'll think of something," he said at last.

That wasn't the kind of answer that made me feel any better. But there was no point getting into an argument. Jason was just as scared as I was, even if he didn't want to admit it. So I settled back in my seat and tried not to think about tomorrow.

Becky was already asleep in my arms, and I held her closer, wanting her to feel safe and loved. But no matter how hard I tried to be optimistic, it seemed as if this were just the lull before the storm. A terrible sense of foreboding came over me, of danger lurking just ahead. I think my fears must have communicated themselves to the baby, because once again she stirred in my arms and began to cry.

"It's all right, darling, Quinn's here," I whispered, gently stroking her cheeks that were so soft and delicate I was almost afraid to touch them. "You don't have any-

29

thing to worry about, Becky. Quinn's here, and she's never going to leave you.''

I looked back at Jason, but he wasn't saying a word. Maybe I should have told him that I would never leave him, either. But somehow I couldn't bring myself to make that promise. Try as I might, I just couldn't say it.

CHAPTER TWO

It was all Warren's fault.

He should never have been born. Smothered in his crib, that's what Bennett Lefland should have done while he had the chance. Only it was too late for that. Fourteen years too late.

But it was still Warren's fault. I should never have tried to find him. For all I know he could have stayed asleep in my head like Rip Van Winkle, and I would never even have realized he was there.

Too late for that, too, though. Much too late.

At least I wasn't so nervous about driving. When I bragged to Quinn that I knew how, I was really just trying to convince myself that I could. But it's like riding a bicycle—or having sex. Once you get the hang of it you never forget how to do it again. Of course, sex on a bicycle might be a little trickier . . . that's a joke, but I guess it wasn't a very good one.

You know me, of course. I'm Jason—Warren's the one who's asleep, deep inside my head. And since I have more of Mom's white pills, I intend to keep him asleep for as long as I can, just so he won't make any more trouble for me.

You know all about the things he's done, so there's no point going over them again. Troublemaker doesn't even do him justice. He burst out of hiding one day like some crazy jack-in-the-box, and ever since then I've tried everything I could just to keep him out of sight. But the pill I took earlier really did the trick, so maybe he's finally under control. Except that even if he is, even if I never hear from him again, I still have to live with myself, knowing what he's made me do.

Mom was all screwed up—you know that as well as I do, but I'm not making excuses for myself. But what she did to me, all that touching stuff and intercourse and things she had no business teaching me, was terribly wrong. Destructive, that's an even better way of putting it.

Now they're all saying she was schizophrenic—I don't even know what that really is because I'm not a doctor. Dad and Aunt Gwen said I have it too, but I'm not about to take their word for it, not when they have everything to gain by making me think I'm crazy.

I mean, come on, let's be honest with each other. There's no reason for me to lie because you're not going to come after me, are you, and make trouble. Of course not. So let me tell you right here and now. The only thing about Warren I invented was his name. But I swear I didn't make him up or bring him into being or anything like that. He was there in my head from the day I was born, only it took him a little longer to start feeling his oats, that's all.

I'm not crazy, that's the point I'm trying to make. I know I've done some pretty weird things, but if you went through what I did you'd probably end up doing those same things yourself. Harry Darby's death was an accident, and no one's going to pin a charge of murder on me and make it stick.

Harry fell and broke his neck. You can ask Quinn if you don't believe me. She was there and she knows I'm not lying. That's just another reason why we had to run away. They wouldn't hesitate to blame everything on me, especially after I made the mistake of admitting what happened the night they dragged Mom away. But you see, that was Warren's fault, not mine.

Only now I'm going to take charge of my life and not let him interfere. He's made too much trouble for me as it is. I didn't ask Mom to do the things she did to me, but it's too late to change all that. I'll just have to learn to live with it, because I don't have any other choice. But as long as Quinn can help me, as long as I know she's there for me, I think I'll be all right.

The big question of course is what do we do now? If I had any answers I'd tell you, but I really don't know what's going to happen to us. To tell you the truth, I'm as confused and uncertain about this whole thing as my sister. Yet what choice did I have? My father would've shipped me off to Dr. Warren's mental hospital in two seconds flat. He doesn't want me around, no matter what he says. And once he got me out of the way he'd do the same with Becky.

She's my daughter, my flesh and blood. Maybe I'm just a kid, I admit it. Maybe I'm much too young to understand what it means to be a father. But it just so happens that I am her father, and that's something no one can ever take away from me. So for her sake, if no one else's, we had to escape while we had the chance.

Only problem, now I don't know what happens next.

"What did the doctor say?"

"He said he'd leave right away, I shouldn't worry."

"Did you tell him what happened?"

" 'Course not. I just said he'd had an accident, cut himself real bad, that's all."

Quinn frowned and looked away. I don't know why she was getting angry at me. I mean, it wasn't as if I'd kidnapped her, dragging her away from the Valley against her will.

"Where are we going, Jason?"

"North."

"North to where?"

I really had no idea, but I didn't say that. Instead I put my arm around her and drew her close, kissing the top of her head that smelled of wildflowers.

"We'll be all right, Quinnie," I said gently, trying to sound more sure of myself than I actually was. "You'll see, everything's going to work out fine, I promise."

I thought I heard something then, and when I glanced in the rearview mirror my breath froze in my lungs, making a rattling sound like ice cubes in a glass.

"Oh shit," I said, half to myself.

Only Quinn heard me. She turned her head back, terrified by what she saw.

Behind us, two rotating beacons—cherries I think they're called—were flashing their red lights, while from the roof of the squad car a siren wailed to beat the band. I looked down at the speedometer but I was barely doing fifty-five.

"Our friend didn't waste much time, did he?" I said bitterly.

But Quinn was too frightened by the highway patrol car to respond.

I had to think fast. I could pull over to the shoulder, ditch the car and make a run for it. But then without transportation we'd really be in trouble. At least with the car we could put some distance between us and the Valley. On foot we wouldn't stand a chance.

"What are we going to do now, Jason? You know what'll happen if they take us back."

Quinn slunk down in her seat and I did the same, just as the squad car overtook us. But instead of hearing a voice calling out to pull over, the patrol car sped right past us. Apparently they were after someone else altogether, and Quinn was so relieved she couldn't stop herself from giggling. Pretty soon both of us were slapping our thighs and laughing so loud we must've scared Becky 'cause she woke up and started to cry.

Quinn rocked the baby in her arms, gently and lovingly lulling her back to sleep. Then she felt Becky's bottom and began to look concerned.

"I have to change her diaper, Jason. And I bet it's time for her to have another bottle."

"Can't you do it in the back seat?"

"I guess so, but it's going to be awfully hard on her. Aren't we going to stop soon? You're not planning on driving all night, are you?"

Actually, I hadn't given it much thought. It wasn't even eight o'clock, and I didn't feel very tired. So I asked her to be patient, we'd drive for another hour or so and then I'd think of something. She didn't argue with me, but I could see how worried she was about the baby. I was secretly worried too, because even I could see that there was more to taking care of Becky than just changing diapers and seeing to it that she got enough to eat. I just prayed Quinn could figure out how to handle such a mysterious creature as we went along.

As we went along to where?

I didn't know yet. But unless I started coming up with some answers, I knew we'd really be in trouble.

Pine Blu f Motel. Vacan y.

It was getting on toward eleven, and we were on a small country road, miles from nowhere. Quinn was half-asleep, holding Becky securely in her arms. The motel looked like a real dump, and I figured they would probably rent a room to anyone who asked. But I wasn't going to take any chances. So I parked out of sight of the office, then nudged Quinn until she opened her eyes.

"Are we there yet?" she asked in a sleepy voice.

That was funny, but I couldn't bring myself to laugh. She used to say that when we were little kids, and Mom and Dad would take us on trips. We used to do lots of things together—until he ruined all that for us. Now, I had no idea where "there" was, no idea where I was ultimately heading. But maybe if we got a decent night's sleep we'd be able to figure out what to do. Anyway, I couldn't drive all night, so I really didn't have any other choice.

"Where are we?" Quinn asked.

"Halfway to Oz."

"Be serious, Jason."

"I'm trying not to."

Before she could say anything else, I cupped her face in my hands and kissed her on the mouth. She tasted good. But when I tried again she pulled away.

I made a move to get out of the car, but Quinn reached out and stopped me.

"What are you going to tell them?"

She motioned in the direction of the office.

"Just leave it to me," I said, trying to project a confidence I was far from feeling.

At least I had money in my pocket. That would have to count for something. So I crossed the gravel drive and went up the steps to the office. The screen door wasn't locked, and as soon as I stepped inside a bell tinkled above my head.

The place was even cruddier than I expected. There was a battered old Coke machine stuck away in a corner, wooden cases with empty bottles piled halfway to the ceiling. At one end a flimsy wooden counter blocked a doorway that led off into another room. I could hear a TV going, and I went over to the counter and rang the bell.

"Anyone home?" I called out.

Something creaked behind the door.

"Hello?"

I thought I heard footsteps, and a moment later the doorknob began to turn.

"Hold your horses, I'm comin' just as fast as I can," an irritated voice called out.

The door opened and this enormously obese man peered at me from behind a thick pair of bifocals. He was so fat that in order to get through the doorway he had to walk sideways.

"What can I do for you, sonny?"

I hate that word, but I had to be polite. So I just smiled and launched into the little speech I'd already rehearsed in advance.

"Sorry to bother you, sir. My dad and I need a room for the night. He's a little . . . well, I think he's had a little too much to drink. I was afraid he wouldn't even make it here, but he did. Only now he's asleep in the car."

I took out my wallet and carefully removed a twenty-dollar bill.

"Will that be enough?"

The owner of the Pine Bluff Motel didn't waste any time snatching the twenty off the counter.

"He's not gonna be sick or anything, is he, sonny?" the man asked suspiciously.

"He's got an iron stomach, my dad. He'll just sleep it off and tomorrow he'll be fine."

"Good, because I don't take kindly to cleaning up someone else's puke. That'll be sixteen even. Checkout time's eleven A.M. No exceptions, neither. You think your old man'll be up by then?"

"Oh, I'm sure of it, sir. He just needs a good night's sleep and he'll be fine."

The fat man managed to wedge his hand into his pocket, pulled out a roll of greasy bills and counted off my change. Then he handed me the key and made a move to step out from behind the counter.

"I can find it, sir," I said hurriedly. "You don't have to go to any trouble."

I didn't like the way he was looking at me. He had these piggy little eyes, and I started to think of that guy in *Psycho* and almost panicked. That's all we needed, some weirdo spying on us through a hole in the wall.

"Number six is around back. And don't play the TV loud, sonny."

"No, we're going right to bed."

I pretended to yawn, then thanked him again and backed away. He just stood there watching me, rubbing his nose with the back of his hand. He was so fat he didn't even have a wrist, and his fingers were like a bunch of sausages. People like that make me sick. But this guy gave me the creeps on top of everything else. I couldn't get out of there fast enough, and when the screen door slammed shut and the bell tinkled I knew he was still watching me. So even as I started back to the car I made sure not to break into a run.

At least he hadn't asked to see a driver's license, so there was no way anyone could trace us. I drove us over to number six, and Quinn was so relieved that as soon as we got inside the room she threw her arms around me and gave me a hug.

"See? That wasn't so difficult, was it?" I said, feeling almost giddy with relief.

The room wasn't too bad, either. At least the TV worked and the sheets looked clean. There was plenty of hot water too, and so the first thing Quinn did was fill the sink so that she could give Becky a bath.

"We'll have to buy her some clothes tomorrow. And maybe a book on baby care, too."

Becky actually seemed to like her bath and was real cooperative, and after it was over, Quinn got her dressed and then fed her. I sat on the bed and watched them, and I had this wonderful feeling that everything was going to be all right.

"Why don't you shower?" Quinn suggested. "Then I'll go in and you can watch Becky."

I stood under the hot water for the longest time, trying to clear my head. I didn't want to worry about tomorrow, or the day after that. One day at a time, just like I'd already said. So much had happened to us, and in so short a period of time, that I hadn't even had a chance to make plans. Tomorrow we'd continue heading north. And after that . . . I didn't know yet, but I didn't want to think about it, either.

When I'd finished, I dried myself off, but instead of wrapping the towel around my waist I just walked right back into the room, purposely standing there without any clothes on.

Right away, Quinn got all red in the face, and wouldn't even look at me.

"Since when have you gotten so shy?" I said angrily. "You've seen me naked before, so why pretend you haven't?"

"I'm not pretending anything, Jason."

She kept her eyes averted, and arranged the pillows on one of the twin beds so Becky wouldn't fall off in the middle of the night. The baby was fast asleep, and Quinn laid her gently between the two pillows, making sure she was comfortable.

"Then why are you acting this way?"

She wouldn't answer me, and announced in a peevish voice that she was going to take a shower, and would I please keep an eye on the baby until she was through. I got into bed and pulled the covers up to my neck, wondering why she was being so distant and aloof. We were more than just brother and sister, and Quinn knew that as well as I did.

"When this is over, and we find out why Father did this terrible thing, what he hoped to gain by it, we'll still have each other. That's the way I want it to be, okay?"

Those were Quinn's very words. She'd told me that earlier in the day, promising me that no matter what happened it wouldn't be over between us. The ritual of the undivided spirit (that was the way I described being close to her) wasn't going to end just because Mom had come back to us. Besides, I hadn't forced her to make that commitment, and now I was getting very upset by the way she seemed to be changing her mind, going back on her word without bothering to tell me why.

When she came out of the bathroom I expected her to crawl into bed with Becky, but I think she was afraid she might roll over in her sleep and hurt the baby.

"You're not wearing pajamas," she said accusingly.

"I never wear pajamas. You know that."

Quinn frowned and got into bed. She was wearing a nightgown, not the sexy shortie pajamas Mom had given her for her last birthday, and which she'd been so pleased with at the time.

I leaned over to kiss her good-night, but she turned her back on me, hugging her side of the bed as if I were a leper or something. I had a good mind to shake her and demand to know what the hell was going on. Instead I turned out the light. Then, without asking permission, I pulled her against me and kissed her hard on the mouth. She tried to push me away, but I wasn't about to let go. Quinn was more than my sister, don't you see? She was my lover too, half the reason why I decided to run away. If she betrayed me now, turned against me, I'd have nothing, and I couldn't bear the thought of being so alone in the world.

"But I love you, Quinnie. You know I do," I whispered.

I reached under her nightgown, slowly sliding my hand up between her legs. Her skin was so soft I couldn't stop myself from groaning. If she'd only relax and give me half a chance, I knew she'd like it as much as I did.

"Stop it, Jason. You mustn't," she begged. "Please, don't do this to me."

She was stammering, and in the darkness her eyes shone with tears that began to spill down her cheeks. I was so surprised that at first I didn't even know what to say. How could she be so afraid of me, especially when we had done this before? Didn't she know how much I cared? Didn't she realize that I'd never do anything to hurt her? By making love we would be joined not just physically, but emotionally as well. I needed that closeness now, more than ever before.

"I don't want to, don't you understand that!" she cried, sounding so desperate I could hardly believe my ears.

"But why?"

"Because it's wrong, Jason."

The words were so final, like a door slammed in my face.

"It wasn't wrong this morning, when you said we'd always be together."

I put my hand on her breasts, stroking her as gently as I could, and trying to get her to calm down. I could feel her shivering, but I couldn't tell if it was fear that made her tremble, or if she liked what I was doing with my hand.

"Just let me hold you," I whispered, kissing her again. "That's all I want, Quinn, I swear. Just to feel you against me, to know you won't leave me."

Quinn reached up, brushing my hair back with her fingertips. I guess she didn't realize the effect she had on me, because even a gesture as innocent as that aroused me. But when I took hold of her hand and tried to get her to touch me, she pulled away.

"I can't anymore, Jason," she said in a sad, faraway tone of voice. "Please don't force me to do something I don't want. It'll be bad for us, just the way it was bad for you when Mother did it. I love you and I always will, but I can't love you that way anymore."

"Then what did we run away for?"

I hadn't meant to shout, not just because the owner of the motel looked like a nosy creep, but also because of the baby. At least Becky didn't wake up, though Quinn glared at me in the darkness, upset by the way I was pressuring her into having sex.

"She's dead, Jason, don't you understand that? She's dead and she's never coming back."

"But we're alive, Quinn. We did everything we could for her. You know how hard we tried to help her. It wasn't our fault that—"

My voice broke, and a thick bolus of grief rose in my throat.

"I know that, but how can you even think of pleasure after what's happened? Haven't we been through enough?"

Having succeeded in making me feel guilty for wanting to be close to her, I knew there was no point in trying to get my way.

"Fine, you want to go to sleep, go to sleep," I told her. "Good night," and I rolled onto my back and stared at the ceiling.

Any moment now I expected Warren to wake up and start passing judgment. But as I lay there in the darkness all I felt was a yawning emptiness in my head.

He was gone, having cleared out without a trace. But I had to be sure, and so I called to him, telling him it was all right to give his opinion of what had happened. But he never answered me, even though I used all of his old tricks to get him to respond.

Who knows, maybe the pills I found in Mom's medicine chest were much more potent than I realized. Maybe Warren was born out of desperation, and now that I'd left the Valley, I could leave him behind.

Being on my own again would take some getting used to. Yet I knew it was probably the best thing that had happened to me in months. I wanted to tell Quinn, but when I glanced at her she was hugging her side of the bed, trying to keep her distance. Even though her eyes were closed I knew she was wide-awake. Was she scared of me, was that it? And if she was, how the hell could I expect her to give herself to me when she probably thought I was on the verge of losing my mind?

"Quinn, I'm sorry," I whispered gently. "You forgive me, don't you?"

I reached out, touching her lightly on the shoulder. She turned over and looked at me, and there was so much sadness in her eyes it almost made me cry.

"I'd never hurt you, you know that. Don't you trust me anymore, Quinnie?"

"I'll always trust you, Jason."

Again I listened to the silence between my ears. There was an empty room up there, and I knew that Warren wasn't coming back to claim it. So I put my arm around Quinn and drew her close. She snuggled up to me, leaning her head against my chest. We didn't say anything after that, but I knew what she was thinking. She was wondering what would become of us, and I was wondering the same thing, too.

CHAPTER THREE

Perhaps I should have given in to him, submitted to the ritual of the undivided spirit that had bound us together in the terrible weeks following Mother's supposed death. I thought of that for a long time, unable to fall asleep. But though I couldn't deny the pleasure I might feel sharing that kind of intimacy with my brother, I knew if we continued to have sex it could only lead to disaster.

Yet it hurt me all the same, for I sensed his need was much greater than just a physical release. Jason needed to give himself to me, perhaps to prove he was still capable of love. He seemed so lost and lonely, so in need of friends, that I struggled with my conscience, unable to decide what to do.

On top of everything else, I was secretly afraid, frightened that Jason might lose control as he had done with Mother. Not once since we'd left the Valley had he mentioned what had happened the night Mother was taken away from us. Not once had he alluded to the desperate confession he had made in Father's presence, admitting the guilt that he'd kept locked inside him.

Mother hadn't tried to harm Jason, not physically that

is. But Jason had tried to harm her, and had nearly succeeded in taking her life that dreadful night when Mrs. Darby locked me in my room, helping Father keep everything a secret from me.

It was Jason who took the bone-handled dirk and brought it down across Mother's wrists, Jason who listened to the malevolent voice that commanded him to punish Mother for her sins, the voice he called Warren.

These were truths that could never be forgotten. All that had happened that night was etched in my memory, and I would have to live with that knowledge for the rest of my life. But though I expected Jason to talk about it, to retell it in less hysterical terms, his silence seemed to say that none of it had ever taken place, that what I had heard just hours before was merely fiction, a horrifying tale that had no basis in reality.

But it *was* real. He had tried to commit murder, and now I lay in bed and couldn't help but wonder if one day he would turn upon me as he had turned on Mother.

Where was the faith and confidence he used to inspire in me? When he asked, I had said that I would always trust him. Yet lying there in bed that night, I was as uncertain of Jason as I was of the future. I could never admit that to him, of course, for I knew he wouldn't be able to understand my feelings. But I was afraid, afraid of everything it seemed. Afraid Father would come after us, and my brother would be dragged away, never to return. Afraid I wouldn't be able to take proper care of Becky, afraid that she, too, would be taken from me. Afraid of so many things I couldn't even close my eyes, for there were fresh terrors waiting in the darkness, creatures which thrived on pain, intent upon destroying what little happiness I had left.

Outside the window of our cabin the pines shifted with

the rhythm of the wind. Shadows moved across the ceiling, branches that took on the shape of bony, clutching hands. Jason was sound asleep as I lay there in the darkness, feeling the same nameless terrors I had known as a child, the fear of the dark, the evil shapes lurking just beyond my reach.

When I heard the scratching at the door I wanted to laugh, certain my lurid imagination had finally gotten the better of me. Of course there wasn't anything there. It was just the wind, whispering through the pines. How could it be anything else when no one even knew we were here?

I tried to will myself to sleep, confident that in the morning I would be able to think more clearly. But the scratching persisted, and finally I could no longer pretend that I didn't hear it. I sat up in bed, peering anxiously in the direction of the door. Was the knob beginning to turn, or were my eyes playing tricks on me?

Oh God, it was turning! But so slowly it was like the ticking of a clock, the imperceptible movement of the hour hand.

Then I heard what surely had to be a key. Had Father somehow discovered our whereabouts? Was he waiting outside, whispering instructions to men in white coats who would carry Jason off before I could stop them? And the baby—what would become of Becky? What plans had he made for her? And what would he do about me, knowing that I had witnessed all his treachery?

The key rasped in the lock. I grabbed Jason by the shoulder and began to shake him, never once taking my eyes off the door.

"Someone's out there," I whispered.

He turned over in bed, still half-asleep and unable to

understand what I was talking about. But by then it was already too late.

A huge, bloated shape filled the threshold, some kind of monstrous apparition I was certain couldn't possibly be real.

But it was real. It was so terrifyingly real that I couldn't even bring myself to scream.

"Little girl, nice little girl," a voice snickered in the darkness.

I started to cry I was so scared. By then Jason was as awake as I was. I saw him reach for something on the nightstand, even as the figure in the shadows closed the door and began to move toward the bed.

"Who's there? What do you want?" my brother suddenly called out.

"You don't want me to call the sheriff on you, do you, sonny? I know what you've been doin', and you're already in lots of trouble."

But Jason refused to be intimidated.

"I don't know what you're talking about," he replied.

"Sure you do, sonny."

The man stood by the foot of the bed, nearly as wide as he was tall. I had no idea who he was, or what he wanted from us. Jason whispered he was the owner of the motel, and that I should just keep quiet and let him do all the talking.

"Who's the cute little girl, sonny? Can I play with her, too?"

He couldn't stop giggling, as if he were enjoying some kind of private joke the nature of which we knew nothing about.

"We haven't done anything to you, so why don't you just leave us alone," Jason told him.

48

"But I want to play a game, sonny. A nice little game."

The man continued to snicker, and when Jason suddenly switched on the light I took one look and couldn't help myself. I sat there on the bed, shivering as a pool of urine spread out beneath me. The man was exposing himself, staring at us as if we were his prisoners.

"Just a nice little game," he said, playing with himself and unable to stop giggling.

"Oh Jason," I whimpered.

"Shh, it's all right, Quinn," whispered my brother.

"I'm wet . . . don't let him touch me, Jason. Please, don't let him hurt me."

"Ain't you seen one before, girlie? Bet sonny here has shown you his."

He reached down and snatched the covers off the bed. Then he pointed at Jason and began to shake his head.

"What a naughty little boy you are, sonny. I bet you make her play with it, don't you?"

I glanced at Becky out of the corner of my eye. She was still asleep and at least the man wasn't paying any attention to her, too busy staring at us to notice we weren't the only ones in the room.

"Take off your nightgown, girlie," the man went on.

There was a threatening edge to his voice, an undercurrent of violence I hadn't heard until now. He was still playing with himself, pulling at his stubby red thing. Behind the thick lenses of his glasses his eyes were opened wide, and he didn't have to say anything to me to know the sick, evil things he was thinking.

"Take it off for her, sonny. I want to see the girlie's little titties."

"Do as he says, Quinn."

"But—"

"Just do as he says."

Jason sounded so calm, so in control of the situation that I didn't hesitate to follow his instructions. I was wet and cold, so terrified of what might happen that when I tried to pull the nightgown over my head my fingers felt numb, incapable of movement. When I finally got it off the man began to grin. Through the gap between his two front teeth I could see his tongue moving. He kept licking his palate, and the sound he made was so obscene I wanted to press my hands to my ears.

His fat, stubby hand moved faster. Jason edged away from me, his eyes never leaving the stranger who'd crept into our room.

"You like to look at her, don't you, mister? She's real pretty, isn't she? Don't you want to touch her? Wouldn't you like to feel how soft she is?"

"Jason, how can you even—"

Before I could get the words out, my brother shot a warning glance at me, and I knew I had to trust him now as perhaps I'd never trusted him before.

"Show me what you do to her, sonny," the owner of the motel whispered excitedly.

The man's voice was dry and bloodless. He kept licking his lips, making that awful obscene sound with his tongue.

"You do it first," Jason challenged him.

The man stepped closer, the buttons on his shirt pulled taut across his pendulous stomach. He bent down and began to rub his hand against my leg. I jerked back, and his leering expression was replaced by one of utter cruelty.

"You shouldn't have been mean to me, girlie, 'cause now I'm gonna have to hurt you," he threatened.

I edged back until I could go no further. The man started to come around to my side of the bed when Jason suddenly threw himself at our assailant. He moved so quickly I hardly knew what happened, but a moment later the man's watery little eyes were no longer hidden behind the thick lenses of his eyeglasses. Jason had managed to snatch them off, and he hurled them across the room.

The man looked wildly about, desperate to recover them. But there was something in his frightened, myopic stare that told me the tables were about to be turned, and now he would be the hunted and not the hunter.

"You son of a bitch, you fucking pervert," Jason swore as he scrambled off the bed.

"Give 'em back to me, sonny, or you're gonna be a very sorry little boy."

"Sure, I'll give it back to you all right. And when I'm through you'll never forget me, either," Jason hissed.

The man squinted at us, barely able to see. He stumbled back toward the door, searching frantically for his glasses. They were just a few feet behind him, but Jason wasn't about to let him find them. Something glinted in his hand, and when I realized what it was I put my hand over my mouth and tried not to scream.

Jason lunged forward, moving so quickly he was a blur. The owner of the motel let out a startled gasp. His hands clutched at his enormous stomach, and blood suddenly sprayed across his fingers.

"Why you little—"

The man never finished the sentence.

Jason darted closer and stabbed him a second time. There was so much blood now I couldn't bear to look. The motel owner began to sway back and forth, while blood continued to drench his shirt. Jason rushed back to the bed and grabbed the lamp off the night table. Brandishing it like a club, he brought it down across the man's head. It was then that Becky woke up and started to cry. And it was then that our attacker collapsed on the floor, landing with a thud that made the entire room shake.

"Dry yourself off and get dressed," Jason said in a breathless voice. "I'll get our things together."

I was still so frightened I could barely move. My teeth were chattering, and when I pulled myself to my feet I had to grab onto the edge of the bed for support. My knees buckled, and for a moment I was afraid I wouldn't even be able to make it to the bathroom. But then Jason took me in his arms and held me close, whispering that everything would be all right.

As soon as I washed myself off I began to feel a little better. Jason hadn't wasted any time getting dressed, and as I pulled on my jeans I watched him tearing one of the bed sheets into strips. These he used to tie the motel owner's hands behind his back, securing his ankles together as well.

By then, the man had come to, groaning but still very much alive. When Jason started to gag him he shook his head violently and tried to pull away. Dragging himself along the floor, he begged my brother to leave him alone. He swore he wouldn't cry out or make any noise, but Jason didn't seem very impressed by his promises.

"You know what they do to child molesters, mister? They lock you up in a nuthouse and throw away the key. So just count your lucky stars that's not going to happen to you . . . this time, anyway."

"I didn't mean nothin', sonny, honest I didn't," the man blubbered.

"Oh sure," Jason said sarcastically. "You just came by to see if we were comfy, right?"

He stuffed the strips of linen between the man's teeth,

tying double knots so it wouldn't slip. But when everything was packed and we were ready to leave, I looked back at our tormentor and couldn't help but feel sorry for him.

"Jason, we just can't leave him here. What if he bleeds to death?"

"Then we'll be doing the world a service," replied my brother.

"But you can't let him die, Jason. Maybe we can try to stop the bleeding before we go."

Jason bent down and unbuttoned the man's shirt. I looked away, not wanting to see how bad the wounds were.

"He'll survive," my brother said when he came to his feet. "He's so fat the knife hardly did any damage."

"But—"

"Quinn, just get your ass out of here and stop arguing! He tried to rape you! Why are you feeling sorry for him? He got what he deserved."

Maybe my brother had a point. But now that the motel owner was lying there on the floor, bound and gagged and covered with blood, he looked much more pathetic than dangerous. As sick as he was—and I didn't need Jason to remind me of that—I couldn't bear the thought of leaving him like this.

"Can't we call someone to come and help him?" I asked.

"This isn't Dad we're dealing with," Jason reminded me. "It's a sick creep who got what was coming to him. Now let's get a move on."

The man had nearly frightened me to death, but all the blood I saw frightened me even more. So I told him we'd leave the door unlocked, he could drag himself outside where one of the other guests would surely find him. He couldn't answer me of course, but there was something in his eyes—a look of gratitude, perhaps—that made me feel a little better.

Jason was tugging impatiently on my arm, and so I bundled Becky up and followed him outside. The light from the cabin spilled across the gravel. I could hear an owl hooting in the distance, and the wind that blew through the trees sent pine needles swirling about my ankles. Becky was sucking on a pacifier, and I could tell it was time for another feeding. I'd just have to do it in the car, that's all, because now the only thing on Jason's mind was getting away.

We'd left the Valley some twelve hours before, and in all that time we hadn't stopped running. Would we ever stop? Or was it going to be like this for the rest of our lives?

"Let's see now," my brother said, consulting the over-sized menu the waitress had handed him. "Ham and eggs, toast, coffee . . . do you want anything else, Quinn?"

"Orange juice, and a bowl of shredded wheat."

"Milk or cream?" the waitress asked.

"Milk, please."

She rattled off the order, then looked at us as curiously as she had when we first walked into the diner.

"You want that bottle warmed up, honey?" she asked while I tried to feed the baby.

"No, I think it's all right, thank you."

"You're the boss," the waitress replied, trying to make a joke of it.

Jason and I kept smiling, not saying a word until she poured the coffee and turned away. Then my brother leaned over the table and whispered we shouldn't stay here any longer than we had to, there was something about this place that was making him nervous.

We'd been driving for several hours, and when I looked at the map I found in the glove compartment I saw that we had already traveled much farther than I realized. Another four or five hours and we'd reach the Oregon border. What would happen once we got there was anybody's guess.

I asked Jason what his plans were, but instead of answering he just sipped his coffee and pretended not to hear.

"Are you sure you're all right?" I finally said. "You're acting like you're spooked or something."

The waitress brought our order, only to return a moment later to freshen our coffee.

"That's some cute little baby you got," the woman said. She jabbed her pencil into the mass of curls piled stiffly on top of her head, then peered at Becky as if she'd never seen a baby before. "How old is he?"

"She," I corrected.

"Looks awfully little," the waitress remarked.

"She is," Jason said coldly.

The woman continued to smile, acting not the least bit put off by my brother's hostile tone of voice. She looked out the window to the parking lot, but I didn't think she knew which car was ours.

"When you bring the check, bring a black coffee and a sweet roll to go," my brother spoke up. He looked at me, but I couldn't tell if he was winking or if there was something in his eye. "Mom'll want some hot coffee when she wakes up," he explained.

His words seemed to have the desired effect. The waitress turned away, and we were finally able to eat our breakfast in peace.

"What was that all about?" I whispered.

"I didn't like the way she was looking at us."

But the waitress wasn't the only one who seemed to be showing an interest in us. Maybe it was my imagination, but as I ate my breakfast I was sure we were fast becoming the object of everyone's curiosity. People kept glancing in our direction and whispering amongst themselves, and finally Jason got so nervous he couldn't take it anymore.

"Let's get out of here, Quinn. Something's going on and I don't like it. Maybe there's been a report about us on the radio. For all we know Dad can be offering a big reward to anyone who finds us."

When my brother noticed the waitress whispering to the cashier, and then the cashier making a phone call right after, he didn't waste any more time. He waved his hand to attract her attention, then asked her to bring the check.

"But you didn't finish your breakfast, honey," she said, smiling sweetly.

Rather than answer, Jason pulled out his wallet and waited for her to add up the bill.

"Come on, a big feller like you must be hungrier than that," she went on, motioning at all the food he'd left on his plate.

Jason ignored her, and when he turned to me he sounded calm.

"Why don't you go wake Mom, Quinn, and tell her we're ready to leave."

By the time he joined me outside I could see the panic in his eyes from ten feet away. For a moment I thought he was overreacting, but when I glanced across the parking lot to the diner, I saw the waitress watching us through the window.

"Just get in the car," Jason said anxiously. "If she sees

me get behind the wheel she's going to call the cops . . . if she hasn't already.''

I did as I was told, and when he tore out of the parking lot and back onto the road I half-expected to see the waitress come rushing out of the diner to try to stop us. But when I looked back there was no one there.

"After this, only one of us is going to eat at a time. Or we'll buy takeout,'' Jason announced.

"After this, I may not ever have an appetite again.''

I tried to laugh, but with Jason staring grimly ahead it was impossible to feel anything but dread. Completing the grim prospect that confronted us was the fact that the gas gauge was dangerously low, which meant we had no choice but to stop and fill up the tank before we ran completely dry.

We were traveling on a dirt road to avoid being spotted, and when we pulled into a rundown service station several miles from the highway, Jason didn't waste any time.. He jumped out of the car and hurriedly unscrewed the fuel cap. But the moment he stepped up to the pump a kid in greasy overalls rushed outside, waving his hands in the air.

"Hey man, you gotta be kidding,'' he told my brother.

I was fully prepared for Jason to lose his temper. But he surprised me and played it very straight. He stared right at the attendant who couldn't have been much older than he was, and asked him to fill her up and check the oil. But the kid just looked at him and laughed.

"Gimme a break, man. You ain't old enough to drive, and you know it. Now who'd you steal the wheels from, your old man?''

Jason smiled mischievously, like he was about to let the kid in on a secret.

"If I tell you, will you sell us gas?''

"Might," the kid said, considering Jason's offer. "Then again, might not."

The attendant stuck his hands in the pockets of his overalls and rocked back and forth, standing between Jason and the pump. He glanced at me and grinned, waiting for my brother to take him into his confidence.

Jason was still playing it very cool, not letting the boy's attitude upset him.

"If my old man comes after me I'm really gonna be up shit's creek. So I'll tell you what. Not only will I pay you for a full tank, but I'll also throw in a ten just for your trouble."

The kid took off his peaked cap and scratched his head, trying to decide whether to accept my brother's offer. He looked at Jason and then at me, looked at the car and then at the pump.

"Make it a twenty and you got yourself a deal," he said at last.

I was afraid the boy might renege once we gave him the money. But no sooner did Jason stuff the twenty dollars into his hand than he went right over to the pump and started to fill the tank for us. Jason asked him the best way to get to Redding, the nearest town of any size—"Without my old man sicking the highway patrol on us"—and the attendant gave him directions that skirted all the main roads into town, something my brother had been trying to avoid all along.

By the time we got back on the road he was grinning from ear to ear, so pleased with the way he handled things he kept smiling all the way into Redding. But getting gas was one thing. Getting a job and a place to stay would be quite another.

I wanted to talk to him about that, but I hated to bring

up anything that might spoil his mood. He was acting like the Jason of old, and even the nightmarish experience back at the motel was something that was behind us now, more like a bad dream than anything else. His carefree mood was infectious, and by the time we got to Redding I was well on my way to forgetting all that had happened to us just a few hours before.

But a few hours before that Father lay on the floor of Mother's bedroom, clutching the wound in his side and begging us to listen to reason. The Valley was hundreds of miles away, but I had the strangest feeling it was just up ahead. If I squinted hard enough perhaps I could see it, beyond the bend in the road, past the break in the trees where the hills scattered the golden light of Indian summer. But no, it was a mirage that shimmered in the distance, for never again would I be able to think of the Valley as home, a place where I was always safe and happy.

CHAPTER FOUR

Redding was awfully pretty, the kind of place you just want to settle down in and stay put. There were kids out playing on bicycles and dogs chasing after them, pretty bright-eyed Moms hanging up the wash, and handsome, dependable Dads mowing the front lawn. I told Quinn it was the kind of town we should've grown up in, then maybe things would have turned out different for us.

I was feeling better than I had in as long as I could remember, and even that creepy business back at the Pine Bluff Motel didn't stick in my mind very long. Not that I hadn't learned a valuable lesson though. From now on in I'd make sure to wedge a chair up against the door, just in case anyone else got the bright idea they could take advantage of us because we were kids.

But those couple of hours we spent tooling around Redding—we needed supplies for the baby—were kind of like a break in the clouds, if you know what I mean. The future wasn't going to be easy, but at least now that my head was screwed on straight I'd be able to face things without being afraid. So with those kind of worries behind me, Quinn and I actually had fun for a change.

Quinn was being extra friendly, just like her old self. We needed this quiet time together, time to figure out what to do next and where to go. But just when I thought we were over the hump, and maybe from now on in things were going to get easier, Becky started having problems.

At first, neither of us thought it was serious. We'd been giving her her bottle every two or three hours, but somehow she was losing her appetite, refusing to eat no matter how much time Quinn spent with her. When we finally reached Oregon early that evening and checked into a motel—''My Dad's in the car, sir. He's not feeling too well. Gets these awful migraine headaches. They just come on out of nowhere''—Becky threw up twice in the middle of the night, and I was afraid the people next-door would call the office and complain that her crying was keeping them awake.

But no one bothered us, and the next morning she seemed a little better. But we weren't on the road an hour when she got sick again and Quinn said we had to take her to a hospital because if we didn't there was just no telling what would happen.

The whole thing was much too chancy, that was the problem. I wanted to steer clear of towns, especially in broad daylight. The less I showed my face, the better I liked it, though when we got a bunch of papers from Fresno, Sacramento, and Bakersfield, there wasn't a word about us. All day we'd listened to the radio, but when the news came on there wasn't any mention of our disappearance. As for that freak back at the motel, we didn't learn anything else about him, either, though Quinn went through all the newspapers with a fine-tooth comb.

Anyway, we had problems, the kind of hassles I never would have anticipated when Quinn and I left home. It wasn't our home anymore, that was the thing. And even if Quinn decided to go back there one day, I knew I never would. I never wanted to lay eyes on Bennett Lefland again. He didn't love me and he never had. Besides, he was probably just as glad I'd run away, because now he wouldn't have to try to explain himself when he and Aunt Gwen got married. And they *were* getting married—she had said so and I believed her. It was just about the only thing she'd ever said that wasn't a lie.

But with the baby sick, I knew I shouldn't even be wasting my time thinking about Aunt Gwendolyn Howe. Becky was a hell of a lot more important, and right now we had to find out what was wrong with her. She was so little, you see, so terribly dependent upon us. And when she got sick in the car I thought my sister would start to cry, Quinn felt so helpless.

"Okay, okay, I'm going to stop, I promise," I told her.

What did she think, I didn't care about my daughter? Of course I cared, and I wouldn't do anything to hurt her. So the first thing I did was have Quinn check out the map. Some ten miles up the road was the county seat, and I figured we'd be able to get help there. I just wondered what I would say to the doctors once we found a hospital.

Josephine County General was right in the middle of town, which meant the risks involved were going to be a lot greater than I cared to take. But I guess we didn't have any other choice. So far we'd been lucky—at least with the police—but driving through town in broad daylight wasn't my idea of a picnic.

But somehow I did it. I just kept my eyes glued straight ahead, never letting anyone look at me for very long. Quinn wanted me to drive right up to the emergency entrance, but I had a feeling it might be too dangerous. So we parked in the visitors' lot, then debated who should go in with the baby.

"You're too young," I told her. "They're going to get very suspicious, and we just can't take the chance."

"Every minute you're behind the wheel we take chances," she reminded me. "So why is it so different now? I know what to say; I'm not stupid."

"No one ever said you were, Quinnie, but it has nothing to do with that. I'll just feel better if I go in with her, that's all. They might not be so condescending."

"I'm not a child, Jason."

"Of course you're not. But they'll probably think you are, and then we'll really be in trouble. A kid comes in with a baby—who knows what they'll do."

What I didn't tell Quinn was that I was afraid she might panic if something unexpected happened. I already knew what I was going to say once I got inside, whereas I don't think Quinn had even stopped to consider that yet.

So finally she agreed to my plan. I left her sitting in the car, and when I looked back she raised her hand and waved, trying to smile though I knew she was very worried about the baby.

I found the emergency room without having to ask directions, but there were three or four people ahead of me so I had to wait my turn. One poor guy looked like he'd been through a meat grinder, just covered with blood. I took a seat and looked away, rocking Becky in my arms so she wouldn't cry. Even though I didn't mean to stare, I couldn't help myself. Every time I glanced at the guy waiting his turn outside the emergency room I kept thinking of my father, lying there in a pool of blood.

Was it wrong what I did? Ever since leaving the Valley I hadn't felt any guilt about what had happened. But now with the baby sick I wasn't living a fantasy anymore. I knew what I'd tried to do to Mom, and I knew what I'd nearly succeeded in doing to my father. And I began to feel very sick and nauseous and dizzy, thinking of the things Mom had forced me to do, and how I must've gotten so nuts I lashed out at her without even realizing it. It was all Warren's fault, of course. But even though Warren had disappeared, he'd still been a part of me, and I knew it was time to take responsibility for my actions.

With rising alarm, my thoughts came back to Becky. She looked pale and listless, and though I tried to get her to smile her eyes were glazed and half-closed. I got real scared then, thinking she might even be dying or something.

Finally it was her turn. When the nurse came out of the emergency room I jumped to my feet and followed her inside. The door closed behind us, and a young guy with a neatly trimmed beard, horn-rims, and a bloodstained lab coat immediately took Becky out of my arms and laid her down on the examining table.

"You're kind of young to be a father, aren't you?" he said.

The doctor was making a joke, only he didn't realize how unfunny it was. I smiled all the same, then motioned vaguely behind me.

"Mom had car trouble, that's why she's not here. She had to wait for a tow truck, and we were afraid the baby might be too sick, so we didn't want to take any chances. I guess she'll catch up to me as soon as they get the car fixed."

I explained Becky's symptoms, but I think what really surprised the doctor was how small she was. I didn't want to tell him she was just a couple of days old, so I said she was born two weeks ago—"Mom had her at home 'cause we live in the country''—and hoped he'd believe me. I don't know if he did, but he went right to work examining the baby.

I told him what we'd been feeding her, and when he asked why my mother wasn't nursing her I pretended not to understand what he was talking about.

"Breast-feeding," said the nurse who was assisting him.

"Oh, that," I said, and I smiled shyly the way boys my age were supposed to whenever people talked about breasts in public. "Gee, I don't know exactly, but the doctor who helped deliver her put Becky on this formula and that's what Mom's been using. Isn't it the right stuff?"

"Oh, it's fine," said the doctor. "But apparently your sister's allergic to it. You wouldn't happen to know the name of that doctor, would you?"

I shook my head, hoping he didn't notice how nervous I was getting.

"Tell you what," he went on. "Why don't you wait outside with your sister. Soon as your mom gets here I'll go over everything with her."

"But what if she doesn't get here for awhile? I told her I'd meet her back at the garage."

"I thought you said she was going to pick you up, soon as your car was repaired."

I knew that's what I'd said, but if I didn't find out what kind of formula to feed the baby we'd be back where we started.

"She said whoever got done first," I stammered.

The doctor took off his horn-rims and rubbed his eyes with the back of his hand. Then I caught him motioning to the nurse with his chin, and the two of them stepped out of earshot.

What the hell were they whispering about? Maybe he

didn't believe my story. But even if he didn't there wasn't anything he could do about it, was there?

When he finally looked back at me I was sure something was up. I could have bolted out the door right then and there, but I didn't want to take any chances, what with Becky so sick and all.

"What was the name of that garage, do you recall?" the doctor asked.

I shook my head.

"It's a couple of blocks from here, that's all I remember. What's the matter, Doctor? If you write it down for me, the new formula I mean, I won't lose the paper."

"I'd just prefer to speak to your mother in person, that's all," he replied.

I could feel myself getting angry, I was so frustrated. But losing my temper was definitely the wrong thing to do. "I can stop and buy the new formula on the way to the garage," I said hurriedly. "That's why she sent me here, 'cause she was afraid if we waited too long the baby might get even sicker. Now you're telling me to sit out there in the hall, when what I should be doing is getting the stuff Becky needs for her bottle. Isn't that right, nurse?" I said, turning to the doctor's assistant.

"But Dr. Palmer thinks it's important he discuss the baby's condition with your mother."

"She'll come in. She'll come back tomorrow if you want. Just tell me what time you'd like to see her."

"But why can't she come in today?" Dr. Palmer argued.

"Because she had too much to drink, that's why," I said with a sob.

I turned my face away and pretended to cry, not stopping until I felt the nurse's hand on my shoulder.

"Don't you worry, Dr. Palmer is going to write everything down for you, all the instructions," she said comfortingly.

"Thank you, miss," I whispered. I rubbed my hands across my eyes like I was drying them, then looked up at Palmer and sniffled loudly. "It doesn't happen often, Doctor, honest it doesn't. But she had a fight with my dad and when he left for work she just couldn't help herself."

By then, Dr. Palmer was already writing everything I needed to know on a slip of paper. I kept sniffling and rubbing my eyes, certain the worst was over. Only it wasn't. The nurse wanted to know if we were on Medicaid, and when I said I didn't know she got all snippy like she was going to have to pay for everything out of her own pocket.

"You don't have to get upset," I told her. "Mom gave me money. I can pay."

Boy, did she change her tune after that. She busied herself preparing the bill while Dr. Palmer went over his instructions with me. When he was through I smiled politely and thanked him for all the time he'd given us, though it couldn't have been more than ten or fifteen minutes. Then I followed the nurse to the cashier's window, feeling so cocky I couldn't stop smiling. And Quinn thought it was going to be so difficult. Hell, the whole thing was a snap.

But no sooner did I pay the bill when the nurse insisted I go upstairs with her, there was someone else she wanted me to see.

"I'm sorry, but I don't have time," I tried to convince her.

She wanted me to speak to this woman who was a social worker, probably to discuss Mom's "drinking" problem. But at that point I just wanted to get out of there, knowing that if people kept asking me questions I was bound to slip up and give myself away.

"I have a headache and I have to meet my mom," I blurted out. Then, before the nurse could say another word I turned and rushed down the hall.

"Young man!" she called after me.

"We'll come back tomorrow, I promise," I yelled back, eyes on the doors that led out to the parking lot.

I don't know exactly what it was, but I kept getting this feeling she was on to me. Maybe I was being paranoid, but I wasn't about to take any chances. So I didn't even look back when she kept calling out to me.

When I stepped outside it was like I'd spent all morning in a movie theater. The sun was so strong I could barely see, and I stumbled on one of the steps and nearly went flying. Becky was bawling her head off, like she understood just what I was feeling.

"Young man!"

My heart started to pound even harder. The nurse and the intern were hurrying after me. I caught a glimpse of Quinn's horrified expression as she stared at me through the windshield, and prayed she'd stay put and let me try to handle things.

"I have to get the formula for the baby and take her home," I tried to explain when they caught up to me. "When Mom sits home alone she starts to drink, but if I'm there she'll be all right. I'll make a pot of coffee and explain all your instructions, Dr. Palmer, tell her how important it is she come in and see you."

I was speaking a mile a minute I was so nervous, but neither of them had any trouble understanding me.

"Are you sure you've told us the truth?" asked Dr. Palmer, eyeing me as curiously as his nurse.

"Truth about what?" I asked.

"Your mother's an alcoholic, isn't she? But we want to help you. Isn't that the real reason her doctor wouldn't let her nurse the baby, because she can't stop drinking?"

I felt like sobbing with relief! At least they believed the story I'd concocted.

"I was afraid you wouldn't understand," I said, making sure they heard the sob that caught in my throat.

"But we do," the nurse assured me. "That's why it's so important she speaks to someone who can help her."

Palmer handed me a card on which he'd written down the social worker's number. I promised to call and set up an appointment as soon as I got home.

"You'll see, everything's going to work out for the best. Alcoholism's a disease, and it's nothing to be ashamed of."

The nurse patted me on the shoulder, glanced at the baby, and finally turned away. Talk about close calls! Any closer and it would've been all over for us, no doubt about it.

But I still had to play it cool, so I didn't make a move until both of them were gone. Then I crossed the parking lot as nonchalantly as I could. All this time Quinn had been watching me, certain the noose was tightening around our necks. When I was sure it was safe, I slipped into the front seat, handed her Becky, and fought to calm myself down.

One crisis was behind us, but what were we to do about the abyss that lay ahead?

CHAPTER FIVE

The narrow road that was leading us farther and farther north looped and coiled around itself like a watchspring. Jason said we were entering the Cascades, but the lush forests, the rolling hills rising to become mountains in the distance, did little to ease my fears, or calm my anxious state of mind.

But at least we now knew why Becky had gotten sick, and how to prevent it from happening in the future.

I was growing increasingly fearful, even though the incident at the hospital had left Jason enormously relieved. Maybe running away wasn't the answer, and never had been.

"Don't worry," Jason kept insisting. "We've been in tough spots before, and we've managed to pull through. And we'll do it again."

But I couldn't be so sure, and I watched him out of the corner of my eye, afraid of what he might think if I began to stare. Despite the terrible hardships of recent months, my brother had only gotten handsomer. His bright silky hair was still a dozen shades of blond and brown, setting off the extraordinary depth of green in his eyes. As a youngster, I think people must have thought Jason too pretty for a boy, his face too finely modeled, too delicate perhaps. But now that he was growing into manhood he reminded me of the faces I'd seen etched on Roman coins. There was a subtle perfection to his features that I imagined disturbed some people, for physical beauty can be a very enviable quality.

Yes, he was beautiful, but manly too, though still in a boyish way. When he smiled, and his white teeth flashed brightly, I was able to glimpse the Jason I recalled from my earliest years, when he always seemed to know exactly how to make me happy. Somehow we'd come full circle, if that's the way to put it. The tables were turned now, and it was I who struggled to please him, to draw him out of himself, to convince him of both my love and my loyalty.

"I feel terrific," he said. "Isn't this beautiful country, Quinnie? Wouldn't it be nice to build a cabin deep in the woods, just live off the land and never have to worry about people again?" He glanced at me and smiled. "Think you'd like that, or would you get bored with me?"

He reached out, rubbing the back of his hand against my cheek. A month ago I might have taken his hand and pressed it to my lips. But now I couldn't, afraid that any display of physical affection would be misinterpreted. Maybe I still wanted that closeness. Maybe I needed it as much as Jason. But I knew I could never allow myself to experience that kind of love with him again.

We'd bought a safety seat for Becky, and now that she was on a formula that didn't make her sick she was sound asleep in the back seat, having finished her entire bottle. I turned my head back and watched her, and once again it amazed me that someone as beautiful as Becky Hope could have been born of so much suffering and anguish.

71

"Don't think of the past, Quinn. It'll only make you unhappy."

It wasn't the first time Jason had read my mind. I knew it wouldn't be the last. There were moments when we were as one, and moments when we looked upon each other as strangers. Now, we seemed to be walking that fine line dividing one from the other.

"It's hard not to," I admitted. "I can't stop thinking about what happened, wondering what steps Father is taking to try to find us."

"Maybe he isn't. Maybe he's glad to get us off his hands."

"You really don't believe that, Jason, do you? He didn't want us to run away. He begged us not to."

"Only because he knew we'd already made up our minds to leave."

"And if we ever make up our minds to return?"

Jason glared at me, and there was so much hostility in his eyes that I found myself shrinking from his gaze. I edged back along the seat, desperate to discuss our situation with him and yet afraid to panic him. He was so unpredictable I could never be sure of what to expect. But the last thing I wanted was to get into an argument, for he needed my support now more than ever before.

"I just think it's important we start making plans for the future," I said, broaching the subject as tactfully as I could. "I'm not questioning you, Jason, believe me. You know I've always trusted you."

Was that cynicism I saw in his expression, or was I just being overly sensitive?

"If you want to go home, Quinn, I can drop you off at the first town we come to. You can take a bus back and that'll be the end of it. But I'm not going with you, just remember that. I know what he wants to do with me, and I'm not going to let him get away with it. He's responsible for Mom's death, and he's going to pay for it, too. How can you even think of going back there after what he did to her?''

"But maybe he thought he was doing the right thing."

Jason slammed a fist against the steering wheel.

"How can you say that?" he yelled. "We've been over this time and time again and you keep coming back to it. Do you want to go home, Quinn? If you miss the Valley so much I'll put you on a bus and you can go back to Daddy and forget I ever existed."

"Please don't say that, Jason. I'm just trying to figure out what to do, that's all. What happens when the money runs out? What happens if someone recognizes us? For all we know the police can be looking for us right now. We have to start thinking about those things whether you like it or not."

He turned his eyes off the road, staring at me as if he didn't even know who I was anymore.

"We're going to make our own lives for ourselves. You promised. You swore to me. You said you'd be like Becky's mother, and that we'd be like—"

He stopped abruptly, his unspoken words dangling in the air.

"We're not husband and wife, Jason. We never will be," I said as gently as I could. "We're brother and sister, and that's all we can ever be."

"But you said you loved me. You told me you did. We made love and you liked it, you know you did, Quinn. You liked it then, so why don't you like it now? Why?"

He was shouting, his face so contorted I could hardly recognize him.

"Jason, you'll scare the baby. Please, just try to calm down," I begged.

"Calm down?" he said with a bitter explosion of laughter. "How the hell can I be calm when everyone's turning against me?"

"But I'm not, I swear it."

"You are so. You don't love me anymore, admit it. When we were together that day at the Temple, when we performed the ritual of the undivided spirit and you became a woman, you liked it then. You wanted to feel me inside you, for the two of us to be like one. And we were, Quinn. No one can ever take that away from us. We were as one. We were so close it was like we were a single person. So why can't we be like that again? What are you so afraid of?"

Back at the Valley we had a secret place, a playhouse deep in the Bottom we'd come to refer to as the Temple. Here we had prayed for Mother's return, worshipping her memory so that we would never lose hope of seeing her again. It was here that I had ceased to be a girl, allowing my brother to make love to me. But I was secretly ashamed of that now, and it was that shame that made me recoil from his touch.

Jason reached over to pull me against him. I tried pushing him away, telling him we couldn't keep living in the past; it would only end up destroying any chance for happiness that might exist in the future. But he didn't listen.

"I want you, don't you understand that?" he cried. "I'm so lonely, Quinn. I lie in bed at night and all I can think of is you, and how much I need you."

"Jason, please, you're not watching the road."

By then he was so overwrought I don't even think he heard me.

"I want you to think about what you're doing to me, Quinn."

I didn't want to get angry, but I couldn't help myself.

"Doing to you!" I shouted. "What about me, Jason? Have you ever stopped to consider that? Do you think I'm doing this out of spite, just to hurt you?"

I glanced nervously at the speedometer. He was going much too fast, and I heard the wheels spinning against the gravel at the shoulder of the road. I begged him to be careful, but he paid no attention to me. It was as if he were in a world all his own, infuriated he wasn't getting his way.

"You're trying to manipulate me, Quinn. Oh yes," he insisted, stabbing his finger at the air. "You're doing just what Mom did. You're just like her, too. You flaunt yourself before me and then—"

"Jason, watch out!" I screamed.

The truck seemed to appear out of nowhere. Jason spun the wheel to avoid a collision, and I could see the driver's startled face as he roared past us. But we were going too fast. Jason was losing control of the car, unable to prevent it from going into a spin.

Thrown back against the seat, I tried reaching for Becky, afraid the safety straps on her seat wouldn't hold. I couldn't reach her, and by then we were already hurtling backwards off the road.

Something reared up before us. A tree, a boulder, it was all happening so fast I couldn't tell. I thought I heard the baby cry and Jason telling me how sorry he was. Then it felt like someone grabbed me by the shoulders and flung me off the seat.

After that I didn't hear anything else, for the darkness came so swiftly I was certain I was already dead.

Mother was calling to me, and I couldn't ignore the terrifying urgency in her voice. It came from faraway, and I wondered how I'd ever be able to get to her in time. I started to race down the hall to her room, but it was like being on a treadmill. My feet kept moving yet I made no progress. There was pain in her voice now, and tears of grief stung my eyes. Someone was hurting my beautiful mother and I had to help her before it was too late.

"I'm coming!" I cried out. "Wait for me, please! Don't leave me!"

I was down on my hands and knees, clawing my way along the floor that felt like rubber, undulating beneath me. I could see the doorknob glowing in the darkness, and when I finally managed to grab hold of it I flung the door back as hard as I could.

There was an explosion, shattering glass, a baby crying. Pain sent feelers down to the tips of my fingers. I started to scream when someone grabbed my ankle and pulled me to the floor. The door slammed shut and I knew there was no escape.

Emerald eyes, hands wrenching my legs apart, Mother laughing in the darkness.

"We shall be as one," a voice whispered in my ear. "Trust me, Quinn. Trust Mom. She knows what's best for you, she always has."

Tears dripped down my cheeks, burning holes in my skin. Mother sat up in bed. The flesh was peeling off her face, hanging in shreds to expose the bones of her skull.

"Trust us," she said with a laugh as hollow as the

sockets of her blind, unseeing eyes. "You must always trust Warren and me, my darling."

"No, I can't!"

The curse, the Lefland curse. The curse of pain and incest, murder, betrayal, and revenge. They huddled over us, watching, laughing amongst themselves. Ephraim and Alethea, Hepzibah and Josiah, Orin, Zenobia, Lavinia, and Bennett Lefland too. They were all there, witnesses to our sin, shrieking with excitement now that it was my turn to become one of them.

"Hold her, boy!" someone shouted.

"Don't let her go, don't let her escape!" someone else cried out.

"Warren loves you," he said as he pinned me to the floor. "Warren will always love his Quinnie till the day he dies."

"You took Jason away. You stole him from me, and I hate you!" I screamed. "I hate you! I hate you!"

The laughter. The pain. The light burning my eyes. Their shadows scattered like leaves caught in the wind. I saw a light fixture above my head, squares of tile with little holes punched across its surface.

Where was I? Where had Warren taken me? Why hadn't Mother tried to stop him?

But he wasn't there anymore. I was all alone now, and as I turned my head to the side I saw a window with white venetian blinds, a glimpse of darkening sky. I was lying in bed, and slowly everything began to make sense again.

Gingerly I eased the covers back, moving my fingers and then my toes. I was alive. Alive! I tried sitting up in bed, only to fall back against the pillows. My back ached and I was still too weak. When I reached up and felt the bandages around my head, I realized I'd better just stay where I was.

But where were Jason and Becky? If I'd survived the accident, surely they had as well. I tried remembering what had happened, but it was all such a blur. We'd gone careening off the road. There was a terrible crash. But I couldn't recall anything after that.

I heard footsteps then, and quickly turned my head in their direction. This wasn't a room in someone's home. I was in a hospital, and when the door swung back I was already prepared to confront my father, his expression one of sadness and reproach.

Instead, a nurse came into the room, smiling cheerfully.

"You're up, that's a good sign," she remarked.

I guess I was still in a daze, because it took a while for the words to register. When I finally realized what she meant I tried to return her smile.

"I don't even know where I am. And what happened to my brother, and the baby? They're all right, aren't they?"

"Shh," she admonished, putting her finger to her lips. "You mustn't exert yourself, dear. You're a very lucky girl, you know that, don't you?"

"But what about Jason? And Becky, what happened to her?"

If the nurse heard the panic in my voice, she pretended not to notice.

"Becky . . . how lovely. We all wondered what her name was," the woman replied.

"Then she's all right?"

"She's doing fine, dear. A little shaken up, of course. But babies aren't nearly as fragile as they look. And that safety seat certainly proved a godsend. She was strapped in good and tight, crying her little head off when they found her.''

I wanted to cry for joy, but I was still afraid that something terrible had happened to Jason.

"And my brother?" I said anxiously.

The nurse cocked her head to one side and peered at me curiously.

"Excuse me?"

"My brother," I said. "What happened to him?"

"I don't know who you mean, dear.''

I could tell she was trying to humor me, but there was nothing funny about what was happening.

"My brother. He was in the car with me. He was the one who was driving.''

I tried sitting up but I was so dizzy I couldn't even move. The nurse warned me I'd suffered a concussion and that it was imperative I get as much rest as I could.

"But you're not listening," I pleaded. "Becky and I weren't the only ones in the car. Why don't you believe me?"

"I think you're still a little confused because of the accident," replied the nurse. "When they pulled you out, you were the one behind the wheel, dear, not anyone else. The baby was in the back seat and you were up front. Now I'm not going to ask what you were doing, because I know you've already been through quite enough for one day. But I must say everyone was quite surprised when they learned you were driving your father's car.''

I couldn't understand what she was talking about. But the more questions I asked, the less cooperative she became. She finally stopped answering me altogether, and busied herself examining my chart and taking my pulse.

What was going on? Of course Jason was in the car.

Then what had happened to him? Had he been thrown out of the car when we crashed? Maybe he was lying unconscious somewhere and no one had noticed him.

If only my head didn't hurt so I could have thought more clearly. But I was getting dizzier and dizzier and finally I couldn't even keep my eyes open.

"That's it, dear. You try and get some rest now. The doctor'll be in to see you later."

The voice came from far, far away. It was part of a dream, that's what it was. None of this had actually taken place. When I woke up I'd be back in the Valley, safe and snug under the eiderdown quilts. Mother would come into my room and tickle my toes, telling me it was time to get up, sleepyhead, Mrs. Darby had breakfast ready and Mr. Finney our tutor had a big day planned for us.

Yes, a dream, that's all it was. A terrible dream that would end just as soon as I woke up.

Someone was shaking me, telling me it was time to get up. Mother, that's who it was. It was going to be a lovely day, I could tell. I felt the bright morning light warming my cheeks, and I yawned and stretched my arms above my head.

"Can you hear me, Miss Lefland, Miss Quinton Lefland?"

I smiled dreamily and opened my eyes.

"Miss Lefland?"

For a moment I froze, not knowing what else to do. A man with acne-scarred cheeks and a big bushy handlebar moustache was hovering over me, watching my every move. I drew back in alarm, just as I noticed he was wearing a uniform. The badge pinned to the pocket of his brown twill shirt reflected the sunlight back into my eyes and I had to look away.

"Miss Lefland?" he said again. "You're up now, aren't you?"

I nodded.

"Fine, then maybe you can answer a few questions for me. We'd like to know exactly what happened yesterday afternoon."

The patch sewn on the sleeve of his shirt read *McKenzie Springs Sheriff's Office*. McKenzie Springs? I couldn't recall passing through a town of that name. But when I asked the sheriff where I was he went right on questioning me without so much as a blink of his eye.

"I've notified your father, Miss Lefland. Now I was hoping you'd want to cooperate with me. But if you don't—"

"I don't even know where I am, or who you are. And I don't feel very well, either," I lied.

I wasn't dizzy anymore, and though the bandages were still in place the headache I'd felt earlier was gone.

"McKenzie Springs, Oregon, population six hundred and eighty-three," he replied in answer to my question. "I'm Sheriff Orickson, and since you're now in my jurisdiction, young lady, it's time you thought about cooperating with the authorities and the powers that be—meaning me. Now what in the world were you doing driving your father's car, Quinton? And what are you doing so far from home?"

"I don't feel good," I said again. "You're confusing me."

I closed my eyes, but the sheriff wasn't about to give up so easily. He tapped me on the shoulder until I was forced to look at him.

"Your father was mighty relieved to know we found you. Said you ran away from home, stole his car in fact. He's in a hospital himself, case you didn't know."

His eyes narrowed suspiciously, and I had a feeling he already thought I was responsible for whatever had put my father in the hospital.

"Why haven't you found my brother yet?" I said, changing the subject.

Sheriff Orickson's face registered confusion.

"What brother?" he asked. "It was just you and the little girl they found. There wasn't anyone else."

"My brother was driving the car when we crashed."

The sheriff smiled patiently.

"I think you *are* a little confused, young lady. You were the one behind the wheel."

"Then maybe he was thrown clear of the car. Maybe he's lying in the woods, and he's too injured to move."

The sheriff's cynical expression left little to the imagination. It was obvious he didn't believe a word of what I'd said, certain I was making it all up so it wouldn't look like I was responsible for the accident.

"My brother was with me, I swear he was! Didn't my father even ask about him?" I shouted.

"Now don't you start yelling at me, young lady," Orickson warned. "You're in a mess of trouble as it is, nearly getting yourself killed like that. So don't make it worse for yourself. Your father's sent two friends of his up from California to bring you and your sister home. But before they get here I want to know exactly what you were doing alone in that car."

"What friends?" I asked.

Sheriff Orickson paused to consult his notepad.

"A Mr. and Mrs. Darby."

My stomach lurched at the sound of those names! The fragile web of lies Jason and I had woven so desperately was beginning to unravel with a vengeance. Mother's coffin had undoubtedly been exhumed by now, and Harry Darby's body discovered inside. And of course, everyone would blame Jason and me for his death. How could I ever explain to them that it was an accident? Harry had been fighting with my brother when he lost his footing and fell into the coffin. Jason and I tried to catch him, but neither of us could get to him in time. The bottom of the coffin was lined with stones Father had put there in place of Mother's body. Harry had fallen onto them, and by the time I jumped down into the coffin to help him, his neck was broken and he was already dead.

"Bit late for tears, young lady," the sheriff said when I began to cry.

"You don't understand," I stammered.

"The hell I don't," Sheriff Orickson angrily replied. The handlebars of his moustache quivered violently and I could see how red his face was getting. "Where the hell did you think you were going, anyway, you and a little baby like that?"

"I think that's quite enough for now, Sheriff."

Orickson glanced back at the doctor who stood in the doorway, looking at him disapprovingly.

"I still have some questions to ask, Doc."

"Save them for later," he said in a tone that didn't invite disagreement. "She needs all the rest she can get. The youngster's in no shape to respond coherently."

With obvious reluctance, Sheriff Orickson put away his notepad and got to his feet. He looked down at me, frowning behind his bushy moustache.

"You and I ain't finished yet, Miss Lefland. Before

you go home I want to know just what you were doing up here.''

"That's enough now, Sheriff," the doctor said angrily.

He started to lead the burly Orickson to the door, but the sheriff didn't take very kindly to being pushed around.

"This little girl ain't as innocent as she looks," he declared.

"This little girl is lucky to be alive. And that's all that concerns me at the moment," replied the doctor.

He held the door open and waited for the sheriff to leave.

"Why hasn't anyone found my brother yet?" I said as soon as we were alone. "He was in the car with me, I swear he was."

The doctor reacted with disbelief, just as everyone else had.

"You're a little mixed up, aren't you, Quinton?"

"I'm not mixed up at all," I insisted. "My brother was in that car!"

"But you and your sister were the only ones the Ettingers found."

The doctor went on to explain that an elderly couple had found me in the car, slumped over the wheel. They'd brought Becky and me back to McKenzie Springs, and had even stayed in town overnight, they were so concerned about us.

"They've asked to see you, if you think you're up for it."

"Yes, I'd like that very much," I said, hoping they might be able to shed some light on Jason's whereabouts.

I was terrified he was lying injured somewhere near the wreck, and that unless help came quickly his very life would be in danger. Yet after I repeated everything I had told the sheriff, the doctor still seemed doubtful. But at least he said he would find out if anyone had searched the woods near the scene of the accident. If not, he promised to personally relay my concern to Sheriff Orickson.

"But he doesn't believe me, don't you understand? He thinks I'm lying, and I'm not. Why would I make up such a story, if he's going to send me home, anyway?"

The doctor started for the door, only to pause a moment and look back.

"If what you say is the truth—"

"I swear to God it is."

"Then if need be, Quinton, I'll go up there myself and look around."

When the door opened a few minutes later a plump woman with curly gray hair peered timidly inside.

"I don't mean to disturb you," she said. "If you're not up for visitors—"

"Oh no, please come in," I told her. "I'm feeling much better this morning, thank you."

"You're sure now, dear? We can always come back later."

"No, I'm all right, really I am."

The woman's smile was as gentle as a caress, and there was something about her that immediately put me at my ease.

"I'm Mrs. Ettinger, and this is my husband Nathaniel," she said as she came into the room.

She gestured behind her, where a tall, somewhat stoop-shouldered man in his early seventies stood in the doorway. He smiled as shyly as his wife and followed her inside.

"You must be the couple who found me. I'm very grateful for all you've done."

"You have a lot to be thankful for, dear. We must have

found you just a few minutes after the accident. The tires were still spinning.'' She glanced at her husband. ''Weren't they, Nathaniel?''

''Perdita has a very sharp eye for details,'' he informed me. ''It's all the mysteries she reads. I think she fancies herself another Miss Marple.''

I didn't know who Miss Marple was, but if she was anything like Perdita Ettinger, she must have been a very nice person. I introduced myself, then asked them to please take a seat. At first they seemed rather uncomfortable and unsure of themselves, though I think that had more to do with shyness than anything else.

A few years younger than her husband, Perdita was by far the more talkative of the two, and began to recount exactly what had happened the previous day. Noticing the fresh skid marks across the road, as well as the torn vegetation along the shoulder, she had insisted they stop their car and investigate. But before she could even examine the ''clues'' as she called them, she heard a baby crying.

''Your little sister, I believe.''

''Becky. She was the last thing I thought of before I blacked out. I'm so glad nothing happened to her.''

''Yes, she was fine, I could tell that right away. It was you who concerned us, dear. You had a nasty gash across your forehead, so we bound up the wound and Nathaniel carried you to our car. He's much stronger than he looks, you know,'' Mrs. Ettinger added with a laugh.

I smiled at her husband, and a faint blush rose in his cheeks. Nathaniel Ettinger's face was weathered and deeply tanned. Below his bushy white eyebrows his bluish-gray eyes had a look of sadness to them, as if he'd seen more than his share of tragedy.

Perdita, on the other hand, bustled with optimism and vitality. Short and round-faced, her animated gestures and manner of speech were in direct contrast to her husband's reserved and somewhat secretive nature. Yet interestingly enough, each managed to complement the other, both in temperament as well as appearance.

"And you found no one else?" I asked.

Mrs. Ettinger looked confused, and turned to her husband.

"Just you and the baby," he replied. "Why do you ask?"

"My brother was in the car with me, and now I don't know what's happened to him."

My voice cracked, and then all my fears came to the surface as my eyes overflowed with tears.

Perdita Ettinger rushed to my side and took me in her arms. She smelled of violets, and when she held me, promising that everything would be all right, I instinctively knew she was someone I could trust. Five minutes before she was a total stranger, but now I felt as if I'd known her all my life, as if she and her husband were the grandparents I had never had.

"You don't understand what happened," I sobbed. "Jason and I had to run away . . . we didn't have any other choice. The things he did . . . the terrible lies he told us . . ."

"There now, dear. You mustn't cry, it'll be all right. Don't you worry, we're going to help you," Mrs. Ettinger said gently.

"The child's terrified, Perdita."

"I know she is, and it breaks my heart. There's something going on here that isn't right, Nathaniel. I've never seen a child so frightened in all my life. Even when poor Kenley—"

Nathaniel Ettinger shot her an anxious glance, and she held her tongue and looked away.

"Perhaps you'd like to tell us what's wrong, Quinton," he asked.

"My father molested her, that's what."

My eyes flew to the door.

"Oh Jason, thank God you're all right!" I cried out, and where there were tears a moment before there was now so much joy and relief I could barely contain myself. "I was so worried I didn't know what to do. Where have you been? What happened?"

His face unnaturally pale, Jason stepped into the room, closing the door softly behind him. He was limping, and there was an ugly bruise along the side of his face. But he was alive and he'd come back to me, and that's all that mattered.

"I'm going to tell them what happened to us, Quinn," he said in a grim and determined voice.

"The accident, you mean?"

My brother shook his head, then turned to the Ettingers.

"My sister hasn't told you why we ran away from home. I think she's frightened of the truth. But now we can't be afraid any longer, can we, Quinn?"

"No," I whispered.

Jason pulled up a chair, and a moment later began to recite the litany of horror that had been our lives.

CHAPTER SIX

The baby was crying. That's what I remember more than
anything else. The baby crying and the wheels spinning
and me wondering if somehow it was all Warren's fault.
Maybe the pills weren't working, that's one of the first
things I thought. But Warren had nothing to do with it. I
just wasn't paying attention to the road, and it was lucky I
didn't get us all killed.

Quinn was slumped over the dashboard, and when I
shook her she moaned faintly but she didn't open her eyes.
I pulled her toward me and propped her up. She was still
groaning and I couldn't get her to respond when I called
her name. That's when I realized I couldn't take care of
her on my own, that she needed to see a doctor and as
soon as possible.

Problem was, the door on my side was crushed in when
we hit the trees, and my leg was pinned between it and the
side of the seat. I didn't think any bones were broken, but
the pain was excruciating. I ripped my jeans pulling myself
free, left a nice hunk of bloody skin behind as well.

Then I crawled over the back of the seat to where my
daughter was still bawling her head off. Boy, that safety

seat sure paid for itself, didn't it? Even though Becky was scared to death she wasn't even scratched. It was Quinn I was worried about, and so the first thing I thought of doing was dragging myself out to the road and flagging down a car.

I got the back door open and sort of toppled outside like a sack of potatoes. Quinn had slipped down on the seat (She was lying right in the middle, so I guess that's why everyone assumed she was driving the car), and when I called to her she didn't say a word. I hauled myself to my feet and started limping back to the road.

That's when I first saw the Ettingers, like they'd gotten there just minutes after the accident. I could have stepped out from behind the trees and told them what happened, but I suddenly realized there were going to be too many questions asked. You know the end result as well as I do. They'd call the cops, the cops would call Dad, and pretty soon we'd be right back where we started.

So I stayed out of sight, watching Perdita Ettinger and her skinny, unhappy looking husband make their way through the woods. They didn't have to look very hard, because of the baby's crying.

When they did find the car, they didn't even seem to lose their composure. Nathaniel managed to pull Quinn out of the front seat while his wife attended to Becky.

"What about all the luggage?" I heard Perdita ask.

"Let's get her to a hospital first. They can always send someone out here later to pick up their things," replied her husband.

As skinny and as old as he was, he didn't have any trouble carrying Quinn in his arms. (Like Will Darby, Ettinger was much stronger than he looked.) I had no idea where they were going to take them, but I figured it had to be the nearest town, wherever that was. So as soon as they were out of sight I dragged myself back to the car.

I checked the map, and sure enough McKenzie Springs was maybe nine or ten miles up the road. I folded the map up and stuffed it in my pocket, then took my suitcase out of the back. I don't even know why I bothered, to tell you the truth, because at that point the only thing on my mind was getting to Quinn. But I also figured the less anyone knew about me, the better. If you remember what happened right before the crash, we were arguing about whether Quinn should go home or not. Maybe now she'd feel she had no other choice. But I wasn't going to go with her, that's the main thing. I just couldn't and I think she understood why.

But at the same time I wasn't going to abandon her, either. So I tied up the wound in my leg, changed my pants so people wouldn't know I'd been in an accident—it wasn't until later I realized I had a black eye that reached halfway down my cheek—and hobbled back to the road.

I must've stood there a good hour and not a single car went by, so finally I decided to walk, even though I could hardly put any weight at all on my bad leg.

I sort of lost track of time after that, so I have a feeling I must have stopped and slept for a while, though I can't even remember. I had a headache and whiplash too I guess, because my neck felt like it was about to snap right in two. Every time I moved my head the pain went through me like an electric shock. But finally, just about the time it was starting to get dark, I managed to reach McKenzie Springs.

First thing I did was look for the hospital. The town

wasn't much bigger than Juniper City, and it didn't take me long to find it. It looked more like a concrete bunker than anything else, just a big pile of cinderblock covered over with white paint. Its three stories made it the tallest building in town, probably the ugliest too. Place resembled a prison, and just walking inside gave me the willies.

There was an old lady sitting behind the information desk, too busy with her needlepoint to even look up when I came in.

"Excuse me," I said, three or four times because either she was hard of hearing or she was afraid she'd lose track of her stitches. "They brought in a girl and a little baby a couple of hours ago. I saw the accident they were in, and I was wondering how they were doing."

The old woman just stared at me as if she didn't have the vaguest idea what I was talking about. So I went over it a second time, all the while trying my best not to lose patience. The third time around she finally got the message, and consulted the current list of patients.

"What was her name again?" she asked.

"Qui—" I caught myself in the nick of time. "I don't know what her name is, I just want to know how she is."

"But if you don't know her name, how am I supposed to?" the woman replied.

So I started from the beginning, trying not to lose my sense of humor though at this point it was just about impossible not to. Sure enough there was a listing for a Jane Doe, and I figured that had to be Quinn. The woman called upstairs to inquire, and when she got off the phone she told me Miss Doe had a concussion but her condition was stable.

I wanted to sneak upstairs and see her, but that's when I caught sight of the tub of lard in a sheriff's uniform, with his ridiculous handlebar moustache. I took one look at the sheriff and knew he spelled trouble. So instead of standing around and waiting for him to introduce himself, I got out of there as fast as I could.

So there I was in the middle of nowhere, tired and hungry and about as uncertain of the future as I'd ever been in my life. There wasn't even a McDonald's or anything like that, and I was afraid if I went anywhere else I'd draw too much attention to myself. So I found the market just before they closed and bought some stuff for dinner, then went off into the woods to spend the night.

Sleeping under the stars isn't what it's cracked up to be, let me tell you. I put on two sweaters and a jacket and I was still cold. But I was really beat too, and I think I probably fell asleep with my eyes open.

In the morning I was stiff and sore but none the worse for wear. I shook the pine needles out of my clothes and went into town, still limping a little though my leg didn't hurt nearly as much as it had the day before. I must've looked pretty cruddy, but at this point I had other things on my mind, namely Quinn.

Of course it was just my luck that the sheriff was already one step ahead of me. His car pulled up in front of the hospital just as I got there, and you could tell just to look at him that he was madder than hell about something. I wasn't certain if he was going up to see Quinn, though I had a feeling that's who he wanted to talk to. So I stayed out of sight until he came down again maybe fifteen or twenty minutes later. As soon as he drove off, the Ettingers showed up. I followed them inside and managed to over-hear them asking for Quinn, though of course they didn't use her name.

They took the elevator up to the second floor while I

snuck up the stairs. When the coast was clear I went down the hall to my sister's room. I could hear her crying, saying something about the terrible lies our father told us. It was then that I made up my mind what to do.

Quinn hadn't stopped worrying about what would happen to us once the money ran out. The truth is, I hadn't stopped worrying about it, either. I didn't want her to know that, of course, but I was just as scared of the future as she was. So when she started to pour her heart out to Perdita and Nathaniel Ettinger, it seemed a perfect opportunity to solve all our problems once and for all.

Of course, Dad had never laid a hand on her, but Quinn was so glad to see me I don't even think she realized what I meant at first. I stepped into the room and made sure to close the door so no one else would hear us. I had an attentive audience all right, because at this point the Ettingers were just as surprised to see me as my sister was.

"My sister hasn't told you why we ran away from home. I think she's frightened of the truth. But now we can't be afraid any longer, can we, Quinn?"

Quinn was so grateful that I was all right—later she told me she thought I was lying in the woods somewhere, bleeding to death—that all she could do was shake her head and whisper, "No."

The Ettingers were staring at me like I was a ghost. I guess my appearance was pretty unnerving, but I had a feeling once they started to hear what I had to say, the way I looked would only make my story all the more convincing.

I introduced myself and pulled up a chair, then glanced at Quinn and hoped she'd understand what I was about to do. It was only because of her and the baby I was going to lie. What she'd said right before the accident was true. We couldn't spend the rest of our lives running away from both our father and the past, and I hoped I'd somehow be able to convince the Ettingers to come to our rescue. Maybe that was awfully naive of me, considering the fact they were total strangers. But at this point it was the only hope I had.

"You know what I mean by 'molest,' don't you, sir?" I began, turning to Mr. Ettinger.

"I believe so, yes," he said nervously.

I knew the subject was making him uncomfortable, though I wasn't sure why.

"Quinn had no way to defend herself, no way to stop him," I continued. "It started a couple of years ago, when he first made her touch him. Sexually, I mean."

Mrs. Ettinger's hand flew to her lips and her eyes opened wide with horror.

"Dear God," she whispered.

She reached over and gripped Quinn's hand, and all the time I spoke she never once let go.

I guess I got carried away, but that too was part of my plan. I wanted to paint the most shocking picture imaginable, and every time I thought Quinn was going to interrupt, my eyes warned her to keep quiet, I'd explain everything to her later.

"When my mother found out what he was doing, she threatened to expose him to the authorities."

That was a phrase I'd heard on television. It sounded very official and believable, and both Mrs. Ettinger and her husband nodded their heads.

"She was going to tell the authorities everything, how he wouldn't leave his own daughter alone, how he forced her to play with him and touch his . . . well, you know," I said shyly, making sure to lower my eyes.

"Jason—" Quinn started to protest.

"It's all right," I told her. I reached out and patted her on the arm. "Don't be scared, Quinn. Everyone knows it wasn't your fault." I turned back to the Ettingers. "He made her have sex with him, and that's when we both decided we had to run away."

I went on to describe how he literally drove our mother crazy, how he convinced us she was dead, and how we opened her coffin and discovered it was filled with stones. Then I related the events leading up to Becky's birth, and how, the night before we left home, he'd forced me to watch him having intercourse with my sister.

The way I explained everything, keeping my voice down and not getting hysterical, made it all sound so convincing I even began to believe it myself. The Ettingers had to realize that if we were sent home we'd be victimized all over again. Worse than before, in fact. When Quinn interrupted to tell me the Darbys were on their way up to McKenzie Springs, I "reminded" her that they were father's friends.

"How can we ever let them take us back there," I asked, "when all along they knew what he was doing and never once tried to stop him?"

Mrs. Ettinger shook her head in dismay.

"But why didn't you go to the police?" she asked. "Surely they would have taken some kind of action."

I sighed loudly, then put my hand over my eyes to make it look like I was about to cry.

"We're all alone, Mrs. Ettinger. We don't have any other relatives. If Quinn and I were separated we'd be worse off than when we started."

"It's true," Quinn broke in.

"The night before we ran away I begged him to leave

her alone," I said. "But he refused to listen. He started to hit me and he wouldn't stop."

I paused to touch the bruise on my face, certain they'd put two and two together without my having to say a word.

"How horrible," muttered Mrs. Ettinger, deeply disturbed by all that I had told her. She turned to her husband, unable to stop shaking her head. "That a father could be such a monster, Nathaniel, it's just too frightening to believe."

"You know what's even more frightening, Mrs. Ettinger? He didn't think he was doing anything wrong. He told me since Quinn was his daughter, he had every right to do whatever he wanted to her. He really believed that, too."

"People like that should never be allowed to have children," she replied.

"Now you know why we can never go home," Quinn said as she lay in bed. She looked over at me for encouragement, and I nodded my head. "He did other things too though, didn't he, Jason?"

"No, please," protested Mrs. Ettinger. "I can't take anymore. I've heard more than enough, enough to last a lifetime."

"There now, Perdita, you mustn't get so upset," her husband told her. "Why, they're a hundred percent better off than they were before, just for being able to get all this off their chests."

Nathaniel Ettinger got up from his chair, went over to the window and looked outside. I kept my fingers crossed, certain he was trying to decide what to do, and what part he and his wife would play in our future. They didn't look like they had any money problems, so I had a feeling that didn't even enter into his thoughts. But would they assume responsibility for two children and an infant? That was probably hoping for a great deal more than they were willing to give.

"What are we going to do?" Quinn started to cry.

She wasn't faking it anymore. The tears that streamed down her cheeks were real. I perched on the edge of the bed and held her in my arms. She clung to me, sobbing so bitterly it broke my heart. I think by now she understood why I had to lie, because if I told the Ettingers the real story they probably would have rushed out of the room and never once looked back.

"What are you thinking, Nathaniel?" Mrs. Ettinger asked.

"About cruelty, and responsibility, and trust. Big words, children, aren't they?" he said, trying to smile.

"When the baby gets older, I'm just so afraid what he'll try to do to her," I whispered.

That was the final straw. Mrs. Ettinger looked at her husband and I knew exactly what was going through her mind.

"We can't let them go back there, Nathaniel. It would be criminal, and I'd never be able to live with myself."

"But what if—"

She didn't even give him a chance to finish.

"There are no buts about it, and you know that as well as I do," she replied in an impassioned voice that made me smile to myself. "It would be a crime to send them home, and even more of a crime if they were separated. They're coming with us, Nathaniel. There's more than enough room on the island. And besides, Kenley needs to be around children his own age. It's just not natural for him to be without friends. Once we've gotten them in safekeeping, we can see about taking legal steps to protect them."

I looked up at Mr. Ettinger, waiting to hear what he had to say. Whatever was destined to happen to us seemed to rest entirely on his shoulders, and he shifted his weight from one foot to the other while he tried to decide what to do.

"How old are you, Jason?" he said at last.

"Fourteen, sir."

"Yes, I thought so. Kenley's our grandson, the same age as you in fact. We've tried our best to protect him from the kind of ugliness you've spoken of. He's a very sensitive youngster, far more perceptive than most boys his age. If you are to be guests in our home, perhaps even part of our family, then you must make me a promise."

"What is it you'd like me to do?" I asked.

"Kenley must never know what brought you to us," he replied. "When and if I think the time is right, I'll tell him myself. But I don't want to frighten him. He's far too impressionable, and I know that if either you or your sister told him of your suffering it would wound him as deeply as it's wounded you."

Talk about leading a sheltered life! This Kenley sounded like he had a few problems of his own. But of course I wasn't going to argue the point. If Ettinger wanted to keep everything a secret, that was fine with me. Besides, who was I to pass judgment, anyway?

"If that's how you feel—"

"I do. Quite strongly, in fact."

"Then I certainly would never go against your wishes," I assured him.

"And how do you feel about it, Quinn?" he asked.

I think she was so relieved to know we could finally stop running that she must have been in a daze.

"You won't say anything to their grandson, will you?" I prompted her when she didn't answer right away.

"Oh no, I won't say a word," she promised, "not if Mr. Ettinger doesn't want me to."

"Nathaniel from now on in," he said with a smile. "Nathaniel and Perdita."

Ettinger stuck out his hand and the two of us shook on it. I think he was a little wacky himself, to tell you the truth, but I couldn't deny he was going out on a limb for us. After all, we hardly knew them, and here they were willing to take care of us, to clothe and feed and shelter us, to act like our surrogate grandparents in fact. So even though I was a little uneasy about what he said about his grandson, I was still very grateful.

"Now, all we have to do is figure out how to get Quinn and Becky out of here," I announced.

Perdita's face dropped. It hadn't occurred to her that we couldn't pack our things and just walk out the door.

"But don't you worry," I told them. "I already have a plan. It may not be foolproof, but I'm sure it's going to work."

"It better," Quinn said, half to herself. "If not, then we'll really be in trouble."

CHAPTER SEVEN

Was I going to have to spend the rest of my life living a lie? Was that what the future held for me? There seemed to be no end to it, the falsehoods and deceptions piled one on top of the other, burying me beneath them. As Jason told the Ettingers his fantastic story I found myself shuddering, knowing that I could easily have stopped him and yet deep down inside I didn't want to. But why didn't he tell them about himself? Why did he have to use me as the pawn in his complicated game of check and double check? Wouldn't it have been easier not to lie, to explain what Mother had done to him, even to reveal the truth of Becky's parentage if need be? But no, he chose instead to fabricate a story that made me the ultimate victim, and that made our father even more of a monster than he actually was.

Yet I didn't question him, for I knew Jason was terrified I would leave him to return to the Valley. But if he convinced Perdita and Nathaniel of the nightmarish existence that awaited me there, they might decide to take us in, sheltering us from the emotional storm he so vividly described. For how long they would be willing to do so was another matter, but even temporary safe harbor was better than nothing.

When they made their decision to help us, I was so relieved I tried not to think of what my brother had told them. To know we would be taken care of again—for however long—seemed more important than anything else in the world. When the time was right I promised myself that I would tell them the truth, if not about Jason then at least about myself.

But there was so much planning to do I really didn't have a chance to think about anything else. My brother had everything worked out, and when I told him about Sheriff Orickson he said we'd have to move quickly, lest the sheriff decide to keep a close watch on me until the Darbys arrived. We had no idea when they would reach McKenzie Springs, and if they got here before we had a chance to escape, it would make everything all the more difficult.

"We'll worry about that when the time comes," he said. "Besides, even if they got here later this afternoon or tonight, you can always say you're still not feeling well and you can't leave until tomorrow."

One of the sheriff's deputies had taken the luggage out of the car and brought it back to my room. I took out what I needed, and when they left the Ettingers carried the suitcases down to their car. I was going to have my hands full with Becky, so it was one less thing to worry about.

For the remainder of the day I lay in bed and tried to get some rest, though I was so anxious I couldn't sleep. Any minute I expected the door to open and Anna and Will Darby to step inside, ready to accuse me of murdering their son.

I decided to write them a letter explaining what had really happened, not wanting them to think that Jason and I had taken their only child's life. Putting it all down on paper was much more difficult than I thought it would be, especially when I realized that Harry would still be alive if Father hadn't tried to deceive us about Mother's death. How would the Darbys feel about him, I wondered, knowing that his actions had contributed to their son's fatal accident? After all, Harry had been told to keep an eye on us, which was why he followed us to the cemetery the night we dug up Mother's grave. Had Father chosen not to involve him in his wretched scheme, Harry would be alive today, and there would be that much less blood on Father's hands. But perhaps it was important he finally realized just how many people he had hurt, for I think he was still convinced that what he did was only for the best.

By early evening I was a bundle of nerves, certain we would be found out before we had a chance to escape. The Ettingers had wanted to tell Sheriff Orickson why we ran away from home, but Jason convinced them it would only make the situation more complicated than it already was. Even if the sheriff believed them, and Jason didn't think he would, the last thing he'd do was give them permission to take me out of the hospital.

I was dressed and ready to go, though I stayed in bed with the covers pulled up to my neck in case one of the nurses came in to check on me. It was after eleven when I finally heard footsteps outside my door. It opened soundlessly and my brother slipped inside. As soon as the door closed behind him I jumped out of bed and hurriedly arranged the pillows so it would look like I was still asleep.

"There's a nurse on duty down the hall," he whispered. "We're going to have to be very careful, Quinn. If she sees us before we get to the stairwell, I don't know what we'll do."

When we first went over the plan, I told Jason it wasn't necessary for him to accompany me upstairs to the nursery. But he was afraid that if someone tried to stop me I'd be at a tremendous disadvantage with a baby in my arms. This way he'd be there to help me in case anything went wrong.

He opened the door and stuck his head out, only to close it again just as quickly.

"What's the matter?" I whispered.

"I think she must've heard something. We'll have to wait a few minutes. You're okay, aren't you? How's your head feel?"

I'd taken off the bandage, and the cut above my eye wasn't as bad as I thought it would be. Jason leaned over and kissed me on the forehead. He told me to be brave; we'd be out of here in no time at all. The Ettingers were waiting for us behind the hospital, and by this time tomorrow we'd be safe.

We'd be safe . . . to think that such simple words could mean so much. There was fairy tale magic in that phrase, and I could hardly believe it would soon come true.

"I'm so scared, Jason. What if we get caught?"

"We won't."

"But if we do?"

My brother smiled patiently.

"I'm here to protect you, Quinn, so there's no reason to be frightened. Besides, who loves you more than anyone else in the world?"

I smiled shyly.

"You do."

"You're damn right," he laughed.

I stood on tiptoe and kissed him on the tip of his nose.

"Forgive me?" he asked.

"For what?"

"Putting you through all this."

"Whatever we've done, Jason, we've done together. You didn't drag me away from the Valley. I went with you of my own accord."

He looked at me for a silent moment, and there was so much love in his eyes, so much trust and tenderness, that I wondered why I'd ever allowed myself to doubt him. He put his arms around me and held me close, the two of us determined to face the future together. When he finally let go he opened the door again and peeked outside.

"Now or never," he whispered.

Jason and I crept into the hall. The nurse was on the phone, so involved in her conversation she never heard us. Staying back in the shadows and praying she wouldn't turn around, we inched our way toward the stairwell. It suddenly occurred to me we should have put on hospital gowns, because at least that way we would have been less conspicuous. But it was too late to turn back. We would just have to chance it dressed the way we were.

My brother reached the stairwell, and waited for me to join him.

"Didn't I tell you this would be easy?" he said with a grin.

In the enclosed space of the stairwell his voice boomed out at me. I looked over his shoulder, afraid someone might have heard him, but there was no one on the stairs.

"We're not there yet," I reminded him.

"But we will be," and without another word Jason started up the stairs to the third floor of the hospital.

Thanks to Perdita we knew exactly where the nursery was. Earlier in the day she'd gone up to look in on Becky, and when she came back to my room she drew us a floor plan so we wouldn't get lost. Nathaniel had said she was addicted to mysteries, and judging from Perdita's enthusiasm for sleuthing, I didn't doubt him.

At the top of the stairs we paused again, for we had no idea how many nurses were on duty. I was afraid to look out into the hall, but once again Jason was there to encourage me.

"I'll be right behind you," he said. "Just think of me as a second pair of eyes, watching out to make sure nothing happens."

I kept telling myself not to be nervous, to just pretend I had every right to be up here. After all, I hadn't seen Becky since the accident. If anyone stopped me I'd tell them that, and if they asked why I wasn't in my room I'd tell them the doctor gave me permission to walk around, he thought it would do me good.

But when we opened the door and peered into the hall, there wasn't anyone in sight. According to Perdita's diagram, the nursery was halfway down the corridor on the right. Still keeping close to the wall, I started down the hallway while Jason kept up the rear.

I heard a baby crying, but there were no other sounds, just my breath coming in short, frightened gasps, and my heart beating so quickly I could feel its pulse all through my body. I was scared all right, but not the way I was back at the Pine Bluff Motel. Thinking about that now made me feel a little better. No matter who I ran into here, my life wouldn't be in danger.

All that seemed so far in the past I could scarcely believe any of it had taken place. The flight from the Valley, the terrible scene at the motel, Jason's close call at the hospital . . . all these things seemed to have occurred in the far distant past. Time was moving so slowly, yet it was only a few days before that we had left Father lying in a pool of blood, begging us to believe him when he said he'd only tried to do what was best.

"There it is," Jason whispered.

The glass door that led into the nursery afforded us a perfect view inside. There was a row of cribs which faced the viewing window farther down the hall, but all of them were empty. For a moment I felt my courage waning, and panic rushing in to take its place. But then Jason reached out and squeezed my shoulder, and I grasped the doorknob and stepped inside.

The air was warm and moist, almost like a greenhouse. I moved cautiously down the row of cribs, wondering where Becky was. Perdita had seen her, so she had to be here. But though I'd heard a baby crying a few moments before, the nursery was deadly still.

"Check over there. I'll cover the door," Jason whispered.

I crossed over to the far side of the large rectangular room. There was an incubator set up with all sorts of electronic monitoring devices, but that too was empty. Then I heard a faint snuffling sound, very much like a sigh. There were more cribs lined up along the wall, and as I made my way toward them a baby suddenly cried out. I was so startled that I stopped in midstep and whirled around to look back at Jason.

Where in the world had he gone?

The door leading into the hall was ajar, but my brother was nowhere in sight. There was no time to lose. For all I knew someone might have already caught him lurking in the hall. Frantic now, I rushed from one crib to the next. The baby cried again, but when I found her it wasn't Becky. The next crib was empty, as was the one after that.

Had she taken ill again, was that what had happened? Maybe they'd transferred her to another ward, because whatever she had was infectious. She hadn't gotten any vaccinations, though I assumed they would have taken care of that while she was here.

"Is this who you're looking for, young lady?"

At the sound of Sheriff Orickson's voice I froze in my place, then slowly turned around to face him. He was standing near the open door, holding Becky in his arms. Her eyes were closed and she looked asleep, more like a doll than a live human being.

"I came to see how she was," I told him.

I didn't want him to think I was nervous, but I'm sure he sensed how I felt from the tone of my voice.

"At eleven at night?"

"She gets a bottle at eleven. I didn't know if the nurses knew that."

"They know more than you give them credit for," he said coldly. "And so do I, Miss Lefland."

I wondered what would happen if I just rushed up to him and tried to grab Becky out of his arms. Would he let go, afraid of hurting the child, or would he pull out his service revolver and warn me not to come any closer? I could see it hanging from his black leather holster, and the more I looked at it, the more frightened I became.

Determined not to let him intimidate me, I took another step closer. What did he think he was accomplishing, anyway? Maybe I should tell him the truth about Becky, how Father didn't even want her to be born, how Aunt Gwen his soon-to-be wife had called the baby a monster. She wasn't. She was an angel, and Jason and I were the only ones who could protect her.

"What do you want from me?" I asked. "So I ran away from home. Since when is that such a terrible crime?"

"Your father's a very powerful man, Miss Lefland.

Very influential in government circles from what I understand. He and I had a very long talk about you. And your brother Jason.''

He paused to let his words sink in, while at the same time I kept narrowing the gap between us, getting closer and closer until Becky was nearly within reach. The sheriff's gun belt was slung low over his hips, and the handle of his revolver bobbed up and down with each breath he took.

"Becky," I called out. "How are you feeling, sweetheart? Becky, it's Quinn. It's Quinn, honey.''

I was the only mother she knew, and at the sound of my voice her eyes opened and she began to struggle in the sheriff's arms.

"She'll quiet down as soon as I hold her," I said.

But instead of handing me the baby, the sheriff stepped back toward the door.

"How come you're dressed, Quinton? Shouldn't you be in your room, trying to get some sleep?''

Becky was still crying, and I knew I had to make my move. If only I knew what had happened to Jason I might have been more sure of myself. But he was nowhere in sight, and I had visions of him sitting in the back of the sheriff's patrol car, guarded by one of his deputies. What had Father told him, anyway, that he was treating me like a criminal?

"You're frightening her," I said angrily. "Now can I please have my daughter?''

I thought the sheriff's eyes would pop out of his head, he looked so surprised.

"That's right, you heard me. She's my daughter," I said again, "and you have no legal right to take her away from me. *Now give her to me!*''

A shadow reared up behind him. I knew who it was, but

I tried not to let my eyes betray me, staring stonily at the sheriff and demanding he hand me Becky. Orickson must have caught them flickering, though, because he started to turn around. He was too late. Jason snatched the service revolver out of his holster and pressed it against the small of his back.

"Don't try to call for help," he warned. "Don't try to do anything. You heard her. Give her the baby."

Orickson tried to look over his shoulder to see who was behind him, but Jason shoved the muzzle of the gun into his back, even harder than before. The sheriff winced and finally did as he was told.

"That's it, you're doing fine," Jason said, so calm and in control of the situation I was amazed.

I took Becky and backed out of the nursery, wondering what my brother would do now that he had the sheriff to contend with. I wasn't worried about his pulling the trigger, but how was he going to overpower a man who probably weighed twice as much as he did?

"Go down the stairs, Quinn. I'll be right there."

"But what are you—?"

"Just do as I say. Everything's under control."

"You're making a big mistake, Jason. You're going to hurt a lot of people by what you're doing," the sheriff told him.

My brother didn't express the slightest surprise that Orickson knew his name. Just as I slipped out the door he brought the butt end of the revolver down against the back of the sheriff's head. Orickson made a sound like air rushing out of a balloon. His legs gave way beneath him, and though he tried to stop his fall I think he was already unconscious by the time he hit the floor.

Jason shoved me into the hall, dropped the revolver, and hurried to the stairs.

"Now you know why I didn't want you to do this on your own," he said as he held the door open for me.

There was no way to get Becky to stop crying. She was bouncing up and down in my arms as I rushed down the stairs, nearly tripping over myself in my haste to get to the ground floor. Behind us we suddenly heard shouts, a woman's excited voice and then a man's. The clatter of footsteps pursued us down the stairwell. But there was no turning back. A few more feet, a few more yards, and the threat of being returned to our father, of Jason being institutionalized and my having to live with the man responsible for Mother's death, would be a thing of the past, never to worry us again.

"Don't let that kid get away!" someone shouted behind me.

Jason was the first to reach the bottom of the stairs. He flung the door open, but the moment he stepped outside a figure jumped out of the shadows and grabbed him before he could get away.

"Just keep going, don't stop!" he shouted as he tried to wrestle free.

It was one of the sheriff's deputies, a lanky man whose long, spidery arms wrapped themselves around my brother, trying to pin him to the ground.

With Becky in my arms there wasn't much I could do. At the opposite end of the parking lot the Ettingers were waiting in their station wagon. Jason had told them not to turn on the headlights until we were safe inside. Nathaniel must have heard the shouts, because the engine suddenly revved loudly and then the car turned around to face us.

Mr. Ettinger flicked on the brights, blinding us in the glare of the headlights.

Behind me the nurse and orderly who'd rushed down the stairs were completely caught off guard. They stumbled to a halt, and unable to see where they were going they shielded their eyes with their hands, powerless to do anything. Jason and the deputy were rolling on the ground, each trying to overcome the other. My brother managed to kick his way free, but he barely got to his feet when the deputy tackled him and both of them went flying.

"Just go! Go!" I heard him shout.

"There she is!" the nurse cried out.

She pointed in my direction and I broke into a run, trying to make it to the car. I wasn't worried about myself so much as Becky. She was frightened, but not nearly as frightened as she would be if Father and Aunt Gwen assumed responsibility for her future.

Perdita had the window rolled down, and as soon as I reached the station wagon I handed her the baby.

"Get in!" she pleaded.

She sounded panic-stricken, but though I was just as scared, I knew I couldn't turn my back on Jason. So instead of doing what Perdita asked I rushed back to help my brother. The deputy had him pinned to the ground, and was shouting at the orderly to give him a hand. As for the nurse, she was standing there with a helpless look on her face, no longer certain what was expected of her.

"Go get Sheriff Orickson," the deputy told her.

The nurse turned and ran back upstairs. The moment she was out of sight I threw myself on top of the deputy, trying to get him to let go of my brother. Jason managed to free one of his hands, rammed the heel of his palm into the deputy's chin and rolled to the side. The orderly tried to stop him, but my brother eluded his grasp. He clambered to his feet, and from out of his pocket came the knife, the same bone-handled dirk he had already used twice before.

Both men froze in their places. Then, just like something viewed in slow motion, I saw the deputy's hand inch down toward his revolver. Like a billy goat, I rushed forward, slamming into him as hard as I could. He went sprawling, his breath knocked out of him. By then Jason and I were running, trying to get to the car before they caught up to us.

If they recognized the station wagon I knew it would only be a matter of hours before Father discovered our whereabouts, but as soon as we jumped inside the car her husband wasted no time racing off into the darkness.

Miraculously, Perdita had brought a bottle and she soon had the baby settled down and eating.

None of us said a word. Houses flashed by, then trees like sentinels standing guard on either side of the road. Hunched over the wheel of what had become a getaway car, Nathaniel Ettinger took the turns at maximum speed, afraid that if he slowed down he would soon find himself in the same position as a fox pursued by a pack of hounds.

"It's over," Jason whispered, breaking the spell of silence.

He took a deep breath, then reached over and cradled me in his arms. We clung to each other like the two frightened children we were, not so much scared of the dark as scared of tomorrow. I tried to tell myself there was nothing to worry about, we were safe now, and no one would ever try to hurt us again.

But even then I couldn't help but think of my father. One day he would come after us. One day he would track us down, as determined to find us as we were to remain hidden. And when that happened, when at last we confronted each other, would it be a time of tearful forgiveness? Or would he demand his retribution, destroying our lives as only he knew how?

PART II

SANCTUARY

CHAPTER EIGHT

The nightmares were over. We were safe now, and Dad and the boys in the white coats weren't getting a strait jacket ready for yours truly. I have to say right here and now that if it weren't for the Ettingers it would've been all over for us. On foot, we would never have stood a chance. So I was really grateful for all they did.

Mr. Ettinger drove like the devil was after him, and though I kept looking back over my shoulder, Sheriff Orickson was nowhere to be seen. He'd have a rotten headache when he woke up, but that's about the extent of it. Do you believe that guy, the way he held onto Becky like she wasn't even ours? I bet Dad was behind that. In fact, I wouldn't be surprised if my dad was offering him a big reward to bring us back.

Nathaniel insisted on driving all night, said he'd taken a nap that afternoon and felt fine. I wasn't about to argue, especially when the man knew his own limits better than I did. Besides, I just wanted to sleep.

When I woke up I don't know how many hours later, Quinnie was still dozing against my shoulder. The poor kid was beat, but I knew in a couple of days she'd be her old self again. But I also knew she was as much a realist as I was. She wasn't about to stop worrying about Dad, and neither was I. Our father was a very resourceful and determined man, and he wasn't the kind of person who gave up easily. One day soon he'd come looking for us, and then the confrontation we were all trying to avoid would finally take place. I wasn't looking forward to it, to say the least. I had nothing more to say to him, and if he didn't realize that by now he probably never would. Besides, he had Aunt Gwen, so what did he need us for, anyway?

As far as the Ettingers knew, he was a child molester and a sex offender, the worst kind of deviant. I don't think my sister was too pleased with the story I invented, and maybe one day we'd sit down and tell them the truth. But I didn't want to think about that now. I just wanted to get through one day at a time.

Now that I didn't have Warren to worry about, there were plenty of other things to make up for it. Like where were we going and what would happen once we got there? The Ettingers hadn't said a word about our destination, and we were so busy planning our escape we never bothered to ask.

It was bright and sunny when I looked out the window, and unless it was my imagination I was sure I could smell the sea. Perdita was driving—I don't even remember them stopping to change places—and her husband was sound asleep in the front seat, his arms wrapped securely around Becky.

"Did you sleep well?" Mrs. Ettinger said softly, not wanting to wake the others.

"Better than expected. You must be pretty beat though."

Perdita glanced back and smiled. She must have been a very handsome woman when she was young, because even though she was what people call "pleasantly plump," you could still see how fine her features were. Even more important than her looks was her character. Without her strength and kindness, Quinn and I would probably have been forced—maybe even at gunpoint—to return to the Valley.

"You know, Mrs. Ettinger—Perdita, I mean—I never even said thank you. But what you're doing for us—I'll never forget it, I promise."

"Now don't get mawkish on me, Jason," she said with a laugh. "You and Quinn are in trouble, and Nathaniel and I are glad to be of help. Besides, we have selfish motives, don't forget."

"Your grandson, you mean?"

She nodded.

"I think you and Kenley are going to get along very well. He's a very easygoing sort of boy, not spoiled or self-centered or anything like that. A little more serious than he should be perhaps, but I hope you and Quinn will change all that."

"Maybe he just needs friends," I said, because I wanted her to know that if she'd gone out of her way for us, we had every intention of returning the favor.

"You know what, Jason? That's just what I've always thought."

"But hasn't he made friends at school?" I asked.

Who knows, maybe Kenley was a real jerk. But then Perdita told me her grandson had a private tutor. Kenley lived with them on an island off the Oregon coast, and taking a launch to and from the mainland every day was too impractical. I'd forgotten all about the island, because they'd only mentioned it in passing. I was real curious to know more, but by then Quinn was up, and so too was Becky.

119

"I gave her a bottle around three this morning," Perdita told my sister.

Quinn busied herself preparing another, and by the time she began feeding the baby, Nathaniel yawned and opened his eyes.

"What time is it?" he asked his wife.

"Six-thirty."

"We should almost be there then."

"Just about," she told him.

He looked back at us and asked if we were hungry. We could stop for breakfast now, or wait till we got to the island.

The island. It sounded so mysterious. I mean, how many people do you know who live on an island, especially year-round? But as Nathaniel explained it, Ettinger Rock had been in his family since the 1850's. His great-grandfather had won it in a poker game, back in the days when Oregon was still a territory, and the Pacific Northwest was an unexplored wilderness.

"I don't think he ever planned to live there," Nathaniel told us. "But after he made his fortune in lumber he built a summer house on the island. When I was a little boy I remember my grandfather telling me about it. It was just a tiny place, he said, very primitive even by the standards of the day. When Great-grandfather finally retired from business he was so attached to Ettinger Rock he decided to move there permanently. I'll show you some of the old photos when we get home. It was quite an amazing undertaking to build a house of that size, especially when you realize everything had to be shipped over by boat. But once an Ettinger sets his mind on something, there's no turning back. They even had to bring mules over from the mainland to haul the building materials up to the top of the cliff where the house is situated.''

''The view's extraordinary,'' Perdita interrupted. ''There's something very special about the play of light on water, and the way you can see the mainland coming out of the mist. It's never the same on any one day. How many times have you painted it, dear?''

''I didn't know you were an artist, Mr. Ettinger,'' Quinn spoke up.

''Please. It's Nathaniel,'' he corrected. ''Mr. Ettinger makes me sound like I'm facing a roomful of students.''

''You were a teacher, too?'' I asked.

He nodded.

''Art history. How long has it been since I retired, Perdita?'' he said, turning to his wife.

''Five years as of last May,'' she said promptly.

Ettinger looked back at us and laughed.

''Didn't I tell you she was a stickler for details? I bet you even remember the day, don't you?''

''May twelfth,'' Perdita said with a grin.

''And since then you've taken up painting? Sounds like a terrific hobby,'' I remarked.

I was trying to be polite, because fooling around with paints wasn't really my idea of fun. I much preferred reading a good mystery—like Perdita, in fact—or just going off exploring. Quinn and I had done plenty of that back at the Valley, even before Mom got sick. I wondered how big the island was, because if it was just this tiny spit of land I had a feeling it might get awfully boring with no place to go.

''And when Nathaniel isn't painting, he builds these wonderful models,'' Perdita told us.

"They're a lot better than my paintings, I'll admit that," replied her husband.

Well, no matter what, living with them was going to be a thousand times better than spending the rest of my life running away from Dad and the head shrinkers. And even if I didn't mind running, I knew Quinn did.

So I decided to just settle back and relax. It might get a little dull on Ettinger Rock, but at least I wouldn't be spending the rest of my life inside a padded cell. Because not only would that have been dreary, it also would've been scary as hell.

Otter Bay was the name of the fishing village where the Ettingers garaged their station wagon and moored the launch that would take us out to the island. Nathaniel tried to point it out to me, but the morning fog was still rolling in, and though he insisted he could see it on the horizon, I couldn't make anything out but sky and water and gulls wheeling overhead.

I thought the village was a pretty neat place though, the harbor filled with fishing vessels, and faded clapboard buildings lining the one main street. It seemed that everyone knew the Ettingers, and judging from the way they were treated, Perdita and her husband were well-liked. When it came to us though, I got the feelings folks were kind of suspicious about what we were doing here. I couldn't blame them, either. We must've looked a sorry sight, what with our bruises and dirty clothes. But Perdita said not to mind if people stared. They were just curious about newcomers, that's all.

She let it slip—on purpose, that is—that we were cousins visiting from the east. But when we went to board the launch, one of the men on the pier asked about the baby.

Even though it was an innocent question, Perdita got flustered for a moment and didn't know what to say.

"Our parents were killed in a plane crash, sir," I volunteered, making it sound as if I were on the verge of tears.

"A terrible tragedy," murmured Perdita.

She shook her head sadly, and the guy helping out on the dock looked embarrassed, and muttered how sorry he was. I'll say one thing, the more time I spent with Mrs. Ettinger, the more I liked her.

Finally, when all the bags were on board, we set off for the island. Behind us, Otter Bay got smaller and smaller, and when it began to resemble a little toy village we were already out on the open sea. Just breathing in that crisp, briny air felt terrific. Salt spray cascaded over the bow, and the launch rolled and pitched in the heavy swells. Mr. Ettinger was at the wheel, and when I got up to join him he asked if I wanted to give it a try.

"You're sure it's all right? I mean, I don't want to capsize us or anything."

He laughed and told me not to worry, if I could drive a car I could pilot a launch. It took about forty-five minutes to reach the island, and by the time it came into view I was well on my way to earning my water wings. It really wasn't very difficult, and it was certainly a lot more fun than driving. When Mr. Ettinger saw what a good time I was having he promised to take me out for another lesson, he'd make a sailor of me in no time at all.

When he took over the wheel the island was no longer a blue-green smudge on the horizon. It rose up before us, much larger than I expected, and not nearly as barren. I could make out thick stands of trees, and from the topmost point something sparkled brightly as it caught the morning light.

"What makes it shine like that?" I asked.

"All that window glass, reflecting the light back at us."

When the house itself was finally visible it kind of took my breath away. It was like a castle—with steeply pitched roofs, twin towers, and more chimneys than I could count on the fingers of both hands. The narrow pointed-arch windows, the elaborate gables and battlements, all suggested a style of architecture more in keeping with the English countryside than an island off the Oregon coast.

Quinn was quick to make the same observation, and Mr. Ettinger explained that on one of his numerous trips to Europe, his great-grandfather had been particularly taken with a house he visited in Sussex. He had his architect copy it stone for stone, re-creating the Gothic Revival manor house we now saw before us, commanding the highest point on Ettinger Rock.

Mr. Finney our old tutor hadn't neglected to teach us some of the basics of architecture. So even though I didn't recognize the style—Gothic Revival, whatever that meant—I still knew a little bit about flying buttresses and stuff like that. The entire house was made of stone, and there was something very cold and forbidding about it.

Of course I wasn't about to make any critical remarks, not when I knew how important it was that I earn the Ettinger's respect. I wanted them to like me as much as I knew they already liked Quinn. So I kept quiet, and let Nathaniel and his wife do all the talking.

Out on the dock a lone figure stood waiting for us, and as we drew near he raised his arm and waved. So that's Kenley Ettinger, I thought, and waved back, knowing that if the kid got to like me, chances were his grandparents would, too.

The house was perched at the very top of a steep limestone cliff, and there was a trail which zigzagged down to the beach far below. I spotted a dog making its way toward the dock, a black and tan Airedale who seemed to bristle with self-importance.

"That's Max," Nathaniel told us. "He's top dog around here."

"He's the *only* dog around here," Perdita laughed.

Now that we were close enough to the dock, Nathaniel threw the painter to his grandson. Kenley caught it, and as he tied the rope around the mooring ring I had my first chance to really take a good look at him. He was about my size, which meant just a little taller than average, with dark curly hair and amazingly piercing eyes. Even from a distance they drilled right through you, seeing what you were all about. I wasn't going to flinch though, so I just stared right back at him, smiling too because first impressions are important.

As soon as we stepped onto the dock, Perdita introduced us to her grandson. By then Max was barking his head off, and though Quinn made friends with him right away, the dog kept his distance from me and snarled when I reached out to pat him.

"He's too protective for his own good," Perdita said, scolding the Airedale for not being more friendly.

Kenley was still staring at me, like he was trying to size me up or something. Perdita was going on and on, making all sorts of excuses for our being there. But I don't think her grandson was paying much attention. He was more interested in me and my sister, and when he noticed Becky his curiosity turned to surprise.

"We'll have Miss Granberry fix breakfast, and then we can sit down and tell you all about our guests," Perdita told him when he started to ask about the baby.

"Are you going to be staying with us?" Kenley asked me.

I glanced at Mr. Ettinger. When he nodded his head I told Kenley we hoped to stay for a while, if that was all right with him.

"All right?" he exclaimed with a laugh. "Why, it's terrific. There are so many neat things we can do together. You guys are really going to have a great time here."

I smiled politely, then picked up some of the bags and followed everyone up the trail that led to the house. At the top of the cliff I paused and looked back. There was sea and more sea, sky and clouds and no trace of the mainland at all. I wondered if we'd made the right decision, or if coming here meant we'd unwittingly exchanged one form of prison for another. It wasn't the most comforting thought, but maybe our luck had finally changed and things would work out for the best. I sure hoped so.

CHAPTER NINE

Those first few weeks we spent on Ettinger Rock made me feel like a child again, and I was grateful for the opportunity to act giddy and carefree, to pretend that nothing terrible had happened to me in the past, and nothing terrible would occur in the future. Even the responsibility of looking after Becky was gently taken out of my hands, for Perdita insisted I needed time to myself, to forget all the troubles I had left behind in the Valley. She and Miss Granberry, the housekeeper, were like two fairy godmothers, each one vying for the baby's attention. They pampered and coddled her, doting on Becky as if she were a little princess.

She blossomed during those first weeks on the island, and I suppose it wouldn't be an exaggeration to say that I blossomed as well. The past was like a crushing weight lifted off my shoulders, and soon I scarcely concerned myself with it at all. And when from time to time it occurred to me how really odd it was for the Ettingers to extend themselves to us so thoroughly, I forced myself not to dwell on it. There were far too many things to distract me, for Ettinger Rock was a marvelous place, with its own little forest, its rocky coves and beaches, even caves

cut away into the cliffs. Kenley mounted expeditions—
that's what he called them—and almost every day found
new ways of occupying our time.

He was one of the most delightful boys I'd ever met,
sometimes shy and reserved, while other times he was the
very opposite, outgoing and ebullient and full of the devil.
Yet between him and Jason there existed a kind of wariness
that all their outward displays of friendliness couldn't hide.

I wasn't exactly certain why my brother insisted upon
keeping his distance, though several weeks after our arrival,
when Kenley and I were lying out on the lawn enjoying
the sun, I looked up and noticed Jason watching us from
his third-floor window. There was something in his
expression, in the grim set of his lips, that frightened me
as nothing had since we had first come here. As soon as he
saw me watching him he let go of the curtain and turned
away. Was he jealous, was that it? Did he think I cared
more about Kenley Ettinger than I did about him? But he
was my brother, and surely he knew that no one could ever
take his place.

Something else happened though, just a few days before
Kenley's tutor was due to arrive on the island. I looked
forward to meeting him and resuming my studies, especially after all that Kenley had told me about Mr. Houghton.
He said the tutor made learning an adventure, and that
once we got used to his methods we'd never be satisfied
with anyone else. Houghton, he explained, made you experience everything firsthand. When he taught biology it was
right at the edge of a tidal pool, and if history was on the
day's agenda, he never spent his time drilling you on dates
and statistics, but described things so vividly it was like
stepping back into the past.

It all sounded very novel and exciting, and I couldn't

wait for Mr. Houghton to return to the post he had left a few months before. But several days prior to his arrival something occurred which made me wonder if once again I'd made the mistake of acting much too naively for my own good.

The Ettingers had given me a lovely room on the third floor of the house, the "Castle" as my brother jokingly referred to it. Jason, Kenley, and I were the only ones on the floor, though when Mr. Houghton returned he too would be living in one of the more than dozen rooms opening onto the L-shaped hall. I never bothered to lock my door, nor did I even think to ask for a key. After all, Ettinger Rock was a far cry from the Valley, and the fears which had consumed my every waking hour no longer existed.

I was so sound asleep that night I never even heard my brother slip into my room. Only when he climbed into bed and put his arms around me did I awaken with a start. At first I didn't realize who it was, but then I heard him whisper that I mustn't make any noise, he didn't want Kenley to know he was here.

"I need to talk to you, Quinn. He's always around. We never get a chance to be alone anymore. Have you noticed the way he looks at you? He just can't keep his eyes off you."

I turned over in bed and looked at him in the darkness. I could see his robe where he'd dropped it on the floor, and when he reached up and touched my cheek his bare arm made me suddenly realize he wasn't wearing any clothes. I edged back, knowing there was more on his mind than just a need to talk to me.

"You're scared, aren't you?" he said accusingly.

I pretended to laugh.

"Don't be ridiculous, Jason. Why would I be scared of you? You'd never do anything to hurt me."

"But Father might."

Father. He hadn't mentioned him in weeks, and just thinking about him made me tremble, doubly so when Jason reached out to hold me. I pulled away, drawing the covers tightly around me.

"Why did you have to do that, Quinn? Couldn't you just let me hold you?" he said angrily.

Although I had tried to explain my feelings over and over again, my brother refused to hear me, turning a deaf ear to whatever I told him. For a moment I even wondered if Warren had resurfaced, if in fact it was he who was telling my brother what to do and controlling his actions.

"Are you still taking those pills you found?" I asked.

Jason's smile was like a peace offering, guileless and completely unstudied.

"Not for weeks now," he admitted. "Funny how he just left, cleared out without a trace. Soon as we left home he vanished into thin air, Quinn."

I had long suspected that Warren would disappear in just such a fashion, that in fact my brother was as sane as I was. Yet the enormous relief I felt was tempered by Jason's very presence. What was he doing here in my bed? Didn't he understand how destructive it would be for both of us?

"What is it you really want, Jason?" I blurted out.

"You."

He said it so simply, so effortlessly, that for a moment I was completely taken aback. But when I felt his hand on my thigh I pulled roughly away. I started to get out of bed, but my brother grabbed me by the arm and held me back.

"Don't you care about me anymore? I need you," he

pleaded. "You've been ignoring me ever since we got here. All I ever hear is Kenley this and Kenley that, like he's the only one on your mind. But what about Jason? Where does he fit in?"

"Kenley is our friend," I tried to explain.

"No, he's *your* friend, Quinn. He doesn't like me at all. He just tolerates me, because he doesn't have any other choice."

His arms tightened around me, and before I could stop him he slid on top of me. I started to cry out but his lips were against my mouth, kissing me so desperately that I didn't know what to do.

"Jason, listen to me," I begged. "I know how much you care about me, and believe me, I feel the same way. But what you're trying to do is going to hurt us terribly. You have to believe that, you must."

He hovered over me, and though I could feel how excited he was, I tried my best to ignore it. I wanted to be a little girl again, not a woman at thirteen, but a child. I wanted a chance to learn about love without having to take lessons from my brother. And it wasn't because I didn't find Jason attractive. That had nothing to do with it. He was my brother, and what had nearly destroyed him was not going to happen to me, not if I had any say in the matter.

"The only reason you're here is because you want to have sex with me. Isn't that the truth, Jason?"

"I want to make love to you," he replied. "That's not the same thing as sex."

"But since I don't want to, it isn't love at all. It's just . . . just fucking," I whispered.

There was no other way to describe it. But in a sense I

was glad I'd said it, because the word was ugly and so too was what my brother was trying to do.

"I don't understand you anymore, Quinn. I used to. I used to think I knew you as well as I knew myself. But now you've put up all these walls around yourself, just to keep me out."

"That's not true."

"It is," he insisted. He edged away from me and lay on his back, staring up at the ceiling. "All I want to do is make love, and you turn it into something dirty."

"It's not dirty, Jason. But it's terribly wrong. It wasn't meant to be, don't you understand that?"

I thought of what he had done to Mother, how in his rage he had lashed out at her, trying to hurt her because of all the hurt she'd inflicted upon him. Didn't he realize that what he was doing now was the very same thing?

Perhaps he sensed what I was thinking. He touched my cheek one last time, then threw his legs over the side of the bed and got to his feet. I looked away, feeling shame and embarrassment where once I had felt nothing of the kind.

"Look at me, Quinn."

"I can't," I said sadly.

"Do I disgust you so?"

The pain in his voice, the bitter disappointment, was more than I could possibly allow him to feel. Slowly I turned my head in his direction. Like a marble statue he stood silhouetted against the darkness, the lean, hard lines of his youthful figure perfect in their symmetry. He was a man now, even more of a man than he had been that day at the Temple, when he first showed me what sex was all about. A thin line of golden hair snaked down from the flat ridges of his belly, fanning out above his genitals. I felt the blood rushing through my cheeks, and yet I didn't look away, flinching from the sight of him. Jason wanted me to see him, to remember him perhaps. I realized then that I loved him even more than I had ever loved Mother. Despite all we'd been through together, that love had only gotten stronger. But now it would have to take on a new face, a new complexion. It would be different than in the past, though no less enduring.

I tried my best to tell him that, but I don't think he heard me.

" 'And if a man shall take his sister, and see her nakedness, and she see his nakedness; it is a wicked thing; and they shall be cut off in the sight of their people.' Remember Leviticus, Quinn? Remember the curse we tried to escape? We can spend the rest of our lives running away from it, but it's never going to go away. It's part of us now. It always will be."

My brother picked up his robe, tied it loosely, and started to the door.

"I do love you, Jason, surely you believe that by now," I called out in a whisper.

"Sure, I know you do, Quinn."

There was no conviction in his voice, no emotion but sadness, deep and unsettling. He left as silently as he had entered, closing the door softly behind him. I lay in bed, staring at the spot where he had stood before me. Tears welled up in my eyes, and before I even realized it I began to cry for the Jason and Quinn who used to be, and could never be again.

The next morning, my brother pretended as if nothing had happened. Warm and friendly and full of good humor, he acted like he didn't have a care in the world. Yet I knew that underneath the laughter and smiles he bore a grudge against me, one that would not fade from memory so easily.

We had turned a new page in our lives, and now there was no going back. If only he understood that. If only he realized how important it was that each of us become our own person, free to grow and mature without the constricting influence of the other. Jason and Quinn weren't an island onto themselves, but existed in a much larger world in which they would have to learn to make their peace. I wanted desperately to make my brother understand that, but when I tried to talk to him he told me not to worry, he knew me better than I realized and that's why everything was going to be all right.

Perhaps it would. Perhaps Jason had already begun to realize that my rejection of him was only for the best—not just for me, but for him, as well. He made no mention of it in the days that followed, and gradually I put it out of my mind, knowing it would only make me even more unhappy if I continued to dwell on it.

When Mr. Houghton arrived on the island my brother diligently applied himself to his studies, far more conscientious about schoolwork than he had ever been under the tutelage of Mr. Finney. Our new tutor was everything Kenley had promised. A big teddy bear of a man, Mr. Houghton had a soft streak a mile wide. Behind his bushy black beard his lips seemed to be permanently fixed in a grin, for he saw humor in even the most mundane situations. The reticence that marked Jason's relations with the other members of the household was quickly put aside when it came to Mr. Houghton. He followed the tutor everywhere, and the friendship that developed between them gave me as much pleasure as I'm sure it gave my brother.

I don't think Mr. Houghton was a father figure though, or even a father confessor. He was more like a big brother, someone Jason could turn to for advice. Often I would come upon them deep in conversation, and there was such a calm and respectful look in my brother's eyes that I was sure the worst was now behind us.

Something in Jason's relationship with the Ettingers seemed to change as his friendship with Mr. Houghton blossomed. Prior to the tutor's arrival my brother had kept his distance, always polite yet vaguely aloof. But now he treated Perdita and her husband as if they were friends of long standing, no longer fearful they would one day turn against him as Father had done.

When I wasn't occupied with my studies, Nathaniel gave me art lessons in his studio. The big, airy room faced north, and seemed always to be bathed in a crisp, bluish-white light. In the very center of the workroom stood his easel, where often I caught him standing in perfect stillness and contemplation. When he painted, and sometimes he continued to work even in my presence, it was almost as if he were in a dream state. The hand that held his brush would rise slowly, moving as I imagined sleepwalkers did. Yet whenever he applied paint to canvas it was never with uncertainty. He knew exactly what he was doing, what effect he was after, and the play of light and shadow which characterized so many of his paintings was far subtler than anything I could possibly have envisioned myself.

Although I very much enjoyed the lessons he gave me, I quickly realized that I lacked the temperament to be an artist. It required such intense concentration that my mind would begin to wander, and instead of trying to capture a still life of driftwood arranged on a nearby table, I started wondering where the wood itself had come from, and how long it had been tossed upon the sea before being washed up on the island.

But painting wasn't Mr. Ettinger's only hobby. He was equally adept at building models, and here I found something at which I too could excel. He was in the process of putting the finishing touches on an elaborate dollhouse, a perfect replica of the house his great-grandfather had built on Ettinger Rock. Not only were the external features identical, but each room was like a tiny mirror, reflecting the exact appearance of its model.

Some of the miniature furnishings he ordered through the mail, while others he made himself. When I noticed that the dollhouse bedroom which corresponded to my own room lacked curtains, Miss Granberry the housekeeper managed to locate a swatch of the original material. It took me several hours to sew them, and though the work was painstaking I took great satisfaction in what I was doing.

When I presented them to Nathaniel—I still felt a little uncomfortable calling him by his first name, even though both he and Perdita insisted upon it—he was so delighted with my little gift that it more than made up for the numerous pinpricks in my fingers.

One afternoon, while I helped him cut wallpaper for some of the rooms on the second floor, he suggested we model a series of dolls to people the house, each one to resemble as closely as possible its counterpart in real life. I thought it was a marvelous idea, and so he ordered the necessary materials from one of the mail-order houses which regularly sent him miniatures.

Within a week they arrived, four adults, three children, a baby, and even an Airedale. The figures were fully articulated, though in their faceless, unpainted state they resembled mannequins more than human beings. But once they were given individual features and dressed in appropriate clothes they would be able to move about the dollhouse just as we did—sitting in chairs or sleeping in beds, studying in the schoolroom or painting before the tiny easel in the dollhouse studio.

Max was the first figure to be completed, and over a period of weeks each of the other miniatures gradually took on life. We even made a beard for the doll that represented Mr. Houghton, and he kindly consented to provide us with a thumbnail's worth of the real thing.

The days were shorter now, and with less light to paint, work on the dollhouse occupied more and more of Nathaniel's time. Some of the rooms were nearly complete, and I made a game of checking the real rooms against those in the dollhouse.

"You'll need logs for the fireplace in the library," I would tell him. "And you forgot to make bulbs for the chandelier in the dining room."

It was almost eerie how perfectly everything was being duplicated, although that was Mr. Ettinger's intention from the very beginning. And when the last of the miniature figures was painted and clothed and set down inside the dollhouse, I found myself gazing into the tiny rooms and imagining that what I saw was life itself, reenacted as if on a stage.

The calm and untroubled world of the dollhouse mirrored my own life. I was busy with schoolwork, with making miniatures, with helping Perdita and Miss Granberry take care of Becky. I had no time to worry about what was, nor even time to think about what might be in the future. Jason and I were part of a family again, and that was the most important thing of all.

But a few days after we proudly showed off our handiwork, and everyone applauded our efforts, I made a discovery I wasn't the least bit prepared for. When I entered the studio I started to tell Nathaniel about a piece of furniture I'd seen in one of his catalogues. The miniature sideboard was a very close match to the one in the dining room, and with a few minor alterations would make a wonderful addition to his collection. But then I realized I was talking to myself, for there was no one else in the studio. With a rueful smile I put down my books, having come straight from the schoolroom, and went over to the dollhouse to see if he'd added anything new.

At first I was so taken with the crib he'd made for the nursery—I knew he was working on it, but I had no idea when it would be finished—that I didn't notice anything else. But then my eyes strayed to the other rooms, until finally I peered into the room that was a duplicate of my own. The Quinn doll lay in bed, the covers drawn up to its neck. I hadn't put her there, but that wasn't what disturbed me.

Hovering by the side of the bed stood another doll, with tawny blond hair and sharp green eyes. I'd painted the figure of Jason myself, and now it stood there with its arm upraised, a tiny piece of metal glinting in the light. I leaned closer to get a better look, suddenly recognizing what it was the doll had clutched in its hand. It was a knife, the blade fashioned out of a strip of aluminum foil.

My first reaction was anger, and when I tried to remove it, my hand shook so that I inadvertently knocked over the doll. It lay on its back, its movable arm still raised in the air and the knife held securely in the little depression of its fist. I finally managed to twist it free, then hurriedly placed the Jason doll back in the schoolroom where I'd seen it last. I was about to do the same with the Quinn doll, only to discover that whoever had done this had first removed the doll's clothing, painting on breasts and genitals where before there was nothing but flesh-colored paint.

It was a stupid and childish joke, I thought, unnecessarily cruel as well. The knife was bad enough, but did Jason honestly think I'd be amused to learn the doll was now anatomically exact? I was certain he was responsible, though whether he meant it as a joke or a warning I had no way of knowing.

The freshly applied paint came off with a damp cloth, and as soon as I dressed the doll and returned it to the schoolroom I hurried from the studio, determined to find my brother and have it out with him.

I thought he might be in his room studying, because Mr. Houghton was going to give us an algebra test the next morning. But as I passed the library on the way to the stairs the telephone suddenly rang, and a moment later I couldn't help but hear Perdita's anxious voice.

I knew I had no business eavesdropping, but there was something in her tone that made me stop short. My suspicions proved correct, for no sooner did I pause by the door than I heard a name I had hoped never to hear again.

"Sheriff Orickson . . . yes, I recall our meeting. It was after we found those children, I believe."

I peeked into the library. Perdita was sitting at the desk, and from the look on her face I knew the sheriff's phone call had taken her completely by surprise. She drummed her fingers nervously on the blotter, picked up the needlepoint canvas she was working on and put it down again without even bothering to look at it.

"No, I don't believe so, Sheriff," she said thoughtfully. She was covering up, I was sure of it. Everything about the way she answered him told me she was lying, though of course the sheriff would have no way of knowing that.

"I'm afraid I have absolutely no idea," she insisted. "No, it's no trouble . . . Yes, I appreciate your concern. Of course."

As she hung up the phone I managed to slip past the open doorway without her seeing me. I started up the stairs, more concerned about what I'd heard than the mischief my brother had done in the dollhouse. That Sheriff Orickson was still looking for us both surprised and disturbed me, for I was certain my father was behind it all. Perhaps Father had promised the sheriff a sizable reward if he managed to locate us. Jason had suspected as much, and the more I thought about it, the more convinced I became. But at least Perdita hadn't given us away. She'd covered up for us, refusing to provide Orickson with any information that might lead him to where we were hiding.

When I knocked on Jason's door, that was the first thing I told him. He put down the book he was reading and leaned back in his chair, listening with a somber expression while I repeated everything I'd overheard.

"Dad doesn't give up so easily, does he?" he said, shaking his head. "It's been nearly two months now—"

"Longer than that," I interrupted.

". . . and he still won't leave us alone."

"But why would he be using the sheriff?" I asked. "If he's so anxious to find us, wouldn't it make more sense to hire a private detective?"

"Probably, unless of course Orickson convinced him he could do a better job. Or for all we know the sheriff might be working on his own, sort of like a bounty hunter. Dad might've mentioned some kind of reward, and then let the whole thing drop. Only Orickson's so greedy he hasn't forgotten it.''

"Do you think Father told him what happened to Harry?''

Jason's eyes darted nervously to the door, but I knew we were the only ones in the house guilty of eavesdropping.

"If he did, then he thinks even less of us than we realize." Jason sighed loudly. "Well, at least we can count on Perdita. Not that I ever doubted her, but it's nice to know she came through for us in a pinch.''

"And what about you, Jason? Will you come through for me in a pinch, too?''

I reached into the pocket of my jeans and removed the tiny aluminum foil knife I'd found in the dollhouse. Jason eyed me curiously, and when I put the knife down beside his book he looked at it with a blank expression, as if he didn't even recognize what it was.

"I don't get it," he said at last.

"You mean to say you've never seen it before?" I said in disbelief.

My brother shook his head.

"It looks like the inside of a gum wrapper.''

"It's not," I said angrily.

My tone of voice surprised him.

"What are you giving me such a hard time about?" he barked. "You throw a piece of tin foil on my desk and the next thing I know you're ready to kill. What's with you, anyway?''

"It's a knife, Jason," and I went on to describe exactly where I had found it.

"Come on, you've got to be kidding," he laughed. "Who would do something like that? I mean, if there was a Bennett doll that might be different . . . sorry, that wasn't very funny, was it?''

I was getting more and more annoyed by his attitude.

"No, it wasn't very funny at all. And neither was what I found."

"And you think I did it, is that it?"

"Well who else would, Jason? You and I are the only ones who know the significance of that knife. It wouldn't mean anything to anyone else."

"And it doesn't mean anything to me, either," he shouted.

He took the strip of foil and crumpled it in his hand, then flicked it off the desk and onto the floor.

"You have no loyalty, you know that, Quinn. And you don't have much of a sense of humor, either."

But I wasn't about to let him talk his way out of it.

"What's so funny about someone standing over my bed with a knife in his hand?" I demanded.

Jason frowned and looked away.

"Okay, so it's not funny. It's tragic, all right."

"Don't be sarcastic."

"Oh come on, Quinn, it's not the end of the world. They're just dolls, not people. The way you and the old man carry on about that dollhouse it's unbelievable. It's become an obsession, you know that?"

"It's a hobby."

"Not in my book it's not. What is it with you two, anyway? It's like you're playing God or something, manipulating those dolls, making everything so letter-perfect that God forbid someone comes along and plays a little joke on you—"

"A knife isn't a joke," I reminded him.

"I didn't do it. Now either you believe me or you don't.

If I'd painted boobs on the doll I'd be the first to take credit for it. But I don't fantasize stabbing you in the back."

I wanted to believe him, even more than he realized. But if Jason wasn't responsible, then who was? I couldn't think of anyone on Ettinger Rock who'd want to hurt me. But maybe someone was trying to warn me, maybe that was it. Perhaps someone on the island, Mr. Houghton for instance, had learned the truth of what happened to us in the Valley. But even if he had, surely he didn't think my brother intended to murder me.

"Have you told Mr. Houghton the real reason why we ran away?" I asked.

"What does that have to do with anything?" he said sullenly.

"Just answer me, Jason. We've argued enough."

"No, I haven't told him. Happy? Satisfied?"

He turned away and buried his nose in his book.

"Are you sure?"

"If there's one thing I don't want to be reminded of, it's what we've been through," he insisted, raising his voice. "Now will you get out of here and let me study."

There was nothing else to say. If he'd put the knife in the doll's hand that was bad enough. But if he hadn't, I knew it was even worse. Either someone on Ettinger Rock was trying to warn me, or else they were determined to turn me against my brother, terrifying me in the process. And if that were the case, then not only was my life in jeopardy, but so was Jason's.

CHAPTER TEN

Boy, she really pissed me off. Quinn was supposed to trust me. More than anything else, she was supposed to believe in me. And she always had, never doubting me for a minute. How the hell could she even think I'd try to hurt her? Sure, I was angry, upset about what happened a couple of weeks back, when I tried to make love. But if you think I slipped into her bed that night just for the sake of sex, you're greatly mistaken. That was the least of it, honest to God. I just needed to be close to her, to know she hadn't deserted me for . . . I don't know, maybe Kenley. See? I'm being truthful.

Okay, I'm going to try to calm down. Anger doesn't do you any good, anyway. She comes into my room, accuses me of trying to terrorize her, and what am I supposed to do? Ignore it? I didn't stuff that crummy piece of foil in the doll's hand. I swear I didn't. But she wouldn't believe me, and that's what hurt more than anything else.

We seemed so apart from each other, know what I mean? We used to be inseparable. We counted on each other for all sorts of things. Now she thinks I'm about to do her in and knife her in her sleep. I'd sooner knife myself, and you know I mean it, too.

The question is, who *was* responsible? You see, on the surface everything was really okay here. The Ettingers were ideal—just sweet and kind and loving. Granberry . . . well, she was another case altogether, sort of hard-faced and sour. But she loved the baby, so that was one point in her favor.

That left Mr. Houghton and Kenley. Now Houghton was absolutely terrific. He was so supportive that if Mom had had a therapist like that, instead of Dr. Warren that shit, I bet she'd be alive today. Houghton was probably the most understanding and perceptive person I'd ever met. You know how adults always pretend to have all the answers, like even when they don't they say they do? Houghton wasn't like that. You asked him a question, and if he didn't know the answer he wouldn't hesitate to admit it. "Let's look it up," he'd say. "Let's find out for sure."

No, it couldn't be Mr. Houghton, it just couldn't.

Which left Kenley Ettinger.

Now Quinn'll probably deny it, but I think she had a crush on him, just like she had a crush on Harry. I'd catch her with this dreamy look in her eyes, and I didn't need to be a mind reader to know what she was thinking. Actually, he wasn't a bad kid. I'd sort of made up my mind not to like him—don't ask me why, but I had—but Kenley had a way of ingratiating himself. Before you even knew it you were on his side, rooting for him if you know what I mean. He was trying so hard to make us feel welcome, like we were part of his family, that I found it very difficult to believe he'd do anything to hurt us, Quinn in particular.

So who *did* stick the knife in the Jason doll's hand? For all the mysteries I read—I was going through Perdita's collection at the rate of four to five titles a week—I still didn't have the vaguest idea. It wasn't a house full of loonies, not as far as I could tell. And if the Ettingers didn't want us around, or if they thought they'd made a mistake inviting us to live with them, I think we would've sensed it by now. But they treated us so well I just couldn't believe one of them actually meant to harm us, or scare us, or whatever was behind the knife in the doll's hand. And that other business, painting on the breasts and everything—taken together with the knife it seemed totally creepy. Although I didn't want Quinn to know how I felt—she was scared enough as it was—the more I thought about it, the more uneasy I became.

One thing was certain though. I'd better find out who was responsible, because there was just no telling what might happen. When someone starts fooling around with dolls, sooner or later they're bound to experiment with the real thing.

Dolls don't bleed, and if they break you can always glue them back together. It's not that easy with people.

Max was acting crazy, like he knew something was up. We were all sitting around the dining table, enjoying Miss Granberry's home cooking, when the dog started barking his head off, wouldn't stop even when Nathaniel lost his temper and yelled at him.

Kenley got up and looked outside, but it was pitch-black out and there wasn't anything he could see.

"Something must've spooked him," Kenley said when he returned to the table.

Or someone, I thought.

But we were all here, the entire population of Ettinger Rock seated around the massive oak dining table.

"Cut it out now, Max," Nathaniel said sharply.

I'd never heard the old man get so angry. Not that I blamed him. Max had this awful high-pitched bark that could really get on your nerves. Although the two of us had finally made our uneasy peace, I knew the dog didn't like me (don't ask me why, but he didn't), and I didn't like him. So we avoided each other, and believe it or not, sometimes when he saw me he just turned around and trotted off in the opposite direction.

"Max, come on, be a good boy," Kenley told him. "Lie down under the table and behave yourself."

But Max was stubborn as hell. He just sat there in the middle of the dining room and kept yapping away like he wasn't about to listen to anyone but himself. Finally Nathaniel got sick and tired of it, and he threw his napkin down and jumped to his feet. He started to grab Max by the collar when the Airedale turned its shaggy head to the side and snapped at his wrist. Mr. Ettinger was so startled that for a moment he froze, not moving a muscle. Then he brought the back of his hand down across the dog's snout, striking him so hard that I think Max was as surprised as the rest of us.

"Nathaniel, you're bleeding!" Perdita said in alarm.

"Just a scratch," he murmured, still glaring angrily at the dog.

Max started to slink away, but not before Mr. Ettinger gave him what-for, warning him that the next time he used his teeth he'd really get a beating he'd never forget.

Kenley looked pretty unhappy about the whole thing. He and Max were just about inseparable. The dog even slept in the schoolroom when we were working, and you hardly ever saw one without the other. Max came over to him, put his head against Kenley's lap, and began to whine.

"See, he's sorry for trying to bite you, Grandpa," Kenley said while the dog licked his hand.

"I don't know what's gotten into him," Nathaniel replied, and I could still hear the anger seeping out of his voice. "He's been acting strange all week."

"Go lie down," Kenley said again.

Instead of obeying, Max suddenly bolted out of the dining room. A moment later we heard him barking, and Kenley finally took him outside where he wouldn't bother us.

"He was just sitting there by the bottom of the stairs, like he was waiting for someone," he told us when he came back in.

Mr. Houghton smiled mischievously behind his beard.

"I think Max needs a nice lady Airedale to keep him occupied," he said with a straight face.

"That's all we need, a houseful of puppies," Nathaniel groaned.

Pretty soon the entire incident was forgotten . . . by everyone except me. Just like a detective, I'd already decided to keep a list of clues, writing down anything that happened that struck me as being out of the ordinary. Maybe a pattern would emerge, and eventually I'd be able to figure out who was responsible for that business in the dollhouse. It was certainly worth a try, because not only did I want to prove to Quinn I wasn't the guilty party, but I also wanted to find out who was.

Even though I hoped it was a joke, I found myself studying everyone at the table as if they were a potential suspect. Behind the laughter, the polite conversation, someone had a secret, and it was up to me to find out what it was. No one had said anything about Kenley's parents, and that was an area that was certainly worth investigating. Were they divorced or separated or what? And why didn't Kenley ever talk about them? He'd never mentioned them to me at all, though maybe he'd confided in Quinn. I'd have to ask her, because the more I knew about everyone on Ettinger Rock, the better my chances of solving the mystery.

Max spooked. Mr. E. loses temper. Kenley's parents??
Granberry's past. The Case of the Sex-Starved Doll.

I put down my pen and closed the notebook. It was late, and tomorrow we had an algebra quiz first thing in the morning. So I brushed my teeth and got into bed. My room had a wall heater because the house was so drafty, but it felt stuffy so I got up and turned it off. Then I went over to the window to open it a crack. The wind was really starting to howl, and I could hear the waves crashing against the beach at the bottom of the cliff. You couldn't see anything out there but shapes and shadows, but just as I started to turn away I thought I glimpsed something moving. It was so dark out it was hard to tell, and though I opened the window and stuck my head outside, whatever I'd seen had already ducked out of sight.

Mysterious occurrences and things that go bump in the night. Not what you want to start thinking about when you're trying to get to sleep. It was probably Max, I told myself, and I pulled the covers over my head and waited for the sandman to get down to business.

When I turned over and opened my eyes, the face of the alarm clock displayed 3:17 in glowing digital numbers. Despite the heavy quilt I was freezing, and debated getting out of bed to close the window. The curtains were beating against the glass, and the tide must've been in because the surf was so loud it sounded like the waves were breaking against the side of the house.

"Jason . . . Jason Lefland . . ."

My eyes jerked to the door. No, the knob didn't turn and the boogeyman didn't step inside. But someone had called out my name. The faint voice was barely audible, and for a moment I thought I'd imagined it.

"Jason . . ."

The voice was so low, so indistinct, I couldn't even tell what gender it was. I eased the covers back and sat up in bed, rubbing the sleep from my eyes. There was a light on in the hall, and even as I looked at the door something moved past the threshold. The shadow came and went. I cupped my hand behind my ear and listened intently. Were those footsteps I heard, or just my heart beating nervously? Maybe it was Quinn, but why didn't she just knock on the door if she wanted to speak to me? And what was she doing up at three in the morning?

Something was very fishy, all right. People didn't go creeping around in the middle of the night just for the fun of it. No, they had to have something specific in mind. Like tampering with the dollhouse? I wondered. Well, there was only one way to find out.

I got out of bed, searching for my slippers because the floor was so cold. Then I pulled on my robe and started to the door. But I wasn't halfway there when I stopped.

You're sure you know what you're doing? I asked myself.

Maybe the best thing to do was just crawl under the covers and forget the whole thing. Maybe it was all a dream, because sometimes dream-sounds can seem so loud they actually wake you up. But when I put my ear to the door I could swear I heard those footsteps again, coming from the far end of the hall near the stairs.

I eased the door open and slipped outside. The hallway was so long I could just as easily have been in a hotel, because that's exactly what it reminded me of. Back in the Valley we had family portraits lining the walls, each one illuminated by its own little lamp. Here on Ettinger Rock the few portraits I'd seen were all hung downstairs in the library, where the floor-to-ceiling shelves were crammed with hundreds of paperbacks, some so old they only cost a quarter when they were new. Perdita told me she'd been reading mysteries ever since she was a girl, and now that she was close to seventy she had quite a collection.

I was just standing out there in the drafty hall, sort of making up excuses why I should go back to my room. I really didn't want to go downstairs and investigate. But maybe there was someone living in the house, someone we knew nothing about. Sure, that would explain things, wouldn't it? Maybe one of Kenley's parents had gone crazy like that woman locked up in the attic in *Jane Eyre*. I hadn't heard crazy laughter yet, but at the rate things were going I probably would in just another few minutes.

I started down the hall, moving as quietly as I could so as not to give myself away. A few minutes before someone had passed by my door, called out my name, and then gone on. Was I expected to follow? I guess so, because that's what I found myself doing.

The stairs didn't creak, but I still took my time, careful not to make any noise. I could hear the wind, really blowing up a storm. I don't think I ever felt so isolated as I did then. There was no place to run, you see, no place to hide.

Except the dozens of rooms you've never even seen yet, I reminded myself.

Just thinking about that gave me the creeps. When I reached the bottom of the stairs I held my breath, not knowing what to expect.

"Jason . . ."

The hair stood straight up along the back of my neck, just like they always say it does when you're scared. And I was plenty scared, all right, even though I kept telling myself I had nothing to be afraid of.

"Who's there?" I called out in a whisper.

There was a light burning in the study, yet when I stepped inside the room was empty. I even looked behind the door—just in case—but there was no one there. I went back to the entrance hall, once again waiting to see if whoever was down here would reveal himself.

"I'm waiting for you, Jason . . ."

Only dead people spoke like that. I swear I'm not exaggerating. It was like a voice from the grave, like those stories of people being buried alive and that's how they sound when they're six feet under. I was so frightened I couldn't stop shaking. Though I tried not to lose my nerve, I think whatever was left was in very short supply.

Someone was waiting for me. Someone who knew who I was. I entered the drawing room, my eyes darting every which way at once. Was someone hiding behind the curtains? Or what about behind the couch? I was afraid to look.

"What is it you want?" I whispered.

The drawing room opened onto a music room, and beyond that was Nathaniel's studio. It was from this direction I thought I heard something, the creak of hinges perhaps, or someone's softly treading feet, tiptoing through the darkness. Something banged overhead and I thought I'd jump out of my skin. It was probably only a shutter, left unfastened and now swinging back and forth in the wind. At least that's what I tried to tell myself.

I took another step forward, then another after that. Suddenly I spun around, just in case whoever was down here was coming up behind me. But once again there was no one there.

The door to the studio was ajar, and as I approached it swung slowly back. I was trembling uncontrollably now, and it had nothing to do with the cold.

Go back upstairs. Lock the door and pull the covers over your head. Forget you ever heard anything.

"Hello? Anyone there?" I called out in a whisper.

Must've sounded pretty stupid, but what else was I supposed to say? I was scared to death, afraid to take another step. Any second now I expected someone to jump out of the shadows, grab me by the throat and squeeze the very life out of me. They'd lured me downstairs, and now that we were alone they were going to take their sweet time, terrifying me in the process.

I stood by the open doorway, trying to recall where the light switch was. Mr. Ettinger's easel was set up in the middle of the room, and with all that expanse of glass it wasn't nearly as dark as the rest of the house. But that wind was something else. I thought it would tear the roof off, it was blowing so hard.

"Well, here I am," I said, giggling nervously, barely able to get the words out, my throat was so dry. My slippers slapped against the tile floor, echoing from one end of the room to the other. I was inside the studio now, reluctant to look behind me lest I discover the way was blocked. The lights, where was the switch?

Moving so slowly, cautiously, it felt like I was underwater, I turned my head over my shoulder, peering into the darkness. Fear was written all over my skin in goosebumps the size of hailstones. I reached out and grabbed onto the switch before I lost my nerve. But even when I turned on the lights I was still too scared to move.

The studio was empty. I felt like crying, I was so relieved. But if someone had come in here, as I was sure they had, how could they have slipped out without my knowing it? I crossed the cluttered workroom and tried the door that led outside. It was locked, the bolt still in place. There was a second door though, this one opening onto an enclosed porch, a kind of sun room that was filled with plants. I didn't want to go in there if I could help it. The room was as overgrown as a jungle, and there were so many places where someone could hide that I didn't want to take the chance. But though I thought I'd open the door and take a quick peek, it too was locked.

Which meant I wasn't alone. Which meant there was only one way to get in, and only one way to get out.

The studio door slammed shut. I bit down on my knuckles because I didn't want to cry out.

"Why're you doing this? I never did anything to you."

"Because it's all your fault, Jason."

I whirled around, certain that's where the voice had come from. When I didn't see anyone I rushed to the door and flung it open. But if someone was in the music room I couldn't see them. The dollhouse . . . yes, of course, I suddenly realized. That's why they came down here to begin with.

It stood there in a corner, a faint light glowing from one

of the downstairs rooms. Strips of colored cellophane were lit from behind to give the illusion of fire. When I peered into the miniature library my breath made the cellophane crackle like flames, and the hearth looked even more realistic than before.

The Perdita doll was sitting in a wing chair by the fire, reading a book. In the studio, the Nathaniel doll stood at his easel, working on a seascape no bigger than a postage stamp. Miss Granberry was in the kitchen, and all that was missing was the aroma of food cooking on the stove. Slowly my eyes moved upward. There was Mr. Houghton, beard and all, writing on the blackboard in the second-floor schoolroom. There was Max, stretched out on the floor between the desks and gnawing on a miniature bone that looked as real as he did.

But where were the rest of us, the other dolls representing me and Quinn and Kenley? Becky was safe in the nursery, asleep in her crib. My eyes darted up to the third floor of the dollhouse. My room was deserted, as was Quinn's. But in Kenley's room there was a party, and I hadn't been invited.

They were lying in bed together, and it didn't take a whole lot of brains to figure out what they were doing. The Kenley doll lay on top of the blonde-haired doll whose painted features closely resembled my sister's. If this was someone's idea of a joke it wasn't the least bit funny. I reached inside, my hand shaking so I knocked over the nightstand, and the miniature lamp hit the floor and broke in two. I didn't care. They had no right, no business doing this. I snagged the tiny scrap of blanket with my fingers and pulled it off the bed.

Oh, they'd had a real good laugh over this one, I thought. Naked, the two dolls were locked in each other's arms, and I didn't have to separate them to know what was painted on their smooth, pink torsos. A pornographic dollhouse! I wish I could've laughed, written the whole thing off as an elaborate prank.

Afraid Quinn or Nathaniel would think I was responsible, I looked around for the dolls' clothes, thinking I'd get them dressed and stick them back in the schoolroom where they belonged. But where was the Jason doll, the one Quinn said had held a knife in its hand, hovering by the side of her bed as if he fully intended to murder her in her sleep?

I looked back into the dollhouse room that was a tiny mirror image of my bedroom. Noticing that the closet door stood ajar, I pushed it all the way open with my fingertip.

"You bastard," I whispered. "You *bastard!*"

He was dangling there, a tiny stool tipped over below his feet, a tiny, perfectly crafted noose tied around his neck. All they'd forgotten was to paint on a tongue, protruding between his bloodless lips, because while Kenley and my sister made merry the Jason doll had hung himself.

I started to loosen the noose to pull him free when I heard footsteps coming from the direction of the music room.

"Who is it? Who's hiding there?" I said loudly, more angry than frightened.

"What are you doing down here, Jason?"

It was Miss Granberry, the unsmiling housekeeper of Ettinger Rock. Dressed in a long flannel robe, she stood in the doorway, eying me suspiciously. Could she have been responsible? I wondered. Maybe she was down here all along, waiting for me to discover her handiwork.

"Someone played a joke," I muttered.

I got the noose off before she could see what I was

doing, then left the doll standing in the bedroom and turned around to face her.

"What are you doing over there, fiddling with Mr. Ettinger's things? Do you know how long he's been working on that dollhouse? Ever since—"

She stopped short, clearing her throat self-consciously.

"Ever since when?" I asked.

She looked at me irritably.

"Never you mind, young man. You should be upstairs in bed, instead of wandering around in the middle of the night." She stepped closer and gave the dollhouse a cursory glance. "You didn't break anything, I hope."

"A lamp tipped over."

Granberry glared at me as if I'd committed a cardinal sin. If she only knew the half of it.

"I'll tell Mr. Ettinger in the morning. There's no sense letting you take the blame, Miss Granberry. It wouldn't be fair."

If she heard the sarcasm in my voice, she never let on. She started to the door, then stepped aside to let me pass.

"I don't know where you came from, Jason, and frankly I'm not that interested. But if you want to stay here, you'd be wise to behave yourself."

Who did she think she was? I really felt like letting her have it, but she'd been suspicious of me since the day I arrived, and the less reasons I gave her to dislike me, the better.

So instead of telling her what a nosy, dried-up hag she was, I smiled politely and nodded my head. She closed the studio door behind her, then led the way through the darkened house. But as she started up the stairs, lifting the hem of her robe so she wouldn't trip and break her neck, I told her I'd heard something and that's why I came downstairs in the first place.

"Heard what?" she demanded.

"Someone called my name. I started to follow them."

Granberry eyed me contemptuously, but I wasn't about to let her intimidate me. She was just like Mrs. Darby, too full of herself for her own good.

"Is there someone else living in the house?" I asked. "Someone I haven't met yet?"

Her hand still clutching the banister, she paused and looked down at me as I stood below her on the stairs. Then she laughed, but it was just as cold and calculating as the tone of her voice.

"What an absurd notion. Do you think someone's hidden away in the attic, Jason? Or perhaps we've got them locked up in the cellar." She smiled slyly. "I think you've been reading too many of Mrs. Ettinger's mysteries."

Having said all she intended to, the housekeeper turned and continued up the stairs.

As soon as I got to my room I turned on the light and went right to the closet. But when I looked inside I didn't find a neatly tied noose waiting to tighten around my neck, nor was there a stool to stand upon so I could hang myself.

I took off my robe and got into bed. Someone had tried to scare Quinn, and now they'd done a hell of a good job on me. But why? That's what I couldn't understand.

CHAPTER ELEVEN

Out in the kelp beds sea otters floated on their backs, using odd pieces of rock to smash the clams and sea urchins they held in their paws. Even as Kenley and I watched, an otter came to the surface and immediately went to work preparing its dinner. Holding a small rock securely on its chest, it proceeded to bang the abalone shell against it to get at the meat inside.

"At night they wrap themselves up in the kelp so they don't float away," Kenley explained.

They were fascinating to watch, their sleek, glossy brown bodies perfectly adapted to life in the water. Gulls wheeled overhead, waiting for an opportunity to swoop down and steal the otters' rich booty. Their raucous squealing cries seemed to have no effect on the otters, who continued to hammer away at the shellfish and mollusks they brought up from the bottom.

I counted several dozen floating offshore, and Kenley said their numbers were on the increase. Since last year alone, the herd that favored the kelp beds off Ettinger Rock had gotten significantly larger. Farther north, along the Alaskan coast, herds of up to a thousand otters had been recorded.

"Do they ever come up onto the rocks?" I asked.

"I'm sure they do, but I've never seen it myself. I remember when I was a little boy, I asked my father for one as a pet. I figured the bathtub was just as good as the ocean, but I'm afraid I had to settle for Max instead."

Kenley smiled shyly, and at the mention of his name Max wagged his tail, having finally given up hope of catching a crab he'd seen slip between the rocks.

"What was his name, your father?"

Kenley had never spoken about him before, and now he looked at me curiously, wondering why I asked.

"Ashby Ettinger, just like that guy in *Gone With the Wind*."

"That was Ashley."

"Well, close enough," he laughed.

Having promised to take me to a spot where he'd seen several sea lions, Kenley led the way down the rocky beach. It was getting on toward Christmas, and the weather had turned cold and blustery. Bundled up in ski parkas, the two of us traced a path among the rocks, heading in the direction of a sheltered cove at the far end of the island. Here, if we were lucky, we might be able to observe the sea lions at close range.

Ever since arriving on Ettinger Rock, Kenley and I had had ample opportunity to get to know each other. Much more reserved and self-effacing than my brother, his shyness was nevertheless very appealing, and had about it a certain charm that had already won me over. Often when we took walks together there were long periods of silence, yet I rarely felt uncomfortable. Occasionally Kenley would reach for my hand, and when I gave it to him there was something in the way he held it that made me feel very special. I can't exactly explain why, because it was just a feeling I had, one that I couldn't easily put into words. But just the touch of his fingers made me feel very close to him, so it didn't matter if we walked along and listened to the silence, rather than ourselves.

Oddly enough, Kenley had never asked me about my past. Jason and I had promised his grandfather we wouldn't discuss it, and I couldn't help but wonder if Nathaniel had decided to keep everything a secret, or if he had already told Kenley the particulars of our family history. Perhaps Kenley knew what had happened to us, and was afraid to bring it up. It wasn't a very pleasant subject, especially after what Jason had told his grandparents, and for all I knew he might be embarrassed to talk about it.

But just as he avoided questioning me, neither did he offer any information about himself. In the first few weeks following our arrival I didn't think much about it. But now that I'd had sufficient time to adjust to my new surroundings, I thought it very strange that he would be so secretive. Again and again I found myself on the verge of telling him why we had come here, and what had happened that had made us run away from home. But each time I remembered the promise I had made to Mr. Ettinger, and so I never said a word.

Several weeks before, Jason had told me about the voice that awakened him in the middle of the night, and what he discovered when he went downstairs to investigate the dollhouse. Convinced someone was hiding in the house, he'd begun a systematic search of all the rooms, though he was yet to uncover anything even vaguely suspicious. Could that mysterious person possibly be one of Kenley's parents, I wondered? I know that must sound crazy to you, but after what I'd been through I was far from ruling *anything* out. I wanted so much to ask him, yet even getting him to tell me his father's name seemed a major accomplishment.

And if Jason were wrong, then who was responsible for what had happened? I needed to confide in Kenley, to tell him my fears, to seek out answers to the questions which troubled me. But I was afraid that if I brought up the subject of his parents, he would think less of me for meddling in things that weren't my concern.

When we reached the cove we found a dry spot on the rocks. Here at the foot of the limestone cliff which rose steeply behind us, we sat and waited for the sea lions. It was very chilly, and when I began to shiver Kenley put his arm around my shoulders. At first I didn't even feel it, and only when I turned my head to the side did I notice where his hand was.

I smiled to myself, for the few boys I'd known had been much more aggressive. I thought of Harry Darby, and how he had kissed me in the orchard, pressing himself against me. Jason too had kissed me, both before and during the ritual of the undivided spirit. But Kenley's shy, fumbling embrace was unlike either of them.

"We're still strangers, aren't we, Quinn? We spend so much time together, and yet we don't know very much about each other, do we?"

I shook my head. I'd let my hair grow, and it swung back and forth against my shoulders. Kenley touched it with his fingertips, marveling at how soft and silky it felt.

"You're very pretty, you know that? You're just about the prettiest girl I ever met."

I laughed nervously, unaccustomed to being complimented about my appearance.

"No, I mean it," he insisted.

Again he reached out to touch me, this time tracing the

faint line of freckles on my cheekbones. I was still cold, but that was no longer the reason why I continued to shiver.

"If you don't want me to—" he started to say.

"No, I do," I blurted out.

Kenley's eyes looked right into my soul, studying me so intently I was sure he could read my thoughts. Then he leaned forward and put his lips to mine. I closed my eyes, and when his arms encircled me and he drew me close I could feel the way he trembled. I don't think he'd ever kissed a girl before, and strangely enough it felt like my first time, as well.

"Did you like that?" he whispered.

I couldn't stop smiling, and I reached out and touched his hair, rearranging the thick curls which fell across his forehead. He was yet to use a razor, because the hair on his upper lip was still very smooth. I parted it playfully with the tip of my finger, and when he took me in his arms again I cupped his face in my hands and responded to his kiss with an eagerness that surprised me.

"I've never done this before," he admitted. "Was it okay?"

"Of course it was, silly. You kiss like an expert, Mr. Ettinger."

He blushed slightly, his lips curling up in a grin.

"Really? You're not just saying that, Quinn, are you?"

"Fishing for compliments?" I teased. "Well, if you must know the truth, that was the best kiss I ever had."

A troubled look came into his eyes, which was the last thing I would have expected. He let go of me and stuck his hands in his pockets, hunching his neck down between his shoulders.

"I know what happened, Quinn," he said sadly. "I've

known about it a couple of months now. Grandfather meant to keep it from me, but I overheard a conversation he was having with Grandmother. What I didn't learn directly from that, I figured out for myself.''

I put my hand on his shoulder, wanting to reassure him that I wasn't upset. What Kenley thought he ''knew'' was, of course, a lie, but how could I tell him the truth without betraying Jason?

''Oh, Kenley,'' I sighed, not knowing what to say. ''I don't want there to be any secrets between us. They have a way of tearing people apart, and I've seen more than my share of that, a whole lot more.''

He nodded thoughtfully.

''I've kept things a secret, too,'' he admitted. ''But I don't want to anymore, Quinn. I think the more we know about each other, the better it's going to be.''

Max curled up at his feet, as if he were just as anxious to hear Kenley's story as I was. I settled back, trying to make myself more comfortable.

''Are they still alive, your mother and father?''

''They died two years ago. It was just a day or two after Christmas, because I remember coming back to the house and sitting in front of the tree, staring at the lights Grandfather had hung and thinking how different my life was going to be, how nothing was ever going to be the same. And it hasn't been. Everything changed, Quinn. But you know what I learned? You can't go back. Oh, I tried, but it just didn't work. No matter what I did, no matter how hard I prayed, I couldn't bring them back. I couldn't even see them again to say good-bye.''

I didn't know what to tell him. The grief I heard in his voice was grief I too had felt. I held his hand tightly in mine, and the two of us sat there and looked out across the water, not saying a word. But at last I found the courage to ask him what had happened.

"Ashby and Gabrielle," he whispered, reciting their names as if they were characters in a fairy tale.

Perhaps they were. Perhaps they had led charmed and golden lives, as perfect a couple as Bennett and Rebecca had once been. From his mother he had inherited his dark curly hair, from his father the sharp and incisive look in his eyes.

"Maybe it sounds corny, but we were such a happy family, Quinn. We had so many good times together. We used to come here every summer and every Christmas. But that last visit we made—"

Kenley's voice broke and he looked away, not wanting me to see the tears that had gathered in the corners of his eyes.

"You don't have to tell me anymore, Kenley. If it's too painful, we can talk about something else."

But now that he'd started, he had every intention of finishing.

"They had a terrible fight, that's what I'll never forget. Just like I was an only child, my dad was, too. He'd always been very close to his parents, and when I heard him arguing with Grandpa that day, I could hardly believe it. They'd never spoken to each other like that before, and at first I thought they were kidding. You know, making it all up, like in a play. But they were serious, and the things they said to each other . . ."

He paused just long enough to dry his eyes with the back of his hand. I nodded encouragingly, sensing how important it was that he get this off his chest.

"I didn't understand half of it, I guess. But there was no

mistaking the hate in their voices, this incredible out-pouring of bitterness and anger. I don't even know what brought it on. Even to this day I don't know. But the next thing I knew, he and Mother set off in the launch. They had some business to attend to, they said, and they'd be back in a few days to pick me up. I never saw them again. Something happened with the launch. No one knows exactly what caused it, but the boat capsized and their bodies were never recovered.''

"Oh, Kenley, I'm so sorry," I whispered.

I wanted to hold him in my arms, comfort him. But instead he held me.

"There was an inquiry, but nothing ever came of it," he went on. "The sheriff of Otter Bay even came out here to talk to Grandfather, though I don't know what they discussed. I think he suspected there was more to the accident than any of us realized, and of course ever since then I've wondered about the same thing myself."

"Surely you don't think your grandfather—"

I couldn't even bring myself to say it. Nathaniel Ettinger was such a gentle, giving man I couldn't believe he was responsible for something as horrible as Kenley had described.

"I don't know, Quinn. Except that ever since then, Grandpa's never talked about what happened that day. It's as if he never had a son, as if he's blotted the whole thing out of his mind."

"And your grandmother?" I asked.

"The only time she ever talks about my father is when Grandpa isn't around. But if she has any doubts about what really happened, she's never let on. As far as she's concerned, it was a tragic accident. Maybe it was, but somehow I've never been totally convinced."

As I mulled over what he had told me, the lie between us was like a palpable presence in my mind. I knew I should tell him my father hadn't molested me the way Jason had claimed, but I was afraid of what might happen to my brother if Kenley or his grandparents discovered our terrible secret.

Just as I turned despairing eyes on Kenley, yearning to open my heart to him completely, yet knowing I couldn't without cruelly betraying Jason, Kenley cleared his throat and announced there was something that had been bothering him, something he'd been reluctant to discuss until now.

It seemed that in the last few weeks he had twice overheard his grandmother talking to someone on the telephone, and each time the subject of the conversation had been me and my brother.

"I heard her on the phone once myself," I told him.

I went on to explain about Sheriff Orickson, and the call he had made, inquiring about our whereabouts.

"Perdita didn't tell him anything then, so why should she now?" I asked.

"But what if she wasn't speaking to the sheriff? What if he'd given the telephone number to your father, and what if he's the one who's been calling, trying to find out where you are? If he ever decided to show up here—"

Kenley left the rest unsaid, but I knew what he thought of my father, and I was more anxious than ever to tell him the truth. Bennett may have been guilty of a great many things, but child abuse wasn't one of them.

I decided to tell him that, finally convinced that he had to know exactly why Jason and Becky and I had come here, when suddenly a few pebbles landed at our feet. I glanced up, only to feel Kenley grab me in his arms and pull me back against the face of the cliff. From high above us came the clatter of stones, striking sharply against each other.

"Max!" he shouted.

Frightened by the noise, Max raced off toward the beach. A moment later, a boulder the size of a basketball landed not three feet away from us, shattering in dozens of pieces as it hit the ground. I tried to look up to see what was causing the rockslide, but luckily there was a narrow ledge above our heads. Even though I heard rocks falling against it, it shielded us from the boulders which continued to tumble down the side of the cliff.

For several minutes we held our breath, not daring to venture out from our makeshift shelter. If the ledge gave way I knew we'd be crushed beneath the rocks. I was so frightened I was even afraid to blink, lest the slightest movement of my body set off another slide. Max whined pitifully as he stood near the water's edge, though he was smart enough to realize he mustn't come any closer.

When the slide seemed to have abated, Kenley warned me to stay where I was and made a mad dash for the beach. I started to call him back, but it was too late to stop him. The waves lapped at his ankles as he peered up at the cliff. A moment later he was clambering over the rocks, urging me to stay behind until he reached the top. Max followed after him, barking a warning to anyone who might still be within earshot.

Cautiously I stepped out from beneath the ledge and watched Kenley make his way up the limestone escarpment. On this side of Ettinger Rock the cliffs were nearly continuous, great stretches of them painted white with the thick droppings of sea birds who used their rocky face both for nesting and roosting.

By the time Kenley reached the top I was already half-way there. As he helped me up the last few feet I could see the troubled look in his eyes, an expression of concern that was to remain etched on his features for hours afterward.

"It was an accident, wasn't it?" I asked, desperate to believe the rockslide hadn't been caused by anything but nature.

Kenley searched the gravel-strewn ground for footprints, but found no clues of any kind. Standing at the top of the cliff, he looked down at the fresh debris littering the beach, saying that if we'd waited a moment longer we would never have managed to escape.

"But these things have happened before, haven't they? I'm sure there are rockslides all the time. The rain, the wind . . . stones are loosened, they start to fall . . ."

Behind us a few gnarled scrub oak held fast to the rocky ground, while farther still a forest of mixed oak and pine formed a crest along the spine of the island, thinning out not far from the house. It was through these silent woods that we made our way back, Kenley far more disturbed about what happened than I was.

I kept telling him it was just a coincidence. After all, he hadn't seen anyone running away from the cliff, nor had he found any clues of a suspicious nature. But Kenley wasn't convinced the rockslide was accidental, and the more he mulled over what had taken place, the more troubled he became.

The oaks had long since shed the last of their leaves, and these and the pine needles formed a thick, spongy carpet beneath our feet. Several yards up ahead a bright spot of color caught my attention, and as we drew near Kenley recognized what it was even before I did.

Snagged on a low-hanging branch, the red woolen tassel

fluttered back and forth in the breeze, looking for all the world like a discarded Christmas tree decoration. Kenley pulled it free and turned it over in his hand, examining it closely.

"It looks awfully familiar, doesn't it?" I remarked.

I was sure I'd seen a tassel like this before, though I couldn't recall where. Kenley stuffed it in his pocket, then reached for my hand and continued in the direction of the house.

"It's part of a muffler my grandmother knit. She was always complaining Grandpa never dressed warmly enough, so last year she made him this muffler with tassels at each end. She said red was a very rakish color. He's worn it ever since."

I fully expected Kenley to discuss the situation with his grandmother, but he never did. Before we reached the house he swore me to secrecy, using the word "coincidence" as glibly as I had a short while before. Nathaniel took walks through the woods nearly every day, charting the changing seasons with a sketchbook and stub of charcoal. I had seen many of those sketches myself, piled high in the studio. For all we knew he could have caught his muffler on the branch days or even weeks before.

Although I made a point of reminding Kenley of that, and he was quick to agree, I sensed that he wasn't altogether convinced. And after what he had told me about the accident which claimed his parents' lives, I must confess that for a while I had my doubts, as well.

Could Mr. Ettinger have been responsible for what had happened to us? It seemed so improbable, especially since he had no reason to harm us. I may not have been the most astute judge of character and human nature, but the more I thought about it, and the more time I spent in Nathaniel's company, the more unlikely Kenley's suspicions became. I just couldn't picture his grandfather sending those boulders over the side of the cliff.

If only Kenley had overheard the argument between his father and grandfather, he might have been able to allay his uncertainties. I saw them come to the surface on more than one occasion in the weeks that followed. There was a coolness to his dealings with his grandfather I hadn't noticed before, a wariness which I'm sure Nathaniel was able to recognize for what it was.

"Do you think Kenley is angry with me?" he asked, putting the question to me one afternoon while we worked on some furniture that would eventually be installed in the topmost floor of the dollhouse, the attic floor whose locked door had already aroused my brother's suspicions.

I tried not to let my tone of voice give me away.

"Why should he be angry?" I replied.

"If I knew the answer I would never have asked," he said with an unhappy laugh.

The impenetrable sadness I had first observed in his eyes when he visited me at the hospital was still in evidence. These days it was even more noticeable than before, and I was sure much of it had to do with the deteriorating relationship he had with his grandson.

I wished the two of them would just sit down and hash things out, for Kenley to discuss his fears and doubts without worrying that his grandfather would think the less of him for it. But though I repeatedly suggested he do just that, Kenley insisted nothing was wrong, and that he loved his grandfather as much—or as little, as I was now beginning to suspect—as he always had.

As Christmas drew near our attention turned to decorations, and here both Kenley and my brother lent their assistance. Handmade pine wreaths adorned the front door and mantelpiece, decorated with cones, nuts, moss, and big floppy velvet bows. Perdita arranged a trip to the mainland, our first since arriving on the island. Otter Bay had the look of a Currier and Ives print, and when we drove into Corvallis, the nearest town of any size, the twinkling lights and merry Santas made me miss more deeply than ever the happy and normal childhood Father had denied us.

But it was Becky's first Christmas, and both Jason and I were determined to make it as memorable as we could. She was growing by leaps and bounds, and at Perdita's suggestion we took her in for a thorough checkup, the doctor who examined her stating she was about as healthy a baby as he'd ever seen.

Each of us had been given spending money. Though cautioned to keep our presents as simple as possible, for it wasn't the gift but the thought that counted, I spent hours in the shopping mall, searching for things that would fully reflect my gratitude to my new family.

Yet for all the gaiety of the season, the festive decorations, the trimming of the tree Nathaniel transported back from the mainland—he was loath to cut down any of the native island pines—I knew in my heart that something was missing. There was a forced and artificial quality to the merriment on Ettinger Rock, as if we were all actors on a stage, playing out our roles only because it was expected of us.

Jason admitted to feeling much the same things I did. He hadn't given up on his theory that there was someone in the house, someone whose presence was purposely being kept a secret from us, perhaps even from Kenley as well. It was this person—or persons, for all we knew—

whom he claimed was responsible for the grisly tableaux each of us had discovered in the dollhouse.

Although I wanted to tell him about the rockslide, I'd promised Kenley I would keep it a secret, and so I refrained from mentioning it to my brother. Besides, he was so calm and even-tempered these days I didn't want to say anything that might cause Jason to look upon our protectors as potential adversaries.

But whatever chance there might have been for us to feel truly "at home" on Ettinger Rock was irrevocably shattered by Mr. Houghton's unexpected announcement on Christmas eve. That night, after a long and leisurely dinner, our tutor got up from the table not to propose a toast, but to tell us that he would be leaving the following morning.

Kenley had mentioned that he usually went on vacation for two weeks after Christmas, and during that time we would be given a reprieve from our lessons. But that wasn't what Mr. Houghton wished to discuss. I think I sensed what was coming even before he told us, for there was no mistaking the troubled and unhappy look that came into his eyes.

"I'm afraid my timing could've been better," he admitted. "It's been a very difficult decision for me, and one I don't take very lightly. But I'm going to have to resign my position here."

At first the words didn't even make sense. It seemed inconceivable that he would leave, especially when all of us knew how much enjoyed his work. There was a moment of stunned silence, and Mr. Houghton shifted his weight uncomfortably from one foot to the other. Nathaniel coughed nervously, and Perdita's hand tightened around the stem of her wineglass, clutching it until it threatened to snap in two.

"A fine time to make a joke," Kenley remarked.

But by then it was obvious Mr. Houghton had spoken in earnest. Our tutor sighed loudly, then tugged at his beard as if it were a disguise he were about to discard.

"But why?" Jason asked, so keenly disappointed there was a desperate quality to his voice.

"Yes, why?" I repeated.

"It's not true, Grandma, is it?" Kenley asked.

Perdita lowered her eyes. She was terribly embarrassed, and I wondered if she was in some way responsible for Mr. Houghton's decision.

He rang his knife against the side of his glass, trying to get our attention.

"Believe me, if I could stay here I would. In fact, I can't think of anything I'd rather do more. But . . . well, for personal reasons I have to leave."

"What reasons?" Kenley demanded.

His grandfather looked at him sharply, but Kenley ignored the warning he saw in Nathaniel's eyes.

"That's an unfair question, Kenley," replied Mr. Houghton. "It really has nothing to do with anyone at this table."

"Actually, Mr. Houghton has gotten an offer he can't afford to refuse," Nathaniel spoke up.

"But you can match it, Grandpa, can't you?"

"I'm sorry, Kenley, but it's a little more complicated than just a question of salary. After all, Mr. Houghton has been with us for over two years now, ever since . . ." He paused to clear his throat. "Ever since you came to stay with us. He feels it's time to move on, and I for one have to agree. But he's been kind enough to recommend a replacement, and I think all of us are going to find

Mr. Davies as likable and conscientious a man as his predecessor."

Actors on a stage, I thought again, reciting their lines to fit the occasion. Mr. Ettinger's little speech sounded so well-thought-out as to be rehearsed. There was more to our tutor's departure than anyone was letting on. But why Mr. Houghton would choose to leave now, as opposed to waiting until summer, was something I couldn't figure out.

Kenley, whom I had never known to sulk or act belligerent, pushed his chair back and sprang angrily to his feet. He looked accusingly at his grandfather, and when he found his voice his words grated harshly against each other.

"I bet you asked him to leave, didn't you, Grandpa?"

"Kenley, how can you suggest such a thing?" Perdita said in a shocked and disappointed tone of voice.

"Because it's true, that's why." Kenley's eyes narrowed, and he glared at his grandfather with unconcealed hostility. "I don't know why you fired him, but it's terribly unfair."

"Kenley, I assure you, your grandfather had nothing to do with my decision," Mr. Houghton insisted.

"Why would you even think that?" Nathaniel asked his grandson.

"Because Mr. Houghton was very happy here, that's why. Because he never said anything about leaving. Just last week in fact he talked about the courses we'd all be taking in the spring. And then suddenly he decides to quit."

"Just hear me out for a moment, will you?" Mr. Houghton asked. "I'll say it again. No one forced me to leave. But you know as well as I do that I can't stay here forever. I've been offered an appointment at a private boys' school. It pays extremely well, but it's not just the money I'm interested in. I'm thirty years old, and it's time I settled down, had a family, met the girl of my dreams.'' Mr. Houghton pretended to laugh, but neither Kenley, Jason, nor I found any reason to join in. ''Max misses having a lady friend, and to be quite honest about it, so do I.''

There was no denying that Mr. Houghton had said this with the utmost sincerity. Kenley muttered an apology to his grandfather and returned to the table.

Into the unhappy silence that enveloped us all, Perdita suggested with false brightness, ''Well, now that that's been taken care of, what say we bring out the dessert?'' She directed a strained smile at each of us in turn.

It was a classic English Christmas pudding, a family tradition Mr. Ettinger explained, trying valiantly to restore some holiday cheer to the gathering. Miss Granberry set it down on the table and poured a snifter of warm brandy over the top. She handed Nathaniel a match, and when he ignited the brandy blue flames danced and shimmered across the surface of the pudding.

We all applauded, though with far less enthusiasm than the Ettingers. It was Christmas Eve, one of the happiest nights of the year. But when I looked at Kenley and my brother, and even Mr. Houghton who would be leaving for good in the morning, happiness was the farthest thing from our minds.

''Come now, it's not the end of the world,'' Nathaniel chided us gently. ''After all, Mr. Davies comes highly recommended.''

''He's really an excellent teacher,'' murmured Mr. Houghton.

"There, you've heard it from an expert," Nathaniel said with a forced and hollow sounding laugh. "I know you're all going to become fast friends in no time at all."

I wish I could have believed that. But despite everything that had been said I still had my doubts. And judging from their glum and dispirited expressions, it was all too obvious that Kenley and Jason felt just as uncertain about the future as I did.

CHAPTER TWELVE

I was real hurt, and for the first time in I don't know how long I felt like crying. Houghton was my friend, and friends didn't desert you at the last minute. Even if he had to leave, why couldn't he at least wait until summer? Then we'd all have a couple of months to get used to the fact he wasn't coming back. But no, here it is Christmas Eve and he gets up and drops a bombshell.

Okay, the guy had a point. I guess when you turn thirty you sort of look back at all the years you've already lived and wonder what you're going to do for the thirty still to come. Houghton wanted a family, and though I could've given him an earful on the subject, I kept quiet since everyone has to learn from his own mistakes. Besides, it wasn't having kids that was so important. Let's face it, he was horny, stuck away on Ettinger Rock when most guys his age were out having fun, if you know what I mean.

But he still could've waited. What difference would a few more months have made to him, when to me it seemed like an eternity? At first I was so hurt, so surprised by his announcement, that all I felt was anger, seeping out of my skin like sweat. But after the anger died down I felt betrayed, cheated almost. I trusted him, don't you see? I liked him so much, respected his every word it seemed, that I just couldn't believe he'd do this to us.

So even though I knew it was probably going to be a lost cause, I went up to his room that night to try to get him to change his mind. He was busy packing, his suitcases laid out on the bed. There was a bottle of wine on his desk, and I was kind of hoping he'd offer me some, but he didn't. But that was the least of it.

"Why'd you have to go and do it, Mr. Houghton?"

That's just how I put it. No beating around the bush, none of that tactful stuff grownups are always harping about. Just the plain and simple, because I figured if I couldn't be honest with him, I couldn't be honest with anyone, Quinn included.

He had a pile of shirts in his hand, and he put them down and sat on the edge of the bed, looking at his hands like he didn't know what to do with them.

"I'm sorry, Jason. I know how disappointed you must feel."

Disappointed? I was ready to get down on my knees and beg him to stay. Houghton cared about me—at least that's what he'd led me to believe—and how can you let someone who cares just walk out of your life without putting up a fight? You can't, that's the whole point.

"Couldn't you wait a couple of months? Mr. Ettinger'll give you long weekends so you can go and . . . you know, meet people and go out on dates and stuff. If they're so hot to have you at this other school, they'd wait a few months, I'm sure they would."

"The position might be filled by then," he said, talking into his beard like he was ashamed to speak up.

"And it might not," I countered.

179

He looked right at me then, but I didn't flinch or lower my eyes or anything like that. Instead I stared back at him, wondering how someone whom you trusted could go and do the very opposite of what you expected.

"I'm sorry," he said again, like a broken record.

"What if I told you our lives might be in danger here, what would you do then? Just turn your back on us?"

My question caught him by surprise, all right. He looked at me in confusion, like he didn't believe I was serious.

"What possible danger could there be here? Besides boredom, that is," he said lamely, giving a half-hearted laugh.

"No, I'm talking about the real thing, Mr. Houghton."

He was still confused, and eyed me questioningly.

"I'm not following."

By the time I finished telling him about what I found in the dollhouse, the voice that lured me downstairs, and all the rest of it, I knew I'd gotten through to him.

"But why didn't you tell me this before?" he asked.

I shrugged.

"Guess I figured you'd think I was going crazy or something. But there's someone in this house, Mr. Houghton, and Nathaniel and his wife are keeping the whole thing a secret. I know it sounds kind of hard to believe, but I can't imagine anyone else being responsible. I mean, it was pretty sick, that doll just hanging there, and that other business, the things that were painted on."

I was a little embarrassed, I gotta admit, but at least Houghton didn't look at me like I was crazy.

"I think we should go downstairs and tell the Ettingers about this," he announced.

"No, you can't do that!" I said, raising my voice. "You just can't!"

"But why? If you don't think they're responsible, and I'm sure they're not, then what harm could it do?"

"The harm it could do is that if someone's hidden away in this castle of theirs, and they find out I suspect, they're going to make us leave, I know they will. And we don't have any other place to go, Mr. Houghton. You know that. So you *can't* tell them. Please, if you're leaving tomorrow anyway, please, don't say anything about it."

Now I was really in a bind. I should never have opened my mouth, but I figured if Houghton thought we were in trouble it might make him change his mind. But I knew then that I hadn't accomplished anything—except for running the risk of having all my fears and suspicions revealed to the Ettingers—which was the *last* thing I wanted. Houghton was leaving in the morning, and he didn't have to continue packing to prove it.

I got up and went to the door, knowing there wasn't much more I could say. He sat there watching me, stroking his beard, his eyes kind of sad and woebegone and filled with all sorts of questions.

"You won't tell them, will you?" I asked again.

"I don't want anything to happen to you."

"Nothing's going to happen, Mr. Houghton. They were just playing with dolls, that's all."

What I didn't say was that dolls were just the beginning. But then he would've gone downstairs and spoken to the Ettingers for sure.

"All right, Jason, I won't say anything. But you've got to make me a promise. When Mr. Davies gets here, will you speak to him about it?"

I frowned and looked away. I didn't even know who

Davies was. What reason was there for me to confide in him or trust him?

"Jason, I'm very serious. If you won't promise to talk to Mr. Davies about this, then I'm going to have to tell the Ettingers. So the choice is yours."

"That's blackmail," I protested.

Mr. Houghton pretended to smile.

"It's just twisting your arm a little, that's all. Besides, Quinn knows, doesn't she? You've talked to her about it, haven't you?"

"Of course she knows. She found some stuff herself."

I didn't want to tell him about the knife the Jason doll was holding in its hand, and how it was leaning over her bed. But he didn't ask for details.

"Then I want you and your sister to discuss this whole thing with Mr. Davies."

"So you're really going then, aren't you?"

Slowly he nodded his head, like it was suddenly an effort to admit what I'd known all along.

"Well . . . we're really going to miss you. You're a real good guy, Mr. Houghton. You've done a lot for me too, and I won't forget it."

I wanted to go over and shake his hand, but I could feel the tears creeping up on me and I didn't want him to see me cry. So I just slipped out the door. He'd made up his mind, anyway. There wasn't anything left to say.

Two things happened right after the New Year. Max disappeared and Franklin Davies showed up on the island to take Mr. Houghton's place. First things first.

We were having breakfast—I'd made my morning check of the dollhouse, but everything looked the way it was supposed to—when Kenley came downstairs, calling to Max and getting no response.

"Have you seen him?" he asked when he came into the dining room.

"Come sit down before your breakfast gets cold," Miss Granberry told him.

She handed him a glass of juice, but Kenley put it down without even looking at it.

"Max?" he called again, glancing in every direction at once.

"Hey, Max. Come on, boy," I called out, and Quinn did the same.

All of us expected to see the Airedale come bounding in, ready for his morning dog biscuit, maybe a strip of bacon too. But if he was within earshot, he was being awfully stubborn.

"Maybe he's outside," Quinn suggested.

"I already looked."

Kenley reluctantly pulled out a chair and took his place at the table. Miss Granberry brought him his bacon and eggs, but after pushing them back and forth across his plate he put down his fork.

"I just don't understand it. It's not like him. He's never run off before."

"Wasn't he in your room this morning?" I asked.

Kenley shook his head.

"The door was ajar when I got up. He must've slipped out."

"Then he's probably still in the house," I replied.

Again he shook his head.

"I looked everywhere, but he's not here."

"He couldn't have opened the front door by himself,"

Quinn said with a laugh, one she immediately regretted when she realized how upset Kenley was getting.

"He uses that special pet door in the kitchen," he reminded us.

"Then you know what?" I said. "Let's organize a search party."

I figured that was the least we could do. Like I've said, he and Max were just about inseparable. The dog couldn't have gone very far, and since Ettinger Rock was an island, sooner or later we were bound to find him. So after we all wolfed down our breakfast, we bundled up and went out looking for him.

Three hours later my legs were about to give out, but there was still no sign of the Airedale.

"Maybe he hurt himself," Kenley said. He sounded so miserable I was surprised he didn't start to cry. "Maybe he fell off the cliff or something, and he's just lying there."

Quinn tried to comfort him, and I had to look away. It bothered me the way she kept babying him. They were getting awfully stuck on each other, if you ask me. I knew I had no right to tell my sister what to do, but I couldn't help feeling a twinge of jealousy.

Anyway, we all trooped down to the beach and walked clear around the island. If Max was nearby he was sure lying low. But someone else wasn't, and when we came upon a pup tent hidden away at the far end of the island, I thought for sure we'd found the answer to all the creepy things that had been happening to us.

The tent was pitched well beyond the high-water mark, and Kenley didn't waste any time checking it out. He threw the flaps open as if he fully expected to find Max hiding inside. What he found instead was a sleeping bag and mess kit, while outside the tent there was evidence that someone had made a fire as recently as a few hours before. The coals were still warm, yet the campsite had a strangely abandoned look about it, as if whoever had come here had suddenly left without even bothering to pack his gear.

"Who do you think all this belongs to?" Quinn asked.

I wanted to say, "Dad," but with Kenley around I figured it wasn't the time.

"Whoever it is, they're trespassing," Kenley replied.

"Has that ever happened before?"

"Not that I know of," he told me. "But if they've done anything to Max—"

He left the rest unsaid, though after what I'd seen in the dollhouse it didn't take much imagination to figure out what he meant.

"I can stick around, if you want. See if they come back," I suggested.

"Might be a good idea," Quinn seconded.

But Kenley was more concerned about Max than anything else, and I don't even think he heard me. Quinn and I exchanged uneasy glances. I knew what was on her mind, but Max's disappearance seemed the more immediate of our problems. So promising myself to return to the campsite just as soon as the opportunity presented itself, we followed Kenley down the beach, calling out to Max and getting no response.

By the time we got back to the house he was really beside himself. Although his grandfather tried to calm him down, reminding him that Max always had a mind of his own, and was probably out in the woods somewhere burying a bone, I knew Kenley didn't believe him.

"You never liked him anyway, so why pretend?" Kenley said accusingly.

Mr. Ettinger was really taken aback by his tone of voice. I think he was a little embarrassed too, seeing as how Quinn and I were just standing there, not knowing what to say.

"I want to speak to you in the study, Kenley."

I could tell he was mad, but it didn't seem to bother Kenley in the least.

"What for?" he said defiantly, like he was going out of his way to bait his grandfather.

"Because it's time the two of us sat down and had a good long talk, that's why."

I'd never seen the old man so angry. Even when Max snapped at him he hadn't gotten this red in the face. He was shaking something fierce, trying to hold in his temper and not having much luck. I was afraid if he didn't start to calm down he'd have a heart attack. So I told Kenley not to worry, we'd keep looking.

I don't know what they talked about, but when Kenley caught up to us maybe a half-hour later his eyes were red like he'd been crying. I was real curious to know what had gone on, but though I was itching to ask I knew it was none of my business.

It was already dark when we finally called it quits. There wasn't a spot on the island we hadn't covered, but we didn't have any luck at all. Max was gone all right, and the more I thought about it, the more I wondered if our mysterious trespasser was in some way responsible.

The next morning I thought for sure Max would finally show up. But he didn't, and when I checked the campsite out it was still deserted. When Mr. Davies arrived a few days later, Max was still missing. By then, I knew we'd never see him again.

Franklin Davies was just about as different from Mr. Houghton as day from night. He was trim and dapper looking, the kind of guy who combs his hair before he goes to bed at night. A real Ivy Leaguer too, never without his button-down shirt and rep tie, chinos and penny loafers and the whole bit. He even had this little device he used to hold chalk when he wrote on the blackboard, he was so afraid of getting his hands dirty. He was also a lousy teacher, just the worst, turned everything into such a big deal it was ridiculous. And the way he treated us, that's another thing. You'd think we were ten years old the way he carried on. He didn't know a hell of a lot either, not half as smart as Houghton, and certainly not half as nice.

"I think he's a real jerk," I told Quinn, less than a week after he arrived to take over for Mr. Houghton.

"You haven't given him much of a chance, Jason."

She was real big on that "benefit of the doubt" stuff, but I wasn't buying it.

"To do what?" I asked. "Prove he's even more of an asshole than I think he is? Next thing you know he'll want us to start practicing our penmanship."

And it wasn't just the way he taught, but his whole attitude toward us, that bothered me. You'd think he'd go out of his way to be nice, at least in the beginning. But no, he acted like he was doing us this big favor coming to the island to teach us. And as if that weren't enough—and it was, I assure you—Davies was much too nosy for his own good.

He wasn't there but a couple of days when I caught him

talking to Perdita. She was in the sun room fooling around with all those plants she kept there, when he came in and sat down like he owned the place. Quinn's always warned me about eavesdropping, but as soon as I heard him mention my name I didn't give a damn about acting like a sneak. He had no business talking about me behind my back, so I didn't feel the least bit guilty about trying to hear what was going on.

"No, I don't think Mr. Houghton knew all the particulars," Perdita was saying.

The French doors that led into the sun room were wide-open. I stood where they couldn't see me, pressing my back to the wall and listening intently. If anyone came out onto the enclosed porch where I was standing, I'd have to do some pretty fast talking. But I wasn't going to let that worry me until the time came.

"I'll be monitoring them very carefully," Davies told her.

Monitoring? What the hell did he mean by that?

"I don't want their studies to suffer, you understand," she replied.

"Oh no, not at all. I intend to follow the syllabus Houghton laid out for me. You know it hasn't been tried before, so we're really going to have to take things one day at a time."

"Experimental teaching methods is one area I know next to nothing about."

Perdita laughed when she said this, yet I knew it wasn't because she thought she'd made a joke. Experimental teaching methods? What was going on here, anyway? This was a house, not a laboratory.

"But I just wanted to take this opportunity to assure you I have their best interests at heart," Davies went on.

Oh give me a break, I thought. He sounded like a total phony. I bet this was his first job, and he didn't have the vaguest idea what it was to be a good teacher.

"They were all very disturbed when he left," Mrs. Ettinger remarked.

"Yes, every time I'm with him I feel I have to prove myself."

Him? Was he talking about me or Kenley? As far as I knew, Kenley didn't think much of Davies, either.

"Naturally, my husband and I are concerned."

"I realize that."

"But now that you've assured me you have everything under control, I do feel a little better about it. You will keep me appraised of things, won't you?"

"Oh, absolutely, Mrs. Ettinger."

When they started to talk about the various kinds of palms and tropical plants that flourished in the sun room I took the opportunity to slip away.

For days afterward that conversation kept reverberating in my thoughts, like a tune you hear that you can't get out of your mind. It seemed to me they were talking about his new duties, but there was something more to it than that. Concerned . . . under control . . . experimental teaching methods . . . monitoring . . . all those words could be interpreted in more than one way. I knew I'd better find out the way they were intended, because if Franklin Davies had any tricks up his sleeve, I wanted to be the first one to know about them.

"He makes me very nervous, Quinn. I don't know what it is exactly, but I just don't trust him."

"He's only a tutor, Jason, not the F.B.I. He's probably just as nervous as you are, that's all it is."

But I wasn't nearly as convinced as she was. We were

189

walking through the woods together, Quinn wheeling Becky in her carriage. It was the first chance we'd had to be alone with each other in a long time. I kept watching her out of the corner of my eye, not wanting her to think I was staring.

The pug-nosed, freckle-faced little girl had done a lot of growing up in the last few months. She was no longer a child, and to see her with the baby you would have thought she was just a very young mother, she acted so poised, so confident of her own abilities. She was also much more beautiful than I'd ever given her credit for, with honey-colored hair that shimmered when it caught the light.

"You're blushing," I said when she noticed how intently I was looking at her.

"You were staring, that's why."

She touched her hair self-consciously, the gesture so unlike her it made me smile.

"You really like Ettinger Rock, don't you? I can tell. It shows on your face, Quinn. You've never seemed happier. I think you'd be content to spend the rest of your life here . . . provided of course Kenley stuck around to keep you company."

If she heard the note of jealousy in my voice, she never let on.

"We have a lot to be grateful for, Jason. Becky's healthy. We're surrounded by people who care about us, strangers who have gone out of their way to make us feel welcome. And I've noticed a change in you, too—a change for the better."

She made it sound like everything was hunky-dory. But it wasn't. There was a nut loose on the Rock, a nut who was practicing on dolls. And when he got his technique refined he'd turn his attention to the real thing, and then all of us were going to be in serious trouble. But when I reminded Quinn of that she didn't seem particularly concerned.

"And what about Max?" I said, in case she'd forgotten. "Don't you think it's strange the way he disappeared without a trace? And Mr. Houghton, the way he suddenly left like that. Doesn't that strike you as suspicious?"

"I think you're looking for conspiracies that aren't there, Jason."

"Then what about that campsite we found?"

She eyed me curiously.

"You've gone back there, haven't you?" she asked.

I nodded.

"More than once. But it's always deserted."

"Kenley thinks it must be some kid from the mainland. Comes over with his girlfriend, that kind of thing."

"Kenley can think whatever he likes, but that still doesn't explain the knife in the doll's hand."

Rather than answer, Quinn bent over the carriage, making sure the blankets were secure so Becky wouldn't catch a draft. She was sound asleep, her fat little cheeks so rosy they looked like they were rouged. She was my daughter, my flesh and blood. But of late I didn't feel like a father—or even a brother, for that matter.

Something very disturbing was happening here on Ettinger Rock, something over which I had no control. I thought again of what I'd found in the dollhouse, the way the Jason doll was hanging there, the noose tied tight around its plastic neck. Someone wanted me dead, and I knew they wouldn't be satisfied until they got their way.

CHAPTER THIRTEEN

Jason's concerns mirrored my own. I hadn't forgotten how Kenley and I had barely escaped with our lives, and though I kept telling myself the rockslide was an accident, deep down inside I was terrified it might have been caused by someone on the island. When my brother and I went walking, and he made no bones about how frightened he was, I was on the verge of telling him what had happened that day. But instead I said nothing, afraid of fueling his suspicions. I knew how unnerved he was by the mysterious incidents which had occurred in recent weeks, and I didn't want to say anything that might get him emotionally upset.

He had already been through enough suffering, and were I to admit how scared I was, his fears would surely expose us to the kind of questions we had gone out of our way to avoid. After all, no one on Ettinger Rock knew the full extent of our ordeal. Rather than expose the truth to them, Jason had told Perdita and Nathaniel a story that relied heavily on shock value. Had he told them who Becky's parents were, I knew they would never have been able to understand, nor would they have consented to invite us into their home. So we kept that part of our lives a secret, just as we made no mention of what had gone on between the two of us. But even though my brother no longer made overtures of a sexual nature, I don't think it was because he'd lost interest. Had I given him the slightest encouragement, I'm quite sure he would have picked up the threads of our tortured relationship, not the least bit concerned about the consequences.

Thus, there was much I kept hidden, afraid of what might happen if I exposed the truth to the Ettingers. Yet time and time again I longed to reveal my feelings to Kenley. He too had suffered a terrible and tragic loss, and I was certain he would be able to understand what I had gone through. If we ever allowed ourselves to be completely honest with each other, I knew the initial discomfort and embarrassment would quickly give way to feelings of sympathy and compassion. But though I wanted to tell him, to lay it all out before him as if unrolling a parchment scroll, I was yet to make that ultimate commitment to the truth.

But with the arrival of Mr. Davies I found not only a sympathetic ear, but a person of great sensitivity and understanding. Despite all that my brother found fault with, and all the negative things he had to say about him, our new tutor possessed certain qualities I couldn't help but admire.

He was acutely perceptive, and seemed to know a great deal about my feelings even before I ever told him anything about myself. I knew he was curious about us, yet it was weeks before he broached the subject of our past, and even then it was with the utmost delicacy and tact. Mr. Houghton was a warm and fun-loving man, and though

Mr. Davies was much more sober-minded, I could tell that he was deeply concerned about us.

One afternoon when we were alone in the schoolroom, he finally touched on the subject both of us had avoided discussing, phrasing his question in such a way that if I chose not to answer neither of us would feel uncomfortable.

"I thought the Ettingers might have said something to you about it," I replied, more eager to confide in him than I had even realized.

"They said you were a woman with a past," he laughed, trying to make a joke of it. "I gather though that things haven't been very easy for you."

Bottled up for so long, the words began to pour out of me. I think I said more than I intended to, but I'd kept everything a secret for so long that now I just wanted to get it all out in the open where it wouldn't continue to fester inside me.

When I spoke of the hurt and betrayal I had suffered at my father's hands, making it clear that though he'd never molested me he had done things equally as destructive, Mr. Davies expressed understanding rather than shock. He also tried to see things from my father's point of view, telling me how difficult it must have been to cope with someone as ill as my mother.

"When Jason told the Ettingers you were sexually abused, do you think that was because he was abused himself?"

I hadn't thought of it that way. But even if it were true, I told Mr. Davies that my brother had gone out of his way to paint as bleak a picture as possible so that Perdita and Nathaniel wouldn't hesitate to take us in.

"And since then you've never heard from him, have you?" he asked.

It seemed such a strange question, I couldn't help but laugh.

"Of course not. If we heard from him, that would mean he knows where to find us. And if he knew that, he'd come and take us home."

"But why should he bother? You said he doesn't love you, so why should he even worry about what's become of you? A man without any love in his heart would just wash his hands of the whole ugly business."

"Maybe he has."

"And maybe he hasn't. Which is something to think about, Quinn, if nothing else."

I recalled what Kenley had told me, the phone conversations he'd overheard. Was it possible Father had gotten in touch with the Ettingers, convincing them he wasn't the monster they thought him to be? But if that were the case, then why hadn't he come to get us?

"What do you think would happen if he and Jason saw each other again?" Mr. Davies asked.

"My brother would try to run away."

"Why? Do you think your father means to punish him?"

I had told Mr. Davies a great deal. But I hadn't said anything about the tragedy that occurred the night Mother invited Jason into her room for what was destined to be the very last time. I didn't intend to bring it up either, for I knew it would be betraying my brother's confidence, something I could never allow myself to do.

"It's all very complicated, Mr. Davies. I'd rather not go into it, if you don't mind."

"Of course, I understand, Quinn. Please, I don't mean to pry. But I do have some advice, if you're willing to hear me out. Maybe now's the time to open a dialogue," he suggested.

I looked at him curiously, not quite sure what he meant.

"It's just what it sounds like," he explained. "Talk to him. Give him a call, or write him a letter if you prefer."

I made a face, but Mr. Davies said that the sooner I started to deal with what had happened, the better off I'd be.

"Tell him what you're really feeling, Quinn, the terrible hurt he caused you. Just getting it off your chest is bound to be helpful."

I knew he was trying to give me good advice, but I wasn't ready to accept it.

"It wouldn't do any good," I insisted. "Besides, if I sent a letter he'd see where it was postmarked, and then he'd be able to find us. I can't let that happen."

"If that's all you're worried about, it's really no problem. I can send the letter to a friend of mine in New York. He can mail it from there."

It all made a great deal of sense, yet I was afraid to take Mr. Davies up on his offer. Putting everything down on paper seemed a very scary proposition. My feelings were so ambiguous, so confused and complicated, that I wasn't even sure I'd be able to express myself coherently.

As much as I wanted to put that part of my life behind me, it wasn't nearly as easy as I had hoped. I was happy here, it was true. But I also knew that my brother didn't share the same opinion. Yet to make peace with himself, Jason seemed to face each day as if it were a major obstacle. On more than one occasion I'd tried to discuss it with him, hoping he'd open up to me. But by this point his concern with the "mysterious stranger" he was convinced was somewhere in the house or on the island—a person whose very presence threatened our lives—had begun to take on the qualities of an obsession, and it was almost impossible to make him attend seriously to anything else.

"Think about it, Quinn. You don't have to decide anything right this very minute, you know," Mr. Davies said with a smile.

"I just don't see what good it would do. I don't want to go back there, Mr. Davies. I don't want to see him again. The Ettingers have given us a second chance. If I open up this dialogue you mentioned, there's no telling what might happen. If Father really does love us, he'll want us to come home."

And then he'd convince everyone Jason wasn't in his right mind. And if he didn't put Becky up for adoption he'd treat her like an outcast, someone he couldn't even bear to look at, knowing who had given her life. The last thing it would be was the joyous homecoming Mr. Davies imagined. On the contrary, it would be like stepping back into the nightmare world my brother and I had tried so desperately to leave behind.

Mr. Davies got up from his desk. He came over to me and put his hand on my shoulder.

"Think about it," he said again. "After all, no one's forcing you to do anything you don't want, Quinn. I've just made some suggestions, that's all. If you choose to ignore them, that's your decision. But I want you to know I'm always here if you need to talk to someone. So don't be shy, okay?"

I tried my best to return his smile.

"Okay."

But it wasn't.

The moment I walked out of the schoolroom Jason grabbed me by the arm and pulled me down the hall. I tried to wrench free, but he wouldn't relinquish his grip.

He dragged me upstairs to his room, and only when he closed the door behind us did he finally release me.

"So you couldn't wait to open your mouth, could you?"

"What are you talking about?"

My arm was sore where he'd grabbed me, but when I told him that he laughed at me and said I was being too sensitive, hurt was a lot more complicated than a black-and-blue mark.

"Why did you start to tell him about us?" he said, glaring at me as if I'd done something awful. "Don't you realize what he's after?"

"Were you eavesdropping on us? Were you spying on me, Jason?"

But if I hoped to make him feel guilty, it didn't work.

"You're damn right I was spying," he said angrily, spitting the words out at me. "And a good thing, too. Any second I expected you to start talking about Mom, and what happened that ·night. That's all we need, people knowing our business. You think the Ettingers are so tolerant and understanding. But everyone has a breaking point, Quinn, and people can only take so much. If they ever find out the truth, they won't wait for Dad to come after us. They'll get on the phone so fast it'll make your head spin."

"I don't believe that."

"Then you don't know the first thing about human nature. How can you be so naive, Quinn? Mom took me into her bed. We made a baby, for God's sake! Do you think if they found out they'd let us stay here?"

"Of course they would. It's no worse than the lies you told them. How do you think it makes me feel, knowing they think he raped me and made you watch? Every time I look at them I know what's going through their mind. Poor, tormented Quinn, that's what.''

"And if they discover that poor, tormented Quinn's brother tried to . . . I mean, he didn't, but . . .''

Unable to get the words out, he gulped loudly and looked away. He was trembling, and I wondered if he meant to remind me of what he had done to Mother, the night they took her away. The knife. The blood that spurted over the walls as he drew the blade across her wrists. But Mother was dead, and the agony she had put Jason through had to finally be laid to rest.

"The bastards, the things they do to us,'' my brother groaned. He sank down on the bed, burying his face in his hands. "Why can't they leave us alone, Quinn? Why must they keep torturing us? We're not hurting them, so why are they trying to scare us like this? All they have to do is ask us to leave, but they won't even do that. They'd rather we suffered instead.''

I sat down next to him and put my arm around his shoulders. He was sobbing, gasping for breath, and I begged him to try to calm down.

"Don't do this to yourself, Jason. Please, don't make yourself so unhappy. They don't want to hurt us. You mustn't even think that. If they didn't care about us they would never have asked us to stay with them. If we were their own grandchildren they couldn't treat us any better than they do!''

He raised his eyes. They were haunted, and in their green, shimmering depths I saw a reflection of my own fears, and shuddered to think they might all come true.

"I bet they're reporting back to him,'' he muttered. "Sure they are. Bennett knows where we are, Quinn, I'm positive. And he's just watching and waiting until the time is right. Then he's going to take me away, lock me up where no one'll ever find me again. One day they'll discover Becky dead in her crib and he'll be responsible. He's here, in this house or maybe even at that campsite. But I'm going to expose him. I'll trap him, Quinn, that's what I'll do. I'll wait downstairs in the studio. I'll wait every night if need be. Because sooner or later he'll sneak in and go right to the dollhouse. He'll take the Jason doll by the neck and strangle it, just like he'd like to do to me."

The words tumbled breathlessly from his lips, one after the other until he was speaking so quickly, so feverishly, I could barely understand him.

"Don't even think that, Jason," I pleaded. "Don't even imagine it. It's not true. You're distraught and you don't know what you're saying. But it's not true. No one wants to kill you. No one wants to hurt Becky. No one wants to harm any of us."

Jason came shakily to his feet. His eyes gleamed dully, his face pinched and prematurely aged.

"And you believe that, don't you?"

"Yes, I do. I believe it as much as I believe in you."

"Then maybe you're right," he said wearily. "Maybe it's all in my imagination."

But there was no conviction in his voice. He took a deep breath, then dried his eyes with the back of his hand.

"That's right, just my imagination," he said again. "I don't even know what came over me. You forgive me, don't you?"

If only I could help him. If only I knew where to begin.

"Jason, there's nothing to forgive. I just want you to be all right, that's all. The rest is unimportant."

"Yes, I know you care, you always have. I shouldn't let

myself get so upset. Davies was only trying to be helpful. And you know what? I think I'll talk to him, too. Isn't that a good idea? I bet he'll be able to give me some great advice.''

He pushed his lips into a smile, but I could tell what an effort it was. He was pretending, and there was nothing I could do but go along with him.

"I got it all out of my system and now I'm fine," he announced.

I left him standing there, still holding onto his grin as if it were a mask. But instead of going to my room to do my homework, I made my way upstairs to the attic. There were several rooms on the topmost floor, and I went from one to the next. Most were used for storage, though one was a sewing room. Miss Granberry had showed me how to work the old Singer sewing machine, and I'd used it on several occasions to make clothes for the dolls.

I knocked and let myself in, but it too was as empty as all the others. But when I tried to enter the room directly opposite it, the door didn't open when I turned the knob. It was locked, just as Jason had already discovered. In a house where no other doors were bolted, why then was this one?

I got down on my knees and put my eye to the keyhole, trying to see inside. But either it was too dark in the room, or something was hanging over the door, because I couldn't see anything at all. I started to get to my feet when I suddenly stopped short. Was that perfume I was smelling, or was it just my imagination? I breathed deeply. The scent was faint yet unmistakable.

From behind the locked door came the lingering fragrance of violets, Perdita Ettinger's favorite perfume.

CHAPTER FOURTEEN

Quinn thought I was making it all up, imagining it, exaggerating. My own sister, and she didn't even believe me when I tried to convince her our lives were in danger. But I was certain they were, and that's why I crept downstairs when everyone was asleep. That's why I slipped outside and made my way down the beach to the far end of the island, determined to confront the person who'd set up camp.

For hours I waited in the darkness, forcing myself to stay awake. But no one returned to slip inside the tent, or cook a solitary meal, revealing their identity in the glow of a campfire.

Maybe Kenley was right. Maybe it wasn't my father, using the campsite as an outpost to spy on us. It could've been some kid from Otter Bay, though I still couldn't figure out why he'd left all his gear behind. Unless of course he came here every weekend, bringing his girlfriend and a couple of six-packs. That might explain why I didn't see a boat, or even the tracks to indicate one had been dragged up on the beach.

I wasn't going to give up so easily though. If the

campsite failed to yield any answers, then I'd turn my attention back to the house. So once again when everyone was sound asleep in their beds I crept downstairs. Huddling in a corner of the studio, I stared at the dollhouse until every gable and battlement, every chimney and tower, was fixed in my memory, never to be forgotten.

The Castle was cold and drafty. I'd worn my robe, but my teeth still chattered as I sat there with my knees drawn up against my chest. Soon my vigil would be rewarded. First there would be footsteps on the stairs, descending from the attic. Then the cautious, wary tread would be heard outside the door. The knob would turn and the door would open, slowly and skillfully so as not to make a sound. A shadowy figure would slip inside. There would be no hesitation now, no uncertainty. Whoever it was, he or she would know exactly what they were looking for. But even then I still wouldn't reveal myself. No, I'd wait until it was over, until the dolls had suffered for the sins of their counterparts. Imagined sins, though that was no concern to whomever was responsible.

Only when they were done and their cruelty laid bare, would I make my presence known. Surprised in the act, I imagined them trying to laugh it off, then arguing heatedly, then begging me to keep it a secret.

"A joke, that's all it was. Just a harmless practical joke, Jason, I swear."

Yes, that's what they'd say, the person responsible for wishing me dead. But I wouldn't buy their arguments and I'd make everyone come downstairs. The entire household would assemble in the studio. The perpetrator of the crime would try to escape. But by then his identity would be known to all of us, so it wouldn't matter anymore.

That was my plan, and that's why I waited night after

night in the darkness, hoping to catch someone in the act. But days went by, then weeks, and nothing happened. Often I was barely able to keep my eyes open. But I was afraid that if I allowed myself to fall asleep the dollhouse would be tampered with without my knowing it. What was worse, I soon realized there was a basic flaw to my scheme, something I'd forgotten to take into account. Whoever was doing this might not have to act under cover of darkness. A few minutes alone in the studio in the middle of the day was all it would take.

When I finally admitted to Quinn what I was doing, she begged me to give it up. But though I didn't need her to remind me of the deep circles under my eyes, and the number of times I'd fallen asleep in the schoolroom, I'd made up my mind to trap the culprit. And nothing was going to stop me until I did.

"Of course he doesn't sleep at night. If you'd been through what he has, you wouldn't sleep, either. In fact, I'm surprised he doesn't have nightmares ."

It was Granberry, that nosy busybody, talking about me behind my back. She was in the kitchen preparing dinner, eager to discuss me with whomever would listen. I made my way to the pantry, and as I stood behind the swinging doors I could hear everything she said.

"I know he's had a difficult time."

"Oh?" Granberry said, sounding surprised.

"Yes, I heard Grandfather mention it. But it's been months now."

If Kenley wanted to know about me, why didn't he come right out and ask? I had a good mind to storm in there and tell him that to his face. Instead, I waited to hear what else they had to say.

A chair scraped across the floor. A pot clattered on the stove. A teakettle whistled.

"It took you a long time to get over your parents' death too, don't forget," Granberry reminded him.

Kenley muttered something I couldn't hear, then asked her what she thought of Mr. Davies. The housekeeper didn't answer right away, and when she did I was sure she chose her words with great care.

"He seems very capable. Why, don't you think so?"

"He's all right, I guess. He's just not a terrific teacher, that's all."

"Everyone can't be as dedicated as Mr. Houghton," Granberry replied.

She sounded very cagy, if you ask me, like she was going out of her way to be diplomatic. Maybe she didn't like Davies, either. I don't know why though. They hardly ever spoke to each other.

"Now what is it?" Granberry asked a moment later.

"I was just thinking of Max, how much I miss him."

Kenley sounded really depressed, and I felt bad for him, too. Max didn't get lost or fall off the cliff. He was too smart for that. Someone must've taken him out into the woods, knifed him or shot him or something like that, then buried him so no one would be able to find the remains. But why? And who? The dog never bothered anyone, except maybe Nathaniel.

"Now just cheer up," Granberry urged. "No sense working yourself into a state. He's gone and there's nothing we can do about it, Kenley."

"If I only knew what happened to him."

"Well you don't, and after all this time I don't think you ever will, either."

"Do you think . . . never mind," he muttered.

But that didn't satisfy her.

"Think what?" she asked, and I could tell how eager she was to ferret out the information.

"Nothing," he insisted.

Even though Kenley didn't want to talk about it, Granberry wasn't about to give up so easily.

"Well it must've been something or else you wouldn't have brought it up."

"Who did it, Miss Granberry?" Kenley blurted out.

"Did what?" she said, still playing it real cool.

"You know . . . Max."

"Kenley Ettinger, it's time you put that poor dog out of your mind, do you hear? It does you no good to carry on like this. Seems to me you put yourself through hell once before, thinking those search and rescue teams would find them after the accident. Remember that? How miserable you made yourself?"

"But they never found them, not even a trace. And no one's ever found Max, either," Kenley told her.

"Some things are best left the way they are, if you know what I mean. And since you're just sitting there working yourself into a snit, you can at least make yourself useful. You know that set of copper mixing bowls in the pantry? I'll be needing them in just another minute."

I heard Kenley get up from his chair, so I didn't waste any time making myself scarce. I didn't want him or anyone else to start accusing me of being a sneak. But someone had to be. All this weird stuff was going on, and I was starting to get so nervous about it that at night I'd taken to wedging a chair up against the doorknob, just like I should've done when we stayed at the Pine Bluff Motel. At least that night I knew who I was dealing with. But here on Ettinger Rock it wasn't nearly that easy discovering who was responsible for what was taking place.

What made it even harder was Quinn's complete lack of cooperation. She could've helped me get to the root of things. But no, all she did was insist that nothing unusual was going on. When I kept reminding her of that business in the dollhouse, she wouldn't even talk about it. Instead, she dismissed the whole thing as a prank, and said the less we worried about it, the better. Funny, I almost got the feeling she thought I had something to do with it.

How could she possibly believe it would all go away? I bet things had happened to her that she hadn't even told me about. I bet she was scared to because then she'd have to admit I was right.

For weeks now I'd been looking for the key that fit the attic door. I'd even managed to get ahold of the big ring of keys Granberry kept on a nail in the kitchen. But though I went through every one, none of them fit. Maybe Nathaniel kept it on him. Or Perdita. Or even Kenley, for that matter. I'd even kept watch on the door, giving up my vigil in the studio to spend several nights hiding in the sewing room. If someone was being kept hidden in the house, sooner or later he'd have to eat. I was hoping to catch Granberry bringing a tray up to the room when she thought everyone else was asleep. But no one came creeping up the stairs to support my theory, and even from within the room itself I didn't hear a single telltale sound.

But I wasn't about to give up. I hadn't back in the Valley, certain Mom's death was all a ruse and she was really alive. I was right then, and I was going to be proven right again. I wasn't imagining things, and the sooner I got Quinn to believe me, the sooner I could count on her to start giving me a hand. Between the two of us we were bound to find out what was going on.

The more I thought about Quinn's unwillingness to believe me, the more unhappy I became. But Leflands aren't easily discouraged, and I figured now was as good a time as any to finally have it out with her. I would tell her about Kenley's suspicions—after what I'd overheard I was sure he felt the same way about Davies as I did—and maybe then she'd start to come around to my way of thinking.

So I went looking for her, first upstairs where I figured she and Davies would be having one of their heart-to-hearts, her asking him for his good advice and all that baloney. But she wasn't there. Then I went on up to the third floor, knocked on her door and let myself in. It was neat as a pin, every paper and book on her desk squared away. But she wasn't there, either.

I went back downstairs, calling her name but getting no response.

"You might try the studio," Perdita said with her nose in a book.

Sure, that was a likely place. She and old man Ettinger were probably busy with their miniatures. They'd been at it for months now, decorating that dollhouse that was giving me so much trouble. I had a good mind to take the dolls and just chuck them over the cliff. The dollhouse looked fine without them, anyway. Besides, it was time my sister gave up playing with dolls and started accepting things the way they really were, instead of pretending everything was wonderful.

"Quinn?" I called out when I reached the studio. "Nathaniel?"

I might as well have been talking to myself, for all the

good it did, though from the look of things Mr. Ettinger had just put down his paints a few moments before. When I picked up his palette and touched one of the blotches of paint he'd mixed, my finger came away with a dab of color.

I glanced at the canvas on his easel. The painting he was working on showed the cliff beyond the studio windows, and where it sheared away there was a suggestion of whitecaps as waves approached the shore. Half in shadow, a lone figure stood silhouetted against the sky. But instead of looking out to sea, his face was turned in the direction of the house. The figure was very small, hardly noticeable at first. But strangely enough, it didn't resemble anyone on the island.

Ettinger wasn't a photo-realist, which Mr. Houghton said was an artist whose paintings were as detailed and realistic as a photograph. But when he showed me his other paintings I hadn't had any trouble identifying who the people were.

I bent over and gave it a closer look. It couldn't be my father, could it? I wondered. It was very hard to tell, given the size of the figure and the way the details were all so fuzzy and unclear. But the eyes weren't green like mine, and they weren't brown like Kenley's or grayish like his grandfather's. He just stood there, staring back at me like he was daring me to guess his identity.

Finally I gave up, knowing it was a little crazy of me to keep thinking I was looking at a portrait of Bennett Lefland, the one person in all the world I was terrified of seeing again.

I looked over at the dollhouse, thinking of that room upstairs, the one across the hall from the sewing room. The last time I'd looked at its counterpart in the dollhouse, it was empty. But it certainly wouldn't hurt to check it again.

If that little door was locked, I'd really freak out, because then I'd know for sure I wasn't imagining things. But it wasn't, even though I kind of hoped it would be. I pushed my finger against it and it opened wide. I bent down and peered inside. Empty. There still wasn't even paint or wallpaper on the walls, just this square little space waiting to be decorated.

I glanced into the schoolroom two floors below. There were the three of us, sitting at our desks, while the Houghton doll stood before the blackboard. What was he writing with that tiny piece of chalk he held in his hand?

JASON IS CRAZY.

I probably would've been, had I been able to read that. But it was just an algebra equation, the numbers even smaller than those on a typewriter.

But where was Max?

Last time I'd looked, the dog was stretched out on the schoolroom floor, gnawing away at a bone. But now the doll was gone. My eyes swept down the hall, going from one room to the next. When I reached the nursery I was shaking so hard I could barely maintain my balance. Where was Becky? The tiny crib was empty, though I could still see the doll's imprint against the pillow, a rounded indentation where its head had rested. I pulled the covers down, but the infant-sized doll wasn't hidden beneath them, nor was she in the carriage that stood in a corner of the nursery, a perfect replica of the one Quinn used when she took Becky out on walks.

Something sparkled, catching the light and bouncing it off the bright yellow walls of the dollhouse nursery. It came from the portable tub and dressing table which I'd even made use of myself, when I helped Quinn give Becky a bath.

There was water in the miniature bathtub, which struck me as carrying realism just a little too far. The white duck apron covering the dressing table part was pulled half over the tub. I tried to grab hold of it between my fingers, but it was wet and slippery and I couldn't get a grip on it. I dried my hand and tried again, flicking it back with my fingernail. The water caught the light, reflecting it into my eyes. For a moment the glare was so intense I couldn't see anything. I put my hand over my eyes and looked again.

The Becky doll floated face down in the tiny tub of water.

I just turned and ran. I flung the studio door open and raced through the silent sunlit rooms, hearing the clatter of my feet and the frenzied beating of my heart.

"Jason? Are you all right, dear?" Perdita Ettinger called after me as I rushed past the study.

I didn't even take the time to answer. The doll was floating in water deep enough to drown it. What I'd seen in the dollhouse was more than enough to send me hurrying upstairs, tripping over myself as I ran down the hall to the nursery.

If the door was locked I had every intention of breaking it down. But when I grabbed the knob and twisted it to the side, the door opened effortlessly and I rushed inside.

The crib was empty, just as I feared. A moment later I was standing at the tub and dressing table, trembling in fright as I peeled the white duck cover back, exposing more and more of the rubber basin which was used to bathe my daughter.

It was filled with water, but thank God whoever had

tampered with the dollhouse hadn't had a chance to turn their sick fantasies into reality. But where was she?

"Is anything the matter, Jason?"

I turned to face Perdita. She was standing in the doorway, and there was something about the way she looked at me that made me wonder if she already knew what was wrong. She was scared, that was it. But of what? Was she here to break the news, to tell me of some tragic accident?

"Where is she? What've you done to her?" I demanded.

"Who are you talking about, Jason?"

"Where is she? Where's Becky?" I shouted.

"Jason, please, calm down. She's fine, I'm sure she is."

"Then you don't know, do you? You're only guessing."

"What are you getting so upset about? Nothing's happened to her."

Maybe she was in on it, covering up for the person they kept hidden in the attic.

"What've you done with my—?"

I caught myself in time, swallowed hard and tried to get ahold of myself. But it was next to impossible. Every second I stood there could mean the difference between life and death.

"Just tell me where she is?" I begged.

By then the tears were streaming down my cheeks, I was so terrified of what might have already taken place.

"I think she's with Nathaniel. He said something about taking her out for a walk."

Perdita's voice cracked, and with it her composure as well. She stepped back into the hall, and I could tell how frightened she was. But she'd have plenty more to be scared of if he did anything to my daughter.

"Is she with him or isn't she?" I shouted.

She shook her head helplessly, her curly hair looking limp and bedraggled. Beads of sweat stood out on her upper lip. She was afraid of me, but I knew that the more fearful she became, the more she would tell me.

"I don't know. I didn't see them leave," she stammered. "But the carriage is gone, so maybe—"

"Maybe what?" I screamed at the top of my voice.

I reached out and grabbed her by the shoulders, shaking her as hard as I could. The tears clouded her eyes and dripped down her wrinkled cheeks. I kept shaking her and shaking her until suddenly I felt someone pull me back. It was Davies, and from the way he looked at me I knew he was just as scared as Perdita.

"The baby, he took the baby. He's going to kill her, I know he is."

"What is he talking about?" Davies said in confusion.

But before Perdita could tell him I turned and bolted, taking the stairs two and three at a time. If they wouldn't help me, then I'd just have to help myself. Behind me I could hear them shouting, Perdita imploring me to wait a moment, Mr. Davies calling out too, saying he'd come with me, and that nothing had happened to the baby.

How did he know? Had he seen what was in the dollhouse? How could he be so sure?

Nothing made sense, nothing at all.

I threw the front door open, didn't even bother to grab my coat. In the Valley it was already spring, but on Ettinger Rock the seasons moved more slowly, and though the sun was out, it was cold and windy.

"Nathaniel!" I started shouting, looking every which way at once. "Nathaniel, where are you!"

And then I knew, just as surely as I did that Becky was in danger. I set off on a run, certain of the one place I would find him. Despite its distance, I managed to reach the campsite in hardly any time at all.

A thin wisp of smoke rose from the campfire. I staggered to a halt, trying to catch my breath. He was here all right, there was no doubt about it. But should I surprise him, or call out his name? Chances were he'd panic, and then Becky might be hurt. So I stole up to the tent, my footsteps muffled by the rubber soles of my tennis shoes.

I didn't even want to think of what he might be doing in there. I didn't even want to imagine it in my wildest nightmare. All I prayed was that I wasn't too late, and when I reached the tent I found myself greedily sucking in air, more winded than I realized.

With trembling fingers I caught hold of the flap, then threw it back and rushed inside.

"What the fu—?" came a startled voice, so scared it couldn't even get the word out.

I caught a glimpse of someone's tits, a bare rump. Then the two kids I'd surprised in the act were trying to cover themselves with their sleeping bag and convince me they hadn't meant any harm. I guess they were just as freaked out as I was, but by then I wasn't about to stick around to hear their explanation.

Chalk one up for Kenley Ettinger, I thought. He figured out what was going on here long before I did.

But even though I finally knew who was using the campsite, just a pair of kids from the mainland, I still hadn't found my daughter. Even before the guy and his girlfriend had a chance to grab for their clothes, I was already clambering up the side of the cliff, heading back in the direction of the house.

There were several trails that led through the woods, any one of which Ettinger might have taken.

"Nathaniel!"

Oh God, what had he done to her? If he'd taken Max here, killed him the way I already suspected, maybe he was going to do the same thing with the baby.

So I kept on running, shouting his name over and over again. If he heard me he never let on. What would he do with the carriage? Send it hurtling over the cliff? Smashed on the rocks, the pieces would be carried out with the tide and no one would ever be the wiser. But was Ettinger as mad as I thought, or was it all in my head, inventing nightmares for myself that didn't exist?

But I surely hadn't invented what I found in the dollhouse. The Becky doll was floating face down in a tub full of water. That was reason enough to panic, and so now I just kept running.

When I reached the path that cut across the width of the island I turned right, and a few minutes later I heard Quinn, her frantic cries echoing through the woods.

"This way, over here!" I yelled.

Like a snake writhing in agony, the narrow path twisted and turned. I tripped over a root and suddenly I was flying, the air exploding out of my lungs as I landed with a thud on the forest floor. There wasn't even time to catch my breath. As dazed as I was, I managed to pull myself to my feet.

What was that up ahead? Something red, bobbing and weaving in the distance.

"Nathaniel!"

My throat was so dry I couldn't even swallow, and it felt like someone was jabbing pins into my vocal cords. There was a stitch in my side but I didn't want to stop. I could see him now, a red muffler twisted around his neck.

He was wheeling the carriage through the woods, oblivious to my cries.

"Nathaniel!"

Why didn't he answer? Why didn't he stop and look back? He wasn't hard of hearing, so why was he pretending to be deaf?

The thud of racing feet came up behind me. It was Quinn, and between the two of us we'd be able to stop him before he hurt her. We'd take Becky in our arms and hold her tight, protect her from all that was evil, from the sickness that was spreading out around me like a stain you can never wipe clean.

"Leave her alone! Don't hurt her!" I begged.

Ettinger finally looked back at me. Behind those sad, bluish-gray eyes I was sure I saw the fever of madness, a gleam of insanity that made his face burn brightly as if lit from within. His bushy white eyebrows rose up in confusion, and as his eyes opened wide I wrestled the carriage out of his hands.

"Jason, what's going on? What's the matter?" he demanded.

As if he didn't know. As if the bastard hadn't guessed by now. He'd taken Max into the woods, slit the poor dog's throat, buried his remains. Now he was going to do the same with my daughter, the child Mom had died to bring into the world. But enough blood had already been shed. I was going to put an end to it, once and for all.

I bent over the carriage. He'd pulled the blankets over her head, trying to suffocate her. I threw them back with a vengeful cry. But I was too late! I was too late!

It was a corpse. Dead rotting flesh, dull scraps of once golden hair, dry withered lips set in a permanent grimace of terror. I was staring at Becky's decomposing remains, and the screams that came out of my throat weren't enough to bring her back to life. The once rosy cheeks were a hideous grayish-green. How long had they kept her like this? How long had they kept it a secret, telling me she was alive when they all knew he'd killed her, drowned her in the tub and then hidden her away in the locked attic room?

I would kill him, that's what I'd do. I'd murder him the way he murdered my daughter. Justice, that's what it would be. Vengeance. I'd rid Ettinger Rock of its sickness, just the way I had purified the Valley.

"How could you, how could you?" I groaned.

I lifted her out of the carriage and pressed her still, lifeless little body against me, trying to warm the dead cold flesh.

"Jason, listen to me. It's going to be all right."

"All right?" I screamed. "Are you out of your mind, Quinn? Look what he's done to her!"

The tears flooded my eyes, and she seemed to be swimming before me. But why wasn't she screaming as I was? Why wasn't she groaning and crying and beating her fists against him? Why was she so calm? She couldn't be part of this conspiracy too, could she?

"Jason, listen, try to understand," she said to me, her response so tempered that I began to back away from her, certain she meant to harm me, too. "Everything is going to be all right. Listen to Quinn. She's never lied to you. Trust me, Jason."

"But . . . but . . ."

I couldn't even begin to say what I was feeling. I was holding death in my hands, cradling it against me, able to smell the putrid decomposing flesh.

217

"My baby, look what he's done to my baby," I whimpered.

But she wouldn't look. She wouldn't believe me, either. And who was that with the evil face standing behind her? Davies, that busy-body, that troublemaker. Davies who asked all those questions about me, who told Quinn to write to Dad and act like nothing had ever happened.

"Let me have the baby, Jason. Let me have our little sister."

Sister? Was she crazy, too? Becky was my daughter, and I was going to tell them so they'd never forget. They'd all know I was her father, that they'd robbed me of half my life.

My head hurt so. Everyone was talking at once, their voices jabbing at me like sticks. I backed off, wondering where I could go.

"Becky is fine, Jason."

"Liar!" I screamed at Davies. "He killed her, can't you see?"

"He didn't, Jason. She's fine. And you're frightening her."

I heard something then, but it was a dream, it had to be. A baby was crying in my head, whimpering in fear. I looked down at the corpse rotting in my arms. Those lifeless shrunken lips opened wide. How could that be? What was happening? I wanted to drop her but I was afraid, afraid of everything, afraid they'd take me away, never let me see her again.

They all thought I was crazy, but I wasn't. How could I be, when the tub was filled with water, and the doll floated face down as proof it had drowned?

Again I heard cries in my head, the dead lips moving, the hollow fish eyes luminous now, dancing with life.

Becky was crying. The rosy cheeks. The little hands pummeling frantically at the air.

"Ohhhhhhhhhhh . . ."

Ever so gently Quinn took her out of my arms. I put my hands over my mouth but I couldn't stop myself from shrieking. And the baby kept crying, screaming now because I'd scared her so.

She was alive. It was all in my head. A trick, that's what it was. They tricked me. Told me she was dead, drowned the doll and made me believe it was real.

"Shh, it's all right, Quinn's here. Quinn'll take care of you."

I clung to her and let her lead me away. I could feel their eyes like a fever in my brain, burning holes right through me.

Make them stop staring, Quinn. Make them go away. They'll hurt me. They'll lock me up, throw away the attic key. Granberry won't even come to bring me food. I'll be all alone. They boarded up the windows, too. No escape. I'll die there, day by day.

"I'm here," Quinn whispered, a soft gentle breeze blowing spring through the air. "You're tired and you're scared, but I'm here, and I won't ever leave you."

"Oh Quinn, what's going to happen? What're they going to do to me?" I cried.

"They won't do anything. You mustn't worry. They'll understand because they all care about you, Jason. We love you. We always will."

"But she . . . I thought . . . when I touched her she . . . but then . . ."

The words were all jumbled up in my head, a pile of broken pieces like a puzzle that could never be solved.

"It doesn't matter now. You'll get some rest, you'll feel much better, I know you will. Everything's going to be fine. Just trust me, Jason. That's all you have to do, and I'll take care of everything else."

"But she . . . when I . . . it didn't . . ."

"It was a dream, Jason, a terrible dream."

"Then he . . . he wasn't the . . ."

I couldn't talk now. Someone was hammering nails into my skull, pounding away as if I were made out of wood. I was shivering, and Quinn draped something warm over my shoulders. It smelled like wildflowers, the way she smelled when I held her in my arms, protecting her the way she was now trying to protect me.

But how could Quinn save me when I couldn't even save myself?

"We're almost home," she said.

Home? I had no home. I was all alone. They'd taken everything away from me, sent me running and running until I'd never be able to stop and catch my breath.

What was happening to me? What in the world was happening?

CHAPTER FIFTEEN

I remembered how something like this had happened before, back in the Valley the day we discovered Great-uncle Orin's corpse. It was tied to a chair in a tiny windowless room hidden behind the attic wall. Jason and I had crept down that narrow passage, where the stink of a rotting possum had us convinced we were about to solve the mystery of Mother's disappearance. We thought that Father had murdered her, hiding her body where no one would find it. But it was Orin we found, a faded note pinned to the tattered remains of his jacket.

EXOD 205. LEV 2011.

Like a secret code, that biblical reference was burned into my memory, never to be forgotten. *For I the Lord thy God am a jealous God, visiting the iniquity of the fathers upon the children . . .*

"We're cursed. It's in the blood, Quinn . . . It can't ever go away."

Moments later Jason had rushed out of the house, confused and frightened and unable to explain what was wrong. And now it was happening all over again, much worse than before. But what was causing it? If only my brother would tell me, I felt certain I could help him.

Kenley and Mr. Davies had chased after me, all of us able to hear Jason's frenzied screams as he ran through the woods. But now they stayed behind, and I was grateful they weren't interfering. I knew what they must be thinking, and I wondered if I'd be able to convince them it wasn't half as serious as it looked. But that wasn't nearly as important as taking care of my brother.

When we got upstairs to his room I urged him to lie down; I would stay with him until he fell asleep. He looked exhausted, not just emotionally drained but physically as well. He was shivering from the cold, having run out of the house without his coat. I pulled the quilt over him, tucking him in and whispering that it would be all right, no one was going to hurt him.

"What was it, Quinn? What made me see things that weren't there?" he whispered.

"Was it Warren? Has he come back, Jason?"

My brother shook his head violently.

"It's not him. It's something else. Besides, he's been gone so long now. And even when he was around, he always made his presence known. He never kept hidden. But he's not in my head, Quinn. I've looked, but he's not there. So it has to be something else. But what? What?"

He tried to raise himself off the bed, but I begged him to stay put, rest was what he needed more than anything else.

"Don't think about it anymore," I said as I kissed him gently on the forehead. "Just try to get some sleep, Jason. When you wake up this'll all be behind you. And we'll start fresh again, I promise."

I didn't know what else to tell him. But at least he'd begun to calm down. Once so young and handsome, filled with vitality, his face was now drawn and prematurely aged. The pain he had felt was written in the circles below his eyes, and the pinched and tortured lines around the corners of his mouth. When I touched his hair it was soaking wet, and even as he huddled under the quilt he couldn't stop shivering.

I brought back a towel from the bathroom and tried to dry him off as best I could. His eyes never left me, as if he had to convince himself that I was real, and not another hallucination.

"It was all in my mind, wasn't it, seeing Becky dead?"

"But you know that now, so it can't frighten you anymore."

"But the dollhouse," he whispered. "Go see for yourself. Tell me I wasn't wrong."

"See what, Jason?"

He licked his lips to moisten them, then asked for a glass of water. When I returned his eyes were closed, and gradually his breathing grew more regular. I pulled up a chair and watched him, afraid to leave his side until I was certain he was asleep. Something about the dollhouse had caused him to believe Becky was in danger. In a few minutes I would go downstairs and look for myself, because if it had been tampered with again I'd already decided to confront the Ettingers with my discovery.

It was time to put aside the secrets I'd kept to myself. I would tell them about the rockslide too, and ask why the attic door was locked. I would bring up the fact that I had smelled Perdita's perfume coming from inside that room, and tell them exactly what Jason and I had discovered in the dollhouse, the knife on one occasion, the noose on another. All these things would finally be brought out into the open, where they couldn't frighten us anymore.

Determined to clear the air, if for no other reason than to protect my brother from the nameless fears which threatened to turn his life into an unending nightmare, I left his room and made my way downstairs.

"I don't care what you call it, Davies. The boy's disturbed, and the longer he stays here the greater the danger to all of us."

It was Nathaniel Ettinger whose cold, dispassionate words reached my ears as I came down the stairs. They were in the library, speaking so heatedly I had no trouble overhearing them.

"Now, Nathaniel, you must try to be a little more tolerant," Perdita spoke up. "After all, the boy was frightened. He didn't hurt you. He certainly had no intention of harming the baby."

"We have no way of knowing that," Nathaniel promptly replied.

There was a note of rancor in his voice, bitterness, that made my heart sink. I had often wondered about the seemingly unquestioning willingness with which the Ettingers had taken us in, welcoming us into their home as if we were their own flesh and blood. If Father ever found us—if in fact he wanted to see us again—the Ettingers would be in legal jeopardy, as well.

But even as I sought to understand what lay behind their generosity, I really couldn't let myself dwell on it too much. If something besides sheer goodness of heart was motivating them—something dark or deceitful—I didn't want to know about it, for that would have destroyed the only peace and safety I had known in months.

But now it looked as if the fragile serenity I had come to depend on at Ettinger Rock was about to vanish. For whatever reasons Nathaniel had tolerated our presence in his home, it sounded to me as if his forebearance had reached its limit.

"I understand what you're trying to accomplish, Davies," Nathaniel continued. "But though your motives are admirable it's my opinion the whole thing has already gotten out of hand."

What did he mean by "trying to accomplish"? And what possible motives could Mr. Davies have other than to teach us to the best of his abilities? My hand tightened around the banister and I remained where I was, standing there on the stairs and listening intently.

"Surely if we found out what triggered this incident," Davies started to say when Mr. Ettinger cut him off.

"Incident?" Nathaniel asked, raising his voice. "Is that all you think it was? Did you see the boy's eyes? They were like a mad animal's. If his sister hadn't gotten to him when she did, I hate to think what might have happened."

"That's only because his first concern was the child," Davies reminded him.

"He called her his baby. What do you suppose he meant by that?" Nathaniel asked.

"Just what it sounds like," Davies answered. "He's taken over the role of father, which certainly isn't unusual under the circumstances."

What circumstances? Why were they talking about us like this, like we were specimens under a microscope, and they could pick and poke and dissect us to their hearts' content?

"I think you're letting your emotions get the better of you, dear, if you don't mind my saying," Perdita commented. "After all, if we were really in danger—"

"That's just it," Nathaniel interrupted. "If none of us can control the youngster, then as far as I'm concerned he does pose a danger. Not only to himself and his sisters, but to all of us on the island.''

''I intend to keep a much closer watch on him,'' Davies replied.

''Small consolation, after what we've been through.''

Closer watch on him? He was a tutor, not a bodyguard. Or was he?

Slowly I made my way down the stairs, anxious to hear everything that was said. There was something in the tenor of the conversation that struck a false note. I couldn't pin it down exactly, but it didn't seem to be the kind of talk I'd expect from them. If Father were behind all this, if somehow he'd gotten the Ettingers to believe that he was the injured party, and everything we had told them was a gross exaggeration if not an outright lie, then there would be no hope for us at all.

There seemed to be no end to the lies and deceptions, the secrets and conspiracies that Jason had worried about ever since we arrived here. Could I have so misjudged Perdita and her husband, perhaps Kenley as well? But that still didn't explain Mr. Davies' role in all this, nor did it answer any of the questions I had decided to raise.

But if I told them what I knew, confronting them with all the evidence I had gathered—evidence which seemed to indicate the Ettingers had much more to hide than we did—they might decide to call Father and have him come and take us away. If that were to happen, I knew that the only future my brother faced was behind the walls of a sanitarium. As for Becky, life would be equally as bleak. Even if Father consented to raise her, as she grew older she would soon come to realize how much he despised her. To grow up in that kind of loveless, stifling environment would be like condemning her to death, an act even crueler than cold-blooded murder.

So instead of confrontation, I chose conciliation. Instead of demanding answers, I would provide explanations, paying particular attention to the questions Nathaniel had already raised.

Thus, when I entered the library it was with a smile, a look of optimism none of them could ignore. As long as I managed to convince them that everything was all right, we might be granted a reprieve, and they'd allow us to continue to stay here.

"Quinn, I was just coming up to see how he was doing," Mr. Davies said when I came into the study.

He stood with his back to the fire, having positioned himself halfway between Perdita and her husband. The Ettingers sat in a pair of matching wing chairs, and though their expressions brightened when I came in, even if I hadn't overheard them talking I still would have been able to tell how disturbed they were.

"How is he, dear? Is he feeling better?" Perdita asked.

The only comfort I took was in Kenley's absence. If he'd been a part of the conversation, I knew I would have found it very difficult to confide in him in the future. When I asked where he was, Perdita told me he and Miss Granberry were in the nursery, seeing to the baby.

"Would you like some tea?" Perdita motioned to the gleaming silver service arranged on a tray near her chair. "A nice hot drink will do you good."

They were all trying so hard to be polite, but I knew what they were really thinking. I glanced at Nathaniel, catching the pained and troubled expression on his face.

"First of all, he's terribly sorry. Terribly embarrassed too, I might add."

"Embarrassed? Whatever for?" Perdita said.

She laughed nervously, and when she picked up her teacup her hand was trembling so that she had to set it down again.

How in the world was I going to explain my brother's behavior without alarming them more than they were already? I couldn't very well admit that what he'd seen was an hallucination. So I tried to gloss over everything as best I could, making light of what had happened.

"He's awfully protective of the baby," I began. "And sometimes I guess he gets a little carried away. But don't we all?" I added, making sure to keep my smile in place. "He went looking for her, and when he couldn't find her he started thinking the worst."

"But why?" Nathaniel asked.

"Well, you know, what with Max disappearing and all."

"Yes, that's understandable," agreed Perdita.

"Did he say exactly what set him off?" Davies asked.

It disturbed me to hear him talk of my brother as if he were a time bomb. I knew Jason better than any of them, and I felt certain he had good reason to fear for Becky's life. But until I had a chance to check out the dollhouse for myself, I didn't want to say anything about it. Jason had come upon something, but I still had no idea what it was. Yet I had a feeling that whatever he had found had already been put to rights, so there would be no clue as to why he believed Becky's life was in danger.

"You know he's had a very difficult time of it," I went on. "We haven't kept that a secret. I think he was afraid our father snuck onto the island and tried to kidnap the baby. That's why he sort of lost control of himself. But he's all right now. He's resting and he's feeling much better. Embarrassed, of course," I said again, looking directly at Mr. Ettinger. "He's terribly sorry if he frightened you, Nathaniel. He thinks a great deal of you, and now he's afraid you're displeased with him."

My words had the desired effect. Nathaniel lowered his eyes, staring glumly into his lap. When he spoke his tone of voice was far more sympathetic than it had been earlier.

"Well, at least no one was hurt," he said with a sigh.

"And that's all that's important," Perdita said brightly, holding onto her smile as tightly as I was.

"But why would he think your father knows where you are?" Mr. Davies asked.

I could have told them about the phone calls, but I didn't want to betray Kenley's confidence. It was enough that Jason and I had already done more than our share of eavesdropping. If they suspected their grandson was in the habit of listening in on their conversations it would only make things more difficult for him, particularly now that his relationship with his grandfather was so strained.

"He's a very persistent man," I replied. "I'm sure he's already traced us to McKenzie Springs."

I glanced obliquely at Mr. Davies, watching him out of the corner of my eye. But when I went on to describe our run-in with Sheriff Orickson, there was nothing in his expression to indicate he was already aware of what had happened to us after the car accident.

"They've had more than their share of problems," Perdita

reminded him. "If the boy's a little hysterical, I for one think that's quite understandable. Wouldn't you agree, Nathaniel?"

She looked pointedly at her husband, and though he nodded his head I knew he was still disturbed about Jason's behavior.

"Perhaps I should have a talk with him," Davies suggested. "Sometimes it's very healthy just to clear the air, if you know what I mean."

"I'm sure he'd appreciate that," I replied, even though I knew my brother placed as little trust in Mr. Davies as he did in everyone else on the island.

"Then it's settled," he said approvingly.

I didn't know what to say after that. I don't think they were totally convinced of my explanation, but at least they weren't getting on the phone to call Father. Yet I knew that the next time something like this happened they wouldn't hesitate to contact him. Were he to arrive on Ettinger Rock, there would be no escape. Not now, and not in the future.

Kenley was in the studio, peering into the dollhouse his grandfather took such pride in. I wondered if he was looking for the same thing I was, though I'd made no mention of it to anyone. That in itself immediately aroused my suspicions, yet at the same time I couldn't bear to think of Kenley as an adversary, someone I couldn't be completely honest with. So I tried to put aside my doubts, knowing that if I couldn't trust Kenley Ettinger, there would be no one left on the island to confide in.

"I went looking for you, but you weren't upstairs," he explained.

I told him of my conversation with his grandparents, and how I had tried my best to allay their fears.

"Grandpa was really freaked out, wasn't he?"

"Worse than that, I'm afraid."

"And Jason?"

I couldn't help but sigh.

"I think he'll be all right," I said, trying to sound more optimistic than I felt. "He was sound asleep when I left him."

"You're very concerned about him, aren't you, Quinn?"

It was more than concern. I was afraid for my brother's very sanity. But perhaps if we managed to learn the truth of what was happening here on the island, Jason would have nothing to be frightened of anymore.

So I began to pour my heart out to Kenley, praying that he would understand. He listened intently, sympathetically too, I could tell, as I related the events which had taken place since our arrival, the inexplicable incidents which had so inflamed my brother's fears.

"And you've kept this to yourself all this time?" Kenley asked. "You haven't told anyone else?"

I shook my head.

"Why didn't you come to me earlier?" he said reproachfully. "Why didn't you tell me what was wrong?"

"I was afraid," I whispered.

His dark eyes widened with surprise.

"Of me?" he asked in disbelief. "But I thought you trusted me. I trust you, Quinn, I always have. If I didn't I would never have told you about my parents, what happened that day."

"It's just that . . . well . . ." I swallowed hard, unable to get my thoughts in order.

Instead of pressing me for an explanation, Kenley reached

231

out and put his hands on my shoulders. His eyes caught me and held me fast, yet there was nothing in his gaze to make me fearful. Rather, I saw such compassion, so much understanding, that I could no longer help myself. I gave a little cry—fear, desperation, confusion, all those things and more—and clung to him with all my might. But I wasn't afraid for myself. Jason's future had never seemed more uncertain than at this moment. If I couldn't help him get better I didn't think anyone else could. That wasn't my ego talking, either. There was a dark, frightened side to my brother's character that no one knew anything about, not even Father. Unless he overcame his fears, his condition would continue to deteriorate, until finally he wouldn't be able to tell the difference between what was real and what was imagined.

I could feel Kenley's hands holding me in their embrace. I didn't want him to let go, and when he began to tell me that everything was going to be all right, there was nothing I wanted more in the world than to believe him.

"You'll see, we'll find out what's really happening around here," he promised. "But you've got to start trusting me, Quinn. Because if you don't then we'll never be able to help each other."

I stepped back and took a deep breath, trying to clear my head. There was something in Kenley's eyes I hadn't seen before, something so kind and loving, protective too, that I realized no matter what might happen in the future, I could always turn to him for help.

Knowing that immediately lifted my spirits. I even managed to smile, and when he touched my cheek I didn't hesitate to return his caress.

"I like you so much," he said, speaking so softly it was as if he were afraid of what he was admitting. "I keep thinking of that time when I kissed you, how good it felt. We were so close, like nothing would ever come between us. And now that you've finally told me what's wrong, nothing will.''

I glanced at him shyly, then lowered my eyes. No boy had ever spoken to me like this before, not even Jason. One day I would have to tell Kenley about that, too. But not now. I had given him more than enough to think about, and I knew it was unfair to keep pouring out my troubles like this. But at least we'd made a start, and in the future there would be no secrets, not when I had already learned how destructive they could be. Even when the truth hurt, it was so much better than keeping everything bottled up inside you.

Whether it was this feeling of finally being able to unburden myself, or the way Kenley continued to look at me so lovingly, I did something I hadn't done before. I leaned over and kissed him, not even thinking twice about what I was doing. I don't even know if it was love I felt. But there was no need to put a label on my feelings. Here was someone who cared about me, and that was all that mattered.

"It makes me shiver," I said with a nervous laugh.

"You're not the only one," he grinned.

We stood there holding each other, so tight I could feel his heartbeat and he could feel mine. It was safe, warm, comfortable, all those good, gentle words I hadn't felt in such a long time. When at last we drew apart our hands reached automatically for each other, our fingers laced together.

"And now the dollhouse," he said, his mood one of utter seriousness.

We began to search the rooms, top to bottom, but

everything looked just the way it was supposed to. Again and again my eyes strayed to the nursery, trying to discover what it was that had caused Jason to react with such fear. But the only thing that caught my eye was the baby's miniature tub, filled with water.

"Seems rather strange, don't you think?"

"Grandfather likes everything to look very realistic," Kenley replied.

"But not that real. And where's the Max doll? It used to be in the schoolroom."

Kenley looked at me sheepishly.

"Well, at least one mystery's solved. I'm the one who took it, Quinn."

"But why?"

Kenley shrugged.

"I don't know, it just didn't seem right. He's gone, so why keep the doll around? I didn't throw it away though. It's in my room. I'll put it back if you think it's important."

"Max was important," I said, "not the doll."

I looked back into the nursery. The doll that represented Becky lay in its tiny crib, pretending to be fast asleep. Maybe that was the key. *Pretending.* Maybe someone on Ettinger Rock was pretending just a little too hard. Pretending to be what though? A murderer? Or maybe a madman, pretending to be sane.

CHAPTER SIXTEEN

Terrible dreams, the worst I'd ever had. Mom stood by the foot of the bed, her arms raised above her head. I didn't want to look but she made me, forcing me to see what I had done to her. The blood was so red it hurt my eyes. It dripped down the insides of her arms, the droplets making angry little sounds as they hit the floor.

"It's all your fault, Jason."

That's all she said, blaming me for everything that had happened. But just because she was the one who said it didn't mean it was true.

"No, it was your fault," I told her. "You did it, not me. I loved you and you turned it inside out, twisted it all up. Confused me. That wasn't love, that was hurt, making me do those things to you."

"So my little man has already forgotten how much he liked it. Shame on you, Jason."

She was giggling, a madwoman's laugh. It scared me to death, and I was so cold it felt like I was standing in the middle of a raging blizzard. But I wasn't. I was in bed, huddled under the covers, fighting off the nightmares that couldn't be dreams because they were so horribly real.

"Why don't you leave me alone?" I begged. "You're dead. I didn't kill you, he did. But I saved the baby, didn't I? So why is it my fault, Mom? I didn't mean to hurt you, honest I didn't. But you had me all confused, frightened. I didn't know what was happening and he hated me, Dad did, and that was your fault, too. Admit it. Please. If I can accept my guilt, then why can't you?"

Her expression hardened, and the corners of her mouth turned down in a frown.

"Guilt?" she said. "I have none, Jason. No remorse, either. Whatever I did, I did out of love."

"Incest isn't love, it's just a kind of punishment, worse than being beaten."

She laughed softly.

"You didn't think that when we made love, when you put your cock inside me."

"Don't say that. Don't talk like that!" I cried out, not even caring if anyone heard me. "Those words . . . they sound so dirty. You were my mother!"

"And your lover. And your whore."

"No, I won't listen to you. You're not real, anyway. You're all in my mind, just like what I saw in the carriage."

"You saw what you wanted to see, Jason. What someone we both know encouraged you to see."

Who was she talking about? Surely not Dad. And she couldn't mean Quinn, could she? But I didn't ask. Crazy people spoke to figments of their imagination, and I wasn't crazy. But she was so real I could even smell her delicate rose perfume, what I used to call the fragrance of remembrance.

"Go away, Rebecca. Go back where you came from."

"The grave?"

She threw her head back, and where there had once

236

been a smooth white throat, silken to the touch, there was now a hideous gash that widened as she tossed her head. The flesh parted, cracking and splitting open even as I watched. Someone had torn her throat out and I slammed my eyes shut, knowing it wasn't my fault. I could never—couldn't even begin to—I wouldn't—

Horrible dreams. And so cold, so icy cold that I'd lost all feeling in my hands. I tried moving my fingers to get the blood flowing, but they were like icicles. My whole body was like that. Ice, shattering at the slightest touch.

"Look who's come to visit, Jason."

Rebecca who was in the grave, who wasn't alive except in my imagination, pointed behind her to the door. It opened wide and there he stood, leering at me and laughing. He was naked, his penis jutting out like a horn between his legs.

"Oh please God! No!" I whimpered.

But he came into the room anyway, taking care to close the door so no one would know he was here. In the house. In my room. In my head.

Rebecca reached up and unfastened her nightgown, the ivory one she liked best of all. She cupped her breasts in her hands and began to fondle her nipples, teasing them between her fingers until they swelled, stiffening at her touch.

"Do it," she told him, her voice trembling with excitement. "I want Jason to watch, so he won't ever forget what he gave up. You were there, darling, don't you remember? You saw what the little bastard did to me. Slashed my wrists and told his daddy I tried to kill myself."

"He was always a liar, couldn't be trusted," he told her.

He stroked himself until he was as hard as a rock. Even

though I closed my eyes, turned over and buried my face in the pillows, it didn't matter 'cause I could still see them.

He came up behind her and she bent over, pressing her bloodied hands against the bed. Then he shoved it in, so hard she started to gasp.

"Oh yes, that's so good, Warren. That's just how Mommy likes it."

"You're not there!" I screamed. "You're all make-believe. You're in my head, and you'll go away when I wake up."

"Maybe. And maybe not," Warren replied. "But it really doesn't matter what's real and what isn't, Lefland. As long as you can see me, that's all that counts."

I tried to get out of bed. I'd run away from them, escape their madness. I'd run and run and they'd never catch me. Not Mom, not Warren, not even Dad who hated me even more than they did. But they pinned me down, refusing to let me go.

"No, please," I begged. "I didn't do anything wrong. Don't hurt me."

"I'm just going to take what's mine," Warren said.

He looked just like me, sounded like me too. And Mom loved him more than me, I could tell. It was Warren she'd taken into her bed, Warren whom she wanted to feel between her legs. Not her son. Not Jason, but the spiteful bastard who lived in Jason's mind, who was so strong now that I couldn't protect myself from him any longer.

"Don't fight it, Lefland. Just relax and let me fuck your brains out," he giggled.

I could feel him burrowing his way inside, like a chigger that gets under your skin. But it was much worse than that. A chigger itches and eventually goes away. But

Warren was here to stay. As they held me down on the bed I could feel him moving through my body, like a message carried in the blood. He seeped into every part of me, every pore, every cell, not content until he'd taken complete control.

"I told you when I was ready I'd come back for you. And now I have, Lefland, and there's not a fucking thing you can do to stop me."

I struggled to break free, but there was no strength left in my body. It was all melting away, and finally I lay still while he sent his cold fingers creeping up into my brain. Then the pain started, like a vise squeezing my skull, squashing and twisting my thoughts until they became his, and I was seeing the world through his hate-filled eyes.

And there I sat, strapped to a chair like Great-uncle Orin back in the Valley, powerless to defend myself. I was in a tiny windowless room, and though I kept screaming for someone to come and get me, he had control of my voice now, and no matter how hard I tried I couldn't make a sound.

I'll wake up and he'll be gone, I kept telling myself. It's a dream, that's all it is. Things like this can't happen in real life. It's all fake, a nightmare. Make-believe, like the games I used to play with Quinn when we were little.

Again and again I told myself that, even as I felt him digging his way deeper and deeper inside me. He was so strong now that all I could do was sit there in that straightback chair, feeling him take control.

"Have fun with him," I heard Mom say. "If anyone deserves it, he does."

Deserves what? To be murdered? That's what it was, even if my heart was still beating and I hadn't shed a drop of blood. What's the phrase doctors use, before they turn off the respirator? Brain death. Yes, that's what Warren had done to me. He'd murdered my brain, emptied it out and filled it up again with all his own thoughts.

I wanted to tell Mom that, hoping she might change her mind and try to help me. But when I looked for her I couldn't see anything but the walls of that tiny windowless cell in which he'd imprisoned me, throwing away the key. Then, like something seen through the wrong end of a telescope, I made her out. She was moving back toward the door, growing fainter and fainter until only her outlines remained, a ghostly silhouette that suddenly vanished, dissolving into nothingness.

Warren yawned and stretched his arms above his head. He lay back against the pillows, playing with himself and smiling contentedly.

"There, that wasn't so bad, Lefland, was it?"

His voice boomed out at me as I strained against the leather straps which kept me confined to the chair.

"I told you this would happen one day," he went on, "but you didn't believe me."

"You're not real. You're all in my head. I'll wake up and you'll be gone."

" 'Fraid not, ole buddy. I'm in your head all right, but it's my head now and I'm here for good. So try to be a nice little boy and behave yourself. But even if you don't, it won't matter anyway, because I'm in control."

Again I tried to scream, desperate for Quinn to hear me. But though my voice rang out loud and clear in the tiny room in which Warren held me prisoner, I knew then that no one else could hear me.

"I don't know why you're complaining. They're all a bunch of fucking hypocrites, so what are you so worried about? We're gonna take care of 'em, every last one,

Lefland. Sure, didn't you know? That's been my plan all along. Why do you think I tried to kill that little cocksucker she likes so much? That's all the cunt talks about, Kenley this and Kenley that.''

"You're making it all up. You didn't try to kill anyone," I told him.

"Lot you know," he laughed. "And the dolls, wasn't that a hell of an idea? I got a real charge tying that noose around your neck. It turned me on, know what I mean? Got me so hot thinking about it I almost came in my pants.''

For a moment I couldn't even breathe, I was so surprised. Here I'd suspected just about everyone else on the island, never dreaming that Warren was responsible for the things that had been happening.

"Then it was you all along!" I cried out. "You used me, didn't you, you bastard?''

"How clever of you to finally figure it out," Warren snickered.

"You made me do things without my knowing it. Made me see things that weren't there, like Becky in the carriage.''

"Why, did you think it was old man Ettinger? I was the one you heard that night, the one who lured you downstairs to the studio. I took you right to the dollhouse, told you what to do and what to see. And of course you were very cooperative, Lefland, a real good little boy. You're gonna stay that way too, because from now on you're gonna listen to me not just when you're asleep, ole buddy, but when you're wide-awake.''

"That's what you think," I shouted, trying to drown out his laughter that was so cold and sharp-edged it was like being slashed with a razor. "I won't let you. I'll stop you. I'll figure out a way.''

"The only thing you'll figure out, kiddo, is that my way is the only way. I'm in charge of things now, Jason. You can try to fight me all you like, but it's not gonna do a fucking bit of good. It's my body now, and I intend to hold onto it. But if you're nice to me, if you start treating me the way I deserve, you'll find I'm really not such a bad guy after all. Who knows, maybe if you play your cards right I might even untie the straps, let you walk around. I could've made it a whole lot worse, you know. Could've shoved you in a coffin like you did to poor Harry."

"I didn't kill Harry and neither did you. It was an accident."

"Accidentally on purpose, you mean."

He was laughing so hard I couldn't hear myself think. I strained against the leather thongs, feeling them cut deeply into my skin. But I knew how to tie knots and so did he. No matter how much I struggled there was no escape, no chance to free myself. And even if Warren decided to release me, how in the world was I going to get out of the cell and regain control of my body?

"There aren't any secrets between us, Jason, just remember that. I know just what's on your mind, every single thought. So don't think you can try any funny stuff, because it's not gonna work."

"You'll never get away with it. They'll find you out, and then you'll really be in trouble. You've put me in a cell, but sooner or later they're going to come and put you in one, too."

"That's a chance I'll just have to take. Besides, even if they put you away, Lefland, they're not gonna get me. I got plans, ole buddy, and no one's going to interfere. Not you, not your sister, not anyone."

He gave another yawn and closed his eyes, snuggling

under the covers. Sleep overcame me just as quickly. Though I wanted to stay awake and try to figure out what to do, I suddenly felt as tired as Warren. Despite the fact the chair was hard and uncomfortable and I was forced to remain upright, my head slumped against my chest and everything began to fade away into darkness.

"Sweet dreams, buddy boy," Warren whispered. "We're gonna need all the rest we can get, because tomorrow morning I intend to start giving them a show they'll never forget."

PART III

MASQUERADE

CHAPTER SEVENTEEN

Jason looked so much better the next morning I could hardly believe my eyes. It was as if he'd cast off all his fears, and was now ready to finally accept our new life on Ettinger Rock. His behavior, his very frame of mind, brought back memories of the Jason of old, long before the terrible events which had forced us to leave our home in the Valley.

I wasn't the only one who noticed how he had changed, for even Mr. Davies remarked how well my brother looked. When we finished breakfast and went upstairs to the schoolroom, Jason's behavior continued to astonish me. He seemed to be going out of his way to make amends, especially to Mr. Davies and Kenley. The playful and exuberant good humor I had seen so little of since Mother's death now returned to give a youthful bloom to his cheeks, a wonderful twinkling quality to his sharp green eyes.

He was alive again, that's the only way I could explain it. Even though I had no idea what had caused this transformation, I was so grateful to find him his old self that I decided not to press him for an explanation. In time I was certain he would come around and tell me himself, for the one thing I'd always been able to count on was the trust each of us placed in the other.

But if Jason was at last on the road to recovery—that is to say a return to emotional stability and peace of mind—there were still numerous other problems yet to be solved. Foremost among these was the business with the dollhouse and, as I reminded Kenley, the question of the locked room on the topmost floor of the house. How we would manage to gain entry to that room without his grandparents discovering what we were up to was something I gave a great deal of thought to in the days that followed. Although I had a good mind to come right out and ask Perdita why the door was locked, Kenley insisted I remain silent, as did Jason.

"No, we mustn't let them know what we're up to," Kenley said. "If they're hiding something up there, they're bound to get rid of it if we start asking too many questions."

"Hiding something or someone?" Jason asked.

Someone was by far the more ominous of the two. We'd gone down to the beach, ostensibly to go clamming, but actually to have a chance to talk things over without worrying about being overheard. The weather had gotten noticeably milder in the last few weeks, and as we waded out into the water it wasn't nearly as cold as I expected.

"Do you actually think someone is hiding in the house somewhere?" Kenley asked.

Jason shrugged. He bent down, retrieved a clam, and dropped it into the bucket.

"I honestly don't know," he admitted. "I know it sounds crazy, but it sure would explain a lot of things. Anyway I don't think we should discount it."

"Then why don't we sneak up there tonight, when

everyone's asleep?'' I suggested. ''After all, the longer we keep postponing it, the more chance they'll have to cover their tracks.''

''They?'' Kenley said, raising his eyebrows.

''Well, somebody's responsible for what's been going on. I mean, it's not a ghost.''

''I almost wish it were,'' my brother murmured.

Having explained to us what had happened at the campsite, Jason's laughter was soon cut short when we told him about the rockslide, and how we'd discovered the tassel from Nathaniel's muffler snagged on a branch not far from the cliff. Fearful for my safety, Jason even talked of leaving Ettinger Rock, though he gave it up when I reminded him we had no other place to go. I was even inclined to discuss the entire situation with Mr. Davies, but my brother vetoed that idea in no uncertain terms. Our tutor would probably go straight to the Ettingers, and if either of Kenley's grandparents were responsible for what was happening they might get nervous about being discovered and do something totally unexpected.

''Such as what?'' I asked my brother.

''Such as handing us over to Dad, that's what,'' he promptly replied. ''No, we have to keep everything to ourselves, Quinn. That's the only way.''

Although I reminded him that nothing unusual had occurred since the unhappy incident involving Becky—a subject over which he seemed to have purposely drawn a curtain—he said it was important not to let our guard down. Even now, as we half-heartedly attended to our clamming, his eyes swept the top of the cliff, as if he fully expected to find someone standing there, keeping tabs on our every move.

''What do you think, Kenley? Should we try to get in there tonight, or should we wait a little longer?'' he asked.

"I agree with Quinn. The sooner the better."

"Then it's settled," my brother told us. "Why don't we all meet in my room at say . . . one? Or is that too late?"

"One's fine," Kenley agreed. "Everyone'll be asleep by then."

With our pail half full of clams we waded back to the shore, dried our feet, and made our way to the house. In just a few hours we'd have an answer to at least one of our questions. And if we were lucky, it might just answer all of them.

Back in the Valley I used to listen to the great horned owls calling in the darkness. When night came sounds emerged from the shadows unlike any I heard during the day. Coyotes sent their sharp, frantic barks echoing through the scrub-covered hills, while poor-wills and crickets made their own mysterious music. But on Ettinger Rock there was an eerie silence to the nights, a silence punctuated by breaking waves and blowing winds, but not a single sound of life.

Alone in my room I listened intently, hoping to catch an owl's muffled wingbeat, or the raspy clicking of cicadas. That might have been a cricket I heard in the distance, but I couldn't be sure. The high keening winds that lashed the island drowned out all other sounds. And with the moon swathed in thick, stormy looking clouds, the shadows were impenetrable, a wall of black that hemmed us in on every side, like a fortress from which there was no escape.

Dread gathered in the corners of my mind, dread that soon gave way to fear and then to panic. Maybe we should just forget about that room, and the scent of Perdita's perfume I smelled the day I crouched in front of the door. Maybe certain things were best left undisturbed, without answers or solutions. But that was fear talking. We had to know what was there, even if it meant breaking into an absolutely empty room. That was what I hoped we'd find, not Bennett Lefland standing in the shadows, ready to take us back to the one place we were determined never to return to.

Of course we won't find him upstairs, I told myself when the panicky feeling I was experiencing threatened to get the better of me. Why, the very idea is ridiculous. Why would he want to hide from us? If he wanted us back he'd come and get us.

But in the past Father hadn't hesitated to do the unexpected, even the bizarre, and so perhaps my fears weren't nearly as foolish as they first seemed. In any event, I wasn't going to be alone. Kenley and Jason would be right beside me, so there was no danger of being forced to confront Father on my own.

Besides, he won't be there, I told myself again. Right now he's hundreds of miles away, too busy with the second Mrs. Lefland to even worry about what's become of us.

I kept repeating that to myself as I opened the door and slipped outside. Mr. Davies' room was just around the bend of the L-shaped hall. If he heard us and got up to investigate, our plan would be ruined. So I took every precaution to avoid making any noise. When I got to Jason's room I found the door ajar. For a moment I was afraid something had gone wrong, and I hesitated to push it open, frightened of what I might discover once I stepped inside. What if Nathaniel were there, or Miss Granberry, or even Mr. Davies, for that matter? How was I going to explain what I was doing up in the middle of the night?

Just say you couldn't sleep, I answered myself. I gave

the door a little push with the heel of my palm. It swung back, and Jason and Kenley immediately got to their feet, motioning me to silence.

"How long have you been waiting for me?" I whispered.

"Just a couple of minutes," Kenley replied.

"We ready?" Jason asked as he put on his robe.

"No, but I guess we don't have any other choice," I said with a nervous laugh, and I waited for him to lead the way.

Together the three of us tiptoed down the hall, mounting the stairs that led up to the attic. I kept looking over my shoulder, but no one was following us. From outside the wind continued to blow, and when I heard something bang I froze in my place, not knowing what it was.

"A loose shutter," Jason whispered, so sure of himself that I finally began to breathe a little easier.

I noticed both he and Kenley carried tools, one a hammer and the other a stout screwdriver with a thick and vicious looking blade. I wondered if they'd attempted to find the key, because if we broke inside there would be no way to repair the damage to the door. I reminded them of that when we reached the attic, but neither Kenley nor my brother seemed particularly concerned, more interested in getting inside the room than anything else.

"But if the door's broken, then how are we going to explain what happened?"

"I looked all over for the key. There has to be one, but it's disappeared," Kenley replied.

"Granberry keeps them on a ring in the kitchen, doesn't she?" Jason asked. "Did you check there?"

Kenley nodded.

"But I couldn't very well take the entire key ring without making her suspicious."

"What about under a doormat? Or above the door? Sometimes we kept keys there at home," I said.

"Gee, I didn't think of that," Kenley admitted.

So before we did anything else, the three of us slipped silently down the hallway, checking the narrow, shelflike lintels above each door. The only light came from a small overhead fixture, the opal glass shade spotty with dead flies and moths. The light it cast was very dim, and the shadows of the insects trapped under the glass made strange patterns across the walls and floor.

I suddenly became aware of the cold, as if someone had opened a window in one of the rooms. Although I was wearing a robe over my nightgown I couldn't stop shivering. Something clattered in the darkness, a sharp metallic sound.

"Well how do you like that," Kenley said with a laugh.

He held up a short, stubby key for our inspection, having found it above the sewing room door.

"Who's going to do the honors?" he asked, grinning at each of us in turn. "Quinn?"

I shook my head adamantly. I was already much more frightened than I cared to admit, and the idea of being the first inside the room was a distinction I could very well do without.

"It's your house, Kenley. Why don't you try it?" Jason told him.

My brother was shivering just as much as I was. I reached for his hand and gave it a comforting squeeze.

"Ready?" Kenley whispered as we crowded round him.

He inserted the key in the lock, and though I was secretly hoping it wouldn't fit, it slid right inside, meeting no obstructions. Kenley turned it, and as the door clicked open I felt an icy wind rushing down the hall. I glanced over my shoulder, but there was nothing there but our shadows, thrown up in lurid relief along the wall.

"We didn't bring a flashlight," Jason suddenly remembered.

"There's got to be a light switch. Every room has one," Kenley said.

He pushed the door open, though he made no move to step inside. I peered over his shoulder, but it was so dark I couldn't make anything out. Then something moved and my breath caught in my throat. White and ghostly, it fluttered in the air. Jason groaned in fear and stumbled back, so scared I thought his eyes would pop right out of his head.

"What the hell is that, anyway?" Kenley said, not nearly as frightened as my brother.

He took a hesitant step forward. Although Jason and I were reluctant to follow, we weren't about to let him go in there alone.

"Where's the light?" I said, barely able to get the words out I was so nervous.

"It should be on the wall near the door."

Blindly my hand swept back and forth, trying to locate the switch.

"Oh, it's only the curtains," Kenley exclaimed a moment later.

He started to laugh he was so relieved, then stopped abruptly when he realized he was making too much noise.

"What curtains?" I asked, still not convinced.

All I could see was this white thing waving at us in the darkness. It looked so much like a ghost—or what I've always imagined a ghost should look like—that I didn't want to take another step until I found the light switch.

Another hand suddenly pressed against my own, the fingers so cold that I jerked back. A bolus of fear clogged my throat, making it all but impossible to breathe.

"It's only me," Jason giggled.

I was so angry I wanted to shake him. But before I could say anything light flooded the room, harsh, cold incandescent light that turned the ghost into a pair of lacy white curtains. The window was half open, and the sharp, biting wind which blew inside sent them swirling through the air. I felt like an idiot, allowing myself to get so frightened for no reason at all.

"Don't tell me this is the big mystery," I murmured, taking care to keep my voice down, especially since Mr. Davies was asleep on the floor below.

There was absolutely nothing else in the room. As empty as its counterpart in the dollhouse, there was no sign that anyone had been here. Yet the window was open, and even then the shutter began to bang, making the same sound I'd heard earlier.

"Maybe they got away when they heard us at the door," Kenley whispered.

But there was no bed, no bedding, no clothes. Nothing in fact but the four bare walls. I glanced down at the floor, remembering the footprints Jason and I had discovered when we investigated the attic back home. But the hardwood floor had been swept clean. There was no dust, and thus no footprints to prove that someone had been here before us.

"What's that smell?" Kenley asked.

He sniffed loudly, like a bloodhound trying to follow a scent. Perfume, was that it? Maybe, but the violet fragrance wasn't nearly as strong as it was the last time I was up here. There was an underlying musky quality to what I smelled, and as we stood there it gradually became more and more unpleasant.

Jason went over to the window and peered outside. Satisfied no one was hiding on the ledge, he turned away. But as he looked back at us his eyes opened wide. He made a horrible choking sound in the back of his throat and started to gag. The next thing I knew he was down on his knees, unable to stop himself from retching.

I had no idea what was wrong, or why he'd suddenly gotten sick. I rushed over to help him, when he raised his hand and pointed behind me, his eyes straining in their sockets.

Kenley saw it just seconds before I did. If he hadn't clamped a hand over his mouth he would have awakened the entire household, because the anguished scream he managed to stifle came from the very depths of his being. It was a cry of pain and terrified disbelief, of unrelenting horror that I would never forget for as long as I lived.

"Dear God," he groaned.

Tears flooded my eyes. Held in the icy grip of something far worse than fear or panic, I stood there, unable to stop staring at what had caused my brother to become so violently ill.

"Don't look," Jason pleaded. "Please, Quinn, close your eyes."

He staggered to his feet and put his arms around me, trying to shield me from the monstrous cruelty that hung on the back of the door. It was Max, his chest laid open from neck to groin. There was no mistaking the dull glint of cracked and shattered ribs, the dark and fetid cavity where he had been disemboweled. Completely gutted, he hung there like a trophy, a wormy carcass a hunter brings home as proof of his marksmanship

When I eased free of Jason's protective embrace my first thought was of Kenley, standing in the middle of the room, the tears streaming down his cheeks. He couldn't stop sobbing, his grief so deep and unsettling I didn't know how to help him.

My brother put his arm around Kenley's trembling shoulders and urged him to turn away.

"It's all right, we're here. You're not alone," Jason whispered, trying his best to comfort him.

"But why? Why would someone do something like this? It's so cruel, Jason. It's so sick, so evil."

"I know it is, Kenley. But don't look anymore. Just try to remember him the way he was, but not like this. That isn't Max anymore. You have to keep telling yourself that. It's the only way."

"I can't," Kenley cried, sobbing more pitifully than ever.

Jason and I held him in our arms, forming a close-knit circle to ward off the horror none of us had expected to find here. We were children, sneaking upstairs in the middle of the night, playing at ghost-hunters and amateur detectives. The room was supposed to be empty. We would all laugh nervously, tell each other how ridiculous it was to be so frightened, and go back to bed. That was how it was supposed to be. But it hadn't turned out that way at all.

Max was dead, butchered, even his eyes plucked from their sockets. Something monstrously evil, something devoid of sanity, walked among us on Ettinger Rock. But there was nowhere to hide from it. Trapped on the island, there was no way to escape the twisted mind that had seen fit to kill a poor innocent animal. And not just kill it, but savage it so sadistically there could be not doubt as to the madness behind such a senseless act.

Kenley broke away from us. His èyes were wild, filled with rage I'd never even suspected him capable of. When he spoke his breath hissed between his teeth.

"I'm going to wake them up, every one of them!" he cried, his voice shrill and vindictive. "I'm going to make them come up here. And then whoever did this is going to admit it. Yes, they're going to tell me, right to my face."

He started for the door, but Jason managed to grab him before he stepped outside. My brother pulled him back into the room, holding onto him so he wouldn't try to run off.

"Listen to me," Jason said in a grave yet gentle tone of voice. "You can't do that. You can't let on that you know. We have to trap them, that's the only way."

"Trap them?" Kenley exclaimed. "But look what they did, Jason. Not only did they kill him, but they tortured him. They took his eyes out, for Christ's sake! They cut him open, and for all we know he could've been alive when they did it."

With a groan of anguish he buried his face in his hands, unable to stop crying. The tears filled my eyes all over again. It was agonizing to see him like this, and all I could do was hold him, whispering over and over that it would be all right.

"You take him downstairs, Quinn. I'll lock up."

"But what are you going to do about—?"

"I'll figure something out. You just take care of Kenley and leave the rest to me."

I nodded dumbly and led Kenley from the room.

"Remember," Jason called after me, "don't let him tell anyone. We can't let them know what we've found."

I wasn't sure if I fully understood his reasons, but there would be time enough in the morning to discuss what had happened. Slowly I led Kenley down the hall, pausing at the top of the stairs.

"I don't know what to say, Kenley. It doesn't just sicken me, it breaks my heart. I know how much you loved Max, how much he meant to you. But whoever did this is going to be punished. You've got to believe that."

Kenley raised his head, his brown eyes cloudy and unfocused.

"How can I even look at them, Quinn, knowing one of them is responsible?"

"It's going to be very difficult for you, I know. But Jason's right. Whoever did this isn't going to step forward and admit it. You know that as well as I do. So tomorrow we'll all sit down and talk it over, the three of us. We'll figure out a way to catch them."

Kenley nodded, drying his eyes with the sleeve of his robe.

"Who do you think it was, Quinn? Do you really think my grandfather could be capable of something like this?"

I didn't know what to tell him.

"You live with people and you think you know them." I shook my head helplessly. "But maybe you don't. Maybe they're really strangers."

Silently we retraced our steps, down the stairs and then down the long L-shaped hall that led to our rooms. I saw Kenley to his door, and when he put his arms around me I could feel his desperation as acutely as my own. There was terror in his embrace, a nameless dread of what the future held for us. But at least we had each other. No matter what might happen, at least we weren't alone.

CHAPTER EIGHTEEN

I saw it all, the whole horrible show. And he was so proud of himself I don't know how the monster faked it. He even made himself gag and start to puke. And then to be so comforting to poor Kenley, to pretend he was just as sickened and disgusted as the rest of us.

How could Warren have done such a thing? Max never bothered him, never got in his way, never even snapped at him like he did at Nathaniel. So why did he have to do this?

"Because I felt like it, Lefland. Because it made me feel real good inside. Besides, the little twirp deserved it."

"But what did Kenley ever do to you?"

"He kissed her, didn't he? For all we know they've already screwed each other. Acts like she's his girlfriend or something, the little prick. That's why he had to be punished."

"So you killed Max, is that it?"

"I didn't kill him, Jason. You did. With your famous stag-handled dirk. Don't you remember how the blood spurted over your fingers? Ohh, it was nice and hot, wasn't it," Warren said.

He was so excited just talking about it that I could feel him getting aroused. He went over to the door, glanced into the hall to make sure they'd gone, then rubbed his hand against Max's bloodstained flank.

"It felt great, Lefland. Like I had all this power, life and death, know what I mean? I was in charge of things, first time in my life. You should've heard the mutt scream, it was fantastic. Sounded just like a woman, honest to God."

Which woman? I wondered. Rebecca? Or maybe he was thinking of Quinn.

"One day I'll kill you, Warren."

"Then you'll have to kill yourself, Jason. And since I run the show, that's not going to be very easy."

I strained against the leather straps, but for all my efforts they remained as tight and unyielding as ever. He hadn't let me go yet, and at this rate I had a feeling he never would. Trapped upstairs in his head, confined to that cell in the darkest recesses of his mind, all I could do was watch him while he played out his sick and deadly fantasies.

"They're your fantasies too, don't forget," he reminded me.

But no, I wasn't going to fall into that trap of believing him. I was Jason, and for all my problems, and all the troubles I'd been through, I would never have imagined the kinds of things Warren was doing. But at least he was letting me see through his eyes. So even though I was stuck away in that room of his, helpless to prevent him from doing whatever he pleased, I wasn't blind to what was happening all around me.

When my sister and Kenley had gone, Warren lowered Max down from the hook on which he was suspended. The dog's body gave off a sickening, putrid stench that nauseated me, but it didn't seem to bother Warren in the least. If anything, he reveled in it as he laid Max's rigid carcass on the floor, then closed the window and looked around as if searching for clues.

"I want the room to look just the way I found it," he explained.

Satisfied that everything was as it should be, he hoisted Max over his shoulder, then made his way downstairs as quickly as he could. But instead of returning to my room—*our* room, as he made sure to remind me—he headed for the front door.

"What are you going to do now? Bury him?"

Perdita's perfume didn't do much good. Even though Warren had sprayed it over the Airedale, it did little to mask the rank and fetid smell of decomposition. Sick to my stomach, I kept gagging and choking back vomit every time I caught a whiff of it, unable to understand why it didn't effect Warren the same way.

"Well? Answer me! What are you going to do with the dog?" I yelled at him.

"Just watch the way you speak to me, Lefland. If you don't, I won't hesitate to tie a gag around your mouth. You be nice, you hear? I don't have to take any shit from you anymore, just remember that."

"Fine. Gag me. Come inside and show your face. I dare you."

"I'll come when I'm good and ready," Warren replied.

For the first time since he overpowered me I was able to detect a note of doubt, as if he weren't as sure of his strength as he'd led me to believe. Maybe that was the wedge I needed, the opening to get at him. If he unlocked the door and came into the cell, at least I'd have a chance to confront him face-to-face, instead of being forced to talk to a disembodied voice.

"What's the matter, Warren, are you scared? Afraid I might be stronger than you?"

"Shut up, Jason."

"I don't feel like it. I think I'll keep talking, for hours and hours and hours. You're just a frightened little bully, Warren, aren't you? You tied me up, so it's real easy for you to be brave. But if you were as strong as you say you are, you wouldn't have to worry about tying me to a chair. Or isn't the door to the cell strong enough?"

"I told you to shut your fucking mouth, Jason, and I mean it!"

Chill night air seeped into the cell. Even though there weren't any windows, it came in through the chinks in the stone walls and under the door. I started to shiver, wishing he'd at least throw a blanket over me. But he had other things on his mind. Max was getting heavy, and he laid the dog's body down on the ground and tried to catch his breath.

"Are you going to bury him or what?" I asked again.

"Who the hell wants to waste time digging a grave? Don't be an asshole, Lefland. I'll throw him over the cliff. Tide's up, anyway. He'll be carried out to sea and that'll be the end of him."

"And what will you tell Kenley in the morning?"

"I'll think of something. I always do."

My fingers were turning numb from the cold. I kept flexing them but it didn't do much good. The soles of his slippers were soaked through as he walked across the damp grass to the edge of the cliff. Between sky and water there was no distinction, no line dividing one from the other. Just a velvety blackness, thick and inky and alive with the sound of breaking waves.

"Here goes," Warren said.

He lifted Max high above his head, his muscles straining as he heaved him over the side of the cliff. He couldn't see the dog's body bouncing against the rocks, but when he heard a splash he began to giggle.

"If you don't watch yourself, Jason, you're going to be next."

"Kill me and you kill yourself," I reminded him.

"I've already killed you, dummy, or haven't you figured that out by now? You're just a voice between my ears, an annoying little voice that doesn't bother me in the least."

Maybe if I could stay awake after he fell asleep, I might be able to loosen the leather straps. But when he started to yawn I couldn't help but yawn, too. And when he slipped back into the house and hurried upstairs to his room, I felt his fatigue just as much as he did.

Stay awake, I kept telling myself as he washed up and got into bed, pulling the covers over his head. Don't fall asleep. Just keep your eyes open.

I started to count the stones that made up the wall directly in front of me. I went from left to right, counting out loud. But by the time I got to the fifth row my head was aching and I couldn't keep track of where I was. I tugged at the straps, raising and lowering my arms to try to loosen them. Was it my imagination, or was I finally making some headway? For the first time since he'd tied me up, I was able to move my arms off the arms of the chair. Not much, mind you. Probably not more than an inch. But an inch was better than nothing.

"Go to sleep, Lefland," he called out in the darkness. "We have a lot to do tomorrow."

"Such as what?"

"You'll see," he chuckled. "After all, if there's one thing you can say about me, it's that I'm not short on imagination."

The stones, keep counting them. Seventy-nine, eighty, eighty-one . . . my head was so heavy. The pillow was so soft. Sleep wrapped itself around me in a warm and comforting embrace. I shook myself out of my stupor, wrenching my arms up as hard as I could. One of the straps gave way and suddenly my left arm was free! I clawed at the leather thong which secured my other arm. I couldn't reach the knots, nor could I bend down to get my teeth around the leather.

"Sleep, Jason, sleep," he kept murmuring, his voice droning on and on.

God knows how hard I tried to stay awake. But I was drained of energy, and I couldn't keep my eyes open any longer.

"That's it, go to sleep, my little man. Sweet dreams, Jason."

But the only dreams I had were his, sick and disgusting pornographic nightmares that were the very essence of depravity. I couldn't block them out or make them go away, and so finally I had to resign myself to what was happening. For the time being he was still in charge. But I didn't intend to give up, even if it cost me my life. Because if it did, at least I'd have the satisfaction of knowing it would cost Warren his life, too.

Warren did a lot of fast talking the next morning, fooling everyone he came in contact with. Quinn and Kenley swallowed everything he told them. As far as they knew Max was still in the attic, because Warren told them that sooner or later the person responsible for killing him would sneak upstairs to admire his handiwork. That's why he suggested they all take turns keeping watch on the room, just as I had done weeks earlier.

When Quinn said the sewing room across the hall would be a perfect hiding place, Warren didn't hesitate to go along with her. As for Kenley, I think he was still in shock, though I had to admit he was handling things a lot better than I would have expected. His anger, his sense of outrage, seemed to give him great inner strength, and I really admired him for it. The kid was a fighter, earning my respect—and Warren's hostility—as he never had before.

Then there was Mr. Davies, whom Warren referred to as Mr. Button-Down Brain. When lessons were over he managed to take Warren aside and started asking him all sorts of questions, like how he was feeling and if he liked living here on the island and stuff like that. I'd always known he was nosy, but Warren seemed to relish being cross-examined. He acted like Davies was his new best friend, even more of a buddy than Mr. Houghton. I don't know how he pulled it off, but he did, because by the time they finished talking he had Davies eating out of the palm of his hand.

To tell you the truth, I didn't pay that much attention to their conversation. Now that Warren was distracted, it was the perfect opportunity for me to get the rest of the leather bindings undone before he realized what I was up to. My right arm was still pinned down to the arm of the wooden chair, but with my left free I managed to untie my ankles. Now that my legs were free I was able to swivel around on the seat, and slowly but surely succeeded in loosening the last of the leather straps.

I was so stiff and sore from having been forced to sit there that it took awhile before I was able to walk around without my knees turning to jelly. Finally my legs were able to support me, and I began a slow and methodical circuit of the cell, trying to figure a way out.

The only source of illumination was an unshaded bulb high above my head. But at least the light was strong enough for me to make out my surroundings. The stone walls were damp and clammy to the touch, and even though I knew the sun was high, the cell existed in a kind of nether world of perpetual twilight. But by now my eyes were adjusted to the dim light. I moved from one wall to the next, searching for a break in the masonry. Earlier, I'd seen a door, a heavy iron one with a peephole at eye level through which I'd already caught Warren spying on me. Yet now that I was free to investigate the cell I couldn't find it. But if there wasn't a door, then how had he managed to wall me up inside this room?

Apparently, reality was something Warren could bend and twist merely by the strength of his will. Perhaps I could do the same. I returned to the chair, sat back and concentrated on the wall directly in front of me. I squeezed my eyes shut, drawing up a picture of a door, one with a judas hole and old rusty hinges. But if I was going to the trouble of imagining a door, why not one that stood wide-open?

I opened my eyes, but all I saw were the stones set in the wall. Then I felt something in my back pocket, something that hadn't been there before. Much to my surprise it was the knife with the antler handle, the same knife Warren had used when he'd taken Max into the woods.

I jumped to my feet and ran over to the wall. I *had* to find a way to escape. I sat down on the floor and used the blade of the dirk to chip away at the loose, crumbling mortar between the stones. I had no idea how thick the walls were, but I wasn't going to let that worry me. At least I had hope now. I would remove the stones one by one and then tunnel my way to freedom.

I set to work with a vengeance.

Either Warren was getting careless, or he had other things on his mind. All morning I worked at removing the stones, and not once did he try to interfere. He was so busy charming everyone that he didn't pay any attention to me at all. That was fine with me, but I was still curious to know what he was up to.

So finally, when my hands felt like they were about to break off at the wrists, they were so tired, I leaned back against the wall and started listening to what was going on.

"I'd really like that, Nathaniel," he was saying. "I'll just run upstairs and put on a sweater. I won't be a minute."

"I'll meet you down by the dock," Ettinger told him as he headed to the door.

"Where are we going?" I asked when he got upstairs to our room and started rummaging through the dresser drawers. "The sweater's hanging on a hook in the closet. Don't tell me you forgot?"

"I didn't forget anything," he said with annoyance.

Was he losing his memory? I couldn't be certain, but if he started to forget things then maybe I wasn't as vulnerable as I imagined.

"Don't count on it," he said, able to hear everything I was thinking. "And don't think I don't know what you're doing, either. You'll never get out of there, Lefland, no matter how hard you try. You know how thick those walls are?"

"Don't tell me, Warren. I'd rather be surprised."

He laughed out loud.

"Oh, you'll be surprised all right."

He pulled the crewneck sweater over his head, combed his hair back with his fingers and raced downstairs. Nathaniel had some errands to run in Otter Bay, and Warren hadn't hesitated to accept his invitation to accompany him to the mainland. I'd managed to remove one of the stones, but now it seemed more important to keep an eye on my nemesis. There was no telling what Warren might do, and I had no intention of sitting back and letting him use me for whatever twisted purposes he had in mind.

"Stop worrying, Lefland. We're just gonna take a nice little boat ride, that's all."

But no sooner did they head off in the direction of the mainland when he started asking Nathaniel all sorts of questions, like why he never talked about Kenley's parents, and how come no one had ever found their bodies or figured out what happened to them.

"It's a very painful subject, Jason. I'd rather not discuss it, if you don't mind," Nathaniel said stiffly.

Warren and I could both hear the anger behind his words, anger that made me more than a little suspicious.

"You think someone murdered them?" Warren blurted out.

Ettinger had given Warren the wheel, but now he suddenly wrenched it out of his hands. For a moment I thought he was going to turn around and head back to the island, but then he seemed to think better of it and continued to maintain his course.

"I don't know what gave you that idea, unless of course you've been speaking to my grandson."

"It's curious though, isn't it?" Warren went on, completely unintimidated by Nathaniel's irritated tone of voice. "You and your son have this big argument, and the next thing you know he and his wife disappear, just like that," he said, snapping his fingers.

"Is that what Kenley told you?"

Nathaniel was getting more and more annoyed, but Warren was having such a good time baiting him he didn't want to stop.

"He talked to Quinn about it, not me."

"And then she discussed it with you?"

"More or less," Warren replied.

There was the faintest hint of smugness in his voice, but I was sure Nathaniel couldn't hear it.

"I've lived a long time, Jason, seventy-some-odd years. I've raised a family, had a career, tried to make some sense out of this ridiculous business they call life. If there's one thing I've learned it's that we're not pawns, or victims of fate, or however you wish to describe it. A man makes decisions and then has to live with the consequences. I could have spent the last two years blaming myself for my son's death, but that would have served no purpose. Yes, we had an argument, a very terrible one in fact."

Any second now I expected Warren to start badgering him for particulars, but for the moment he managed to keep his mouth shut.

"And if we hadn't argued, he and his wife wouldn't have left so precipitously. But they did, and I was so angry that day I had no desire to stop them. And they had an accident. An *accident*, Jason.''

"You don't have to convince me, Nathaniel. I believe you.''

Nathaniel's eyes, bluish-gray like the water which surrounded us, searched Warren's face, staring so intently I was surprised Warren didn't turn away. But instead of flinching he stared right back, a cocky grin plastered across his lips.

Was the old man lying? I didn't think so, but Warren wasn't nearly as convinced.

"Why don't you leave him alone and forget about it?" I asked.

"Because he's just like Benny, a fucking liar from the word go.''

"He's an old man, Warren. Don't you think he's suffered enough?''

"No one suffers enough, Jason. Not you, not me, not anyone. There's always room for a little more hurt, a little more pain. And I'm just the guy to give it.''

"To whom?" I asked.

"To everyone.''

I sat down on the floor of the cell, pulled out my knife, and went back to work removing stone number two. From the way Warren was talking I knew that time was running out.

"I'm here to pick up the mail for Ettinger Rock.''

Nathaniel had gone off to the general store, having sent Warren over to the post office to collect the mail. It wasn't much more than a weathered clapboard shack, divided in two by a long wooden counter. Behind this partition the postmistress held court, a mousy-haired woman with a wen on her nose like the witch in *Snow White*.

"On whose authority?" she asked.

I knew she was only trying to make a joke. But Warren had no sense of humor and so he figured she was serious.

"If you don't believe me, ask Mr. Ettinger. He's in the general store. Do you want me to bring him here or what?" he said sharply.

"That won't be necessary, young man."

The postmistress turned away in a huff, and when she returned she had a stack of mail half a foot high. Warren snatched it off the counter and didn't even bother to say thanks. Then he headed for the door.

As soon as we got outside, he started flipping through the mail like he fully expected to find something addressed to him.

"What are you looking for?"

"Evidence."

"What are you talking about, Warren?"

"Don't start acting dumb, Lefland. You know damn well."

His fingers moved more quickly, past bills and garden catalogues and copies of *Time* magazine, insurance brochures and pitches for this charity and that.

"Maybe now you'll start believing me," he said when he found what he was looking for.

It was a letter addressed to Mr. Davies, and though there was no return address, and nothing suspicious about the Los Angeles postmark, Warren removed it from the pile and hurriedly stuck it under his sweater.

"Why'd you go and do that for?" I asked.

"You'll see."

Those two little words sounded so ominous that I redoubled my frantic efforts to pry the stones from the wall. I had to get out before Warren fulfilled whatever course of madness he had already embarked upon. Because if I couldn't stop him in time, it might be too late for both of us.

Mr. Ettinger suggested they grab a quick lunch before heading back to the island. Warren excused himself to wash up, and as he walked through the dining room of the Otter Bay Inn, he told me he was finally going to get some answers.

The moment he locked himself in the men's room he couldn't get at the letter fast enough. I kept telling him to wait till we got back so he could steam the envelope open. That way he could glue the flap down and Mr. Davies would never be the wiser. But Warren was in too big a hurry. He tore off one end of the plain white envelope and pulled out the folded sheet of paper he found inside.

"Dear Dr. Davies . . ."

Doctor Davies? But how could that be?

"Your last progress report left me greatly encouraged," the letter began. "Although I've tried to express my profound gratitude to the Ettingers for agreeing to this unorthodox plan, words alone cannot convey the extent to which I am in their debt. Without their consent, your presence on the island would be an impossibility, and any hope for my son's continued improvement would be all but nonexistent."

"What the hell is going on here, Warren?"

"Let's keep reading, Lefland. We'll find out."

"The only suggestion I might make is that you continue the course of treatment you discussed in your last letter. Therapy in such a non-therapeutic environment must surely present a unique challenge, but Dr. Warren assures me that if anyone on his staff can accomplish miracles, it's you. As long as the children never discover the real purpose behind your unexpected arrival—Yes, that was rather sticky, I agree, though Houghton has been amply compensated and is quite content in his new position—I don't foresee any further difficulties.

"When and if the desired breakthrough occurs, and I keep praying it will happen sooner than any of us dare to expect, it might be wise to finally let Quinn in on our arrangement. Despite all you've written to me about her, I'm far less concerned for her mental state than my son's. Quinn's emotional difficulties can't be dismissed, but neither are they rooted in mental illness. Others of your profession may argue that schizophrenia is a disorder for which no cure can possibly exist. But as long as there's a breath left in my body, I refuse to believe that.

"Sincerely yours, Bennett Lefland."

The paper crackled like fire, singeing our skin. Warren's fingers tightened convulsively. I could feel him getting redder and redder, and if he weren't careful he'd soon lose control completely.

"You wouldn't believe me, Lefland, would you?" he shouted. "You wanted to be just like Quinn, giving everyone the benefit of the doubt. But I *never* doubted he was a spy. Have you already forgotten what he said to the old lady?"

No, I hadn't forgotten, and now the conversation I'd overheard between Davies and Perdita began to make sense.

My husband and I are concerned . . . that Jason will find out you're really a psychiatrist.

I'll be monitoring them very carefully . . . just in case Jason shows signs of going off the deep end.

Experimental teaching methods . . . is just a nice, polite way of describing a shrink who poses as a tutor.

"But you're forgetting one thing, Warren, maybe the most important thing of all," I reminded him. "If Dad's gone to all this trouble, doesn't that say something about him you've never accepted before?"

"Such as what?" Warren asked suspiciously.

"Such as maybe he really does care about us, more than we ever thought."

"The only thing he cares about is getting rid of us. And the sooner you start believing that, the better."

"But if all he wanted to do was stick us away in a hospital, he would've already done it by now. Don't you see that?"

Warren didn't answer. He stuffed the crumpled sheet of paper into his pocket and returned to the dining room. I don't know how he managed to get through lunch, because every time he took a bite the food got stuck in his throat.

"I thought you were hungry," Nathaniel remarked, noticing how Warren hardly touched his lunch.

"Stomach's a little queasy. Guess I'm still a landlubber at heart." He tried to laugh, but he was so upset by what he'd read that what came out of his mouth sounded more like a whimper. "Do you think we could head back now?"

"Of course. I didn't realize you weren't feeling well. Just let me take care of the check and we'll be on our way."

Ten minutes later the nose of the launch was pointed straight at Ettinger Rock, a faint, greasy smudge so far in the distance it looked like it would take forever to get there. Warren was huddled in a corner of the bow, his arms wrapped around his knees. He was talking silently to himself, and the things I heard him say were so scary and I didn't know what to do.

For a moment I put down my knife and started pounding on the wall, begging him to let me out. But it was as if I weren't even there. He paid absolutely no attention to me, thinking about the letter he'd read, and the way he would soon take care of Dr. Davies.

It was late afternoon, and though dusk was still an hour away, the sky kept darkening and Mr. Ettinger said he could smell a squall. The launch was at full throttle, but the increasingly heavy swells cut down on our speed, and it was all he could do just to maintain our course.

"You want to give me a hand here, Jason?"

"Not particularly," Warren muttered to himself.

"I'm sorry, I can't hear you," Nathaniel shouted, trying to make himself heard above the clamor of waves which broke against the bow.

The launch rolled and pitched like a bronco trying to unseat its rider. Warren reached up and grabbed onto the safety rail. He hauled himself to his feet, and as the boat continued to battle its way through the breakers it pitched starboard and he was sent crashing against the wheel.

"Just hold on tight and you'll be fine," Nathaniel advised.

He was less concerned about the weather than Warren, and kept his eyes peeled straight ahead, trying not to lose sight of the island.

"We'll get back before it really turns ugly. I've been through worse, believe me. This is just a typical spring storm, nothing to get concerned agout."

Warren was still too busy thinking about the letter to pay any attention. His mood was even darker than the weather, and when he finally blurted out what was on his mind his voice was like a raw wound, his words dripping with blood.

"Why'd you lie to me about Davies?" he demanded, taking Mr. Ettinger completely by surprise. "He's no teacher; he's a fucking psychiatrist, sent here by my father to spy on me."

"I don't know what you're talking about, Jason. Whatever gave you that idea?"

There was panic in the old man's voice, and Warren seized upon it with a laugh.

"This letter, that's what!" he screamed.

He pulled out the crumpled sheet of paper and rammed it in Nathaniel's face, shoving him back with all his might.

"Warren, don't!" I pleaded.

"You're dead, Jason, so just stay out of this."

Nathaniel's fingers slipped off the wheel, and the next thing I knew he'd fallen back onto the deck.

"Jason, please, I beg of you. You'll get us killed," he cried out.

But Warren wasn't listening to anyone but himself. He threw himself on top of Mr. Ettinger, pinning the old man's arms down with his knees. Nathaniel was scared to death, and I was afraid he'd have a heart attack. His eyes were bulging with fear, and all the blood had drained out of his face. His skin was so gray he looked dead already, and he started panting like he couldn't breathe.

"You murdered your son and now you want to murder me, don't you?" Warren shrieked. "I know what you're thinking. Poor crazy Warren, I'll just shove him overboard, tell everyone he fell out of the boat and got lost at sea. But I'm not gonna let you. You got away with murder once, but you're not gonna be so lucky the second time."

277

"Jason, please, you've got to believe me," Nathaniel groaned.

"I wouldn't believe you if my life depended on it. You're just like all the others, fucking liars trying to hurt me, send me to that place they tried to put my mom. But I'm too smart for them. I put Jason where I wanted him and now I'm gonna put you there, too."

By then I was screaming at Warren, pounding on the wall and begging him to let Ettinger go. We were already straying from our course, and if Nathaniel didn't take over the wheel we might not make it back before the storm broke.

"You forget, he showed me what to do. I can get us back without any sweat," Warren assured me.

He grabbed Nathaniel by the collar and hauled him to his feet. Both of them were soaking wet, their clothes as heavy as lead. Nathaniel clawed at him, trying to break free. But Warren relished the way the old man was putting up a struggle, and held on even more tightly than before. The launch pitched violently, and suddenly the two of them were tumbling across the deck, rolling back and forth as each successive wave butted against the bow. Water poured over them, making it all but impossible to regain their footing. Mr. Ettinger was shouting, but I couldn't hear what he was saying. Warren still held onto him, and as the boat leaped and plunged through the angry swells, he shoved Nathaniel up against the safety rail, trying to push him over the side.

Stones shattered beneath my fists. I was breaking out of my cell, and I slammed myself into the wall, feeling it crack like an eggshell. Again and again I threw my weight against the stones, trying to make good my escape before Warren could stop me.

He knew what I was doing, but faced with the choice of dealing with me or dealing with Nathaniel, he chose the latter. Ettinger was screaming into the face of the wind, his words lost in the gathering storm. Warren's hands slipped lower, locking around the old man's knees. As the launch tipped in their direction he wrenched Nathaniel's feet off the deck and sent him toppling backwards to disappear below the waves.

"Grab him, Warren! Throw out a life line!" I screamed.

I was outside the cell, yet instead of freedom I found myself in a corridor, one that stretched endlessly in both directions. I had no idea which way to turn, and so I just stood there, screaming at Warren and begging him to listen to me. The life ring was just a few feet away. Warren pulled himself along the railing and managed to reach it just as Mr. Ettinger came up above the water, choking and coughing but still very much alive.

"Throw it to him!" I shrieked.

The life preserver went sailing out across the choppy water. Struggling to stay afloat, Nathaniel made a desperate attempt to reach it. From where we stood on the deck we could see his hand stretching out to the ring as it bobbed up and down not more than a foot away from him.

"Closer, closer, you can do it!" I was yelling, hearing my words coming out of Warren's mouth for the first time since he'd taken control.

Nathaniel's fingers caught the ring. His hand tightened around it when suddenly a wave came crashing down on top of him. The water foamed and bubbled as if it were boiling.

"Hold on!" I begged.

His head slipped below the churning water. For a moment I was sure he was going to be all right, but then he lost his grip on the life ring. I rushed back to the control console and cut the engine, but by then he was nowhere in sight. I searched for him until my eyes grew bleary, burning from the saltwater. But he never came up again. Despite everything I'd tried to do, Warren had gotten his way.

Like his son and daughter-in-law, Nathaniel Ettinger had drowned at sea. Only this time it was a matter of murder. How in God's name was I going to convince everyone it wasn't my fault?

CHAPTER NINETEEN

The darkening sky was a mirror reflecting Kenley Ettinger's unhappy mood. Late that afternoon we sat on the dock, eyes on the wind-tossed waves and the storm clouds building up ominously in the east. On clear days one could catch a faint glimpse of the mainland, far off in the distance. But now it lay hidden behind an impenetrable scrim of mist and low-lying fog, fog whose chill, wet tendrils were already moving up along the beach.

Despite my sweater and parka, I still felt cold. The day's warmth had vanished, replaced by sharp and biting winds which stung my cheeks. Kenley saw me shiver and put his arm around me as the two of us waited for the launch to return from Otter Bay.

"We don't have to wait for them, you know," I reminded him. "We can go back to the house if you'd like."

Kenley shook his head, his dark eyes as moist as the winds which sent whitecaps surging up along the rocky shore.

"It's Max, isn't it?" I asked, broaching a subject I knew was terribly painful, yet one I sensed he wanted to talk about. "I know how upset you are, Kenley, but you can't expect it to go away overnight. It's going to take time, just like it did with your parents."

As he held me in the crook of his arm I saw the grief that was written so clearly on his face. I put my hands on his cheeks, feeling the faintest suggestion of stubble. He and Jason had only recently begun to shave, and though I imagined they took great pride in what they undoubtedly saw as an act of manliness, I still thought of them as boys, playing at being grownups.

"You can't change what happened, Kenley. It's too late for that. All we can do now is try to find out who's responsible."

"Before he left this afternoon, Jason said he was going to speak to my grandfather, sort of feel him out and see what he could come up with." He glanced out across the water, and when he looked back at me there was even more uncertainty and confusion in his expression than before. "What's taking them so long? They should've been back an hour ago."

"They'll be here, don't worry," I tried to assure him. "Your grandfather's an expert sailor, you told me so yourself."

"But if the storm breaks—"

He left the rest unsaid, but I could see worry written all over his face. Max was still in the attic, and though each of us had taken turns earlier in the day keeping guard in the sewing room directly across the hall, no one had tried to sneak upstairs.

I knew that Kenley suspected his grandfather, but I really couldn't believe it was possible. Although there were many unanswered questions regarding the accident which had claimed his parents' lives, I still strongly doubted that

Nathaniel could have sent them to their death. And I found it just as unlikely that he'd had anything to do with the hideous mutilation and killing of the dog. But if Nathaniel weren't responsible—and I was convinced he wasn't—then who was?

"There they are, and just in time, too," Kenley called out.

He raised his hand and pointed to the launch, finally visible through the mist.

"Who's that at the wheel, can you see?" I asked.

"Doesn't look like Grandpa, does it?"

Suddenly the sky opened. The rain came down in thick surging sheets, and in less time than it took to get to our feet we were both soaking wet.

"Why don't you go back to the house and dry off?" Kenley suggested.

"I can't get much wetter than I already am," I laughed. "So I might as well stay and help them unload."

By then I could make out Jason standing at the wheel. He gestured frantically, waving his arm from side to side to try to attract our attention. He was shouting something, but he was still too far off to make himself heard.

Kenley stood by the end of the dock, ready to tie up the launch the moment she came in. He seemed oblivious to the rain, and never once took his eyes off the boat. But where was Nathaniel? I searched in vain, but saw no sign of him. Maybe he was sitting in the bow, trying to keep dry. Sure, that was it. He was probably huddling under a tarp while Jason steered the launch up to the dock.

Thick, hail-like pellets of rain continued to descend. My clothes clung to my skin, and beads of icy water dripped into my eyes and over my cheeks. The wind-driven rain came down with ever increasing force, muffling the boom of the waves, breaking over the rocks.

The end of the narrow pier was already awash with water. It moved beneath us, swaying violently as the sea battered against it. Kenley begged me to go back to the house, but by now the launch was just a few yards away.

My brother cut the engine and threw the painter onto the dock, where Kenley retrieved it before it was washed over the side. Jason was shouting, but I still couldn't hear what he was trying to say. After hurriedly tying up the launch, Kenley reached down and gave him his hand, helping Jason onto the dock. My brother was shivering uncontrollably, barely able to speak.

"Accident . . . grandfather . . . went over . . . the side," he said in halting tones, gasping as if he were out of breath.

My eyes darted back to the launch. Where was Nathaniel? Had something happened to him? Was he hurt, was that it?

"Where's my grandfather?" Kenley shouted, trying to make himself heard above the ear-splitting roar of the storm.

"Accident . . . went over the side . . . both of us . . . I climbed back in but . . . I looked everywhere . . ."

No, this wasn't happening. This wasn't true. I wasn't hearing him correctly, that's what it was. The words didn't make sense, and I grabbed my brother by the arm and pulled him along the dock, urging him back in the direction of the house.

The narrow trail that zigzagged up the side of the cliff was a river of mud. Kenley kept asking my brother what had happened, but it was all any of us could do just to maintain our footing. I slipped and fell flat on my face, felt someone pull me to my feet, only to lose my balance all over again.

"What happened to him!" Kenley yelled at the top of his voice.

I glanced back. He'd grabbed my brother by the arms, shaking him as he tried to get Jason to explain himself.

"The storm . . . this enormous wave came up. We didn't see it in time. It just lifted us off our feet and sent us over the side. When I came up I started calling to him, but he didn't answer. I swam all around the boat trying to find him. But he never came up again, Kenley. I climbed back in and cut the engine, but by then he was gone."

This wasn't happening, I thought again. It couldn't be. If Jason had managed to haul himself to safety, then why hadn't Nathaniel? Had he struck his head when he went over the side? But even if he had, wouldn't my brother have spotted him floating in the water? Surely someone who was unconscious didn't just sink like a stone. What about the air in a person's lungs? That would keep him buoyant for at least a couple of minutes, wouldn't it?

I clawed my way up the trail, hauling myself inch by inch over the muddy scree. I couldn't stop my teeth from chattering, and my jaws began to ache as if someone had punched me in the mouth. I wasn't able to see very much of anything either, forced to keep my head down while I negotiated the path.

By the time I reached the top and saw the lights of the house glowing cheerfully through the rain, the reality of what had happened finally began to take hold. When Perdita opened the front door and saw the three of us standing there, I think she realized instantly what was coming, even before any of us said a word.

Kenley put his arms around her, trying to soften the

blow, but she pulled roughly away from him and stared at my brother, at once horrified and incredulous. She didn't seem to know what to say or what to do. Her fingers tore at her curly gray hair, tugging at it as if she needed to feel pain to prove to herself she wasn't dreaming.

"What are you saying to me?" she began to scream. "He was a good swimmer, a strong swimmer. He knew the sea like the back of his hand. You're not saying he drowned? You can't say that to me, Jason. I won't allow it. I won't hear of it!"

Miss Granberry must have heard her cries, as did Mr. Davies. A moment later the two of them hurried into the vestibule where we were all crowded together, wet and shivering and still very much in a state of shock.

"Why was he so stubborn? The errands could have waited another day. He must've known a storm was brewing, so why did he insist on going out?"

Tears streamed down Perdita's cheeks, but she paid no attention to them. Her voice hoarse and accusing, she demanded that Jason tell her exactly what had happened, questioning him so closely it seemed to me that she didn't believe my brother's story. But why would Jason lie about a thing like this? He too was crying now, clutching Perdita's hands and begging her to believe him, it was just as he described.

Finally she couldn't take anymore. Always so lively and good-natured, as quick with a joke as with a compliment, Kenley's grandmother had grown old before my eyes. The woman that Miss Granberry led away bore little resemblance to the woman I had come to love, trusting Perdita as I had once trusted my own mother. Sobbing pitifully, she dragged her feet across the floor, leaving behind a trail of tears to mark her grief.

"You're sure you didn't see him?" Davies asked as soon as Perdita was out of sight. "Maybe the current carried him off. Maybe he's still out there."

Jason shook his head.

"I looked everywhere, Mr. Davies," he said miserably. "But the swells . . . you can't believe how rough it was. They must've been six, seven feet high. They just tossed us around like a bottle, like we didn't weigh anything at all. One minute we were standing there by the wheel, trying to hold onto our course, and the next it was all I could do just to keep my head above water."

"But he could still be out there," Davies said again.

He glanced behind him in the direction of the library, and Kenley seemed to know what he was thinking even before Mr. Davies said anything.

"I'll try to get through to Otter Bay. Maybe they can send out the Coast Guard."

"But how will they know where to look?" I asked.

"Grandpa used to say there was only one way to get to Otter Bay. Just draw a straight line between the Bay and the Rock and then follow your nose."

I knew he was clutching at straws, but unless a search party combed the waters between Ettinger Rock and the mainland there would be no way to know for sure if Nathaniel had drowned.

"Are you all right?" Davies asked my brother.

Jason lowered his eyes, watching the water drip from his clothes to form a puddle at his feet.

"How can I be all right when he's dead?" he replied, his voice choked with emotion. "He was so good to me and Quinn, and now he's just . . . just . . ."

Jason covered his face with his hands, sobbing that he

blamed himself. He should have stayed out in the storm and kept looking, instead of finally giving up.

"You mustn't be so hard on yourself," Davies told him, putting a fatherly arm around my brother's trembling shoulders. "You did everything you could, Jason. It was an accident. At least be grateful you're still alive."

I reached for his hand, and as his fingers clutched at mine I urged him to follow me upstairs. I was anxious that he get into some dry clothes. But no sooner did we reach the second-floor landing and were safely out of Mr. Davies' earshot, when my brother turned to me and revealed something he hadn't dared to mention earlier.

"It was him, Quinn. He was the one. We had lunch at the inn and he decided to have a drink, said he hadn't had a martini at lunch since he could remember. Only one wasn't enough. He had to have another, and then another after that. I knew he was getting drunk but there was nothing I could do."

"Are you saying that's why you had the accident?" I asked, Jason's story taking me completely by surprise.

"No, you don't understand," he whispered, fearful of being overheard. He dragged me up the stairs to the third floor, our wet clothes weighing us down and making it difficult to move quickly. "We were heading back home when he started bragging about what he'd done."

"What do you mean?"

"Max," my brother said.

I looked at him in horror.

"My God, you can't mean that, Jason. Do you know what you're saying?"

"He was the one who said it, Quinn, not me."

He glanced nervously about, then hurried down the hall

to his room. Once he closed the door he began to pour out his story, repeating everything Nathaniel had told him.

"He was drunk, that's what did it. I don't even think he realized what he was saying, Quinn."

It wasn't shock that made me shudder, so much as disbelief.

"It can't be true, Jason. It just can't."

My brother shivered and said, "I didn't want to believe it either, but after what he told me I knew he couldn't be lying. He knew exactly how Max was killed, even the way he was blinded. And the business with the dollhouse—he knew all about that, too."

Jason pulled his sweater over his head and tossed it on the floor. His shirt was plastered to his skin, and he quickly unbuttoned it and added it to the pile of wet clothes.

"He said Max was getting on his nerves, always barking and snapping and making a nuisance of himself. He said he blamed it all on Kenley; his grandson was too disrespectful and had to be taught a lesson. I knew he was crazy, Quinn, but what could I do? I was afraid he might try to hurt me, so I just kept quiet and let him do all the talking."

I started to sit down on the edge of the bed, then thought better of it. I was cold and wet, but that seemed the least of my problems. After what Jason had told me I didn't know what to do, or even what to think. How could Mr. Ettinger have done such things? It was inconceivable. I needed some time to myself to sort things out, to try to make sense of what had happened.

Jason made a move to unbutton his fly and I turned my head away, grateful that he didn't chide me for being shy.

He peeled off his jeans and wrapped himself in his robe, then added his socks to the pile.

"I'll take everything down to the laundry room," I told him.

"You better get out of those wet things yourself."

"I will," I promised, barely knowing what I was saying.

"It's never been very easy for us, Quinn, has it?"

"No, it never has."

The tears I hadn't shed for Nathaniel suddenly filled my eyes. What was going to happen to us now? I wondered. Would Perdita ask us to leave? Would Jason tell her what her husband had said before his death?

"You mustn't say anything about this," I blurted out.

I bent down and picked up my brother's clothes, waiting for him to answer.

"No, of course not."

"Because there's no need for her to know, Jason. It would only hurt her, and there's no point to it."

I started to the door.

"Are you going to tell Kenley?" he called after me.

"I guess I'll have to." I glanced back. "What should we do about Max?" I whispered.

"I'll take care of it. As soon as the rain lets up."

I dropped the pile of clothes and ran back to him, burying my face against his chest.

"Oh, Jason, why do these things have to happen? Why can't everything be the way it should?"

"Because it's in the blood," I thought I heard him say.

I drew back, staring at him as if to reassure myself he wasn't a stranger.

"What is?" I asked.

He shook his head.

"Nothing. I barely know what I'm saying." He managed to find a way to smile. "We'd better change our clothes. No sense catching our death of cold."

He was still standing there, smiling confidently, as I turned and hurried out.

By the time I changed my clothes and went downstairs to the laundry room, all those emotions I hadn't allowed myself to feel were finally coming to the surface. Yet there remained an air of unreality about what had happened. I still couldn't believe Nathanial wasn't coming back. I just refused to. Any minute now he'd come through the front door, grumbling about the weather, and what an old fool he was, not to have worn his slicker.

That was all in my head, of course, my imagination. There was an awful stillness to the house, as if each of us had already gone into mourning. All I could hear was the rain, coming down even harder than before.

I put the clothes down on the laundry room counter, mechanically going through pockets before shoving everything in the hamper. For a moment I thought it was a pack of cigarettes, but Jason didn't smoke. I pulled the crumpled ball of wet paper out of his pocket, and was about to toss it away when I caught a glimpse of typewritten letters, the ink bleeding through the paper. I smoothed it out on the counter, and when I saw the salutation my eyes locked onto it. I found myself reading it over and over, not being able to believe my eyes.

Dear Dr. Davies . . .

I must have read the letter three or four times before it finally began to sink in. So what Jason had worried about all along was true. Mr. Davies wasn't a tutor, he was a psychiatrist, sent here to treat my brother. Kenley had suspected his grandparents were in contact with my father,

though when he told me about the phone calls he'd overheard I didn't really believe they had anything to do with
him. But now I realized how naive I was to think we had
succeeded in escaping the horrors we had tried so desperately
to leave behind. Father would never leave us alone. Never.

*"I understand what you're trying to accomplish, Davies.
But it's my opinion the whole thing has already gotten out
of hand."*

That's what Nathaniel had said after Jason chased him
through the woods, convinced he meant to harm Becky.
But surely he did mean to harm her, for after what my
brother had told me I knew that Mr. Ettinger was hopelessly insane. Or was he? And how had Jason managed to
get ahold of this letter? Apparently he had no intention of
returning it to Dr. Davies, for why else would he have
crumpled it into a ball unless he meant to throw it away?
And if Ettinger *was* out of his mind, why had he brought
us here? Or was that the whole point?

"You okay?"

I thought I'd jump out of my skin and give everything
away, I was so startled. But at least I had the presence of
mind to hide the letter, throwing Jason's sweater on top of
it before turning to Kenley.

"Not very," I admitted.

"Me neither. I just got off the phone. The sheriff wants
to come out here and question Jason. I told him that was
fine, we weren't going anywhere. I think that calmed him
down a little."

"You mean he was suspicious?"

"Well . . . sort of," Kenley said reluctantly. "Seems
our family's had more than its share of tragedies at sea."
He gulped loudly, and a sheepish expression flashed across
his face. "Sorry, that must've sounded awful. I didn't

mean to be glib. It's just that . . . I still can't belive it, Quinn."

"You're shivering. You should get out of those wet clothes before you catch a cold," I said, trying to change the subject.

"Funny, I've kind of gotten used to them this way."

He tried his best to laugh, but when that didn't work he grinned sideways, smiling gently into my troubled eyes. I lifted my shoulders, then let them fall in a gesture of resignation.

I had run out of small talk, and could only stare at him, the wet curls of his hair forming tight ringlets across his forehead, his luminous brown eyes startling for their depth, as if they were capable of seeing things without his even knowing it.

How could I be thinking how handsome Kenley was when there were so many other things to worry about? But though I felt a twinge of guilt, I couldn't deny my feelings. Or my fears.

Dinner was a grim and painful affair, Nathaniel's absence made even more noticeable by the empty place at the head of the table. Miss Granberry had set the table the same way she always did, though I think it was less out of habit than a sense of respect. As for Perdita, she remained in her room, and I was sure Dr. Davies had given her a sedative to help her sleep.

When I looked at him sitting there at the table, picking at his food and obviously troubled, I no longer saw the neat and well-groomed Ivy Leaguer who had arrived on Ettinger Rock to be our tutor. Rather, I saw a young and perhaps even brilliant physician, a psychiatrist who for whatever reasons of his own had eagerly embraced my father's desperate scheme.

How I longed to tear away the lies, that web of deceit from which there seemed no escape. It had ensnared me back in the Valley, and though for months I had thought I was finally free, I now realized my liberty was just an illusion, something that could be snatched away from me at any moment.

But there was much more to it than that.

The lies from which I had so desperately struggled to free myself rose up before me like an impregnable barrier. Who was I going to believe? Jason had stolen the letter addressed to Franklin Davies, but was that all he was guilty of? Was Nathaniel really the psychopathic monster my brother would have me believe? Had he actually admitted killing Max? Or was Jason lying, taking advantage of Nathaniel's death—accidental or otherwise—to cover his own bloody tracks, concealing the truth not just from me, but perhaps even from himself?

The specter of Warren, lurking behind my brother's chair and watching his every move, made me shudder to myself. But Jason had insisted Warren was gone, and there was nothing about his behavior to suggest otherwise. Besides, even when Warren was around my brother had never lied to me about him, so there was no reason to think he would do that now.

Yet my doubts persisted. What if it were Warren who sat across from me, pretending to have no appetite when in fact he was ravenous, not the least bit upset by Nathaniel's death?

I put down my napkin and pushed my chair back, ignoring the startled look that came into my brother's eyes.

"Are you all right, Quinnie?"

Quinnie. He hadn't called me that in months. And now, when he said it, that term of affection no longer rang true.

"I'm just not hungry," I murmured. "I think I'll look in on Becky."

She was asleep in her crib, but as soon as I came into the nursery she opened her eyes, and even raised her pudgy little arms, wanting to be held. I lifted her gently out of the crib, then slowly paced the nursery, rocking her in my arms.

Jason's daughter. My sister. My niece.

In the past, the tears I'd shed had always been a balm, a safety valve that once opened, allowed me to express my feelings without keeping them bottled up inside. But now my eyes remained dry, as if I needed to see everything as clearly as I could. I had to find out what was happening, had to learn the truth no matter how painful it might ultimately prove.

If Jason were lying, if Nathaniel Ettinger's death hadn't been accidental, then I knew I would have no choice but to turn to Dr. Davies. But I was afraid to make that move until I had figured out whether or not Warren had returned. But just how I would do that I still had no idea.

The rain had finally stopped, and the night air which blew in through my open window once again carried with it the promise of spring, of green leafy things, of flowers unfurling their fragrant blossoms, and songbirds trilling overhead. After the raging moon went out like a match, snuffed between the fingers of dawn, I told myself I'd awake to a world washed clean of despair. We would be at peace again, Jason and I, safe from the tortured memories that pursued us, dogging our steps as stubbornly as our shadows.

Lying there in bed I made myself that promise, yet even then I knew it wouldn't do much good. In the morning nothing would have changed. The sky might be clear, but death would still be in the air, the threat of further violence hanging over all of us.

When I heard a faint, tentative knock on my bedroom door I hoped it was my brother, for I was ready to confront him with my suspicions. But when the door opened it was Kenley who stuck his head inside, peering at me through the darkness.

"Quinn, you still up?" he whispered.

I sat up in bed. It was nearly one and yet I was wide-awake, unable to close my eyes.

"I couldn't sleep," he said shyly.

"I couldn't either."

I slid over and made room for him. He sat down on the edge of the bed, swiveling around to face me.

"It's like nothing is real anymore, like I've been dreaming. I just can't believe he's gone, Quinn. I know we weren't on the best of terms recently, but I never stopped loving him. Even when I doubted him, I still loved my grandfather."

Kenley's eyes glistened, and he seemed confused almost to the point of tears. When he reached out, taking my face between his hands, our lips were just a few inches apart. Suddenly he shuddered and pressed his mouth to mine. For the first time since we had known each other, there was nothing shy or hesitant in his embrace. One hand slid down off my upturned face to move across my breasts, stroking them so delicately I couldn't help but shiver.

Kenley moved up on the bed. He lay alongside me, kissing my lips and my eyes and the tip of my nose. Ever so gently he unfastened my nightgown, pushing it down off my shoulders. I thought I would feel self-conscious, but I didn't, for what I saw in his eyes was something that not even Jason had ever shown me. It was a kind of reverence, or awe, that we were finally allowing ourselves to reveal some of the mysteries of our bodies, trusting each other as never before.

"There are things I feel for you I can't even describe, not even to myself," he said softly. "I know I love you, Quinn. I know that's what I'm feeling, because I've never felt anything like it, not ever. Does that embarrass you, my saying this? It's just that I want to share my feelings with you. That's all right, isn't it?"

"Oh, yes, of course it is," I said, feeling a smile spread across my lips.

When he leaned over me and began to kiss my breasts, the pleasure I experienced was frightening in its intensity. Nearly a year had passed since Jason had unlocked the door to that mysterious hidden room where the woman I was to become waited for her freedom. *"No one will ever love you as I do,"* he had promised. And now, after all those months, someone else had come along to prove him wrong.

I arched my back, my body seemingly moving of its own volition. Kenley was doing things with the tip of his tongue, the edges of his teeth, that made me want to cry out.

"I want to see you, too," I said when he finally raised his head, pausing a moment to look at me in the darkness. "I want to know you that way, Kenley."

What embarrassment I might have felt had vanished. Certain that Kenley would never hurt me or do anything to betray my trust, I pulled my arms free of the nightgown, pushing it all the way down to my waist. He glanced at me nervously, then pressed himself against me, kissing me so feverishly it made me dizzy.

The letter. I knew I had to tell him before anything else. It reared up before me like a barrier in the middle of the road, a fallen tree that would take both our strength to move aside.

I caught his face in my hands and held it, telling him there was no hurry, we had all our lives to learn about each other. Maybe that sounds overly romantic, but I meant every word of what I said. Jason had taken me in the Temple, that secret place that was hidden away in the Valley. It had been an act that went far beyond the loss of my virginity, for he imbued it with vague religious and mystical connotations, insisting it was the only way we would be able to fully commune with Mother's spirit. Since then I'd come to realize there was an element of selfishness in what he had done, something that struck me as irresponsible, as well. He had done to me what Mother had done to him, even though he knew how destructive it could be. But with Kenley it would be different, if only because when and if it happened I would be the one to make that decision, to use my body as I saw fit, giving of myself of my own free will.

Struggling to find words to express my feelings, I haltingly told him what I had discovered in Jason's pocket. For a moment Kenley was so stunned by my revelations that he couldn't even say anything, and just stared at me questioningly.

"Who is this Warren? What's he all about?" he finally asked. "Is it like a split personality or something like that?"

"I think so, yes. I think he was always there, a facet of my brother's personality. But he never really assumed his own identity until last summer, when all those terrible things began to happen to us.''

I had told Kenley a great deal about what had taken place back in the Valley, though there were still many gaps in the story, things I was afraid to reveal to him. Eventually I would tell him everything, including the incestuous relationship I had shared with my brother. But for the time being the letter Father had sent Dr. Davies was of prime importance.

"And yet he insists he's managed to overpower this Warren of his?" Kenley asked.

"Not exactly. When we left the Valley, Warren stayed behind. At least that's what Jason told me, and there wasn't any reason for him to lie. Besides, you've seen how he's been acting. He's fine, just like his old self. But then how did he get ahold of that letter, and why is he keeping it a secret?"

"There's a pile of mail downstairs, most of it soaking wet.''

"You think he read the letter in town and—?''

I left the rest unsaid, because to start accusing my brother of cold-blooded murder was something I refused to accept.

Kenley scooted up along the bed and held me in his arms. I rested my head against his shoulder, unable to stop myself from trembling. That special moment between us had passed, and yet what remained was still a bright, comforting light in the darkness. We held each other snugly, tenderly, seeking answers to questions we both realized would change our lives forever.

If only I had known what was coming. If only I could have stopped it in time.

CHAPTER TWENTY

Warren made me watch. I didn't want to, hating the idea
of being a spy like Davies. But I didn't have any other
choice. I roamed that corridor of my mind, looking for a
way out. I'd walked along the narrow hallway for hours
now, ever since I managed to break out of my cell. But the
walls were as smooth and unyielding as polished glass,
offering no means of escape.

Crouched before Quinn's door, fondling himself in the
darkness, I felt the heat of Warren's gaze as he peered into
my sister's room. She and Kenley were going to make
love. I couldn't bear to look, knowing that what I tried to
give her hadn't been enough. She needed something entirely different, something I wasn't able to provide.

"Maybe he's got a bigger dick than you," Warren
giggled as we crouched in the hall, one eye to the keyhole
that afforded an unobstructed view of my sister's bed.

Even when I looked away and closed my eyes, I could
still see them, Quinn whimpering now as she arched her
back, pressing her breasts against his mouth.

"He's slobbering all over her, the little prick," Warren
said angrily.

For a moment I thought he was going to barge right in and put an end to what he saw as their treachery, a form of deceit his ego had no means of coping with. Sordid images flickered along the walls of the corridor. Again, I tried not to look, but he had a way of making me see things even when my eyes were closed. He could have blinded me and I still would have seen the horrifying slideshow he put on for my benefit, flashing pictures of blood and gore as if violence were the only thing he understood. And it was. His world was black and white, with no room for compromise, and even less for compassion. He smiled into the camera of his mind, holding Kenley's severed head up for my inspection. The boy's castrated body lay on the rocks at the base of the cliff, a faceless, sexless corpse over which my sister wept in agony and despair.

"And then it'll be her turn," Warren whispered excitedly.

"How can you even think such things, even in your wildest imagination!" I cried out.

I was sickened by what he insisted on showing me. Yet no matter how hard I protested, pounding my fists against the walls of the corridor, he wouldn't stop. The grisly display continued. Quinn would be punished for taking Kenley Ettinger into her bed. He would torture her slowly, methodically, savoring each scream and each precious drop of blood. And when she paused in her love-making to talk about the letter, Warren's hand reached for the doorknob.

"Don't!" I screamed, over and over again.

The black glass walls rippled, and the floor beneath my feet moved up and down like something in a funhouse. He heard me all right, because I could see his fingers twitching convulsively as he tried to clutch the knob. I concentrated with all my might, trying to prevent him from making good on his threats.

He'd listened to me once before, when I begged him to throw out the life preserver and try to save Nathaniel. But now he wasn't obeying me because he realized I was right. Desperate to step inside Quinn's room, he continued to struggle for the knob. A crack appeared in the smooth surface of the wall. I squeezed my eyes shut, clearing my mind of every thought but one.

"For God's sake, leave my sister alone!"

When I opened my eyes the wall had miraculously repaired itself. Warren was breathing hard, the effort to overpower me having sapped him of some of his strength.

"You got away this time," he said, "but don't think I'm gonna make a habit of it, Lefland. She'll get hers. Maybe not now, but one day real soon, my little friend."

He started down the hall, and just as he reached our room footsteps sounded in the darkness. Warren hurriedly slipped inside, leaving the bedroom door ajar so he could see out into the hall. At the same time I broke into a run, feeling my strength return even as Warren's diminished. If only I could reach the end of the corridor, I was sure I'd find a door leading to the outside. I half-expected Warren to throw up walls to stop me, now that he knew what I was trying to do. But he was too busy listening to the footsteps.

A moment later Dr. Davies came into view. He was wearing a robe and slippers, yet there was something about his appearance that immediately aroused Warren's suspicion. Davies moved furtively down the hall, and it didn't take much intelligence to figure out how anxious he was to avoid being seen. When he reached the stairs he paused and looked back.

"I told you he combs his hair before he goes to bed," Warren said with contempt.

He remained by the door, holding his breath lest Davies

hear him. Satisfied he wasn't being followed, the doctor started downstairs, and Warren didn't waste any time hurrying after him.

We were halfway down the stairs when we heard the front door open. Not about to lose his quarry, Warren ran the rest of the way, skidding to a halt when he reached the vestibule. Cautiously he opened the door and peered outside. It was cold and damp, but at least the storm had abated. The smell of salt air drifted down the corridor. I wanted to keep looking for that doorway I was certain existed, but I was also very curious to know what Davies was doing up in the middle of the night.

"See? We're not always at odds," Warren reminded me. "You seem to forget that I'm you, Jason. By denying my existence you deny your own."

"You exist in a nightmare, Warren. You're not flesh and blood. You never will be."

"Oh really?" he said sarcastically. "Then how come I'm on the outside and you're not?"

I didn't answer. The less time I spent arguing with him, the better. Again I looked down the hall. I couldn't give up, not now when escape seemed so close at hand. I would reach that door at the end of the corridor if it was the last thing I ever did.

"Rest assured, it will be."

Warren's smug, self-satisfied voice echoed and re-echoed off the black glass walls. He was reading my mind. Then a light flickered, and both of us stood motionless, waiting to see what would happen next.

Davies was carrying a flashlight, and as he stood on the top of the cliff he sent its beam out across the water. Much of the trail leading down to the dock had been washed away in the storm. So I wasn't surprised he remained where he was, rather than try to find his way down with only the flashlight to guide him.

"I'd like to shove him right over the edge," Warren said as we kept our attention riveted to Davies. "What a nice sound that would make, his bones cracking."

"Then why don't you just do it and get it over with?" I said, testing him.

"Because I'm a lot smarter than you, Jason, that's why. I'll pick them off one by one, but I'll take my time. Besides, the sheriff from Otter Bay might come out here tomorrow. I have to be on my best behavior."

Out on the water a light suddenly shone, and for just an instant we could make out the shape of a launch. It was heading straight for the dock, and Davies signaled again, turning his flashlight on and off in rapid succession.

"We've got visitors, Jason. Do you think it's the sheriff, come to pay a midnight call?"

"Doubtful."

"Then who the hell is it, the boys from the funny farm?"

The light went on again, illuminating the launch as well as its passengers. There were two people in the boat, but only one of them stepped onto the dock. Suitcase in hand, he started up the trail, guided each step of the way by Davies' flashlight. At the same time the launch turned around and headed back toward the mainland.

"Can you see who it is?" Warren whispered, his teeth chattering from the cold.

Whoever had gotten off the launch was no longer visible.

"Watch your step, it's very slippery," I heard Davies call out in a hoarse whisper.

"I don't like it, Jason. I don't like it one bit."

I didn't either, but I decided to reserve judgment until I

saw who our visitor was. Warren, however, wasn't about to take any chances. He started back to the house, never once taking his eyes off Dr. Davies.

"Welcome to Ettinger Rock," the doctor said as he helped his guest up the last few feet of the muddy trail.

There was no mistaking the irony in his voice. When the person to whom he was speaking finally came into view, I understood why Warren was suddenly behaving so skittishly.

Tall, with a square, angular jaw and large teeth that could fashion a grimace as easily as a grin, Bennett Lefland paused at the top of the cliff to catch his breath. He glanced warily about as if to get his bearings, then pumped Dr. Davies' hand.

Warren took one look at him and broke into a cold sweat. I'd never known him to be afraid, not of anyone or anything. But now the terror he was experiencing made his breath rattle in his chest, and he couldn't get back to the house fast enough.

"What now?" I asked, pretending to be calm when in fact I was feeling the very opposite.

"What do you think, shithead? We're leaving on the first boat out. Fucking asshole thinks he can shut me up in a padded cell, he's got another guess coming. Warren's getting out of here, and he's taking you with."

"I think I'd rather stick around and enjoy the show."

But by then my snappy comebacks fell on deaf ears. Warren ran up the stairs, and the next thing I knew he was packing a bag. I wondered if I should try to stop him, then realized it was probably an exercise in futility. Right now he was calling the shots, and if Dad spent any time with him it wouldn't take long before he realized Warren wasn't the son who'd left home months before. The two of us would be packed off to Dr. Warren's Institute, and once there I knew we'd never be allowed to leave.

No wonder Warren was so scared. He was seeing his future from behind the walls of a cell. But maybe if I managed to reclaim my identity before he succeeded in leaving, I might be able to convince my father I wasn't nearly as crazy as he thought.

So as Warren packed his suitcase I raced down the corridor, desperate now to find a way out before it was too late.

All my arguments fell on deaf ears. No matter what I said, Warren wouldn't pay attention. Like a creature possessed—and I knew damn well he was—he threw things into his bag, hardly even noticing what he was packing.

"You know you won't get very far. Why don't you just give up while you're ahead?"

"And let you run the show? Fat chance," he sneered. "You know what your problem is, Lefland? You're getting soft, too damn trusting for your own good. Do you think if you make up with him he's just gonna pat you on the back, tell you how glad he is to see you again, let bygones be bygones? Don't kid yourself. He wouldn't be here if Davies hadn't alerted him to what was going on."

"And what the hell is going on, if you don't mind my asking?"

"Life and death, Jason," he hissed at me. "The stuff of the universe. Real first-class elemental bullshit, get the picture?"

I didn't, and I was so exhausted from running that every time I took a step my knees dissolved and I could barely stay on my feet. I had a stitch in my side that was doubling me over, so finally I sat down in the corridor to catch my breath. I leaned my head against the wall while Warren snapped the suitcase shut and glanced around the bedroom, making sure he hadn't forgotten anything.

"Now what?" I asked.

"I'm getting my kid, that's what."

I pulled myself to my feet. As tired as I was, what Warren had just told me made escape even more imperative than ever.

"Leave her out of this, Warren, please," I begged. "You want to run off to God knows where, I don't think I can stop you. But she's just a little baby. You don't know the first thing about taking care of her."

He stood by the door, and for a moment I thought he was going to change his mind. But when I looked into his eyes I saw the green fire that was burning out of control. Was this madman really me? Was this cruel and sadistic little boy a part of myself, a distorted reflection of what I had actually become? It couldn't be possible, and yet there he was inhabiting my body and my mind while all I could do was run and run and never seem to get anywhere.

I started jogging down the corridor, even as Warren crept into the hall, glancing nervously in both directions. Satisfied he wasn't being followed, he tiptoed down the hallway to the stairs. As he passed Quinn's room I screamed out, trying to attract her attention. Warren's mouth opened, but all that came out was a mouselike squeak, so faint it was all but inaudible. But it was me! I was still there, still alive is what I'm saying. He'd cried out Quinn's name, even if I was the only one who could hear him.

Just as surprised as I was, he gulped loudly, then shook his head as if to jar me loose. I half-expected to go tumbling head over heels down the corridor, caught in the middle of an earthquake. But his anxiety didn't translate into physical terms. The walls of the corridor remained as they were, untouched by his dismay.

"If I were you, I wouldn't try that again," he warned. " 'Cause the next time you get any bright ideas it's back to the cell, and this time for good."

A few days before I might have believed him. But now I knew I had nothing to lose by challenging his authority.

"Try it. I dare you, Warren. If you're so fucking powerful then why don't you come down here and have it out with me, once and for all?"

"You forget, I already did have it out with you, Lefland. And guess who won?"

His laughter was like thunder. I slammed my hands over my ears, crying out in pain and rage, but that didn't stop him. The more I hurt, the more pleased he became. He gripped the banister with his one free hand, the suitcase heavier than he realized. Then he started down the stairs, moving so cautiously it seemed to take forever before he reached the second floor.

"What about Becky's clothes, all the things she needs? How the hell are you going to carry her and the suitcase and all the rest of that stuff?"

Warren was too preoccupied now to even listen to me. With narrowed, suspicious eyes he glanced down the hall, making sure the coast was clear before he headed for the nursery.

When the door swung back he held his breath, staring at the night light glowing cheerfully from a skirted table next to the crib. Then he slipped inside, leaving the suitcase near the door. He went straight to the crib, and when he looked down at the baby I realized there was at least a side of him that was still human, capable of feeling love and compassion.

"Daddy's here," he whispered softly. "Daddy's come to take you on an adventure, Becky. We're gonna go far away, sweetheart, where no one can ever hurt us again. It'll just be you and me, and I'll take care of you and we'll always be together."

When the baby opened her eyes and saw him leaning over her, I thought she'd burst out crying. But Becky recognized him—recognized *me*, that is—and gurgled happily as Warren lifted her out of the crib, wrapping the blankets around her to keep her warm.

"I know you love her, Warren, because what you're feeling is what I feel. But you can't take her with you, don't you understand that? She breaks, Warren. She's not a doll. She's flesh and blood, and she gets colds and she cries and—"

"SHUT UP!" he roared. "She's *mine*, so don't start laying all your guilt on me, Jason, because I'm not listening. She's all I have left now, and I'm not giving her up, not for you or anyone else."

"Put her down, Jason. Just put her down where you found her and we won't say another word about it."

Warren spun around, glaring at Miss Granberry. She must have been dozing in the rocking chair, but now she was wide-awake. As she came to her feet the pinched, mean look I'd seen in her eyes was replaced by an expression of utter determination. She didn't look worried at all, as if she already knew she was going to get her way.

"I know just what you're thinking, Jason. But you're not going to make that innocent little baby a part of it, do you hear?"

She pointed to the suitcase Warren had left by the door. Drawing her faded wrapper tightly around her, Granberry glared at him and repeated what she had said, ordering him to return Becky to her crib.

"Don't make trouble for yourself," he warned her. "This isn't your concern, lady."

"Don't you talk like that to me, young man," the housekeeper replied, affronted by his tone of voice. "I'm Miss Granberry to you, and don't you ever forget it. Now put your sister down."

"And if I don't?"

"I won't hesitate to wake the entire house, if necessary."

"Big fucking deal," Warren muttered.

But I knew he was scared, because I could see how his eyes darted nervously to the doorway, afraid someone would hear them arguing.

Her patience exhausted, Granberry took an angry step forward. "Put your sister down this instant!"

"She's not my sister, you ugly bitch. She's my daughter, and I can do whatever I goddamn please with her."

A flush of surprise spread rapidly across the housekeeper's wrinkled cheeks. Yet I had to give Granberry credit. She held her ground, refusing to allow Warren to intimidate her.

"Whether that's true or not is no concern of mine. She's an innocent child, and so I'll ask you one more time. Put the baby down, Jason. If you want to leave the Rock, I couldn't be more delighted. But you're not taking Becky with you."

Warren bit down on his lip. He glanced at Becky, and then at Granberry, trying to decide what to do.

"You won't tell them, will you? You'll keep it a secret, if only for her sake?"

His voice was so conciliatory that Granberry's expression softened. She nodded her head with a little jerk, and

Warren lowered Becky into the crib. I was about to congratulate him on using his head for a change, when instead of turning to the door, he went over to the table where a frosted bulb glowed beneath its pleated shade.

Warren suddenly wrenched the lamp off the table. As the plug was pulled from its socket and the nursery went dark, Granberry gave a startled cry. Warren lunged forward, and just as I'd used a lamp to overpower the owner of the Pine Bluff Motel, Warren did the same, swinging it wildly through the air.

The base of the lamp struck Miss Granberry across the shoulder. With a terrified groan she stumbled back, trying to shield herself behind the rocking chair. She started to scream, and Warren slammed the lamp down against the side of her head.

Her bony fingers clutching the back of the chair, the housekeeper made a last desperate effort to call for help. Warren eyed her spitefully and held the lamp in readiness. But before he could use it again the woman slowly crumpled to the floor, letting go of the chair only when her legs could no longer support her.

The rocker wobbled back and forth, creaking loudly in the darkness. Warren took one deep breath after another, sucking air into his lungs. He set the lamp down on the table, then bent over Granberry to make sure she was still unconscious.

"You never liked me, from the very first day," he whispered. "All you ever wanted to do was make trouble for me. But now you've made a lot of trouble for yourself, haven't you?"

For a moment his concentration wavered. An image took shape in his mind's eye, blurry and unfocused.

"That's what I should do, just nail you to the floor," he

hissed. "But the thought of sticking it into you makes me want to puke."

He straightened up and took another deep breath. Then he went back to the crib, wrapping Becky in her blankets before lifting her out.

"What about her things? You don't have any clothes for her, or diapers, or anything else," I reminded him, hoping he might still change his mind.

"I'll buy her whatever she needs once we get out of here."

He reached down and grabbed the handle of the staircase. With Becky snug in the crook of his arm, Warren hurried down the hall. If only the baby would start to cry maybe someone would hear her and try to stop him. But Becky seemed perfectly content to be in his arms.

"Don't you worry now," he whispered as he made his way down the stairs. "You're Daddy's best little girl, and he's gonna love you 'til the day he dies."

Then let it be soon, I prayed. Not for my sake, but for Becky's.

CHAPTER TWENTY-ONE

At first I thought it was part of a dream, the noise I kept hearing. I turned over in bed and pressed my face into the pillows. But the sound wouldn't go away. Like a mosquito buzzing fretfully in my ear, it droned on and on, and the more I heard it, the more awake I became. When I opened my eyes it was still dark out, and for a moment everything was so quiet I was certain I was imagining things. But then it started again, a grating mechanical sound, popping and sputtering in the distance.

I pulled myself into a sitting position and rubbed the sleep from my eyes. I was all alone, Kenley having returned to his room hours before. But when I glanced at the clock near my bed, I saw that it hadn't been hours at all. Not more than forty-five minutes had passed since we'd said good night.

But what was that racket I was hearing? I got out of bed, started to turn on a light and then thought better of it. I could barely keep my eyes unglued. With a light on I'd be blinded for sure. I stuffed my arms into my robe, shivering from the cold. The noise came from outside, and I raised the window and stuck my head out, trying to see what it was.

Somebody was down by the dock, trying to start up the launch. I could just about make them out, hunched over the wheel. But for some reason they couldn't get the engine to kick in. That's why I kept hearing that sputtering noise, like a car makes when the battery is dead.

But who could it be? Surely not Perdita, nor Kenley. I couldn't imagine Dr. Davies going off in the middle of the night, either.

The letter! I suddenly thought. Now that Jason knows who Davies really is—

I hurried down the hall to my brother's room. There was no response to my anxious knock, and when I opened the door I found his bed empty, just as I feared. All I could think of was getting to him in time. I ran down the stairs, threw the front door open and rushed outside.

"Jason!" I cried.

Where would he go? What would he do? Obviously he was terrified by what he'd learned, and his only thought was of escape. But I couldn't let him run off like this. I had to talk to him, had to try to reason with him before it was too late.

I kept calling his name, even as I ran toward the edge of the cliff. When I reached the top of the trail I looked down at the dock, relieved to see the launch was still tied to its mooring ring. But my brother was no longer at the controls. The boat bobbed up and down in the water, and all I could hear were the waves, scattering foam across the rocks.

By the time I got back to the house, Kenley and Dr. Davies were waiting for me by the front door. They'd heard me shouting Jason's name, and I wasted little time explaining what had happened.

I don't know why I felt so afraid, but I did. After all, Ettinger Rock was an island, and without the launch there was no other way to leave. But I had no idea what kind of state my brother was in. If Warren had returned, forcing Jason to do things against his will, there would be little that any of us could do to help him.

For a moment I even considered telling Dr. Davies that I knew who he was, and why he had come here. But if Jason meant to keep that information a secret, I didn't want to betray his confidence until I was certain it was absolutely necessary.

"No doubt he's very upset over Mr. Ettinger's death," Davies told me. "Maybe if he has a chance to be alone for a while—"

"You don't understand. He tried to leave. He's not in—"

Control of himself was what I intended to say. But until I had proof I couldn't let Davies think my brother had already lost his grip on reality. He would call Father, and the next thing I knew Jason would be taken off the island, dragged away by force if need be. If only I could find him first, talk to him, try to get him to open up to me. But if he were responsible for what had happened to Nathaniel— No, I wasn't going to allow myself to think along those lines. First I would speak to him, making no decisions and drawing no conclusions until then.

"Do you think he could've taken the baby with him?" Kenley asked.

His question caught me completely by surprise. Rather than stand there a moment longer, I rushed back into the house and up the stairs to the second floor. The nursery door was ajar. I pushed it all the way open, my eyes darting to the crib.

Why wasn't the night light on? I stepped inside, my hand searching blindly for the light switch. I didn't want to wake the baby, but now I was so anxious I couldn't help myself. Flooded with light, everything I saw became hard-edged, sharp and almost forbidding.

The crib was empty!

A faint cry made me spin around on the ball of my foot. Half-hidden behind the rocking chair, Miss Granberry lay stretched out on the floor. Even as I drew back in surprise she groaned feebly and struggled to sit up.

I hurried to her side, urging her to remain where she was. An ugly bruise discolored the side of her forehead, spreading from her temple down to her cheekbone. I grabbed the pillow out of the crib and used it to prop up her head, then ran into the bathroom and soaked a towel in cold water. By the time I returned Miss Granberry had managed to pull herself up into a sitting position, and was leaning awkwardly against the rocker. I helped her into the chair, applying the wet compress to her forehead.

"The lamp," she muttered, motioning with her bony chin.

It was unplugged, its upturned shade lying at the foot of the table. Although I was afraid to ask, I knew I had to.

"What happened, Miss Granberry? Was it Jason? Did he take the baby?"

She nodded slowly, looking at me with troubled eyes.

"I tried to stop him. He wouldn't listen." The housekeeper reached out and clutched my hand, and I could tell by her grip that her strength was beginning to return. "Is it true, Quinn, what he told me?"

I looked at her blankly, afraid to show any emotion.

"He's so frightened, Miss Granberry. You have to understand that. He thinks our father is coming after him."

The housekeeper shook her head.

"Not that. He said . . . Becky was his daughter."

316

Was that shame that made my cheeks suddenly burn? I don't think so. I don't think I could ever be ashamed of my brother, knowing that he had been a pawn, someone Mother had used for her own twisted and perverse desires.

"Yes, it's true," I said sadly.

"But why didn't you ever let us know? We wouldn't have thought less of her for it. Or less of him, either."

That's what I was ashamed of, that we hadn't trusted the Ettingers as much as they were willing to trust us.

"It's very difficult to talk about. It's all so terribly complicated, Miss Granberry. But he was concerned about Becky, that's what you have to realize. I can't apologize for what he did to you. He's very confused and unhappy, but we know he's still here on the island, hiding somewhere. We'll find him. And the baby."

Her grip on my wrist relaxed, and she dropped her hand into her lap and closed her eyes. Such a strange woman she was, her response to what had happened so different from what I expected. She actually did care about us, after all. Underneath that seemingly cold and brittle exterior lay a warm and forgiving heart. It saddened me that I had never had the time nor inclination to sit and talk with her, and get to know her better.

"I'm sorry for what happened, Miss Granberry. Jason hasn't been . . . well, he's just not been himself lately. I know that must sound like a lame excuse, but I'm sure he didn't mean to hurt you."

Her eyes opened wide, and what I saw in their pale, watery depths was a kind of dread, that same nameless terror which gripped me even as I knelt before her.

"Find them and bring them back," she whispered. "I saw something, Quinn. When you find your brother, you'll see it, too."

"See what, Miss Granberry?"

"He's not Jason anymore. He's someone else."

Miss Granberry had seen the one thing I feared most. If she could recognize what had happened to my brother, a trained psychiatrist such as Dr. Davies would have no trouble discerning it as well. Then was it all true, the terrible things Warren had done, the crimes he'd committed?

I got dressed and went downstairs. In that mysterious half-light that just precedes dawn, the mist which flowed across the lawn glowed with a faint blue phosphorescence. I stood by the dining room windows, watching the slow creeping movement of the fog as if it were a creature, a malevolent presence responsible for all the nightmarish events that had happened since our arrival on Ettinger Rock.

How easy it would have been to blame it all on some disembodied spirit, some supernatural force holding my brother in its sway. Perhaps a thousand years ago mental illness was looked upon that way. But in these more enlightened times—and sometimes I wondered if they really were—it wasn't the Devil to whom we pointed the finger of blame, but ourselves. Yet if Mother had acted any differently, I was certain Warren would never have been born. Nor would we ever have found ourselves running away from all that we once held so dear.

Off in the distance I thought I heard something. Could it be Jason, holding Becky in his arms as he ran through the fog? I peered out into the swirling mist whose ruddy underglow told me that dawn was just minutes away. Was he still out there in the cold and damp, or had he already managed to sneak back into the house?

I was about to go upstairs, thinking that perhaps he might have hidden himself in the attic, when a faint creaking of floorboards made me turn suspiciously in the direction of the studio.

"Jason, it's me. I'm all alone," I called out in a whisper.

From the dining room I went directly to the drawing room, then on through the music room to the studio. As soon as I entered I made sure to close the door so no one else could hear us.

"Jason, you don't have to hide from me. I just want to talk to you. Everyone is terribly worried, you know that. Is it Warren? I know about the letter you found, the one from Father. But we won't let him hurt you, I promise. If Dr. Davies won't help us, we'll find someone else who will. But don't let Warren hurt the baby, Jason. You mustn't listen to him, I beg of you."

There was no response, no movement in the shadows, nothing but the sound of my tearful voice reverberating sadly in the air. I glanced at the dollhouse, and suddenly had this maddened urge to sweep it off the table and crush it beneath my feet. Maybe by destroying the replica of the house, I could destroy the twisted replica of Jason, leaving him forever free of Warren's malignant influence.

I stepped closer, wondering if he'd left me a clue to his whereabouts. When I saw that the Jason doll was missing from its usual place in the schoolroom, I began to methodically search each of the rooms, even going so far as to open closet doors in hopes of finding it.

Jason's bedroom was empty, as were all the rooms in the attic. The second floor was undisturbed as well, as was the first. Then where was the doll? He'd already been here, I knew that now, for why else was it missing? Had he taken the doll with him? I couldn't understand why, unless he wanted to convince me his only option was to leave the island.

My eyes strayed to the easel, and for a moment I even pretended that nothing was wrong. Soon Nathaniel would come down for breakfast, taking his coffee with him into the studio where he would spend the remainder of the morning hard at work.

His palette lay on the worktable where he kept his paints. Something caught my eye, and I stepped forward, unable to explain the chill I suddenly felt in the air, as if someone had opened a window or a door.

I think it must have been fear that made me shiver, for it was blood, bright red and freshly spilled, that formed a tiny pool across the paint-stained surface of the palette. And right beside it, propped against one of the many coffee cans in which Nathaniel stored his brushes, lay a bloodied little arm, clutching a tiny foil knife in the hollow of its fist.

Pieces of the Jason doll were strewn across the worktable. The severed head was the most gruesome of all, for Warren had scraped the green paint off its eyes, smearing blood over its face until the doll was barely recognizable.

"Don't you see what he's doing?" I cried out. "He wants to kill you, Jason, just like he wants to kill everyone else who's dear to you. You can't let him win. You have to fight him, you must!"

For one fleeting instant I wondered if Nathaniel were responsible for what had happened. Perhaps he'd torn the doll apart before he and Jason left for Otter Bay. But no, the blood was still wet, and when I looked over at the easel, and saw the bloody W that Warren had scrawled in a corner of the canvas, I knew my worst fears were realized.

Jason wasn't running away from us. He was running away from himself.

CHAPTER TWENTY-TWO

We were right outside, and she never saw us. We were so close I could have touched her, but she never even knew we were there. I tried to stand up and bang on the window, but Warren wouldn't let me. I tried to get him to pinch the baby so she'd start to cry, but though his hands trembled he still maintained control. I screamed too, over and over again, calling to Quinn as we crouched below the studio windows. But this time Warren didn't utter a sound.

"I don't understand you anymore, Lefland. Don't you know what's going on around here? Benny's back, and when he leaves he intends to take you with him whether you like it or not. So why don't you just sit back and relax, let me do what I have to."

"And what's that?"

"Come on, Jason, don't be naive. Just what you tried to do back home. Only this time we're gonna finish the job."

He reached into his pocket and felt the knife, the same one I'd used to break out of my cell. I didn't even realize he'd taken it, but as soon as his fingers curled around the bone handle a smile lit up his face and he began to laugh, he was so damn proud of himself.

"And then what?" I asked. "You still won't be able to get off the island. If you couldn't start the launch this morning, you're not going to be able to this afternoon."

"Then I'll just have to take the sheriff's launch, that's all."

"Just like that?" I said, and now it was my turn to laugh. "Talk about being naive. You're worse than me."

"But unlike you, Jason, I never give up," he said smugly. "Maybe you're ready to let Benny ship you off to an asylum, but I sure the hell ain't. And when I find him that's the first thing I'm gonna let him know."

There was no reasoning with him, probably because there was nothing even vaguely rational in his makeup. Warren was like a hunted animal, and now that he felt trapped he was about to turn the tables on everyone and go on the offensive.

"At least put Becky back in her crib until you're done," I told him. "She's only going to get in your way."

"They'll steal her."

"How can anyone steal her when there's no place to go? We're all trapped here, Warren. If something's the matter with the launch we're going to have to wait for the sheriff, anyway. So at least put her back in the nursery until then."

He glared at me suspiciously, his eyes burning so brightly it was hard to look at them.

"If this is some kind of trick—"

"It isn't, I swear."

"Well, maybe it's not such a bad idea," he reluctantly agreed. "But I'm warning you, Jason. You try anything and this time I'm really gonna take care of you, you hear? I'll lock you up for good, and that's a promise, buddy boy."

I didn't think he could, not now when I was free to roam this endless corridor in which I found myself a prisoner. But sooner or later I'd reach the end. I just had to, because the closer he got to Bennett, the closer he got to deciding our fate. Not just what would happen today, but what was going to happen to us for the rest of our lives.

He'd hidden the suitcase in the woods, and as he cradled Becky in his arms he crept around to the back of the house. I think at this point I was as confused as Warren. My father's presence on the island could mean only one thing, because I didn't need Warren to remind me he wasn't here to pay a social call. It would be off to the hospital for sure, and once there we'd be guarded so closely they'd never let us out of their sight.

I remembered how he looked at Becky, the day we all left home. No way in the world was he going to get me to believe he cared about her. So even if he locked me up for the rest of my life, I was less afraid for myself than for my daughter. Quinn understood that, but without my help she'd be powerless to prevent Father from doing whatever he pleased.

Yet murder wasn't the answer, either.

"Then what is?" Warren asked.

I didn't know, and Warren wasn't about to stand around while I tried to think of something. He slipped in through the kitchen door, then made his way up the back stairs to the second floor. He wasn't very happy about returning Becky to the nursery, but if he wanted to go looking for Bennett and still keep out of sight, it would make much more sense to put her back in her crib.

"Fucking battery. We'd be long gone if it wasn't for that."

He paused on the landing, and I could feel his nervousness like a change in the weather. The air in the corridor turned damp and musky. It was cold sweat I was smelling, Warren's not mine. Voices drifted toward me. For a moment I thought I had visitors, but then I realized I was listening through Warren's ears, not my own.

He ducked into the linen closet near the top of the stairs. Everything suddenly smelled fresh and clean, and he breathed more easily.

"Of course I didn't tell him," we heard Kenley whisper as he and Quinn came down the hall. "Davies has no idea we know. I was waiting for you to say something, but you didn't."

"Not until I speak to Jason."

Good old Quinn, thank God I could still count on her. I tried to get Warren to go out into the hall and take them into his confidence, but of course he didn't fall for it. He didn't trust anyone, my sister included.

"Where the hell do you think he's gone? Warren won't try to hurt Becky, will he?" Kenley asked.

"God, I hope not."

"Then what do we do now?"

"Keep looking, I guess. Try to find him before Davies does."

"Maybe he's called your father. If he shows up here that's only going to complicate things even more."

Quinn sighed loudly.

"I guess we'll just have to deal with that when the time comes," she told him.

Their voices receded. Warren counted to ten before venturing out into the hall. He ran the rest of the way, and as soon as he put Becky in her crib the tension that had been building up along his shoulders and the back of his neck slowly began to subside.

"Daddy'll be back for you, I promise," he whispered as he rearranged the blankets to make her comfortable.

She opened her eyes and stared at him with a solemn expression. They were crystal blue, and when he looked at them pictures of Mom flickered across the walls of the corridor. Even as he stared at the baby her face began to change, growing older, more calculating, sharp and even cunning.

Warren pressed his knuckles to his lips, then bit down hard to suppress a groan. Something was happening to him, something that might work to my advantage. He was frightened, you see, but I wasn't scared at all. As long as he kept looking at Becky and seeing Mom, I might still have a chance. And sure enough there was a light glowing at the end of the tunnel, a warm and comforting light that bounced off the smooth black glass walls, scattering its rays in dozens of directions.

I ran faster, trying to get to it in time. Was that a door I saw? Yes, it had to be! But something else was happening too, and now I found myself just as scared as Warren.

He was seeing Mom, and his fingers probed deeper and deeper into the pocket of his jeans. He gripped the handle of the knife and I ran as fast as I could, trying to reach the door.

If I broke his concentration there was just no telling what might happen. For all I knew the door might vanish. Worse than that, he might try to reenact what had happened back in the Valley, the night Mom took him into her bed for the last time.

The door was some kind of highly polished metal, not gold but the same color. Set flush into the wall, there was no knob, no bolt, nothing at all but a panel of metal that resisted the frenzied pounding of my fists. I looked back into the window of his mind, that cloudy mirror through which he saw the world. Warren was pulling the knife out of his pocket, breathing hard and not saying a word.

"It's not Mom, it's the baby! It's Becky!" I screamed when the blade flashed in the morning light that streamed into the nursery.

Warren blinked rapidly as if he had something in his eyes. He cocked his head to one side, listening intently.

"It's me, Jason!" I cried, unable to understand why he wasn't answering me. "It's Becky, not Mom. Look again. It's the baby, your daughter!"

Warren looked down into the crib. Mom's features began to melt and rearrange themselves. They grew younger, softer, traveling back in time until all that remained of her was the crystal blue of Becky's eyes.

I waited for the door to sink back into obscurity, but it didn't disappear the way I expected. The light began to fade, yet the door remained intact. I sank down onto my knees. I could stop running now. I'd finally found a way out. All I had to do was get the door open and I'd be free.

I don't know how long Warren stood there by the crib, staring at the baby until she fell asleep. It seemed like hours, though I'm sure it couldn't have been much longer than five or ten minutes. At last he turned away. He was sweating so profusely his shirt was soaking wet, and I could feel the sweat trickling down his chest and arms.

"You did that to me, didn't you, Jason?" There was so much anger in his voice, such uncontrollable rage, that I knew there was no way I could start to reason with him.

"You're playing tricks on me again, aren't you? Well, I'm going to show you a thing or two, you little prick."

Bolts of lightning crashed overhead. I pushed myself into a corner by the door, drawing my knees up to my chest. The chlorine smell of ozone filled the corridor, making it difficult to breath. It was a wild emotional storm I was witnessing, the lightning bolts glowing hotly in the dim, uncertain light.

Any one of them could have struck me, and yet none did. Was that because Warren's hold on me was getting weaker? I swiveled around, probing the edge of the door with my fingers. Surely there had to be a way to get it open, if only I could figure out how.

"That's just for starters," Warren cackled.

Was he laughing out loud? I couldn't tell, but he had me so scared now that I figured the best thing to do was just sit tight until he exhausted himself.

The sharp and acrid stink of ozone lingered long after the last of the lightning bolts had passed overhead. Warren's trembling fingers tightened around the doorknob. He let himself out of the nursery, glancing anxiously in both directions. There was no one in the hall.

It was at this point that I decided to stop talking to him. Let him see what it was to be all alone. It would serve him right. He was so damn sure of himself, so certain he had the upper hand, that I wasn't about to contribute one iota to his sense of self-confidence.

Sensing that I was withdrawing from him in a way I never had before, he got so upset he lost control. He slammed his fist against the wall, and though I wanted to warn him he was making too much noise, I'd already made up my mind never to communicate with him again.

You see, by talking to him I was just encouraging

his madness, because that madness was mine, as well. That was something that was hard for me to accept, because all along I'd seen Warren as a separate person, distinct unto himself. But he really wasn't. He was actually a part of me, and maybe what kept him alive was the fact that I believed in him. But if I stopped believing, stopped talking to myself, maybe I'd find a way out of here.

So even as he ranted and raved and pounded on the wall, I didn't say a word. Instead, I turned all my attention to the door, trying to figure out a way to get it open.

Back home, by twisting one of the moldings in the attic I'd exposed a secret passageway, behind which Great-grandfather had condemned his son to a slow and merciless death. But this door was smooth and faceless, a solid sheet of yellow metal, so shiny I could see my reflection wavering before me.

Between the door and the wall into which it was set there was no more than an eighth of an inch of space. I reached into my pocket to get my knife. Maybe by using the blade to probe along the edge of the door I might hit upon some kind of mechanism to get it open. But just as I remembered I no longer had the knife in my possession, I heard footsteps, sneaking up on me from the end of the corridor.

Warren heard them, too. He gave a startled cry and looked wildly about, less sure of himself than ever before.

"Now just calm down, Jason. Everything's going to be all right, I promise," Dr. Davies told him.

His voice dripped like syrup, each syllable rolling slowly off his tongue. Warren backed away, once again reaching for the knife he'd stolen out of my pocket.

"It's all right, Jason. I'm going to make sure no one hurts you, I promise."

I stumbled back against the door. There was a sound like a lock clicking open, a whoosh of trapped air, blinding sunlight filling the dark, cavernous length of the tunnel. I spun around, trying to get my bearings. Warren was coming toward me, his arms outstretched.

I backed away, terrified of what would happen if he touched me. He'd lock me up again, and this time I'd never find my way out.

"Go away!" I screamed. "Leave me alone!"

"I'm a doctor, Jason. I'm here to help you."

"Make him go away!"

I didn't want to go back into the tunnel. I couldn't take that anymore. But Warren kept coming closer and closer, and there was nowhere else to turn.

"Hey, ole buddy, don't be scared. It's just me, your old friend Warren."

"You need to rest, Jason, that's the most important thing," the doctor was saying. "You'll get some sleep and you'll be able to think more clearly."

I darted to the side, trying to avoid Warren's outstretched hands. But he was just as fast as I was. He grabbed me by the shoulders and held me tight. Only it wasn't Warren anymore. It was Franklin Davies, so close to me I could see the pores of his skin, the stubble where he hadn't shaved.

"You need to sleep," he said in the soothing, syrupy voice.

Davies jabbed something into my arm. I pushed my hand into my pocket, trying to pull out the knife. But something was wrong with my fingers. They were turning

330

to rubber and the floor suddenly fell away beneath my feet.

"Thorazine," I heard him say.

Wasn't that what they'd given Mom, so she wouldn't act crazy?

"You guessed it, buddy boy," Warren snickered.

Suddenly he vanished like a bubble that goes pop. Alone now, and grateful for my solitude, I floated through the black empty spaces of my mind, finally at peace with myself. But I knew it wouldn't last very long, for when I woke up I was sure I'd find myself in hell.

CHAPTER TWENTY-THREE

By the time I heard the commotion and ran upstairs, Jason was already unconscious, stretched out on the floor like a corpse.

"Don't worry, he's going to be all right," Dr. Davies tried to assure me. "I gave him a sedative. He'll be out for five or six hours."

So the masquerade was over. Davies was making no bones about being a doctor. But that was the very least of it. Even as I heard the baby cry, the schoolroom door opened and a familiar figure stepped into the hall. Yet oddly enough I wasn't at all surprised. No wonder Jason had tried to run away. He had probably seen Father arrive on the island, and his only thought was to get as far away from him as possible.

He looked the same, and as he stepped closer he held out his arms to me. But before he even had a chance to say hello I turned away and slipped into the nursery.

Becky lay in her crib, squalling loudly for her bottle. Maybe Warren wasn't as insane as I thought, for he had done nothing to harm the baby. I lifted her out, remembering that dreadful day months before, when Father had returned to the Valley to confront the nightmare he alone had set in motion.

"I'll take care of the baby, Quinn. There's a pot of fresh coffee waiting in the study. Why don't you take your father downstairs? Kenley and the doctor'll help carry Jason to his room."

I put down the baby, and turning to Perdita my eyes filled with tears. Her sadness was mine. Her terrible grief could never be erased.

"There now, dear, you'll be all right, I know you will. You're much stronger than you ever let on, Quinn. And you remind me of myself when I was your age. You wear your heart on your sleeve, but I've never thought there's anything wrong with that."

Perdita held me in her arms, stroking my hair and whispering that everything would work out for the best. Did she already know what Jason had done? Should I tell her about Warren, or was it better to leave things as they were?

I didn't know, but the pain I heard in her voice was like a wound that wouldn't heal. We had brought tragedy and heartache into her life, for despite all my efforts I hadn't been able to unmask Warren in time. Yet I knew she bore me no malice, for there was in her very touch something permanent and abiding, as if the love we felt for each other would only grow stronger in the face of adversity.

Perdita wiped the tears from my eyes. "You're not a child anymore, Quinn. There comes a time in all our lives when we have to face the truth, not only about ourselves, but about those we love. He wants to take you home. It's all he's ever wanted."

"Don't make me leave, Perdita. This is my home now,

the only home I care about. I can't go back. There are so many things I haven't told you."

"I know that," she said gently. "I think I knew it from the very beginning. But you were so frightened, and if I started asking too many questions I was afraid you'd run off again. I couldn't bear to think of you that way—all alone, with no one to turn to. Talk to him, that's all I ask. He does care about you, Quinn, more than I think you realize."

He was waiting for me in the library, the man I couldn't bear to think of as my father. I closed the sliding doors behind me, pressing my back to them as I stared across the room.

"Hello, Quinn. I've missed you."

Jason had told me I was a woman, all grown up now, ready to face the world. But it was much easier to be a child. A child could run to her father and let him make all the decisions that would affect her life. But a woman, an adult, was responsible to herself.

Caught between the two, I chose my words carefully, trying to find even a shred of affection I might still feel for my father. But I found nothing but bitterness and contempt. As familiar as he was, he was a stranger, an impostor who had come here pretending to be someone who was concerned about my future. But it was a lie, and realizing that I drew myself up to my full height and stepped forward, demanding to know what his plans were.

"I think you already know what has to be done, Quinn."

Was that sadness in his voice, or was I making the mistake of projecting my own feelings onto him? I couldn't be sure, but I knew I had to at least listen to what he had to say.

"Jason is very ill. He has been for a long time now,"

he went on. "I don't doubt that a great deal of it is a result of what happened with his mother—"

"My mother too, don't forget," I interrupted.

"Yes, of course. And my wife, Quinn. The woman I fell in love with. And love still."

"I don't believe that."

He looked away, and from where I stood I could smell the English toilet water he had worn ever since I was a little girl. The faint woodsy scent made me think of lazy Sunday mornings, and how I used to watch him while he shaved. Father would spread the thick white lather over his face, discussing the plans for the day. There were picnics in the hills, rides into the countryside. A visit to a winery. A trip to the beach. One Sunday he took us to a farm where game birds were raised; fancy pheasant and quail, dove and squab cooing mournfully from their dovecotes. It was always the four of us, Jason and I in the back seat of the dark-green Lincoln, Mother and Father sitting up front.

I shook my head, trying to clear away the cobwebs of the past. That life was gone now—the security of a loving family, feeling safe and content in Father's arms.

"What are you going to do?" I asked.

He motioned me to join him on the couch, but I felt more comfortable standing, and remained where I was.

"I tried, Quinn. I tried very hard. Why do you think I asked Dr. Davies to come here, why I arranged it this way? I wanted to see if he could help your brother overcome his problems."

"Problems that might never have surfaced if you hadn't taken Mother away from us, lied to us," I reminded him.

He lowered his eyes, studying the whorls in his fingertips. There was a marked resemblance between him and Jason

335

that I had never noticed before. Not in the eyes—for Jason's were uniquely green, unlike either of our parents—but in the shape of his face and the texture of his hair, so thick and straight that all it took was a toss of the head to get it to look neat. Although Father was taller and more ruggedly built, I didn't doubt that in the next few years my brother would become his equal. And when he looked at Father eye to eye, would they finally understand each other? Probably not, for Mother would always be there like a shadow to warn him of Bennett Lefland's selfish and deceitful ways.

Father cleared his throat self-consciously. He poured himself a cup of coffee, but made no move to drink it.

"I tried," he said again. "The last thing I wanted was to see your brother institutionalized. But there's no other choice, Quinn. Mr. Ettinger's so-called accident—surely you don't think it happened the way your brother described? And what about poor Harry Darby? Do you have any idea what it was like when we opened your mother's coffin and found him there?"

"I wrote to them. I told them exactly what happened. I didn't lie about a single thing. It was an accident. No one pushed him."

"Anna and Will don't believe that. They think Jason murdered their son."

"Harry would still be alive today if you hadn't tried to deceive us. You asked him to spy on us, or is that something else you've conveniently forgotten? Because if you have, I'll make sure to remind them if I ever see them again."

"You will see them again," he said with certainty.

"No, I don't think I will," I replied with just as much confidence. "I'm not going back there, Father."

"You're upset. Everything is going to take time, Quinn."

"Time?" I said, and I couldn't help but raise my voice. "How much time did it take before you remarried? And not just a stranger, but Mother's own sister, for God's sake!"

"You're shouting."

"I don't care. Let everyone hear. I want them to. I want Perdita to know just what kind of person you really are. And what about Becky? You haven't said a word about her, have you?"

The look of determination I had seen in his face was being chipped away at from within. And as his expression changed, everything Jason and I had feared seemed about to be confirmed. I held myself stiffly, wondering if Father would once again try to make excuses for himself.

"Well?" I demanded when he failed to answer me. "If I go back to the Valley, and I'm not saying I will, where does Becky fit in?"

For the first time since Jason and I had run away, I was unburdening myself. But it was more than just the satisfaction of getting things off my chest. The questions I was raising couldn't be taken lightly, and Father knew that as well as I did.

"Your stepmother and I have given that a great deal of thought," he finally replied. "We're willing to take the child into our home."

"The child!" I was outraged, and I could barely control myself. "That *child* is a Lefland. She's not a stranger, someone who was just left there on our doorstep. And I don't believe you anymore, not a word of it. You want your way, though why you're so anxious for me to leave here is something I don't think I'll ever understand. But in order to get me to go with you, you know you have to take Becky as well. So now you say you will. But what about next week, or next month, or even next year? What's to prevent you from turning your back on her? Nothing, and that's just another reason why the only home I have is here, on Ettinger Rock.''

His lips were trembling, and the anger that was building up inside him brought the blood rushing to his cheeks.

"And if Mrs. Ettinger asks you to leave?''

"She would never do that.''

"But if she does, if she feels that it's best?''

"You can drag me home, Father. You can tie me up and carry me off. But you'll never keep me there, or earn back my respect.''

"You have no love for me anymore, do you, Quinn?''

He already knew the answer. But there was a time when I had loved him. Oh yes, I had loved my father so very much. He and Mother and Jason were my entire world, and what a happy and carefree world it was, too. But that was in the past, and though the past could be exhumed like a coffin, it could never be brought back to life.

"I can't stop you from taking Jason. I know that, and I know it's best for him, too. He's invented an entirely different personality for himself, and this other person he becomes, this Warren he calls him, is as much a danger to Jason as he is to all of us.''

Although Jason had mentioned Warren the day we left home, Father still reacted with surprise.

"But though you can take my brother off the island, you're not going to take Becky and me.''

There was nothing else to say. I had searched my heart, examining my feelings like something observed beneath a microscope. Yet nothing remained of the love and admiration, the unquestioning devotion, I had once felt for my father. There was an emptiness there, as if someone had ripped those very feelings out of my breast, grinding them into the dust. And the person who had done that, who had turned love into loathing, was Bennett Lefland himself.

How calm and peaceful Jason looked. So untroubled, so safe from Warren's dreadful influence. I sat beside his bed, trying to tell myself that he was going to get better, that unlike Mother his condition was not incurable. One day he would leave the hospital, whole and well, ready to begin his life anew. Dr. Davies had told me there were all sorts of experimental drugs to be tried, several of which were proving particularly effective in the treatment of schizophrenia and multiple personality disorders.

Yes, that was the way I was going to think of it. As a disorder, not a sickness. His mind was disordered, jumbled up and confused. But he was still very young, and with medical advances occurring every day, surely something could be done to cure him.

"I know how afraid you are, but we can't let Warren destroy your life. They want to help you get better, Jason. No matter what Father did to us, he does want you to get well. You must believe that."

Although he couldn't hear me, I needed to tell him these things, for when he awoke he might not be able to understand what I was trying to say. So it was as much for my own peace of mind as his that I sat and talked to him, trying to put everything that had happened to us in proper perspective.

In the morning the launch would come to take him off the island. Right now, Father and Perdita were discussing my future. Though I thought it unfair not to be included, Perdita said it was best this way. My presence would only make it difficult for them to speak freely while they tried to reach a decision.

But as far as I was concerned, that decision had already been made. The fork in the road was behind me. I had chosen to go one way and Father had chosen to go another. There could be no turning back.

CHAPTER TWENTY-FOUR

We floated in darkness. Borne along by an unseen tide, we traveled back and forth in time, reliving the past, experiencing the future. And what we saw terrified us as few things ever had. Like an animal in a circus menagerie we paced the padded floor of our cage, waiting for the keepers to come and feed us. To experiment on us. To jab us full of needles and shock us with their electrodes.

Oh yes, it would happen, we had no doubt. We were brothers now. We would live together and die together. We were as one, whole and complete, unique unto ourselves.

We opened our eyes, breathing a collective sigh of relief when we saw where we were. Our room on Ettinger Rock, not Dr. Warren's three-ring circus of the insane. Had Quinn come and spoken to us, told us his plans? We couldn't remember, but we thought she had.

We wanted to say good-bye to her, knowing our love for her was even stronger than it ever was for Mother. But there was too much to be done, and so little time to accomplish it.

We sat up in bed, still feeling the aftereffects of the Thorazine. We were woozy, and when we got to our feet it was hard to maintain our balance. We had to hang onto the edge of the bed for support, waiting until the dizziness passed.

"Better?" we asked.

"Yes," we answered.

We practiced walking until we were certain we hadn't forgotten how it was accomplished.

"That most useful art of ambulation," we said, laughing to ourselves.

Then we moved to the door, pausing a moment to look back at the clock on the nightstand. Midnight. The infamous witching hour. Davies must have given us one hell of a jab with his hypodermic, because we'd been out much longer than we realized. Unless he'd given us a second shot while we slept. We glanced at our arm. Sure enough, there were two distinct puncture marks. So Dr. Warren's protégé wasn't taking any chances.

Alone, we might have slept until dawn. Together, our strength raged in our blood. We were all-powerful now, answerable to no one but ourselves, and we knew just what had to be done.

Somewhere in this house he lay sleeping, dreaming of our death. But we would find him, even if it took all night.

No stone unturned. No door unopened.

Quinn cried out in her sleep, and though we wanted to tell her what we were about to do, we knew she would try to stop us. Not because she loved her father, but because she loved us, and always would. So we let her sleep, let Kenley sleep, let Perdita and Granberry and Davies sleep, all safe in their beds, dreaming their pitiful little dreams.

But where was the spider? we wondered. Where had they hidden him? He wasn't on the third floor, nor the second, where we stood by the crib and watched our beautiful little daughter, her tiny lips turned up in a smile as she slept.

One day Quinn would tell her the story of the spider and the fly. She'd reveal each and every one of his evil deeds, explaining how the web had tightened around us, trying to ensnare us in its cruel and heartless strands.

"We're doing it for you," we whispered. "It's your future we're concerned about, not ours. No matter what might happen, you must always believe that, Becky."

We kissed her silken cheek and didn't want to leave her, but we had to. The witching hour wouldn't last forever, and there were two or three guest rooms on the topmost floor we still hadn't checked. But as we started up the stairs we suddenly paused.

"Did you hear something?"

We held our breath, listening to the creaking of the house, the waves breaking far below us at the base of the cliff.

"What do you think it was?" we asked ourselves. "A door opening? Footsteps?"

There it was again, faint but audible. We turned and hurried down the stairs, barefoot and silent as the house yawned in its sleep.

There was a light on in the study. So the spider was as sleepless as the fly. But he wasn't alone, because we heard him talking to someone. But who? We'd already looked in on everyone else in the house.

". . . sorry to call so late," we thought we heard him say.

Call who? Orickson? Dr. Warren? Maybe the Darbys, convinced we were guilty of murdering their son.

". . . very difficult, Gwen . . ."

Aunt Gwen! He was speaking to the second Mrs. Lefland, that evil, conniving bitch we should have killed when we had the chance.

"Yes, tomorrow morning . . . No, Davies shot him full of Thorazine . . ."

We rubbed our hand against our arm, feeling a slight soreness where the needles were jabbed into our skin.

". . . worse than I imagined . . . Of course the poor woman's distraught. She just lost her husband, and now she knows why . . ."

He deserved it. He was going to make trouble for us. He wasn't our friend, and we were glad when he went under and we never saw him again. Oh yes, we were so glad we wanted to clap our hands and do a little dance, laugh out loud we were so pleased with ourselves. But we kept quiet, listening, spying on the spider as he swiveled back and forth in his chair, unable to get comfortable.

". . . she knows how I feel about the baby. How can she not? She's been through so much, she just doesn't trust anyone anymore . . . What good would it do, Gwen? She'd only run away again. At least this way . . . what? No, I haven't even spoken to him yet. I don't think he knows I'm here . . ."

Of course we knew. What did he take us for anyway, a pair of idiots? We knew he was here from the very beginning, but now we waited until he finished with the treacherous bitch who had hated mother as much as he did. But as soon as he got off the phone . . .

"He's not very optimistic, no . . . She understands that. After all, she probably knows him better than any of us . . ."

He tapped his fingers nervously against the desk, nodding his head as the second Mrs. Lefland jabbered in his ear.

"I will," the spider said at last. "Yes, the worst is finally over . . ."

Not quite.

"I love you, too . . . Tomorrow evening. Sleep well, my darling."

He set the phone down, then suddenly buried his face in his hands. Were those sobs we heard? No, of course not. He wasn't sad; he was tickled pink, thrilled to death he'd finally caught us in his web. But now we were about to escape, and we stepped inside the study, pulling the doors shut so no one else would hear us.

Startled, he raised his head. When we saw his eyes, wide and surprised and tinged with fear, we couldn't stop ourselves from smiling.

"Good evening, Daddy," we giggled softly.

"Jason . . . how are you, son?" he stammered.

He was trying to recover his composure. But we could smell his fear now, and we moved closer, knowing we had nothing to be frightened of. We were all-powerful, and no one was going to stop us from doing what had to be done.

"How are you feeling?"

"Fine."

"You're not surprised to see me?"

We shook our head.

"We saw you last night, when you came ashore."

"You and Quinn, you mean?" he said uncertainly.

"Quinn was sleeping, but we were wide-awake. That's why we tried to leave. Only now it's too late for that, isn't it?"

"You'll see, everything's going to work out for the best, I promise."

"You used to promise lots of things. But they were all lies, weren't they?"

"Come, let me take you upstairs to your room."

He came to his feet. He looked a little bit like us, but we saw through his disguise. He wasn't our father, because our father loved us and this man with the nervous grin hated us through and through. We felt it, smelled it, saw it in his eyes. But we weren't afraid. All-powerful, we weren't scared in the least.

We felt the knife resting against our thigh, rubbing back and forth and making us shiver it felt so good. The blade was nice and warm, as sharp as the needles Dr. Davies had jabbed into our arm.

He stepped closer, holding out his arms to us. We were ready for him, but still we waited. First there had to be a sign, and we looked all around, wondering why she was keeping back in the shadows. Hiding from us.

He saw the way we were looking over his shoulder, and glanced behind him.

"Can't you see her? She's standing right there," we told him.

"Who?"

The word fell on the floor and broke in two. We stepped closer.

"She wants us to go away with her. Don't you, Mom?"

Of course she did. She was waiting for us, arms outstretched. Her long ivory nightgown, the satin one she used to wear whenever she invited us into her room, billowed about her ankles. Such pretty little feet, the toes painted a ruby-red. Her crystal blue eyes stared right through him, seeing us and no one else.

"For the sins of your fathers you, though guiltless, must suffer."

That's what she told us, and we knew it was true. When we did what she asked she would take us into her arms and her bed, and we'd be safe from him at last. We took another step forward, glaring at the demon hiding behind his mask.

He moved to the side, afraid of us now, and that was good. That was very, very good.

"Let me call the doctor, Jason. It'll be all right, I promise. No one's going to hurt you.

We rubbed our hand against the bulge in our pants. Our knife was bigger than his, sharper and far more lethal. We pulled it out of our pocket and laughed to see the terror dancing in his eyes.

"Scared?" we giggled.

"Not of you, son."

"Liar!"

We rushed forward, but he darted out of our way.

"Don't let him get near the door," Mom warned.

This was fun. We laughed and laughed to see the spider scurrying across his web, trying to elude our grasp.

"Jason, listen to me! I'm your father. I don't want to hurt you, you know that."

"Liar. Fucking filthy liar. She died because of you!"

"But you were the one who tried to kill her, Jason. You were the one who used the knife."

"And we'll use it again. Again and again and again!" we laughed. "And then the sins of the fathers'll be avenged, and there won't be a curse on us, not ever again. And Becky and Quinn'll be safe from you. Yes, that's right, safe from the spider who eats his own children."

"Davies!" he shouted, cupping his hands to his mouth so his voice would carry.

"Hurry, before they hear him!" Mom cried out.

We tried to corner him, but the spider managed to avoid the flashing blade of the knife. He clawed at the sliding doors, trying to get them open.

"You lied to us!" we screamed. "You said you loved us!"

"I do," he sobbed. "Dear God, I love you and I always will. Put that down, son. Please. I beg of you. Your mother's dead, Jason. She can't come back. But I'm here for you, I swear."

"Liar!"

If only we could plunge the blade between his shoulders or deep into his heart, the web would fall away and we'd be safe at last. But as we lunged forward he caught us around the wrist, trying to wrestle the knife out of our hand.

"Drop it, please. I don't want to hurt you."

"You already have!"

He was pushing us down to the floor. We struggled to stay on our feet, but he was as strong as we were. He pinned us down, first one shoulder and then the other. But we still had the knife, clutched tight in our hand. We jabbed it at him again and again, trying to work the blade into his arm. His hold on us weakened as blood gushed down his sleeve. We rolled to the side, forcing him to relinquish his grip.

The spider scrambled back along the floor. We threw ourselves on top of him. The blade was poised, ready to go in. He tried to deflect its path, pushing it aside with the heel of his palm. He wanted to kill us, we knew that now, and Mom knew it, too. But when we looked up she was gone. She didn't care about us anymore, and the sharp bloodstained blade slowly turned in our direction, shaking violently as he gripped our wrist.

Yes, it was time. There was no one else we could turn to. We were all alone, Jason and I. Mom had gone, and Dad. Quinn, and the baby too. And it was so much easier this way, so much better than being shut up in a cage.

We threw ourselves against him as hard as we could.

The mask fell away, and the spider showed us his true face for the first time. Dad cried out a warning, but it was too late. The knife slid into our chest, a sharp, tingling icicle that wouldn't melt until we were dead.

Yes, better. So much better this way. And cold, so very cold. But soon it it would be all right.

We were safe now.

EPILOGUE

It was my wish that Jason be buried on the island, where, if only for a brief time, he had found some small measure of happiness. I couldn't bear the thought of being without him, yet Father would have none of it. Leflands had always been buried in the Valley. Even Great-uncle Orin's remains had finally been laid to rest in the family plot, around whose sad and accursed precincts a sagging picket fence defined the territory of the dead.

There was so much I wanted to tell my brother. Yet when I knelt beside his bed, the words I intended to speak died in my breast. It was too late to tell him of my love, and pointless to swear that I would revenge a death none of us could have foreseen, nor prevented.

I had doubted Father's story, the heartrending way he retold the events which had occurred even as I slept, dreaming of a time when my brother would be well. Rather, I preferred to believe that it was his hand which had thrust the knife deep into my brother's heart, unwilling to sacrifice his own life for his son's.

Yet those initial feelings of rage had passed, and with the dying of my anger there came grief, welling up in my soul like an uncontrollable tide. I knelt beside the bed where my brother lay in deathly silence, sobbing now and cursing myself for being unable to help him. Stalked by demons of his own design, love alone could not have cured Jason of the sickness he had seen fit to put an end to, tired of battling for his sanity.

Understanding that was one thing, accepting it quite another. When all the tears had dried, when sorrow became a dull ache that would forever remain a part of my life, there would still have to be a final accounting, a reckoning of deeds both good and bad.

So it was that I stood by the nursery window, cradling Becky in my arms. Far below, where waves crashed against the rocky beach, and a launch bobbed in the swells, a sad and forlorn figure stood upon the dock, his eyes turned seaward.

Was Father looking for salvation, proof that the decisions he had made were just and wise? Or was he merely gazing into the future, when the tragedy he had brought into our lives would fade from memory, and the guilt he now felt would slip away, never to trouble him again?

I had no way of knowing what my father was thinking that day, nor what he would do in the years to come. Although I prayed I would never see him again, those prayers were destined to remain unanswered. One day we would find ourselves pitted against each other, for the Lefland curse was in our blood, and always would be.

The road leading back to the Valley is strewn with pitfalls, upon which the faint of heart dare not tread. When I returned ten years after my brother's death, I found no trace of his grave, no monument erected to his memory. In vain I searched the rubble of that graveyard, refusing to believe that it was so. Yet there was nothing there that bore his name, no proof that he had ever lived, no vestige of his dying.

But even though I found no marker before which I might kneel and say a silent prayer, I felt his presence in the very air I breathed. Somewhere, just beyond the borders of my sight, I could see his green eyes sparkling. And if I listened carefully, I could hear my brother's laughter, echoing through the hills that shimmered magically in the golden light of a distant summer's day.